AN ARTHURIAN LEGEND

LEGEND OF MIST AND BLADE

A.M. ROSS

Ebook ISBN 979-8-9915926-0-4

Paperback ISBN 979-8-9915926-1-1

Cover design by Miblart

Map by Shepengul

No AI was used in the creation of this book.

I've worked very hard with an editor, alpha and beta readers, and a proof reader to catch all possible errors; however, this is a creative piece of work created by a human. Any resemblance to actual people either living or dead or events is purely coincidental. The use of actors, artists, movies, TV shows, and song titles/lyrics referenced through the book are for storytelling purposes only and should not be seen as advertisement or endorsement. If you see any issues, please contact me at info@amrosswriter.com.

For those who make their own destiny

Contents

Author's Notes and Trigger Warning

Dear reader,

Being thrust into an unexpected role as the "Chosen One" hits a bit differently when you're in your mid-thirties. Our main female character is everything I love in a heroine - humorous, sassy, vulnerable, quirky, and loyal. I hope you enjoy reading about Gwen's journey as much as I enjoyed writing it.

Our heroine learns quickly that everything is different from the literary tales about King Arthur. The majority of this book is set in a very different version of Avalon than the traditional description. You will see references to much more traditional names for locations and individuals like Camelot and Excalibur. This is done intentionally to honor the roots of the original Arthurian legends.

The creatures in this book are pulled from myths and stories from around the world. If you run into a creature that you're not familiar with while reading, please reference the Creature Glossary at the back.

This is a dual point of view book with a few flashbacks. The chapters swap between the heroine's point of view and one of the other main character's point of view. This book is an adult romance and meant for readers 18+.

Happy reading!

POTENTIAL SPOILERS

I have tried to treat any potentially emotional triggers with sensitivity. The majority of the emotional triggers listed below are discussed in detail in the first three chapters. The strong language is scattered throughout. The battle scenes occur in the latter part of the book. This story includes the following:

- Discussion of emotional neglect by the main character's parents

- Mentions of a potential divorce of the main character's parents

- Mention of the death of an important family member due to cancer

- Strong language

- Minimally gory battle scenes

- Fade to black intimacy

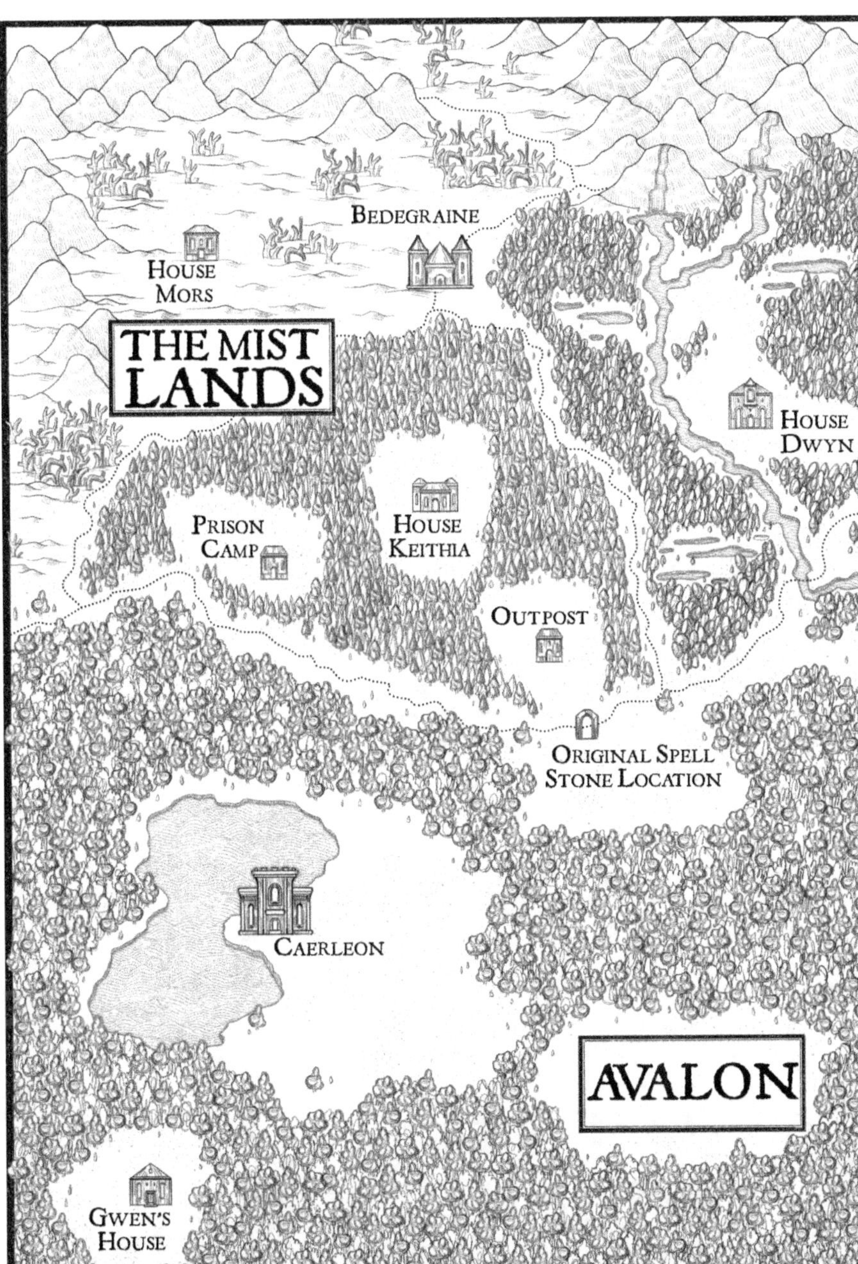

BEDEGRAINE
HOUSE MORS
THE MIST LANDS
HOUSE DWYN
PRISON CAMP
HOUSE KEITHIA
OUTPOST
ORIGINAL SPELL STONE LOCATION
CAERLEON
AVALON
GWEN'S HOUSE

CHAPTER ONE

GWEN

I hate working on the weekend, Gwen McMillan thought as she raced down the stairs. Saturday shifts ranked right up there with decaf coffee, algebra, and Mondays.

She had slept through her alarm, barely dodged two phone calls from her narcissistic mother, and didn't have a lick of coffee in her house. If she didn't get her butt in gear, the chief was going to have a fit, and her police partner, Logan, would tease her mercilessly. Even though today was another normal patrol day, Gwen was loath to be late.

Being a community guardian was a joy she'd chosen, unlike the heavy responsibilities that had chased her since childhood. Gwen shook her head as the memory of the prior night's dreams dogged her heels. Nothing like watching a werewolf maul a man's face to ruin a good night's sleep. If it wasn't for that stupid hunk of metal hidden in the wall of her bookshelf, she wouldn't look like death warmed over every morning.

"Saxon, let's go!" she hollered up the stairs, bouncing on one foot as she pulled on her black tennis shoe. Her ebony-furred German Shepherd police dog thundered down the stairs, almost taking her out at the knees. "Sax," she scolded. His tongue lolled out in a canine laugh. "All right, all right, let's go."

They bundled into her black-and-white police SUV, leaving her old, white farmhouse in the rearview mirror as she pointed the vehicle toward Littleton, where she was one of eight police officers. Gwen had fled New York City and her socialite mother's clutches and sought out small town USA as a welcome alternative to the hectic yet emotionally devoid lifestyle expected by her family.

The only good thing about New York was the plethora of coffee shops, she thought with a huff. As soon as she and Sax grabbed Logan from the precinct, they were going to head straight to Depresso, the coffee and romance bookshop down on Main owned by old Miss Hannegan. Gwen was going to order a bucket of their delicious bean brew.

"Oh, thank God," Gwen muttered, seeing Logan leaning against his blue Ford F-150 in the precinct parking lot. The stolid-looking, red-brick building cast a shadow across him. She rolled the SUV's window down. "Get in, loser. We've got coffee to find."

The big man laughed, folding his bulk into her car. He'd always reminded her of the tales of old with Viking raiders. Logan even kept his blond hair long and tied back in a short ponytail or man bun, sides shaved close to his head. Give the man a sword and shield, and he'd fit the part perfectly. Logan had told her once that he had tried live action role playing, or LARP, once in his early twenties but found it wasn't realistic enough, whatever that meant. Still, the man loved movies like *Lord of the Rings, The Green Knight, A Knight's Tale*, and oddly enough, *A Connecticut Yankee in King Arthur's Court.*

Gwen shrugged, thinking that giving any man, but especially her prankster of a partner, a sharp and pointy object was a bad idea. Chief was *this close* to putting Logan on probation for the pranks he pulled at the precinct. The only one safe from them was Gwen because she was his best friend, but that also meant he teased her without mercy instead.

"Damn, girl, you sound desperate. It's a bit early to go out on a quest. Late night?" He winked with a leering smile.

The look Gwen leveled at her best friend would have peeled paint off the side of her farmhouse. "No, just . . . a lot of bad dreams." She swallowed harshly, sweat pricking out on her hairline as her heart sped up.

She didn't need to relive the nightmares that were actually visions of the mythical realm of Avalon. Those dreams were an unwelcome gift for being the guardian of Caliburnus, King Arthur's legendary sword. According to Gran, the dreams helped the sword's guardian understand what King Arthur and his people protected the world against—the fae. From hauntingly beautiful to absolutely monstrous, the fae came in all shapes, sizes, and power levels. Their fae king, Mordred, sought to enter the mortal realm to expand his kingdom.

That was where Caliburnus came into play. Gwen's gran had been convinced that one day the legends would be true. Arthur would need the sword, and someone from their familial line would be the one to return it to the One True King. As the current guardian, Gwen held the secret close to her heart, trying not to let the ever-present exhaustion that ravaged her body affect her work. With enough coffee in her system, she mostly succeeded, and Logan picked up any slack without complaint.

"Want to talk about it?" Her partner's voice had changed from jovial to serious with the question while his gaze swept over her, assessing.

That right there was why they were besties. Logan may be a tease and a prankster, but he was loyal, and he cared fiercely about those he considered "his" people. Gwen was lucky enough to be one of them.

"Nope." Gwen emphasized the *p* with a pop of her lips as she drummed her fingers against the steering wheel. She never asked to be the guardian after her gran, and being "the Chosen One" sucked. Gwen couldn't remember the last time she had an uninterrupted night of sleep. Her weariness went beyond simple tiredness to straight-up fatigue.

Add in this constant, nagging crush she'd developed in her dreams on one of Arthur's high-ranking knights—because of course her fickle heart chose an unattainable man—and she was in *a mood*. Neither of her parents believed in this burdensome responsibility that her gran had passed on to her. Gwen's mother had scoffed at her childhood tales of the dreams and told her to be quiet and not embarrass their family at social events. Gwen's father had never been around long enough to care. He was too focused on his studies and career (and truth be told, avoiding his wife). Luckily, the sight of the coffee shop broke Gwen out of that train of thought.

The brick building was painted a cheery blue with a matching blue-and-white awning spread across both the glass door and large window, offering shade to those who sat at the café tables while they read and drank their beverage of choice. Compared to the two traditional red-brick buildings on either side, Depresso stood out as a welcoming beacon of caffeinated bliss. Miss Hannegan leveraged her renowned gardening skills to fill two pots on either side of the door with draping greenery and bright-pink petunias. A very disgruntled looking gargoyle statue peeked out from the middle of the pot between the door and window while a Green Man mask peered out of the other flower pot.

"Awesome, there's a spot right out front." Gwen whipped the SUV into the parking space, lowered the windows a bit for Sax, then sprang out and hustled toward the glass door where the shop's name was painted in bright gold letters.

"I don't know if 'My birthstone is a coffee bean' is as good as last week's 'Coffee makes me do stupid things faster,'" Logan commented, waving his hand at the white letters scrawled on the blackboard sign hanging next to the coffee shop door. Someone had drawn a dancing coffee bean holding balloons next to the words.

"Right, like you need any excuse to do anything stupid," Gwen joked as Logan held the door open for her. "I did like last week's drawing of the coffee mug running with scissors, though. That was a nice touch." The scent of coffee, vanilla, mocha, and cinnamon rolled out, assaulting her nose. Her mouth watered as the breath stuttered in her lungs. Delicious, delicious coffee. Gwen wove between the polished, blond-wood tables, eying the stacks of romance books that sat on the other side of the building. The brightly colored covers and book spines taunted her. When was the last time she read something for pleasure?

Logan gasped, grasping at his chest, then grinned widely. "You wound me. I think that means you should pay."

"Fine, whatever. Terry, my very favorite teen in the whole wide world, good morning. Please make me the biggest coffee ever." Gwen pulled out her wallet, fully prepared to pay for both her and Logan's drinks, plus a pup cup for Saxon.

The red-haired teenager's bright smile flashed, showing off chrome-and-green braces. "Absolutely, Officer McMillan."

"Uh, Terry, you got something right here." Logan tapped his front teeth as if the teenager had food stuck in his braces.

"Yeah, I had to go to the orthodontist yesterday and decided to change things up. My friend Piper got hot pink, and it looked like old bubblegum by the end of the first week. Not sure I like the green, but I'm stuck with it for at least a month. You want your usual, Officer Houlihan?"

"Nah, Gwen's paying, so make me the most expensive, floofiest drink possible." Logan shot Gwen a shit-eating grin and winked. His dimple flashed as he leaned on the counter.

"Logan!" Gwen laughed, her hand flying out to smack him in his stomach, but she still nodded at Terry. "Whatever the man wants."

"Sure thing, Off–" Terry broke off as the Cruella de Vil theme song blared out of Gwen's phone.

She groaned, throwing her head back to stare at the ceiling while she counted to ten. Gwen had dodged the earlier two calls because, well, one, she hadn't had coffee and no one needed to speak to her mother unless properly awake, and two, it was easy to ignore the phone if it was in another room.

Third time's the charm, Gwen thought, a shudder running through her athletic frame. Her mother was nothing if not persistent. Looking back at the teen and man staring at her in bemusement, she shoved a twenty and a ten at Logan then waved her phone at him.

"I need to take this. Can you get the drinks and the pup cup, please?" Gwen heard both the desperation and despair in her voice and winced, trying to avoid Logan's knowing gaze. He was only a few years older than her, but there were times when her best friend's knowing looks gave him an air that spoke of a much older soul than thirty-eight.

"Sure, partner." Logan nodded slowly, straightening and turning toward Terry to give Gwen the chance to disappear from Terry's curiosity.

"Great, thanks, bestie." Gwen graced Logan and Terry with a quick smile before striding outside to get back into the SUV. Saxon snuffled up behind her, putting his nose into her neck under her ear. "Pup cup will be out shortly, Fur Face, promise." Gwen looked down at her phone. The call had been forwarded already to voicemail, but her mother had hung up and immediately redialed. Okay, fourth time's the charm.

"Hey, Mom." Gwen took a deep, bracing breath.

"Gwenhwyfar." The voice was cold and none-too-pleased sounding, reminding Gwen that Mom was far too casual a moniker for their relationship.

"How are you, Mother?" Gwen corrected herself, keeping her eyes closed and trying to lose herself in the repetitive motion of scratching the black fur under Saxon's chin. Her gut tightened with anxiety as the strident voice on the other end of the line rose an octave in outrage.

"I would be fine, except your father insists that he cannot attend the divorce hearing Tuesday because he will be in England! England of all places! I want you to call him and talk some sense into him." From the rapid staccato of heels coming across the line, Gwen could picture her mother pacing across the marble floor of the New York penthouse. Her mother's old family money had been well spent on updating every feature to showcase luxury.

"So it's final this time?" Gwen asked, dropping her forehead against the steering wheel. Exhaustion weighed heavy in her tone.

Her parents had been going through the motions of getting divorced for more than half her life. Arty McMillan spent all of his time in books or on dig sites as one of the world's foremost experts on ancient British history and culture, a fact that displeased her mother. Whereas Arty's time focused on knowledge, Beatrice Brookes-McMillan spent the same time seething over the fact that she had married the absent-minded professor and not a dashing and charismatic Indiana Jones. Setting a court date was the furthest they had gotten through the divorce proceedings.

"Of course it is, if you can get your father to show up! He needs to be on a plane this evening. Make it happen!" Gwen's mother delivered this edict in a terse tone that grated across Gwen's nerves.

Gwen didn't even bother sighing. As was typical, her mother had gotten in the last word simply by hanging up the phone. Phone calls with her mother never ended well. Gwen was, as her mother often told her, a huge disappointment that had never lived up to the Brookes family name. Her mother never understood, nor expressed any interest in understanding, why her only child would give up the privileged life of the wealthy to become a small-town cop.

"Here." Logan's large, scarred hand came into view, bringing a huge to-go coffee cup into her line of sight as he settled back into his seat and closed his door with a resounding thump.

"Thanks," Gwen told him, grasping the cup and letting its heat warm her chilled hands. While the weather outside sat at the perfect T-shirt and jeans temperature, the call with her mother left her cold.

Logan shifted in his seat, blue eyes focused on her as if cataloguing every micro-sign of distress and fatigue. "Terry added a shot of vanilla with it. Said you might need your day sweetened because the call looked bad."

"Aww, he's a sweetheart." Gwen waved at the teenager through the window, smiling a bit at his cheery wave back. "Did you get Sax's pup cup?"

"Do I look like an amateur?" Logan scoffed, handing it to her, Saxon's whines and drool landing between them.

Gwen's smile wavered from sad to sly. "Do you really want me to answer that?"

"No, no I do not. Who was on the phone?" Logan asked, lifting his own coffee to take a sip as Gwen twisted to give Saxon his pup cup. The all-black German Shepherd shoved his large snout straight to the bottom. "Geez, man, slow down," Logan cackled as whipped cream went flying around the cab. "Right, so again, who was that on the phone? Hell of a ringtone."

"That was my mom. Being her usual cantankerous self." Gwen took a sip of her coffee before glancing around and backing out onto the street to head off for their patrol.

"So you made her ringtone the Cruella theme song?" His eyes widened at the level of pettiness Gwen had stooped to.

While he may be her bestie, Gwen had glossed over any discussions of her family throughout the life of their friendship. Gwen hated to admit it, but she was embarrassed by the sheer level of dysfunction she grew up in, even with Gran's attentiveness during Gwen's childhood. Logan had a large, gregarious family on the other side of the country, with siblings and a plethora of cousins, including both a sister and a cousin he apparently was very close to.

"Eh, it's fitting. I've told you how horrible she is." Gwen turned toward the high school, and the quaint storefronts of Main Street gave way to a small parking garage and a large, white Baptist church with a tall steeple staring imposingly down at passersby. Still, the town council made sure that the large hanging flower baskets that adorned Main Street continued. This year, they went with pink and purple petunias. Gwen liked these better than the yellow portulaca flowers and sweet potato vines of last year's baskets.

Littleton turned on the charm for the tourists and the locals alike, ensuring flowers and trees lined the streets and that at least two festivals were held each year. The town's charm and its low crime rate had been the two big selling points for moving here. She could help people as a police officer, and the fact that Gwen hadn't had to use her service weapon was a point of pride. Gwen had spent the last decade getting to know the majority of the townies and could usually talk people out of doing something dumb. Their worst cases were typically calls of a bear in the trash, a brewing bar fight, or kids causing mischief.

"Do you have specific ringtones for other people?" Logan asked, intrigued.

"Yep. I consider it one of my more quirky charms. My dad is the *Looney Tunes* theme. He's brilliant but lacks any form of common sense," Gwen said, smirking at her partner.

Logan chuckled, twisting to get a better look at her. He stroked his chin, grin widening, as he asked, "Okay, so what's mine?"

"It's that weird noise from your *Dr. Who* show. The phone booth noise." Gwen drove by the high school, noting the single-story building was understandably quiet other than the band practicing in the adjoining field. The kids marched in rows, turning whenever the band director blew a whistle. Gwen expected that the practice was focused on preparing for the upcoming homecoming game.

"The TARDIS?" He sounded pleased.

She nodded, her mind drifting to her mother's phone call as she answered absently, "Uh-huh." Gwen couldn't believe that her dad would finally be free of her mother, assuming he'd actually come up for air long enough to sign the divorce papers.

"So what's the captain's ringtone?" Logan asked, running his hand down his chin. "It's got to be something scary like *The Dark Knight* theme or something, right?"

Mischief glittered in Gwen's eyes as she pulled her attention back to the conversation, glancing at her partner before returning her eyes to the road. "It's the *Scooby-Doo* theme song."

Logan whistled. "If she ever hears that, she will kill you."

"Why would she ever hear her own ringtone?" Gwen's brows drew together. "There's no reason for her to call me while my phone is in earshot of her."

"That . . . is an excellent point. Captain would still kill you." Logan scratched under Saxon's chin as the dog thrust himself into the conversation, and the canine grumbled in pleasure at the attention.

"Well, Shaggy, as long as no one tells her, you'll still have a partner," Gwen pointed out sagely. "Maybe we should rename Sax to Scooby."

Logan shook his head. "That would just be a crime. Our big boy deserves to have a big, manly name, doncha, boy? Yes, you do," Logan cooed in a high-pitched, baby voice. Her bestie lavished attention and praise on the dog, much to Saxon's delight.

"You're going to spoil him," Gwen chuckled, rolling slowly through the area with older homes. The houses had been here since the forties and fifties, but the pride of the community kept the houses in good shape. She waved at the high school principal Mr. Morris, busy planting bright orange and deep-red mums around his black mailbox. Maybe today would get better if she kept drinking her coffee and driving around. They focused the rest of their shift on light banter, that week's grocery specials, and whether or not Wonder Woman or Thor had the best hair.

"I still vote for Wonder Woman," Gwen told Sax as they pulled into their farmhouse's gravel driveway as the sun lay lower in the sky, turning the first autumn leaves bright gold. She and Logan had parted ways back at the precinct. Now, Gwen was looking forward to changing into her running gear and heading out into the woods to hit the trails behind her house; they had about an hour or so of daylight left before it would be too dark to run safely. Saxon woofed as if he read her mind. The dog loved three things—kibble, running in the woods, and Gwen.

Well, she thought, *four if you counted Logan.*

Her house stared at Gwen as if inviting her to leave her worries at the door. Every time she came home, she found the house more charming, an elegant old lady with laugh lines in her eaves and faded yet lovely colors. Rather than the regimented gardens of her mother's house in the Hamptons, Gwen's gardens displayed a colorful mix of any and all flowers. She'd planted what struck her as pretty and ended up giving the old house a colorful skirt made of both practical-looking and romantic flowers. With a contented nod of her head and a jingle of keys, Gwen stepped up the whitewashed porch steps to the weathered front door painted a cheery turquoise.

The dreaded Cruella de Vil song slunk across the porch again. Gwen's exasperated sigh rolled out right behind it. She looked at her dog. Her dog looked at her.

"Yeah, I'm not answering that. Let's go for a run."

The late afternoon sunlight filtered through the trees as she and Saxon ran along the familiar wooded path. The breath labored in her lungs as she pushed herself through the last of her three miles for the day. Music blared from her headphones, an eclectic mix of Celtic, country, and rock and roll. Saxon's tongue lolled as he kept up with her, jumping over logs and dashing off into the bushes to investigate an interesting smell before galumphing back to Gwen. They slowed to a cooldown walk on the last quarter of a mile. She listened to The Cottars harmonize as her back porch came into view.

Life wasn't great, but it was good. It was solid. She didn't think she could ask for more than that.

Did it get lonely out here in the woods? Sometimes. Did she talk to her dog too much when she wasn't at work? Gwen wasn't even going to admit that to herself. Well, except when she drank too much wine; on those nights, she talked his ears off about her frustrations with her mother's need for control, the fact that her life wasn't where she thought it would be by her mid-thirties, and those damn Avalon dreams. If he was human, Sax would be rolling his eyes and telling her to pull on her big-girl panties and ignore her mother. He couldn't help it that the woman knew what words to use to strip Gwen emotionally raw, and Gran wasn't here any longer to help tend the wounds. Then the dog would probably tell her to drink more wine so she could actually sleep. Too bad it didn't work that way.

"Thankfully," Gwen panted, bopping the dog's nose, "you are not human." Saxon growled and lunged into her legs, sending her staggering. "Oh, so we're not tired, huh? We'll see about that after dinner."

She strode into the house and started the process of settling herself and the dog in for the night. Self-care, she reminded herself, was an important part of her evening routine, so she took a quick shower, lit the vanilla candles she had scattered around her house, and fed Saxon his kibble before leaving him to chew on his favorite plastic hamburger squeaky toy. Gwen turned on her stereo, letting the speakers she had installed through the house filter violin music into the evening air. Then she headed into the home library and music room she had built in what was meant to be the farmhouse's formal living and dining areas.

Gwen let her fingers trail across the spines of her favorite novels. The book choices were as eclectic as her music. Romance, science fiction, historical fiction, nonfiction. They all stuffed the bookshelves. She tried to keep them neat and tidy, but eventually gave up and stuffed every available inch of the shelves with books. Her mother would be horrified. Perhaps that was half the point to her collection. Gwen's fingers *tap tap tapped* their way to one of her favorites, its spine creased with lines and pages hanging onto the glue through sheer will. It was a retelling of the King Arthur legend and a book her gran had introduced her to. Compelled for some reason, she pulled it off the shelf and stared at the worn cover. The illustrator had drawn a white stone castle next to a still, dark lake.

In the distance, she could have sworn she heard shouting and the long, visceral howl of a wolf. Odd. Gwen looked up as the light from the window wavered, and the floor jerked beneath her feet. She heard Saxon growl from the kitchen as she scrambled to the door, perplexed at the thought of an earthquake happening here of all places. There were no nearby fault lines. As she grabbed at the doorframe, the floor seemed to leap up out of nowhere to acquaint itself with her face.

Gwen woke to find herself face-first on the floor, the book mere inches from her eyes. She blinked and rolled over, groaning. Nearby, the vanilla candle had sputtered out. It looked like it'd hardly burned at all since she lit it. Thank goodness it hadn't burned her house down.

But the light was weird in the room. It should've been gloomy, inching toward dusk. Instead, bright daylight met her squinting eyes.

Saxon whined and thrust his nose against her throat.

"Oh God, Fur Face, what the heck happened?" she croaked, pushing his face away. "Your breath stinks. We need to brush your teeth more." Gwen rolled over onto her stomach again and pushed up, her head hanging as if she had a hangover. "How long have I been out, buddy?" She stood, legs shaking, and stepped over to glance out the window as her mind registered that the music had stopped playing. Her gaze fastened on the trees.

Gwen's breath caught in her throat. The trees gracing the edge of the clearing were not her trees. Her trees were tall and skinny loblolly and longleaf pine. But these trees were dark, with large trunks and dull leaves. Saxon's favorite pink azalea bush, usually growing at the edge of the forest, was nowhere to be seen.

She blinked.

The trees stayed where they were.

"Did I . . . hit my head harder than I thought?"

She glanced back at the room. Everything remained the same, no sign of her fainting spell other than the book on the floor . . . the book with the same dark trees on the cover as the ones outside her window. Gwen licked her lips as her nerves hummed, and she bent and picked up the book, her eyes fixated on the cover. Then she glanced out the window again.

"No way." She shook her head, but the trees stubbornly refused to change back to her beloved pines. "The heck?" she muttered and strode over to open the window to stick her head out. *As if that would change anything,* Gwen thought to herself as a weird feeling settled in the pit of her stomach.

As soon as she had lifted the window, she heard it. The shouts and roars of battle. The same sounds that had haunted her dreams for years. Gwen shook her head in denial.

"Just a dream, just a dream," she muttered as a compulsion rose in her.

The urge to move fixed around her heart and sent it thudding heavy against her ribs while adrenaline rode wild in her blood. The urgent need to find the battle and do something drove her back into the house and to the upstairs bedroom where she kept her guns locked and her weaponry collection—ancient swords and knives from Britannia and France—on display. Gwen's shaky hands opened the gun safe and pulled out her hunting rifle and her service weapon, which she attached at her hip as if in a daze. She shoved her feet into her hiking boots and tied the laces, fingers shaking. Gwen cursed as the time spent on the laces stretched out.

The compulsion grew until all she could focus on was the person or people screaming. A fog rose in her mind, leaving her vision fuzzy around the edges. She could hear her labored breathing as she opened the back door and strode off into the sun-drenched, dense trees, but Gwen could do nothing except follow the sound of battle. Saxon trotted beside her, but her throat locked up as she tried to speak to him.

Hurry, hurry, hurry, her mind told her muscles, and she found herself moving into a fast jog, moving deeper into the trees and toward whoever was in trouble.

CHAPTER TWO

ORIN

The day has gone to complete shit, Orin thought as he thrust his sword into the chest of a Redcap trying to rip his throat out. The Redcap gurgled, grasping with clawed hands at the wound before toppling to the ground. Its black blood stained the coarse tan-and-green tunic that had camouflaged the monster from the knights.

This should have been a routine hunting mission, out at dawn with the intent of being back at Caerleon before midday. Instead, Mordred's fae patrols ran them to ground, herding them away from their home and closer to the boundary between Avalon and the Mist Lands, Mordred's kingdom. The tyrant sent out daily patrols of werewolves, monstrous fae like gorgons and vampires, and mages from the three different fae courts he ruled without mercy.

Orin and the other two knights were sore, tired, and bleeding from dozens of wounds, large and small. As he stumbled back-to-back with his fellow knights and closest friends, Cae and Tor, three werewolves circled them while a manananggal hung from the branches of a near-by tree, hissing as she flared her wings and split her abdomen open to reveal bloody intestines. Orin had no desire to be sucked dry by the vampire-like fae or have his throat ripped out by a werewolf. He already carried three raw-edged scars across his face from a werewolf attack four centuries prior.

Tor dodged a lunging attack from the large gray werewolf harrying him. Orin grunted and wavered on his feet, trying not to fall. The eyes of the wolf stalking him flared with predatory intensity as it rushed forward. Orin snapped his sword point up, aiming for the wolf's throat while bashing the werewolf's claws away with his round shield. The wolf snarled and retreated, weaving back and forth on large paws while watching for another moment of weakness. At this point, Orin knew it was only a matter of time before he or his comrades faltered and offered that opportunity. Still, they'd take as many of the fae with them as possible, though that would be little comfort to Cae's wife and children or Tor's brother. He had no one who would miss him. He gritted his teeth, willing his muscles to keep his sword and shield aloft.

Sweat and blood rolled down into his eyes, and he dashed it away with an impatient hand, gripping his sword hilt in the other. The sword felt too heavy at this point; his muscles burned with the effort. He lifted the blade up in a defensive stance with an exhausted grunt, the other two knights mirroring his pose.

The wolves towered over them, well over six and a half feet tall. Orin estimated the one before him had to be over seven feet. Their narrow jaws and piercing amber eyes sent terror shivering down the knight's spine. Three clawed fingers graced their outstretched paws, and they used these to feint and slash at the knights.

Orin clumsily brought his sword up, parrying the bloodstained claws. Then thunder rolled through the woods, and the head of the gray wolf in front of him jerked to the side, blood spraying in a fine mist.

"What . . . ?" He gaped as the wolf's body toppled over.

The crack of thunder snapped out again, reverberating through the woods, and the manananggal shrieked as blood and ichor blossomed on her chest. Her wings crumpled, and her claws lost traction on the branches, leaving the fae to plummet to the forest floor below. The remaining two wolves snarled and crouched, looking for the source of the noise and death.

A slim figure stepped out farther from behind a tree, a long metal weapon held in their arms and notched against their shoulder. The weapon fired, and the nearest brown and gray wolf crumpled to the ground. The once bright, amber eyes dimmed in death. The final wolf launched itself from a crouch, aiming to run into the forest. The back of its head exploded as the figure, a dark-haired woman he realized, swung her weapon to follow its escape.

"What the hell!" Her eyes were wide on her pale face as she lowered the weapon to point at the ground and stared at them. A large black dog growled next to her. She dropped her free hand down, settling the dog as she swung her gaze around the forest. The woman brought her eyes back to look at the three men, who were just as surprised. She blinked and shook her head, as if shaking something off, and then focused on them.

"You guys look like death warmed over. Are you okay?" Her voice was laced with concern as she moved closer.

Orin raked his gaze over her. She wore a large green shirt with short sleeves that hung off one shoulder, showcasing a bright tattoo of flowers. Tight black pants encased lean legs. Her brown hair hung in loose waves over her shoulders, the color matching her umber eyes. The weapon now slung over her shoulder looked somewhat similar to the firearms Henri had with him when Avalon had claimed the man nearly two hundred years prior.

She was also very clearly a human and possibly the most stunning woman he had ever seen. The strange woman took his breath away, and feelings he thought lost long ago surged to the foreground. He coughed, shifting as unexpected attraction raced through him.

"Who?" he asked, his voice hoarse.

"Um, Gwen," she said, almost hesitantly, and flushed pink, which he found oddly endearing considering he and the other knights were dripping blood onto the forest floor. The woman darted her eyes to the side and then back to him. "Gwen McMillan. This is Saxon," she added, placing a hand on the large dog's head. The dog sat panting at her side, not quite growling. "You're Orin, Cae, and Tor, right?"

"How did you . . . ?" Cae snarled, backing away from Gwen, suspicion heavy in his voice. Orin trusted Cae with his life, but the man was a skeptic on his good days and a bastard on his worst. Today definitely qualified as "worst."

How did she know who they were? Orin firmed his grip on his sword hilt, though what they could do against her weapon, he wasn't sure.

She hurried to calm them, throwing her hands in the air in placation. "It's . . . a really long story. But I swear I'm not going to harm you. So, do you want to come back to my house and get patched up or sit here and wait for something else to come by to kill you?" Gwen jerked her thumb over her shoulder in the direction she had appeared from. Tor eyed her and then turned to Orin, shrugging. "I don't think we have a choice. I'll grab the horses," he said and limped away.

Cae's eyes were suspicious. "What's the short version?" he growled at Gwen.

"The short version of what?" she asked, looking flustered.

"The long story," Cae clarified, suspicion still stamped on his face. Orin noticed his friend's grip on his sword hilt was white knuckled.

"Oh." Gwen closed her eyes and took a deep breath as if to center herself. "The condensed version is either I'm in a really shitty dream, or it's time for my family to return Caliburnus to Arthur?" She said it as if questioning her own words.

The two knights jolted at the mention of the fabled sword.

"So it would be grand if you told me this is just a really awful dream," Gwen continued, rocking a little bit on her heels while her lips pressed into a grim line. Her eyes flicked around the woods and then back to Tor as he emerged from the dense forest with three horses in tow. "I've had enough of them to last a lifetime. That's how I know who you guys are." Her eyes flicked to Orin's scars. "That's how I know what you fight, who you've lost. About Arthur and Caerleon."

Orin looked at Cae, who shrugged fatalistically. They had done this dance dozens of times. Avalon brought new soldiers through the mists at least once or twice per century, though hearing about the dreams was new. The last soldier to join them at Caerleon appeared forty years ago but lasted only two days before he left the safety of the castle, trying to get back home, and was torn apart by an ogre. Orin and the others had told the man that what Avalon took, Avalon kept, but he wouldn't listen. Eventually those who survived—like Henri, a Frenchman who was exploring the American frontier when he was taken—were incorporated into the ranks of the remaining knights. Some even started families with the women Avalon had taken when bringing Caerleon through the mists from the mortal realm.

"I'm afraid not," Orin murmured, realizing that Gwen was on the edge of panicking. He couldn't blame her. Although it had been centuries since it happened, he remembered the visceral fear when the residents of Caerleon had woken to find themselves in the strange land of Avalon, threatened by creatures out of stories. Orin looked at the others, who had dragged their bleeding and tired bodies into their saddles.

"Lead on then. Let us see if Avalon did indeed bring your home." He waved at the woods behind her.

"Okay," Gwen said with a terse nod. "Right, home. Okay." She swung around, looking for her tracks then said a soft command to the dog. "Sax, home."

On command, the dog started off into the woods, Gwen right behind him. Orin climbed into the saddle, exhaustion settling in his bones. The knights glanced at each other one last time, then fell into a single line behind the woman and her dog. As the trees began to thin, the outline of a two-storied structure could be seen.

Gwen glanced over her shoulder and pointed. "We'll go around back to the kitchen door. That's where I have my Search and Rescue first aid kit stored."

Orin had no idea what a Search and Rescue first aid kit was, but she seemed so focused on taking care of their wounds that he continued following her. Perhaps she was an herbalist or midwife? If so, then Avalon had brought them someone truly useful. It was rare when the magic here did something helpful, so he would take this boon and be glad of it. Orin's eyes meandered over her body. She had an incredible figure showcased in those tight black pants. He jerked his eyes up, shaking his head at himself. That way lay danger. No, he was not going to get drawn in by any of that nonsense.

True to her word, she led them around to the back of the well-maintained, white house and motioned for them to dismount and come inside. Orin noted they'd need to tether the horses away from the flowers circling Gwen's home creating a riotous array of colors. The dog huffed and his nose wrinkled, showing a glimmer of ivory fangs, as Orin went to take the first step onto the wraparound porch.

"Sax, come," Gwen said, her voice firm. The dog entered the house but not before glancing over its shoulder at the knights one last time. "Come on in and have a seat at the table. Let's see what we can do to stop the bleeding and get you cleaned up."

They limped inside while Gwen pulled open a door that looked to store boots and jackets and pulled out a red, square box with a shoulder strap. Orin looked around the room. The three of them sat at a round, light-wood table with matching chairs while the kitchen sported white and gray colors. The entire space felt soothing after their time in the woods. Except for the bright-red splotches of blood on the floor. Those were more concerning than soothing. Orin blinked, realizing that exhaustion was making him muzzy.

"All right, let's triage the worst on each of you then start on the smaller wounds," Gwen said, placing the first aid kit on the table. Orin watched as she pulled out odd-looking bandages, clear bottles, scissors, and other items he didn't recognize. She was gentle but efficient in her work, Orin would give her that. Though the clear liquid from one of the bottles burned like fire as she wiped it around the wounds to "kill the germs," whatever that meant.

"The rest can wait," Orin ordered, stilling Gwen's hands as she went to tend to his bloody knuckles. "You need to pack what you can, and then we need to head to Caerleon. The fae are out in force today. It's not safe."

Gwen blinked at him. "Right, okay. Um, wait a minute." She wandered through the pristine kitchen, pulling out a drawer and grabbing three towels. Then she opened a large silver box against the wall, pulling out three more clear bottles. She brought them back to the table, cracking each of the bottles open. He realized that each one was a cold bottle of water, and he marveled at the magic contraption that kept things cold. "Here. You can at least wipe off the blood while I pack. I'll be quick. Sax, let's go."

Cae waited until the strange, striking woman and the grumpy black dog had headed out of the room and up the stairs before turning to his companions as he poured water on the towel and began wiping the blood off his face. "This is new. Avalon has never brought a structure along with a person. Do you think she actually has the sword?"

"I have no idea," Orin replied.

"Guess we will see. At least Avalon brought a pretty one this time," Tor said, standing up with a wince and wandering toward the rest of the house.

"What are you doing?" Orin hissed. Tor had always been nosy, and the last thing they needed was the knight wandering upstairs and upsetting Gwen.

"Just curious." Tor vanished through the door into the front of the house.

Cae sighed. "We should probably keep him out of trouble." He groaned a bit as he stood, hobbling after Tor.

Orin followed, his eyes glancing around the house. The next room over was some form of large sitting room that led to the front door and the stairs to the second level. White bookshelves stuffed full of literature lined the walls. Tor was already reading the book spines and pulling random books off the shelf.

"Do you think the lass will let us take some of these? I'm bloody bored of the books we already have. No idea what all of these are, but anything new is good." He started piling the books on the small table next to a comfortable-looking teal chair.

Cae ran a finger across a beautiful violin displayed in an open case on a table under the large front window. His eyes glanced at the guitar leaning against a stand next to it. "We should take these with us if we can manage. Doesn't matter if she's any good. Music would be good for morale."

Orin gave a sharp nod, so Cae closed the violin case and moved to put the guitar into the case sitting behind the stand. The man turned and took the instruments to set them down by the back door. Tor was still pulling books down, staring at the covers before filtering them into piles, so Orin looked up the stairs to where the woman, Gwen, had gone.

He wondered about her. Why had Avalon brought her? Did she really have Arthur's lost sword? How was she going to handle the transition into life here in Avalon? Was she currently upstairs quietly panicking? Was she claimed by someone?

His brow furrowed at that thought. Why should he care if she was wed to someone? Orin couldn't afford to entangle himself again with a woman. His grief-ridden heart couldn't take it. The fact that another part of his anatomy thought they should see if she was available both irritated him and had him assessing the staircase again.

Orin gave her ten minutes before he headed up the stairs while his friends continued to poke around the lower level, learning what they could of Gwen from what they found in her house. Two large bags were already stationed at the top of the stairs, ready to be tied to the back of the horses.

Three white doors lined the hallway. He glanced into the first one, seeing a bedroom with a meticulously made bed. Soft, soothing shades of blue, gray, and forest green drenched the room. He got the impression that Gwen did not have a soothing personality so this room must be where she went to calm herself. A small smile graced his face as he thought back to her staring at them in alarm while barking "what the hell." He wasn't sure what the next room was, but he thought it was a lady's dressing and bathing room. The third though, that's where he found Gwen.

She had changed out of those tight black pants; *more's the pity* he thought. Now she sported rough, light blue pants with tall, brown, laced boots and a short-sleeved, fitted, purple shirt that covered both shoulders. He wondered if she had more tattoos, his brain stuck on the colorful art that was showcased earlier in the woods. Over the shirt, Gwen wore odd black armor with the word POLICE written in bold, white letters on the back. Her dark brown hair was captured in a long braid. She stood in front of a table with an array of weapons spread out before her as she handled a strange looking bow. Her black dog lay on the floor next to her and growled at his presence.

Gwen glanced over her shoulder, met his gaze, and told him, "Almost ready."

Then she turned back to the table and placed the bow down. With practiced ease, Gwen belted a long knife and a sword around her waist then slung a quiver over the dark armor, working to settle it more comfortably. The firearm she had used earlier and some more knives went into a long, soft tan case, and she placed a small, similar-looking weapon in a holster on her hip. Picking up the bow, she turned and looked around the room as if to ensure she wasn't leaving anything important, her brown eyes still a bit wild.

Orin dropped his eyes from her striking face down to the sword on her hip, and his breath caught in his throat. A dark-indigo gem graced the pommel, the round cut edges reflecting the sunlight from the window. Supple black leather wrapped the bronze hilt. For a moment, power seemed to pulse from the long, sharp blade, curling around Gwen before dissipating. Orin exhaled heavily as the brief show of magic tingled across his skin.

"Caliburnus," he murmured. He looked at Gwen. "You were telling the truth."

CHAPTER THREE

GWEN

Gwen wasn't sure what to think as she and Sax padded upstairs, the hunter-green carpet runner softening her footsteps. She felt the breath backing up in her lungs as panic rose. When she got to the top of the stairs, she blindly walked the sage-green hallway of mismatched frames holding pictures of Saxon, her and Logan, her and Gran, and her college diploma.

Okay, deep breath, she thought. *Gran used to say in all her stories that Avalon was known for having a mind of its own, with a few peculiarities. Apparently being able to grab people and transport them here happens to be one of them. Time to think logically; I'm awake, in Avalon, and knights of the Round Table who I have been dreaming about are sitting in my kitchen, including the man I have the hots for. What the hell?*

A hysterical laugh bubbled up out of her throat before she could choke it off. Just to be sure this wasn't some weird dream, Gwen pinched herself, hard. The skin on her bicep throbbed in pain.

"Ow, shit," she hissed, rubbing at it and swinging into her bedroom. Sax's claws *tick tick ticked* beside her on the hardwood floor. The sound grounded her, as did the fur on his head when she buried her fingers in the thick pelt. She took one quick glance out of her window, but the strange trees still remained.

"Not a dream then, Fur Face?" Gwen whispered, still not quite convinced. *But even if it was a dream,* she thought, *I could be practical.*

"Okay, first things first, let's get some clothes and toiletries." Thanks to her mother's propensity for whisking her away on their travels at a moment's notice when she was younger, Gwen was adept at speed packing. Shirts, pants, sleepwear, undergarments, socks, and a pair of leopard-print flats and her favorite light-blue sneakers went into her two canvas duffel bags. The bags were gifts from her father when she turned sixteen—a birthday he actually remembered. Her dad claimed they were for when she joined him on his digs, but he never invited her. Gwen swung into her bathroom and grabbed her toiletries—toothbrush and toothpaste, brush, hair accessories, razors, makeup, and the most important menstrual items. She couldn't exactly pop down to the store for more when she needed them, after all.

Gwen dragged the two bags out to the hallway and left them at the top of the stairs and moved to what should have been her guest room. Since she wasn't in the habit of inviting her parents for a visit—not that they would come if she did—she'd converted it into a workout room and, for lack of a better term, an armory. One half of the room was graced with a treadmill and a set of weights and yoga gear. The other half held her gun safe while her bows and quivers hung on the wall alongside her sword and knife collection. An innocuous-looking, small white bookshelf stood under the bows and next to the gun safe.

Gwen moved over to the bookshelf and pushed it to the side, revealing a hidden safe built into the wall. With quick fingers, she keyed in the combination and pulled out a gray cloth-wrapped bundle. Unwrapping it, Gwen pulled out a sheathed sword and what she suspected was the reason she was here.

For generations, her family watched over the sword. Family legends said that after Arthur's last battle, one of her ancestors scoured the battlefield and found the fabled Excalibur—properly called Calibur-nus—and vowed to keep it safe until the Great King returned. The sword was then passed down to whoever had dreams of Avalon, and Gwen happened to bear that burden after her gran. Unbidden, a memory surged to the forefront.

The strange mix of peppermint and lilac that she associated with her grandmother surrounded Gwen as firmly as Gran's arms. At nine years old, Gwen found the strong presence of her grandmother still soothing.

"Easy, easy," her grandmother murmured, stroking Gwen's hair as the child buried her face in the woman's shoulder. The pink cardigan Gran wore felt scratchy under her cheek, but it matched the bright pink of her grandmother's hair. Gran's unconventional hair color tendencies irked Gwen's mother, but Gwen found it fascinating how easily and how often her gran could change her close-cropped gray hair.

"Just a dream, honey, it was just a bad dream." Gran pulled the covers up around Gwen and tucked an old, worn teddy bear into her grand-daughter's hand. "You know, the best thing to battle a nightmare is a story." Her grandmother's warm brown eyes looked steadily at her as she settled into the nearby rocking chair. "Once upon a time, there was a place of trees and mist called Avalon. It exists alongside our world, but the people who live there live in a big castle by a lake."

"The place where King Arthur went?" Gwen asked.

"Yes, exactly. Arthur still rules there. So one day, Arthur and his knights went along the lake shore, searching for a lady. She is tall and very thin and very pretty." A small smile graced Gran's face as if she personally knew the woman and was describing a friend.

"She has blond hair, really long blond hair," Gwen told her Gran. Her voice became timid. "The Lady of the Lake, right?"

Gran turned shrewd eyes on her granddaughter but kept rocking. "That's right, Gwen. Very good. Yes, the Lady of the Lake. They were searching for her because they thought she could send them home to Britannia." Gran leaned over and brushed the hair out of Gwen's face. "Do you remember the stories of the wee folk and the lords and ladies of the fae, sweetie?"

"Yes, ma'am." Gwen nuzzled into her grandmother's touch.

Gran smiled, pulling the rocking chair closer to Gwen's bed and reached out to grab the child's hand. "Not all of the wee folk are nice, unfortunately. Arthur and his knights are supposed to protect us from the fae who aren't nice." Gran rocked slowly, the creak of the old wood rhythmic on the floor. Then she patted Gwen's hand. "Wait here, honey. I have something else that will help with the nightmares."

Gran rose, the light casting her shadow regally on the wall. She gave her granddaughter a penetrating glance before walking out of the room, her footsteps pattering away. She was back shortly, a long thin bundle in her hands. She sat on the edge of Gwen's bed and placed the cloth-wrapped bundle on Gwen's lap.

"Here, honey, this is yours now. It will be yours to guard until a new guardian in the family is identified, or Avalon summons the blade home." Gran peeled back the cloth, revealing a long sword with a gold, black leather-wrapped hilt.

A vision slammed into Gwen's young mind of a large, stone cavern with a pulsing stone standing in front of an archway, sending the child reeling back from the honor her gran wanted to bestow upon her. The cavern called to her, but Gwen didn't want to answer.

Shaking her head to clear the memory, Gwen moved over to the gun safe and pulled out as much ammo as she could safely stuff into her tan gun case and police vest pockets. She grabbed her favorite compound bow off the wall, putting everything onto the table in front of the window. Despite what her gran had said, the sword hadn't helped with the nightmares. They came slowly at first until sometime in her mid-twenties; then the dreams were a nightly occurrence. Occasionally, Gwen lucked out and the dream allowed her to interact with the slim, blond woman known as the Lady of the Lake. Gwen dared to say that she could even consider the Lady a friend. At this point, she and the fae woman had talked over the last decade and a half regarding Gwen's life, the burden of protecting the sword, and the Lady's loneliness at being constrained to the lake around Caerleon yet not being part of Arthur's court.

Saxon alerted Gwen to Orin's presence, and she turned to look over her shoulder at him. Of the three knights in her house, he was the oldest, with gray starting to creep into his dark hair at the temples and peppering through his close-trimmed beard. Three scars marred the left side of his face, leaving it in a perpetual scowl. Orin was tall with broad shoulders that filled the doorway, and he wore his armor, a dull black chain mail and a round shield and sword, with ease. Her fickle heart beat a little faster at the sight of him. God, she loved a sexy silver fox.

"Almost ready," she told him, turning back to the secondhand, scarred table to hide her hot cheeks and how flustered she felt. At thirty-five, she would have thought she could handle being around a man she was attracted to without being a ninny, but apparently not. Shaking her head at herself, Gwen belted Caliburnus around her waist, pulled on and adjusted her quiver, slid her rifle along with a few of her favorite fighting knives into its case, and added her service weapon to her belt. She adjusted her quiver again; it felt odd over her police armor, but she would make it work. Then she slid on Saxon's K9 vest and large DO NOT PET collar.

"All right, I think that's it," she told Orin, her eyes bouncing around the space one last time to make sure she wasn't forgetting anything. Then she looked at the knight, but his gaze was on the sword belted around her waist.

"Caliburnus," he muttered. "You were telling the truth."

"Yeah, I try to do that as much as possible. Surprise." Gwen wriggled her fingers in the air with a small, mocking smile. "So, I guess I'm ready to go. Can you help me get my duffel bags downstairs?"

Orin held her gaze for a moment then gave a quick nod, disappearing from the doorway. Gwen looked down at Saxon.

"Talkative fellow, huh," Gwen whispered, not sure what to make of Orin now that she had met him in person. "All right, let's do this," she told the dog. His furry eyebrows twitched as he stayed sitting. If a dog could look skeptical, Saxon managed it. Gwen sighed. She was pretty sure Saxon was too smart for his own good. She was definitely sure he was too opinionated for his own good. "Come on, Fur Face. I don't have any desire to run into any more of what we saw in the woods."

The dog heaved his own sigh but stood and followed. When they got to the top of the stairs, the bags were missing but she still paused, listening. The quiet murmur of the men's voices wafted up from the main floor, and she strained to hear what they were saying. The words were elusive, but the tone grew increasingly urgent.

Guess that's our cue, Gwen thought, steeling herself for whatever came next. She and Saxon headed downstairs, Gwen letting her fingers trail over the family photos hung on the wall as she went. Fear and grief battered her heart for a moment as she passed the final picture of her and her gran. *Let's hope your stories can help me here, Gran.*

Swinging around the bottom of the stairs, Gwen felt the fear and grief change rapidly to annoyance, and her eyes flashed as she surveyed the destruction of her library. Tor gleefully pulled books down, setting some in a growing pile but putting others back seemingly at random.

"What the hell are you doing?" Gwen stomped down the last step and hurried into the room.

Tor flinched at her barked question before flashing a quick, disarming grin. "Finding something to read. The options have been limited the last few centuries." He waved a book at her, one she recognized as a steamy sports romance novel. "Do you have something we can put these in?" he asked.

Gwen blinked at him, registering the fact that the citizens of Caerleon hadn't had anything new to read in that long. Her annoyance dissipated. "I guess, yeah, let me grab a bag from the closet."

After she gave Arthur back his sword and Avalon sent her back to the mortal world, Gwen would straighten everything up and replace whatever Tor took to Caerleon. Her bank account could handle it. She brought a book bag over to Tor and helped him load it up, explaining the different books quickly and helping the knight weed out a few. She didn't think the Caerleon library would ever need *Auto Repair for Dummies.* Tor hefted the heavy bag and led her out as she noticed her violin and guitar were missing.

"Cae's already got them strapped to his horse. Haven't had new music in ages either," Tor said over his shoulder with another grin. The dark-haired, dark-skinned knight headed out the back door to help Orin finish strapping the duffel bags and book bag to the back of the horses while Gwen paused and looked around her house. She hoped that it would be okay, that the fae would leave it alone, and that somehow, she, Saxon, and the house would make it back home to Littleton. Then she followed, locking the door and giving it a tiny pat farewell.

The men were already mounted, and Orin moved his bay horse over to stand next to the steps, holding out his hand. "You'll ride behind me," he ordered.

Gwen raised an eyebrow at the command but nodded, slinging her bow over her shoulder before grabbing his hand and using his foot to swing herself up behind him. It took a moment for her to settle. Then she wrapped her hands around his waist to steady herself.

"All good," she told him. "Sax will follow with no issues."

"Good. We move quickly back to Caerleon." Orin kicked his horse, and they moved off at a slow trot. Cae and Tor fell behind them in a line. It took a few strides, but Gwen's riding lessons from when she was a teenager came back to her, and she found herself moving with the rhythm of the trot. She dared one last look back at her house in time to see mist swirl around it. A strong breeze blew through the clearing, and when the mist dissipated, her farmhouse was nowhere to be seen.

"Well . . . crap," she muttered.

"What?" Orin asked, stopping and turning his mount. The others glanced back, then turned to look at Gwen and Orin, their faces a study in disbelief and fear. Avalon was normally a jealous mistress. The fact that She had brought Gwen's residence and then snatched it away was unsettling.

"Something is brewing," Cae said, the wind ruffling his auburn hair. "Everything is off today. Let's get going."

They stayed quiet as the horses picked through the bracken-strewn forest floor. Gwen tried to pay attention to the woods as they wound their way through them. The thick forest and undergrowth forced the men and horses to take the few game trails they could find as they made their way toward Caerleon. Light filtered down through dense foliage, and birdsong surrounded them. Small streams criss-crossed the forest floor like quilt threads. Unlike the fae kingdom that bordered Avalon, the forest's air and landscape was damp but not shrouded in mist. Verdant plants and mushrooms in a wide array of colors dotted the ground, providing both sustenance and hiding places for small rodents, reptiles, and forest mammals.

After two hours of riding, they broke out of the trees, and Gwen was dazzled by the brilliantly blue lake that spread out before them. Down the shoreline, the land jutted out into the water, creating a small peninsula.

A large, white stone castle consumed the entirety of it. The walls climbed three stories high, bordered by low crenelations across the battlements. Between the merlons and crenets, Gwen could see small figures patrolling the stone parapet that led to four large bastions which jutted out from each corner to improve the knights' and soldiers' firing range. The tower keep could barely be seen over the battlements. A massive dark-iron portcullis hung over the thick front gate lined with murder holes to repel invading forces.

The sight of it took Gwen's breath away.

She had dreamed about this place ever since she was a child. Seeing it in person was mind-blowing. Gwen wasn't too proud to say that seeing it freaked her out a little bit. The dreams had always been a bit hazy, as if the edges were shrouded in mist, but her view now was crystal clear.

I wish this was a dream. Her hands clutched at Orin's belt as Gwen drew in a sharp breath.

Orin patted one of her hands. "We'll pass you over to the women when we get there, and they'll get you settled while we report to Arthur."

Gwen frowned. "Shouldn't I give him Caliburnus?"

"I'll take it to him." The man patted her hand again, and Gwen frowned at his back.

"Like hell you will." Gwen shifted behind him while Orin looked over his shoulder at her in irritation. She scowled right back. "My family didn't keep it safe for centuries, and I didn't get stuck here, for you to waltz off with it."

Orin snorted, turning back toward the keep as he steered the horse around the edge of the lake. "That's not up to you. You'll be in the women's quarters until we can figure out what to do about you."

"Are you forgetting the fact that I saved your lives earlier? Patched you up? Isn't that worth something?" Gwen demanded.

Orin sighed in irritation. "There is a hierarchy and certain expectations for those of us who are left. The expectation is that the women and children stay within the bounds of their assigned duties and safe within Caerleon. They are few in number and more precious for it, so you will abide by our rules."

"Lovely," Gwen muttered. "I'll have to introduce you all to the concept of feminism."

Orin grunted. "Of what?"

Gwen's lips twisted in an unamused smile as she looked out over the lake. "The concept that men and women are equal. I can protect myself." Her gaze focused on the water as odd ripples shivered across the water near them. "Is that normal?" she asked Orin, pointing.

"Is what normal?" Orin asked, looking where she pointed. He tensed. "No, no it is not." He moved to kick his horse back into a trot as a tall, thin, blond woman emerged from the lake and strode out of the water.

Water dripped down her azure dress, the cloth drying as the rivulets chased their way towards the lake. She sparkled as a smile lit her face, highlighting the angle of her sharp cheekbones. The fae tucked her straight, blond hair behind her slightly tipped ear then raised her hand in greeting.

"It's her," Tor hissed, pulling out his sword. "What are you doing, woman?" he snapped at Gwen as she slid somewhat inelegantly off of Orin's horse and started jogging toward the shore.

"Be right back!" she called over her shoulder. Gwen focused solely on the woman, who waved again at Gwen. "Hi," Gwen said, her voice high and breathy. Saxon sat next to her, his tail thumping on the ground as he stared at the fae woman.

The fae held out her elegant hands in welcome with a wide smile on her face. "Young Gwenhwyfar, I did not expect to see you except in dreams but well met indeed." She grasped Gwen's hands tightly, her slight build hiding an inner strength. "I wondered which of the guardians Avalon would choose to return the sword, and I am ever so pleased it is you."

Gwen's face stretched into a matching smile, remembering that in the last dream, she and the Lady of the Lake had discussed Logan's last office prank and how some of the squires and pages had started dropping stones into the lake from the walls, forcing the Lady to shoot water geysers at them. The boys had not been amused, but both women got a good chuckle at the thought of the young boys and teenagers scurrying away, dripping wet. "It's good to see a familiar face, Lady. I'm freaking out a little bit to be honest. Actually, freaking out a lot. Is this really real?"

"Now that you're here, call me Viviane, child, and yes, I'm afraid it is. Avalon has decided it is time for changes, and you will be at the center of it." Viviane's grip loosened as the fae glanced at Caerleon.

"That doesn't sound ominous at all," Gwen commented, rocking back and forth on her feet, tension in her shoulders. She pulled her hands away. "What exactly does that mean, especially for me?"

Viviane's eyes flicked over Gwen's shoulders to the knights who were drawing closer. "They don't want me talking to you, but anytime you need me, come to the lakeshore, and I will be there as quickly as I can. I will answer your questions then. Here come your gallant defenders." She winked then turned and slid back into the water, disappearing from sight as the water rippled against the shoreline from her passing.

"Well, that wasn't useful." Gwen looked down at her dog then turned to find Orin looming right behind her, anger stamped across his face. "Oh, hi. Sorry. I needed to talk to Viviane."

"How do you know her?" he snarled, pointing at the water.

"The Lady of the Lake? She's been in my dreams since I was nine. Long story, remember? I told you that I used to have dreams of this place." She put her hand up to hover over his facial scars. "I was eleven when I saw how you got these." She pointed at Caerleon. "I've dreamed enough about the castle that I know its layout, and I've seen the variety of fae you fight." Gwen's eyes turned serious. "I know about Mordred and his plans to destroy Caerleon in order to rule Avalon and find a way to the mortal world. Mordred uses his magic to dominate the fae courts and force his people to fight each other and you."

Orin reared back in surprise while Tor cursed under his breath. Cae surged forward as if to hit Gwen but paused when Orin put his hand out. Gwen knew Cae hated anything to do with the fae, and she no doubt worried him with her strangeness and the knowledge she possessed. She wondered if he thought her a fae spy. Gwen could only hope to get Cae and anyone else on her side; how else was she to get home without their support?

"Look, I know you don't have any reason to trust me other than maybe the fact that I have Arthur's sword, but I don't want to be here, and I didn't want the dreams. I was given no choice but to bear this burden, okay? Don't forget that I did kill those fae for you. I am a friend of Caerleon's, not an enemy." Gwen nodded for emphasis.

"She's no friend," Cae snapped as he pointed to where Viviane had disappeared.

"Well, maybe not to you, but Viviane and I have talked for roughly two decades, and she's been nothing but friendly in my dreams, so . . ." Gwen shrugged. "I consider her a friend. Orin, are we going?" she asked and pointed at the castle. "Sorry for the detour," she added, trying for a conciliatory tone.

Orin sighed and scrubbed his face. "This day has been the worst."

"You're telling me," Gwen commented, waving her hands to take in everything then the men. "This . . . is a lot to deal with. I'm one more surprise away from having a total meltdown. I'm supposed to be prepping for another day at work, and then I was supposed to tell my dad that my mom wants to end their marriage. This..." She waved her hands around again. "Yes, this is the worst. But, we can get through this as long as you trust me and also let me talk to Viviane." Her glare matched Orin's at this point. God, why did he have to look so sexy when he was angry? She probably looked like a frazzled and indignant chicken.

"Let's get going then," Tor said. He looked up at the parapets and the men watching them. "They've got to be wondering what's going on. I'm tired and hungry, and the lass is right. This has been a lot to take in for all of us, so let's at least go process it with a mug of ale. I've got a new barrel we can tap and try."

"Fine," Orin muttered. Gwen could practically hear him grinding his teeth in frustration. He turned and headed back to his horse, forcing her to trail after him. The knight hauled her into the saddle behind him as the mare fidgeted.

"Thanks," she murmured, glad that they were almost at Caerleon. Riding double was not the most comfortable, especially with all her gear and Orin's armor.

Gwen peered up at the stone walls as they drew close to Caerleon. She knew from her dreams that the walls hid multiple buildings, gardens, and the main keep, but seeing it in person was intimidating. Where her house always felt welcoming, the castle felt heavy with age and sorrow. She couldn't help but shiver a bit as they passed through the shadows of the gate, under the ominous murder holes, and headed toward the stables. Gwen felt the stares from the men on the parapets, and she tried to smile at the children who stopped their games to watch the four of them pass through the courtyard. When Orin drew the horse to a standstill, she was already sliding down out of the saddle, her hand going to Saxon's fur as the dog sat and leaned against her leg.

They stood in a large bailey, or courtyard, that was ringed by buildings safely nestled against the walls. Green areas abounded inside the walls and even on portions of the buildings' roofs, maximizing garden plots so the castle could be self-sufficient during times when hunting in the woods meant facing droves of Mordred's forces. Inside the keep was the main dining hall, Arthur's war room and his chambers, and the armory.

The kitchen, chapel, library, training grounds, and living quarters were attached to the tower keep in smaller stone buildings. Adjacent to the walls lay the wooden stable, right next to the wattle and daub barracks.

"Tor will see that your bags and instruments are taken to the women's quarters," Orin said, standing next to her as he passed the reins to a gawking stable boy. The warrior sighed, brows furrowed, and stared at Gwen as if he was trying to decide something. She stayed silent and waited. He seemed to finally make up his mind, nodding decisively. "He'll take you there as well. Cae and I will let Arthur know you're here and take the sword to him." Orin held out his hand for Gwen to hand over Caliburnus.

"Like hell you will," Gwen repeated, crossing her arms and frowning. She flicked her fingers as if dismissing his plan. "I told you, my family didn't bear this burden, and I didn't suffer for the majority of my life for you to run off with it."

"We could take it," Cae growled at her. He used his height to loom over her, sneering. Clearly Cae was not one to be won over easily.

Gwen spared the belligerent knight a glance before shaking her head and shifting her weight to her back foot. The audacity of this guy. "You could try."

For the first time, she saw Cae smile, and it wasn't a nice one. "With pleasure." He reached for the sword as Gwen rolled her eyes. Gwen had tired of such testosterone-driven antics long ago.

As Cae's hand landed on the hilt, Gwen grabbed his wrist and moved to lock his elbow, her foot shooting out to kick his leg out from under him. She twisted, using the momentum to throw Cae into Orin, sending both men thudding to the ground. The horses snorted and danced away, held in place only by the stable hands holding them. Saxon rushed in front of Gwen, snarling at the men as she held on to the handle of the dog's vest.

"Easy, Sax. Fuss," she commanded, bringing the dog back to heel with the German command. Gwen looked down at Cae and raised an eyebrow at him. "You done?" she asked, keeping her hand on Saxon as the dog continued to rumble growls deep in his chest.

Cae shot up, towering over Gwen. "What are you playing at?" he snarled, poking a finger toward her.

"Playing at? I'm not playing at anything. I told you that I'm taking the sword to Arthur, and damn it, I am going to. It's not my fault you underestimated me and landed on your butt." She batted away his hand and poked back at his chest. "In case you forgot, I saved you guys just a couple of hours ago. That should at least earn me something."

"It'll earn you a trip over my knee," he ground out.

"God, you're such a grumpy asshole. What the hell, Cae? I've been nothing but nice since I landed here, and you've been nothing but a raging, paranoid dick. I told you that I don't want to be here. I want to give Arthur the sword and go home." She poked him again. "You want to go another round? I'll be happy to put you back on your ass to prove whatever point I need to, but you're not funneling me off to sit in a part of the castle while you guys trot off with my sword and possibly my way home."

Cae scowled at her as Orin muscled the other knight out of the way, looking now with more interest at Gwen. "Fair point. You've proven more useful in your first few hours here than most who've been taken by Avalon." He scratched at the salt-and-pepper stubble adorning his jaw. "Fine, you can bring the sword. Arthur needs to know you've got something going on with that lake fae anyways. You can explain it to him so I don't have to."

"Wonderful," Gwen said, eying Cae to see if he was going to try something else. "But the firearms go with me. I won't have an accidental discharge happening and someone getting hurt." Orin nodded, letting her grab the rifle case from where it hung off his saddle. She slung the case over the same shoulder as her bow, jostling both around until she was comfortable.

"This way," he said with a jerk of his head. Gwen took a deep breath and followed.

Here goes nothing, she thought as they headed into the main keep.

CHAPTER FOUR

ORIN

Orin had to admit, he was not expecting Cae to come flying at him, so he didn't brace himself. The courtyard ground was unforgiving as the two men tumbled to the ground. He blinked at the sky for a second, hearing the snarling of Gwen's Saxon and her quiet command to calm the large black canine.

"You done?" she asked, her tone calm and rich with confidence while she raised a mocking eyebrow at them.

She's a healer and a warrior? he thought, heaving himself off the ground as Cae leapt to his feet to yell at Gwen about her "attitude." As she and Cae argued, Orin took stock of her again and the weapons and armor she wore.

He had to admit that Arthur would find her presence interesting, though he had to wonder how the king would react to her name. Arthur's Guinevere had died centuries ago. Having another Gwen here might bring up sorrowful memories, which was not something he wanted for his king. Then again, maybe having the same moniker would make Gwen more intriguing to Arthur, and Orin scowled at that. He had very conflicted feelings for Gwen at the moment, and tossing in someone's else's interest felt . . . threatening. He shook his head at that.

Orin shoved Cae away from the woman. Cae had a wicked temper when provoked, and Gwen was provoking it with just her presence. Orin had to admit that he sided with Gwen; Cae was being difficult solely to be difficult.

"Go see to your family, Cae, and have your wife tend to your wounds," Orin ordered his friend. "I'll be taking Gwen to see Arthur, it seems." Cae threw him a frustrated look, then a cold one at Gwen before limping off.

Gwen sighed, looking up at him. "I swear I'm not trying to cause trouble, Orin." He scratched again at his chin, liking the way she said his name. Where had that thought come from?

"Look, where I come from, I'm a police officer. They're basically the equivalent of a knight. We're peacekeepers, protectors," she continued, making him raise an eyebrow in surprise. "I've had martial training since I was nine and the dreams started. My gran made sure of it. I won't insist on much, but I won't let you treat me like a doormat."

"A what?" he asked, brows drawn together in confusion.

"You know, the thing you put in front of your door to wipe your feet. It means that I won't let you guys walk all over me. Avalon brought me for a reason, right?" Her brown eyes stared up at him intently, as if willing Orin to understand.

He didn't, but at this point, he was tired, hurting, and wanted some ale and time in a relaxing bath and solitude in his room. Orin jerked his head toward the keep and turned, expecting her to follow. Her footsteps fell in quietly behind him, and the dog's claws *tap tap tapped* against the stone hallway as they entered the keep.

Orin wound his way in and up the keep, heading toward the war room. "Show Arthur respect," Orin told her over his shoulder as he put his hand on the large wooden door to the war room. He turned to look at her, catching her frown.

"I've shown you guys nothing but respect except when you showed your asses." Gwen plopped her hands on her hips, mouth pursed as she scowled at him. Saxon chuffed at her feet, echoing his owner's displeasure.

His mouth quirked in a small smile. Damn, this woman was bold and irritating by turns and nothing like Arthur's Guinevere. Orin wondered again how Arthur would receive their newest citizen. "If you say so," he responded, wanting to see if it lit her up. He wasn't disappointed as anger flared in her eyes, and she hissed out a frustrated breath. The door swung open as Orin moved into the room, not waiting to hear a reply.

Arthur didn't look up from his reports as they walked in. The man's authority blanketed the room. His king stood as tall as Orin, with slightly broader shoulders, dark hair, and keen green eyes that rarely missed things. Crow's feet and strong worry lines dug into his skin.

Arthur had held Caerleon together against Mordred's attacks for centuries through sheer will power. While Orin knew his king felt like their demise was inevitable, the man still tried to find ways to keep his people safe. Arthur spent his days in the war room, poring over maps, the scouting reports, and Caerleon's inventory lists, trying to ensure his people survived. Their exile to Avalon plus the warriors they had lost to the fae's aggression left Orin's king with an odd mix of paranoia, apathy, and grit.

"Summary report?" Arthur asked, his voice a low rumble that Orin knew could bellow across a battlefield with ease.

"The fae are out in force today, and Avalon brought us a new one," Orin replied. Arthur's eyes flashed up from the report to land on Gwen, who stood slightly behind and to the side of Orin. Orin lifted his hand to hide his widening smile as Arthur gaped at Gwen. He couldn't remember ever seeing his king taken so completely off guard. Then again, Orin knew the feeling. He hadn't known what to make of Gwen when first seeing her in the forest.

"Who is this?" Arthur asked, still blinking in shock at Gwen.

"Hello," Gwen said, stepping over to the desk Arthur was sitting behind. She held out her hand toward him. "It's nice to meet you." She cast a quick look at Orin, narrowing her eyes. "I guess you could say I'm Avalon's latest victim."

His king looked in bemusement at the hand, reaching out to take it. Gwen gave it a firm handshake before re-curling her hand around the bow string and gun case strap hanging off her shoulder. Saxon sat next to her, pressed tightly to her leg.

"Where did you find her?" Arthur looked over at Orin, who schooled his face back into an impassive mask.

"She found us in the woods as we were fighting against the third patrol we ran into this morning. The woods are crawling with fae today. We thought we were done for when she showed up and took them out. She's got weapons like Henri's, only better I think. Avalon brought her home as well, so she took us there and tended to our wounds. We brought her and some of her things back before her house disappeared." Orin shrugged and looked at Gwen. He pointedly looked at the sword at her hip.

"Right," she said, reading his body language perfectly. "I think this is yours," she continued, unbuckling the sword from her belt. Gwen put it on the desk in front of Arthur. She tapped the hilt once, looking at Arthur intently. "My family kept it safe for you. That is, if you still want it."

"Is that Caliburnus?" Arthur breathed as he stared at the sheathed sword. His eyes flew back up to Gwen, who nodded. Orin noted the slight tremble in Arthur's hands as they reached for the blade, pulling it out of its sheath. Just like back in Gwen's home, the sword blade reflected the light from the nearby windows while the gemstone in the hilt flared to life.

"I thought this lost long ago," Arthur said, voice pensive. He touched the blade with light fingers.

"One of my ancestors found it after your last battle. It's been passed down through the generations to whoever had dreams of Avalon." She dared another glance at Orin. "And whoever had a connection with the Lady of the Lake."

"*Her*." Arthur ground the word out. Menace flashed in his eyes as he focused on Gwen as if assessing if she was human or fae.

"She's been a good friend to my family through the centuries and to me as well," Gwen said, staring back at him. "Viviane has also been a good friend to you and your people. Remember, she's the same person who gave you Caliburnus in the first place so you could save your kingdom." She tapped the gemstone again, and Orin sucked in his breath as power shivered in the air around the blade. Arthur dropped his gaze. "Your Majesty," Gwen said, "I'd like to formally return your fabled blade and end my family's guardianship."

Arthur graced her with a bemused look. "Thank you and your family for keeping it safe for me," he told her, curling the blade toward him possessively. The king placed it on the desk in front of him, heedless of the reports scattered underneath. He dropped his eyes to it for a moment before continuing, "Do you have a name?"

Orin braced himself. It was anyone's guess how Arthur would act. Gwen seemed to wonder the same thing as she paused before introducing herself.

"Gwenhwyfar McMillan. But most people call me Gwen." The woman's quiet voice matched her rigid stance, as if expecting a blow.

Arthur's hands stilled, and his eyes closed briefly as if in pain. "What?" His voice was a low growl, laced with sorrow.

"Gwen?" she said, though her voice was hesitant. She gave him a shrug and a kind, small smile when the king stared at her again. Then she sighed, shifting her weight from foot to foot. "I hope this doesn't make things weird. My family had a tendency to pick historic names, and Gran insisted on this one for me." Gwen winced. "My father's name is Arthur actually."

"Of course," Arthur muttered. Then he raked his eyes across her, taking in her odd garb, the weapons slung on her shoulder, and the quiver on her back. His brows knit together in confusion. "These are yours?" he asked, waving his hand at them.

"Yes. Orin was right. I have more modern firearms than Henri." She pointed at the bow. "This is a compound bow."

"She can fight," Orin added helpfully.

"What?" Arthur blinked at them. Orin nodded, rolling his lips together to prevent a smile at Arthur's flabbergasted expression. Centuries of war meant Arthur was typically unflappable, but the surprise of Caliburnus and the one who borne it here was enough to pierce even Arthur's usual taciturn exterior.

Gwen turned slightly so she could look at both Orin and Arthur, ignoring the flummoxed look on Arthur's face. "So, Orin wants me to talk to you about my friendship with Viviane, but I seem to keep hitting you with surprises, so that can wait if you want."

"But you just arrived in Avalon. How do you already have a relationship with that . . . fae?" Arthur asked, pausing to swallow what was probably a very unflattering description of Viviane.

Gwen hummed a bit and then looked around before divesting herself of the gun case and bow on a nearby table. She rubbed at her shoulder a bit as she turned back. "I have to start by explaining how my family came to have Caliburnus to explain how I know Viviane. Can we sit? I'm tired and heading toward an adrenaline crash, and Orin is standing there trying to be stoic when he's been chewed on by a couple of werewolves like a rawhide bone."

"You're hurt?" Arthur whipped his eyes over to his second-in-command, assessing quickly and seeing the few bandages peeking out underneath Orin's armor and clothing.

Orin tipped his head toward Gwen as she dragged over a couple of chairs for him and herself. "Tor and Cae took some wounds as well, but the worst were tended to at Gwen's home, thanks to her." He looked down at the scrapes across his knuckles. They were crusted over with dried blood and dirt. Maybe he should have let Gwen take care of that before heading back to Caerleon. He'd have to see to it himself once he reached his rooms.

"So you're a healer?" Arthur asked, sitting down in his own chair. His fingers ghosted across Caliburnus as if he couldn't bear to touch the blade.

"Not exactly. I mean I know basic first aid because I used to do Search and Rescue and at one point wanted to be an EMT before I decided to be a cop. So the guys probably should get looked at by someone else."

As she talked, Orin scratched at the back of his head in confusion. He had as little an idea as what an EMT or cop was as he did Search and Rescue, though now that he had time to think about it, the last one appeared to be self-explanatory. Arthur seemed as puzzled, but Gwen was already forging on.

"So back to the family story. One of my ancestors was a farmer in ancient Britannia, and after your last battle, she and her children were combing the battlefield and found Caliburnus. She must have known how important it was, so she took it and hid it. If the family legend is true, one of her children started seeing visions of Avalon in their dreams. I have no idea if this is accurate or not because oral history is always suspect, but considering the last few generations of guardians had dreams, I would assume the first guardians did too." She paused to take a breath, her hand falling to her dog's head as he laid it in her lap.

"Anyways, so my gran was the person before me. She used to tell me stories about this place, much to my mom's displeasure and my dad—well it depended on when he was paying attention or not, which wasn't often—he always enjoyed the stories because he's a historian and archaeologist, but he thought they were just stories. Gran passed the sword on to me around the time I turned nine, when I had my first dream. That was when I started talking to Viviane." She noted the men's displeasure and rolled her eyes. Then she flushed as she realized she had done so in front of royalty. Orin's reminder about respect flashed in her mind, but she forged on. "You realize that she's as much a victim as you guys are, right?"

"What does that mean?" Arthur growled, slamming his hands down onto the table and leaning over it to glare at Gwen.

Gwen blew out a long breath, looking as if she was trying to figure out how to explain it. She rubbed the back of her neck then dropped her hand back to Saxon. Whenever she needed comfort, it seemed to Orin that she looked to her dog for it.

"Okay, so I know Viviane is a fae, and you're fighting the fae, but hear me out. They're not all bad. No, you wait," she said sharply as Arthur opened his mouth to argue, and Orin muttered a curse. "Do you know what Caliburnus is?" Arthur and Orin both looked at each other, confused at the turn of the conversation.

"A sword?" Orin asked, feeling ridiculous at the obvious answer.

"Well, yes, but it's an artifact of power, right? You can feel it? When Arthur touches the sword, the air gets heavier as if a storm was coming. I assume that's what magic feels like," Gwen said, waving her hands in front of her for emphasis. The king nodded for Gwen to continue.

"So according to Viviane, it's an artifact of power that the fae used to use to open a gateway between this world and the mortal world. That's what Avalon is. She's a bridge between the human world and the fae lands beyond the mists." Gwen shifted uncomfortably in her chair and tossed her gaze between the two. "I know that speaking about him probably isn't your favorite topic, but this ties into Mordred and his rise to power."

Arthur sucked in a breath at the name of his nemesis. "How do you know . . . ?" he trailed off as she raised a finger to stop him.

"The dreams, remember, and what Viviane told me in them. As Mordred was gaining power and taking over the Mist Lands and subjugating the three fae courts, he had to do something with those who rebelled. He used the magic stored in Caliburnus and its ties to Avalon's magic to rip open a portal from Avalon to our world." Gwen paused, looking speculatively into the distance. "I would assume that's why we have cryptid sightings in our world. They're probably exiled fae who are still alive and hiding from humans. Huh, never thought of that before. That's kind of neat."

Once again, Orin felt like Gwen was talking a different language. *What the hell was a cryptid?*

"Viviane was one of those exiled," Gwen continued. "Only she was powerful enough that she managed to grab Caliburnus as she was chased through the gate. I don't know why she gave it to you. You're going to have to ask her, but I'm sure she thought it was necessary . . . or maybe she wanted to help you defend your home." She raised an eyebrow at Arthur, who frowned at her.

"This part is a little fuzzy to me because Viviane says she doesn't know how this works either, but at some point, Avalon's magic became partially sentient? She's connected to it somehow; I think because Viviane's the only fae to have passed through the gate twice, once to the human world and then back here. She has a unique tie between the two worlds that Avalon uses to keep finding people to bring here. Pretty sure that's also why Viviane's tied to my family and whichever one of us is chosen to be the sword's guardian. Something about her magic, Avalon's magic, and the sword creates a link with each of us who protects Caliburnus so we can talk to Viviane in the dreams we have of this place."

"That's quite a tale," Arthur said slowly.

Gwen nodded at him. "I know. It sounds like a story for a novel or something, but needless to say, I've been dreaming of this place and talking to Viviane in those dreams since I was a little girl." She turned and looked at Orin. "That's how I knew who Orin, Tor, and Cae were when I found them in the forest. Though, I have to admit, I was really hoping this was a dream." She turned back to Arthur. "I'm still trying not to freak out about all of this because what the hell? Just because I had the sword, the stories, and the dreams, I never once imagined myself actually here." Her voice rose, edged a bit in panic. Gwen shook her head, clearing her throat. "I'm hoping that now that I've completed my family's mission, Avalon will pop me back home the same way She did with my house."

"Say I believe all of this," Arthur said. "Why would Avalon choose you to bring me the sword and not one of your forebears?"

Orin noted the rapid pattern of Arthur's fingers on the table. The king stared at Gwen as if she were a grand puzzle to unravel.

In turn, the woman shrugged again, dropping her hand to Saxon's head where it lay in her lap. "I have absolutely no idea, but Viviane said something at the lake about a lot of changes coming. Maybe that's why your knights kept running into fae patrols today? It's normally a lot quieter, right?"

Arthur grunted a yes at her. "Mordred's left us alone for over a century. We're far beneath his notice as he continues to tighten his rule of the Mist Lands."

"Things felt off today as we patrolled," Orin told Arthur. "It wasn't just that there were significantly more fae out in the woods. Even the air felt different, as if something is coming."

Gwen shifted again in her chair and steepled her fingers in front of her chest. "About that . . . Viviane's last words were that I may be the catalyst for the change, but I don't know what she meant. Orin and Cae scared her off before I could ask."

Orin scoffed. "I did no such thing. She's a fae. I thought I was protecting you."

Gwen scowled at him, and Orin tried to ignore her as she leaned forward to make her next point. She smelled like flowers and something both spicy and sweet.

"I told you I was going to be right back after I talked to her, which implied that I knew what the hell I was doing and would be fine." Her crisp voice told Orin exactly what she thought of him, and damn if he didn't like the jolt of attraction that her fire sparked in him.

"But what if you weren't?" Orin asked, trying to keep his voice reasonable and not doing a great job of it as her eyes pinned him in place. He might like her spunky attitude, but Orin also knew what kept their people safe and talking to the fae wasn't it.

"Then I would handle it. I handled the patrol this morning and Cae's hissy fit, didn't I?" Gwen huffed out a breath and turned back to the king.

"Hissy fit?" Arthur asked, looking at Orin. The knight sighed and shook his head at Arthur, trying to move the conversation along. "Did something happen with Cae?" Arthur continued, not dissuaded in the least.

"I don't think he likes me, and it shows," Gwen said before Orin could answer.

"Girl," Orin growled, frustrated that she was still controlling the conversation. He wanted to protect Cae from Arthur's attention. Cae was a solid knight but not the most personable. How he managed to have a family while some of the other more genial knights hadn't paired off yet was a mystery to Orin. Cae's wife was a saint.

"What? It's true. Also, I'm thirty-five, so don't call me a girl. You can tell anyone else that needs to know; if they try to touch me without permission, I'll be handling them in a similar manner. I'm not going to be pushed around just because I have tits instead of a dick." Gwen folded her arms, which made Orin drop his gaze momentarily to her breasts before wrenching his eyes back up to her face. He flushed as he realized she had noted the lapse.

Arthur snorted a laugh at Gwen's frankness. "Are women in your time and place always this bold?"

"Some of us, yeah. Others may not curse, but they're allowed to have their own opinions and stand up for themselves. Women can fill traditionally male occupations and vice versa. There are always the usual holdouts, with some men being jerks about it, but I'm in a job that used to be only open to men." Gwen wilted a bit, exhaustion evident in the way she slouched down a bit in the chair and crossed one leg over the other.

"What is it you do?" Arthur asked. "If you're not a healer and not a warrior, then what are you?"

"I'm a police officer," Gwen explained, using that term again. Peacekeeper, Orin remembered her saying, and she continued on with that exact phrase for Arthur.

"We're not that different from your knights, to be honest. It's our job to ensure our communities are safe. We make sure people follow the laws, help people who need to get out of bad situations, and try to prevent bad things from happening if we can. Me and Sax," Gwen looked down at her dog with a smile. "We're part of the K9 unit, so we do a bit of everything. Community outreach, finding illegal substances, catching criminals. He's trained for Search and Rescue along with me, which means if someone gets lost in the national forests near our town, we go out and help find them."

So that's what Search and Rescue means. Orin scratched at his beard. It sounded like Gwen had a lot of experience handling herself. The human world wasn't Avalon though, and human criminals weren't the fae. Her overconfidence could get her killed. He, Arthur, and the other knights had seen that before with some of the men brought to Avalon over the years.

Arthur looked at her speculatively. "Avalon has always brought someone useful, so there must be something to Her bringing us a . . . police officer, you said? We don't have much room for a peacekeeper. Mordred's not one for peace, but maybe you can be useful."

"Damned by faint praise," Gwen muttered under her breath.

"Orin can see you to the women's portion of the castle, and the women can get you settled into one of the empty rooms. I need some time to process everything you've shared." Arthur ran his fingers again across Caliburnus, then he took a deep breath. "I do appreciate what your family has done for me, keeping this safe. Thank you."

With that, Orin knew they were dismissed and rose to his feet, ready to show Gwen out.

CHAPTER FIVE

GWEN

Gwen followed Orin, exhaustion grinding down into her bones so much so that she couldn't even appreciate the view in front of her. Several hours had passed since she'd awoken in Avalon, meaning it was well after nightfall back home. Since Gwen had been up before the sun, she'd gone to work, done her multi-mile run, and had multiple adrenaline-inducing moments on top of that. She was as close to done as she had been in a very long time. The last time she was this exhausted may have been after the one all-nighter she pulled in college junior year.

Gwen's mind wandered in her exhaustion. Would Logan have to handle their shift solo tomorrow? What would the captain think when Gwen didn't show up on time? After things settled here in Avalon, would Gwen be able to get home? How was she going to explain everything when she did? A dull throb set up in her temples as her thoughts swirled. Did she even have the brain cells to worry about this right now?

She was thrilled when Orin finally led them to the kitchen where women bustled about while a few younger children were being minded in a corner, kept out of the way but close by if they needed their mothers. Gwen hoped this meant she could finally sit down and stay sat, or even better, someone could show her to a bed.

Maybe if I go to sleep, I'll wake up and this will all have been the weirdest dream ever, she thought wistfully. If she was really gone, she wondered what Logan and the chief would think. Would they think something bad had happened to her or that she had packed up and disappeared with no warning? She doubted her parents would notice. Would anyone else though?

"Bronwyn," Orin said, getting the attention of the oldest woman in the kitchen. The steel-gray-haired matriarch turned from where she was chopping vegetables and pushed a few hairs that had fallen from her severe bun out of her eyes. Then her keen blue eyes landed on Gwen. Her gasp drew everyone's attention to Gwen, and there was a flurry of muttered conversations between the women present.

"This is Gwen. She's . . . new, obviously, and Arthur would like you to help her get settled in." He turned to Gwen. "The women will see to you." Then, he nodded and left.

Into the lion's den, Gwen thought and smiled at Bronwyn, shifting her gear on her shoulder. It was starting to hurt.

"So, hello. I'm sorry to interrupt." She sighed wearily. "It's been a long day. May I sit?"

That seemed to snap Bronwyn and the others out of their surprise, and Bronwyn, along with another much younger woman with light brown hair and friendly hazel eyes, rushed forward. Gwen was pretty sure her name was Eidytha.

"You poor thing. Of course," Bronwyn said. "We've never had a woman join us before from beyond Avalon! What a wonderful surprise for us. We've already got your things put into a room for you, and Tor told us about your dog, so it's one of the few rooms that leads out onto a small courtyard." Gwen realized that Bronwyn was one of those scarily competent people. The matriarch bustled around the table, pulling together a small meal as she dragged out a chair for Gwen, all while talking quickly.

"It was definitely a surprise," Gwen agreed. She nodded at Saxon, sitting calmly at her heels, his nose snuffling the scents in the air. "Is it okay if he stays with me? We're a package deal. Is there somewhere I can put my weapons that won't be a danger to the little ones?"

"Maybe I should help her get settled into her room?" Eidytha asked helpfully. She flashed a warm smile at Gwen, who smiled back.

Bronwyn simply nodded. "A wonderful idea, Eidytha."

Got the name in one. Gwen congratulated herself for remembering it. She was rubbing her tired brain cells together as fast as possible at this point to stay upright and coherent. She recognized what this was. A major adrenaline crash coupled with her normal end-of-day tiredness.

"Thanks, that would be lovely. I'm dead on my feet. It was evening time when I was taken, so this is the end of my day rather than the middle."

"Poor thing, you do look exhausted. Those who are brought to Avalon always look somewhat shocked and take some time to settle," Bronwyn said in a soothing tone. She shoved the plate of food at Eidytha, who took it and winked at Gwen.

Okay, Eidytha has a sense of humor. Gwen was glad of that.

"Maybe you can rest between now and dinner. Then, Eidytha can come get you so we can all eat here and you can meet everyone. Well, not everyone. We'll let the menfolk eat in the large banquet room." Bronwyn eyed Gwen, taking in her outfit and the weapons. "Needless to say, they'll be all aflutter to meet you. Is that the normal garb these days for women?" Her brows furrowed a bit.

"'Fraid so," Gwen said, resigned to the fact that this would be a frequent question. "It's been several centuries, and a lot has changed. Women wear pants, hold a variety of jobs, and are allowed to be fighters."

"Well, we've known of women warriors, haven't we, Bronwyn?" Eidytha asked, her smile widening. "Just haven't had one here at Caerleon. How exciting. Come along, young Gwen!" Her cheerful voice beckoned as she turned and headed out of the kitchen. Gwen flashed a thankful smile at Bronwyn, nodded at the other women, and hustled to follow Eidytha.

"Bronwyn means well," Eidytha commented over her shoulder as Gwen caught up with Saxon trailing along at her heels. "She doesn't do well with change, even after all these years. Now we've got you next door to me in the single women's quarters. Three of our rooms look out on a triangular courtyard that butts up against the wall. Doesn't get much sun, so we don't use it really. Your fine-looking lad—it is a boy, right?" She pointed at Saxon.

"Yes, his name is Saxon."

Eidytha smiled. "Well, your fine-looking Saxon can use it instead. The nice thing is it does let some light into our rooms through the windows, so you won't need as many candles, unlike with some of the interior rooms."

"I appreciate that." The fact that the women were being so welcoming soothed her frayed nerves, unlike her time with the knights.

"Here we are," Eidytha said with another bright smile, pulling a key out of a small bag hanging off her belt. She unlocked the door then turned and handed Gwen the key. "This is yours. Tor mentioned you might have some things the children should stay out of, so you can keep the doors locked." She opened the door and swept in, putting the plate of food down at a small two-person table under the window.

Gwen blinked at the room then looked down at Saxon before divesting herself of her weapons and police vest on the sole table in the room. The room was furnished simply with a bed large enough for two people, a roughly hewn table with two chairs, a chestnut wooden wardrobe, a comfortable looking tufted blue cushion, and a blond wooden chair that faced a cold fireplace. A door out to what Gwen assumed was the courtyard was next to the table, so she led Saxon over to let him out to do his business.

"Now, we've put clean linens on the bed. You can put your clothes in the wardrobe. I guess we will need to talk to someone about getting you a weapons and armor rack?" Eidytha nodded at that, as if committing the request to her memory. She looked at Gwen. Her voice was softer as she said, "Welcome to Avalon, Gwen. While this isn't what you ever wanted, we'll do what we can to make the transition to living here with us as easy as possible."

Gwen felt tears prick in her eyes, and she blinked rapidly while letting out a long breath. "Thank you, Eidytha. This is so overwhelming, and well . . . the guys were nice enough I guess, though a couple need to pull their heads out of their rears. You and the other women thinking so much through for me really helps."

"Our pleasure," she said, clapping Gwen on the shoulder. "The garderobe is down the hall if you need to relieve yourself. I'll be back right before dinner to get you. Just rest now." Then she swept out of the room.

Standing in the doorway to the small courtyard, in the shadow of the castle, Gwen finally let herself breathe. The panic she'd been holding at bay sped right in, and her knees almost buckled as she watched Saxon explore the tiny bit of grass.

What the hell was this day? What does the future hold?

"All done, Fur Face?" Gwen asked. Saxon huffed as he came over to sit in front of his mistress, looking up in focused adoration at her. She ran her hands over his face and behind his ears, scratching in his favorite places and bringing comfort to both of them. "How about a nap? I think we could both use one."

She turned, closing the door as Saxon entered the room and began nosing around and learning the smells. With a weary sigh, she pulled his vest and collar off and then stripped out of her boots and bra and laid down on the bed, staring up at the stone ceiling.

Saxon hopped up on the bed, nosed at her, then turned three times and sighed as he curled up. His eyebrows wriggled at her and his tail thumped until she put her hand on his head.

With another sigh, holding Saxon for comfort, Gwen let herself drift off to sleep.

She awoke several hours later to a knock on the door. A soft gloom flooded in from the small-paned window, and light kaleidoscoped through the multi-colored blue, red, green, and clear glass, heralding the evening hour and nighttime's approach. Gwen blinked, trying to figure out where she was. It all came flooding back as a second knock came and Eidytha's voice floated through the door.

"Gwen, we'll be congregating for dinner soon. Are you well and awake?"

"Move, Fur Face," Gwen told Saxon, trying to untangle herself from the blankets and her dog. He looked at her, unimpressed, and moved down to the foot of the bed before lying back down again.

Gwen staggered over to the door and opened it to Eidytha's smiling face. Gwen knuckled sleep out of her eyes and grinned back at the other women. It was hard not to. Eidytha had that kind of energy about her that invited people in. Gwen could see the two of them possibly becoming friends.

"Hi," Gwen said, "I need a couple of minutes to wake up and get myself together."

"Wonderful. Come next door when you're ready, and we can go together." Eidytha beamed. "We've already sent the squires and pages out with the men's food, so we can eat peacefully in the kitchen." With a wave, Eidytha headed to her room.

Gwen closed the door and leaned against it for a moment. Her wish of waking up back in her own room hadn't been granted, so it was time to put her big girl panties on and deal with her new reality. Or at least that's what she told herself as she straightened up, ran a brush through the hair she'd loosened from her braid and put on the dreaded bra again as well as the flats she dug out of her duffel bag. Then she looked at Saxon, who stared at her with his head on his paws.

"You want to go out?" she asked him. The dog rolled onto his back. "I'll take that as a no. Stay, then, and guard. Don't eat any of my stuff. I'll bring you something after I get done." He chuffed again and closed his eyes.

"Lazy dog," Gwen muttered, grabbing the uneaten food. She let herself out into the hall before locking the door and pocketing her key. She stuck her head into Eidytha's room.

Where the room she had been assigned to was sparse and utilitarian, Eidytha's was anything but. The woman had obviously used her time here to create a cozy and warm room. Rag rugs covered the floors and plush blankets mounded on her bed. Candle sconces were installed on the walls, so the evening gloom was washed away in golden light.

"Ready? Let's go then." Eidytha let herself out of her room and beckoned for Gwen to follow. "You'll be meeting both the married and single women and a few of the younger children. You'll find that we age slowly here, so many of us are still able to bear children. Don't be surprised by the babies and toddlers. The married women and some of us single women have birthed children over the years, but the last two or three years have seen a significant number of pregnancies."

"Okay, that's cool. There's only like fifteen or so of us women, right?"

Eidytha nodded. "Yes, so we've got nine of us paired off in marriages and six of us who are like me. We've been married but lost our husbands to the fae."

"I'm so sorry," Gwen murmured, grimacing. Gwen's mixed feelings toward the fae stood in direct contrast to those in Caerleon. Whereas all fae were the villains for Eidytha and the others, Gwen knew from her time talking with Viviane that the fae suffered under Mordred's rule, and that rebellion brewed under his tyranny. These facts did not bring back those who had been lost, however, and Gwen squeezed Eidytha's arm in support.

"We appreciate the sympathy. Our time here has been horribly hard. There's been a lot of grief, but the new burst of life in the babes has made things easier. The men don't mind keeping us company if we so choose." Eidytha cast a wicked and knowing grin at Gwen.

Oh yes, Gwen thought as she stifled a small laugh, *Eidytha and I could be friends.* Eidytha was obviously not a prude and had a good sense of humor.

They reached the kitchen, where the hustle and bustle of earlier had calmed. The women and their small children were arranged around the main cooking table, chatting as they started to eat, keeping toddlers in their laps. In the case of one mother, Gwen could see a baby probably not much more than four months old in a sling across her mother's chest. The quiet noise died down as everyone turned to look at Eidytha and Gwen.

"There you are!" Bronwyn said, waving the two over to the empty chairs next to her. "Come, sit. We'll get you some food and then start introductions."

With that, Gwen was ushered into the fold. The women welcomed her with warmth and enthusiasm, with laughter and so many questions that Gwen could barely keep up, let alone eat. She met Cae's wife, Alodie, a sunny-dispositioned woman who wrangled twin toddlers with the help of the woman, Isola, next to her. Then there was Aislinn, Fiona, Brea, Maebh, Kyla, Agrona, Blaine, Avina, Demelza, Hertha, and Idina. With Gwen's brain back online post-nap, she finally remembered everyone's names.

"I heard you brought books?" Kyla, a dark-haired woman with light brown eyes, asked. "We haven't had anything new for entertainment in ages."

"Tor pillaged my personal library, and then I helped him get a little something of every genre. I can go grab the bag and show you some?"

"That would be amazing!" Kyla practically vibrated in her chair. Her excitement was contagious as the other women started chattering about the possibilities while Gwen made her way back to her room. Thankfully, she didn't get lost.

Saxon barely opened his eyes when Gwen came in and grabbed the backpack next to her duffel bags. She patted his head affectionately then hurried back to the kitchen with the bag slung over her shoulder.

"Okay, here we are." Gwen put the bag down next to her chair and began fishing books out. "This one's a mystery, no gore. It's a straight-up whodunit art heist with a female detective tracking down the art thief. This one's good, another mystery, but it's a murder mystery and kind of gory with the murder scene, and it has a broody male detective main character."

She pulled another one out and flicked a glance at Eidytha. "This one is a romance, but it's what's known as an open-door romance, so it's . . . well, it's kind of graphic about the bedroom scenes." Gwen grinned at the gasps around the table. "Maybe we won't let the guys see this one, but it's really good. The main male character messes up and has to do a lot of groveling to get the main female character's affection back." She handed it to Eidytha, who looked rather pleased and thumbed through the pages while Gwen pulled out some more books.

"This one is another romance, but this one is a closed-door romance. You get the gist that they're going to be intimate but no details. This one is a historical fiction from ancient Rome. Oh, and this one is fun . . . it's a romantic comedy so there's a lot of funny misunderstandings that keep the main characters from getting together until the end."

She passed out more books, giving a quick synopsis of each as the women laughed, gasped, or exclaimed at the contents. Gwen looked around the table as they chatted about the books, commented on the cover artwork, and the clean print on the pages. As they talked and laughed, she realized how much she took modern amenities for granted.

This was how Orin found them when he stuck his head into the kitchen. The laughter died down as the women all turned to look at him. Gwen found it amusing when he cleared his throat and shuffled his feet as Bronwyn stood.

"What brings you down, Orin?" she asked. It was clear that Bronwyn ruled here, even if it was Arthur's castle.

"Arthur wishes to see how much martial training Gwen has." He looked at her. "So, I'd like to see you at the training arena tomorrow after breakfast."

"All right." Gwen nodded. "One of the ladies can bring me down probably, or I'll find my way."

Orin cleared his throat again. "Good, good. See you in the morning then. Ladies." He disappeared quickly, leaving the mood of the room dampened.

"Well, I guess we should finish up and ensure you have a good night's rest then," Bronwyn said, clucking her tongue in disapproval at Orin's interruption. "Let's get this all cleaned up. You ladies take whatever books you'd like, and Gwen can take the rest back to her room. We will get them to the library tomorrow sometime." She patted Gwen's shoulder. "I know you don't want to be here, but we welcome you and are glad to have you. Tonight's been one of the happiest in a long time."

Gwen smiled wanly but acknowledged Bronwyn's point. "Thank you all so much for being welcoming. This has been overwhelming, but this dinner really helped."

"Let's get you settled in for more sleep then," Eidytha commented, standing and motioning for Gwen to follow. Gwen looked down at her empty plate and then around the kitchen, looking for where to put it.

"Oh, don't worry about that, dear. We'll take care of it tonight and work you into the chore roster over the next few days," Bronwyn told her. "Off you go with Eidytha. Oh, and here are some meat scraps for your shadow."

Gwen chewed on her lip and took the bowl to her room, where Saxon heartily approved of Bronwyn's offering. As her dog scarfed his food, Gwen paced.

Days? Would she even be here long enough to land on the chore roster? Gwen dragged her hands through her hair, huffing out a breath as she thought back to Bronwyn's last declaration.

Surely now that Arthur had Caliburnus, Avalon would return me home . . . right?

Once Saxon finished, the canine hopped up onto the bed, turned three times, and lay down, licking his teeth clean while eying Gwen as she slowed her pacing. He woofed, catching his mistress's attention. Gwen sighed, shoulders slumping as she ran a hand over his head.

"Well, Fur Face. We survived day one. Let's hope we survive the future." Gwen shook her head, knowing that fretting anymore would get her nowhere and crawled back into the bed. While her time in the kitchen was enjoyable, it was draining. She fell asleep quickly and slept a dreamless sleep until Saxon woke her up at dawn.

CHAPTER SIX

ORIN

There was a pervasive smell to the training room that even having the double doors open to the practice grounds couldn't quite dissipate. It smelled of sweat, leather, metal, and earth. That scent swirled around Orin as he stood with Tor, Bedevere, and the two Frenchmen, Henri and Louis. Orin wasn't sure exactly how he was going to follow Arthur's orders.

"She's obviously . . . different from our women," Arthur had said at dinner. "She can fight, so let's see what else she can do. Have her report to you tomorrow and run her through the normal exercises we do with the other newcomers."

So here he was, waiting for Gwen with an entourage because of course the men were curious. The women had descended on Gwen last night, and not a single one had been in the main dining hall for dinner. They had all eaten in the kitchen, making Gwen feel welcome and keeping her from being overwhelmed by the entirety of the castle population. The men outnumbered the women three to one, and many of the women were permanently paired off, like Cae and Alodie. The few unpaired women usually ended up in semi-long relationships without the fetters of marriage before moving on to another relationship. Some of the men had paired off with each other as well. Orin expected many of the men would be interested in pursuing something with Gwen. He couldn't stop his frown at that thought.

"She killed the fae that were attacking you, you say?" Henri repeated. The man stroked at his blond-and-gray beard, his blue eyes intense in his tan face. "With a rifle? Do you think the mademoiselle will let me see the weapon? I am curious how they have changed since my time."

"Are you interested in the weapon, Henri, or are you using this as a way to wrangle an introduction before everyone else?" Orin grunted.

Henri grinned and shrugged, the action quick and light on his lanky frame. "If it allows me both, then I see no harm in it."

"Right, well that's not what we're here for today," Orin retorted, looking out in the courtyard. Based on the light slanting in the doors, he expected Gwen to arrive any minute.

As if on cue, light feminine chatter drifted through the door that led to the rest of the keep. It sounded like Gwen was being accompanied by a few of the women so she wouldn't get lost finding her way. He could appreciate the gesture, but the women never came here. It seemed out of place as their laughter rang through the room. Three of the women stood with Gwen at the door as they finished their conversation. Gwen turned her back on the room to say something in a low tone that had the others giggling before they disappeared back into the keep.

"Damn, that ass," Louis muttered, eying Gwen as she stood with her back to them. The crow's-feet adorning his gray eyes crinkled as he leered. Orin rolled his eyes. Avalon had absconded with the dark-haired man when Louis had been in his early twenties and, despite the centuries, he was incorrigible as ever. Unlike his fellow Frenchman Henri, not a single gray hair bespeckled Louis's black hair. The fact that Louis kept his face clean-shaven only hammered home his continued youthful appearance.

Orin smacked him in the chest. "Show some respect."

Henri flashed another quick, wide grin and winked. "We can always show something else."

"Don't be crude. She is to be treated with respect the same as the other women," Orin snapped. "She might kick your ass if you don't," he added under his breath.

Even with his words about respect ringing in his own ears, Orin couldn't stop his gaze from raking down Gwen's body as she said farewell to the other women and turned. Her own gaze flitted across the room, taking it all in, before it landed on the group of men. She was wearing another pair of black skintight pants, some form of short puffy shirt with another shirt hanging out underneath it, and odd gray shoes that stopped at her ankles. Her hair looked to be braided and then twisted into a low bun at the nape of her neck. One of her large black travel bags was slung over one shoulder. She hiked it up a bit and headed over toward them.

"Morning." Her voice was cheerful as she surveyed the group, not looking intimidated in the least, despite the fact that all but Henri towered over her. Even Henri still had her by a couple of inches in height, and she was taller than the average woman.

"No dog?" Orin asked, adding a quick, "Good morning," as he tried not to be rude.

"Nah, left Sax in the room because I didn't know what we'd be doing, and I never take him with me when I go sparring. I'll take him out later wherever I'm allowed to and let him run a bit and do his daily training exercises."

"I'm Henri," the Frenchman said, shoving forward and holding out his hand. Gwen looked at him in bemusement and went to shake his hand, but he brought it to his lips for a quick kiss instead. "It is nice to meet you, mademoiselle."

Gwen cleared her throat and extricated her hand from Henri's. "Hmm, it's nice to meet you, Henri." She swung her eyes immediately back to Orin, and he couldn't help the small smile at Henri's crestfallen face.

"So, what's the plan today?" she asked, cocking one hip out as she hiked the bag's strap again up her shoulder. "I already warmed up back in my room so I'm ready whenever you are to get started."

"We typically ask each man what their martial experience is, and then we give him a chance to prove what he can actually do," Orin said cautiously.

Gwen nodded, all businesslike. "Great. I've studied tae kwon do since I was nine and picked up jiujitsu about a decade ago when my police partner dragged me to a class, and I loved it. I'm comfortable with knife fighting and the bo staff, and while I can use a sword and buckler, I'm not great with either. I prefer knives. I'm proficient with a bow, but I haven't had a chance to practice in probably close to six months. Due to my job, I'm proficient in the firearms that I brought. However, I won't be showcasing those because I want to save the ammunition for when I really need it."

Orin blinked a bit at the skill rundown as the other men muttered among themselves, eying Gwen with increasing interest. He wasn't sure exactly what tae kwon do or jiujitsu was, but it sounded like it was maybe hand-to-hand combat.

Gwen nodded when he asked. "Yes, tae kwon do is more about repelling an opponent while jiujitsu is more about grappling. Combined, they can work well together for fights, depending on the situation. Do we want to focus on unarmed combat today then?"

Orin rubbed his beard as he thought. "That and the knife and staff fighting if we have time. We can focus on the bow tomorrow. Bedevere here can assess those skills." The man nodded a hello to Gwen, who smiled back. Orin frowned at the bright smile she bestowed upon Bedevere, then glowered at the man. Objectively, Orin could admit that Bedevere stood out with his hazel eyes and copper red hair. Still, Orin shifted partially in front of him, pleased when Gwen's eyes skated away from his friend.

"Okay, where can I drop my bag? I'll get my hands wrapped up real quick, and then we can start." Gwen's eyes flicked over to Henri and Louis, who were speaking rapidly and quietly to each other in French. She raised an eyebrow and shot something back at them in the same language.

"You speak French?" Louis gaped at her.

"*Oui*." Gwen nodded. "So if you're going to be talking about my butt and showing yours, at least do it somewhere I can't hear, okay?" The two men looked abashed enough at this and then cowed as Orin glared at them.

Orin ground his teeth in frustration. Granted, he had had some thoughts on Gwen's body, but at least he kept them to himself. "I told you two to be respectful. For that, Louis, why don't you have a chance at sparring with Gwen?"

"That is a punishment?" the younger Frenchman asked, a lightning-quick grin crossing his face as he turned back to Gwen.

Her returning grin was sly and a little wicked. "Guess you'll have to see." The men snorted in amusement at Gwen's bravado, but she ignored them as Orin led her over to a bench against the wall. She dropped the bag and tugged the puffy gray shirt over her head as she toed off her shoes.

"Uh, what?" Orin blinked as the shirt came off, revealing more of the undershirt, which hung off her shoulders with two thick straps but left her toned, muscular arms bare. The floral tattoo he had caught a glimpse of on her shoulder was showcased with its brilliant pastel colors. The shirt dipped low in the back, showing some form of black band going around her chest and back. Another pastel tattoo snagged his full attention. It was a flower-and-vine-wrapped sword that followed the length of her spine. The pale gold, blue-jeweled hilt started beneath her neck. He wondered how far the blade went down her back as the tattoo disappeared beneath her shirt.

"What? Oh yeah, the sweatshirt? I was wearing it to keep my muscles warm and loose. Wasn't sure how long it would be before we hit the mats," Gwen said as she tied a knot in her shirt at her hip, drawing the loose teal garment tight against her. Then she reached into the bag and brought out long strips of bright white fabric that she began winding around her hands and wrist in practiced, deft movements. Once both hands and wrists were wrapped, she pounded her knuckles together a couple of times and bounced on her toes three times before turning to Orin.

"How are we doing this? Until someone taps out or until you call it?" Her brown eyes bored into his, and his attention drifted as his thoughts stuttered.

"Taps out?" Orin's brows wrinkled as he tried to follow the jargon.

Gwen tapped his arm, setting his skin buzzing. "You know, like when someone is in a grapple, and they tap the mat or their opponent to signal that they're yielding?"

"Ah, no, we usually go until I call it, but if you are more comfortable with tapping out, we can do that too." Orin rubbed at the warm spot where her hand had touched him. Even with the quick touch, he had felt the calluses on her hand. Gwen wasn't a pampered lady by any means.

"Nope. Let's do the normal way. What's allowed? Kicks, hits, elbows, grapples, throws?" Gwen strode by him, heading toward the mats.

Orin hurried after her, catching her elbow to make sure Gwen was listening as he said, "Yes. Let's see what you would do in real hand-to-hand combat. Louis has three centuries of experience on you, so he will make sure he doesn't hurt you."

Gwen ran her tongue over her teeth and gave Orin a measured look. He wondered what she was thinking.

"All right," she finally responded. "Let's do this."

Orin escorted her over to the round sparring area, where rush mats that were stitched tightly together padded the dirt floor. Louis was already there, barefoot and, much to Orin's disgust, without his shirt. Louis smirked at Orin, making a show of stretching in a way that showed off his muscles for Gwen. She seemed unfazed, stepping into the ring and stopping near Louis.

"Until I call it," Orin said as the other men stood next to him. "You may begin."

Louis winked at Gwen. "I promise to go easy, mademoiselle."

"I don't." Her voice was crisp, gaze focused. She raised her hands into a defensive position in front of her face and beckoned him forward. He grinned lazily, shrugging, and strode toward her.

Orin almost missed it, Gwen was that fast, but as soon as Louis was in range, she lunged forward with a devastating kick that landed mid-thigh and sent the man staggering back and falling to the mat.

"Interesting," Tor said as he stood next to Orin. They exchanged a look as Louis surged to his feet, eyeing Gwen warily.

She stood waiting for him, hands still in front of her face. Louis circled toward her, his own hands up. He swung at her face, and she ducked under his arm, landing three quick blows to his ribs before pivoting behind him and kicking the back of his knee, sending him thudding back to the ground.

The man growled something in French, clambering to his feet before rushing to Gwen to grapple with her. As he reached for her, she grabbed his wrist and then shoulder and tossed her body toward the ground. She twisted, using her body weight to throw Louis and slam him into the floor. She held on to his arm as he landed and twisted, using her momentum to keep him rolling, so he was pinned beneath her with his arm locked behind his back. Gwen wound her legs around his waist and then down to lock around his legs, effectively keeping him from pushing up. Her other arm wrapped around his neck in a choke hold.

"Go get Arthur. He needs to see this," Orin muttered to Tor. Then he strode into the ring. "Gwen wins this bout." Orin nodded as she immediately let Louis go and stepped back. "Louis, you want to go another round?"

"Yes," the man ground out, tossing a look at Gwen. She met his gaze impassively. Orin had to give her credit for her calmness.

"All right, then, back to positions." Orin left the ring. "Begin."

Gwen and Louis moved around the ring, Louis cautious this time. He feinted a few punches toward Gwen, but she dodged and batted them away, not being drawn in by his attacks. Then she went on the offensive, and Louis found himself being pushed around the arena as she punched and kicked out at him. They exchanged blows, Gwen landing more than Louis. Louis landed a punch that rocked Gwen back onto the mat, but she rolled with it, coming back to her feet as Arthur strode up to stand next to Orin.

Orin was glad that his king arrived in time to see what happened next because he knew he wouldn't be able to explain to Arthur how Gwen did it. She rolled back to her feet, and as Louis pressed his advantage, she lunged up, using Louis's leg as a steppingstone to twist around his shoulder, then wrapped her legs around his neck before throwing him across the mats as she twisted her body down like a fulcrum. It was a flashy move and utterly impractical on the battlefield, but it was effective. Orin recognized the level of control and training Gwen had to pull off such an attack without breaking Louis's neck.

Which, he thought, *was probably the point of her using the move.*

Louis hit the ground with a thud that drove the breath out of the man. Then he lay there as she stood and waited. When he didn't get up, she looked to Orin.

"Round two to Gwen," Orin stated, his respect for the woman growing. He hated to admit it, but so was his interest.

Gwen strode over to Louis and looked down at him, hands on her knees. "You okay?"

He grunted at her.

She grinned. "I don't speak gruntese. Does that mean 'yes,' 'no,' or 'I'm still not sure'?"

Louis groaned and sat up. "That is undoubtedly my least favorite experience between a woman's thighs I've ever had." Gwen snorted a laugh, braced herself, then offered her hand to help him up. As he stood and loomed over her, his gaze held begrudging respect.

She nodded at him then walked over to the other men, taking in the fact that the king had joined them. Orin noted Gwen's energy remained high as she said good morning to Arthur.

"You have a tattoo?" Arthur asked, startling a bright laugh out of Gwen.

"That's what you guys keep getting hung up over?" Her wicked smile was back for a moment. "I have four actually."

Well, shit. Orin flinched as his mind wondered where the other two tattoos were. The clothes she wore were way more revealing than what he was used to, but only the two tattoos he'd already seen were on display. He caught Henri looking speculatively at Gwen and knew he was having the same thoughts. Actually, the other men all gawked, even Arthur.

Gwen huffed another laugh out. She knew what was going through their minds, damn it, and didn't seem fazed.

Well, that's good, he mused. *Maybe she won't be overwhelmed by everyone's attention.*

Her eyes flitted back to Orin, assuming he was still in charge even though Arthur was here. Orin couldn't help standing a little taller at that and preen at the attention. Then he wondered what the hell he was thinking. He wasn't interested in impressing Gwen. She had just gotten here. Everyone else was falling all over Gwen, but he didn't want to be like the other men. What was he supposed to say anyway?

Gwen saved him from his running thoughts by asking, "So do I actually seem to know what I'm doing?" Then she winked and grinned cheekily at him, tapping her knuckles together. "Or you want to go a couple of rounds to double-check?"

His thoughts screeched to a halt. *Is she flirting with me?*

She continued, nodding at Louis. "He wasn't expecting it, so I had a leg up. But now you know, so do we need to spar some so you're comfortable with my skills or not?"

He was a gentleman, he reminded himself. He did not need an opportunity to touch her. He did not need an opportunity to be more interested. Somehow though, something in him yearned for that opportunity.

"You said you know how to fight with knives?" Orin knew what she'd said, but he didn't want to admit to himself that he was interested. "Tor here is our best knife fighter. He can test your skills."

"'Kay," Gwen said easily, starting the process of unwrapping her wrists. "I didn't bring my knives down, so I assume you've got some practice weapons we will be using?"

"Tor will get you situated." Orin turned to his friend. "Let's have you test both knife and staff skills while I talk to Arthur." Tor nodded and motioned for Gwen to follow him. She gave Orin another measured look he couldn't translate before walking over to the weapons racks with Tor.

"So, what are your thoughts?" Arthur asked. "Will she be a help, or will she be a danger to our people? I'm still not sure how I feel about her being friends with that fae."

Orin rubbed the back of his neck with one hand, watching Tor and Gwen pick through the practice weapons. "She's fast, obviously skilled. Not sure how good her fighting style would be on the battlefield though. We'd have to see how she spars with multiple opponents. Once she gets settled in, it might not be a bad idea to add her to the normal training rotations. She'd be good for protecting the women and children if we ever have a breach."

He narrowed his eyes as Gwen and Tor bantered and laughed about something. Tor flipped a knife and then handed it to Gwen, who shook her head while grinning as if they had shared a joke. She spun the knife in her hand, testing its weight.

"She seems to fit well with the other women?" Arthur asked, scrubbing a hand along his chin as he watched Tor and Gwen.

Orin grunted at that, remembering Bronwyn's steely gaze in the kitchen. "She has. I believe Bronwyn is planning to incorporate Gwen into the women's chores."

Arthur shrugged. "Well, that's something. Maybe her presence won't be as disruptive as we expected."

"Maybe," Orin murmured, remembering that the Lady of the Lake had referred to Gwen as a harbinger of change. "Are you staying to watch?" Arthur nodded, crossing his arms as Tor and Gwen made it back onto the mats.

Tor had the advantage of reach and strength on Gwen, but she had speed and a mostly unknown fighting style. Orin ran them through three bouts with Tor winning two and Gwen the other. For the staff test, they ran another three bouts with Gwen leading two to one simply because of her speed. By the end, both Tor and Gwen were drenched in sweat, and it was approaching mid-morning. Arthur had left after the first staff fight, but the others remained.

"That's enough for today," Orin told them as Gwen and Tor paused to catch their breath. He looked at Gwen, weighing his next words carefully. "Arthur and I agree that you've got useful skills though we're not sure if they'll be useful for anything other than keeping the women and children safe if the fae manage to get inside the walls."

"All right," Gwen agreed readily.

Orin raised an eyebrow. He hadn't expected such a genial response. "All right?"

"Sure. Your men have centuries of experience working together and know the area around Caerleon. You know how the fae fight. All of which I don't, other than what I've watched. So, if I'm at least helpful here, that's good enough for me." Gwen shrugged and pushed some sweaty hair tendrils out of her face.

A mental image of her sweaty and out of breath for other reasons flitted through his mind, which he shut down hard. *No, absolutely not,* he thought to himself.

To distract himself further, Orin continued, "Well that's good then. Let's plan on you meeting Bedevere at the archery range tomorrow morning, early. Bring your strange bow too. He'll probably be interested in seeing it." At this, the other man nodded.

"Sounds good. I'll put my gear back and get out of your hair. Bronwyn probably wants me to check back in with her." Gwen flashed them a grin and jogged over to the armor rack. She placed her staff back in the weapons rack before sliding on her shoes, scooping up her bag, and heading out the door with a cheery wave.

Orin blinked for a moment.

"Is she always like that?" Bedevere asked.

"Like what?" Orin asked.

Bedevere chuckled. "A whirlwind. Breezing in and out and knocking people off their feet."

Orin grunted. That was as accurate a description as he could think of for Gwen. He wondered who she'd knock off their feet next.

CHAPTER SEVEN

GWEN

Gwen was tired, but it was the good kind of tired . . . the kind that led to loose muscles and quiet thoughts. She worried that she wouldn't put on a good showing this morning but was pleased with how it went.

Slow and steady wins over hardheaded men, Gwen thought. She'd keep proving her usefulness and trustworthiness and maybe then she'd be allowed out to talk to Viviane. If anyone knew a way home, it had to be the Lady of the Lake. Arthur and Orin's asinine insistence that she couldn't see her fae friend could only last so long. If they continued to obstruct her opportunities to find a way out of Avalon because they didn't trust Viviane's intentions, well . . . surely there was a way to sneak out of the castle to talk to the fae.

Saxon was waiting for Gwen, shoving his face into her belly as soon as she opened the door. He sniffed all over her, as if ascertaining who she dared spend time with without him. Gwen laughed and rubbed her dog's ears.

"No need to be jealous, Fur Face. You'll always be my one true love." She leaned down, almost nose to nose with the German Shepherd. "Best dog a girl could ever ask for."

Gwen let him out in the small courtyard as she stretched in the middle of her room, finishing her cooldown routine. Muscles still limber but definitely feeling gross with sweat, she dug out an outfit for the day and headed to the ladies communal bathing room. That was definitely going to take some getting used to. It was like living at college all over again, only magnified by the number of women and small children.

Clean and with Saxon happily trotting at her heels again like a shadow, Gwen headed to the kitchen. It was almost lunch, and she was both hungry and willing to help with whatever Bronwyn assigned her. Whereas the approach last night to the kitchen had been quiet, today Gwen could hear a cacophony of voices talking, a baby wailing, and what sounded like two or three toddlers crying. Entering the kitchen, Gwen walked into barely contained chaos.

Alodie and Hertha were corralling Alodie's crying twins, Stockton and Athelred, into a corner. Isola paced with her wailing baby on her shoulder while still trying to stir multiple pots over the fire. Bronwyn looked almost frazzled, which meant this had been going on for a while. The older matron looked up as Gwen stepped into the room.

"Gwen, I didn't expect to see you yet. It's a bit busy right now so perhaps we can talk after lunch?" she asked, pushing a stray gray curl back under her blue cloth wimple.

"My hands are free, Bronwyn, if you want to put them to work now. I can manage stirring those pots for Isola or whatever you need. Unless me being here means I'm underfoot." She glanced at Alodie and Hertha.

Alodie had the exhausted look of a boy mom. The twins must've been running her ragged. "I'm good with kids if that's more helpful."

Isola's head whipped around so fast, Gwen was worried she'd broken a vertebrae. "Have you ever held a babe?" the woman asked desperately, patting her crying child's back.

Gwen smiled and walked over to Isola to take the rag draped over the mother's shoulder and put it over her own arm. "Yes, I babysat all through college, so four years of handling children ages three months to ten years old. I love kids. Gimme." She made a clutching motion with her hands.

"Oh, thank you. She hasn't stopped crying since dawn." Isola looked close to tears.

"Mommy sensory overload is a thing. Let me take her. What's her name?" Gwen asked.

"Bea," Isola said.

"Come to Auntie Gwen, beautiful Bea," Gwen crooned. Carefully, Gwen transferred the crying baby from Isola's shoulder to lying on her tummy on Gwen's forearm, making sure Bea's head was supported. She headed back to the door and empty hallway. "Is it okay if I walk her in the hall and out of the kitchen bustle? I'll come get you if there's issues."

Isola gave her an exhausted nod and wiped sweat from her brow, pushing hair that had escaped her braids out of her face. "Yes, thank you so much, Gwen."

"My pleasure," Gwen told her, rocking back and forth and bouncing softly in a constant rhythm. Gwen smiled down at Bea's back. She couldn't count the times she had seen frazzled moms in the grocery store doing the same "keep the baby happy" dance.

Gwen started humming as she walked up and down the hall with Bea, making soft shushing noises occasionally. As she walked, Bea's cries eventually started trailing off into soft hiccups. Gwen started singing quietly, continuing her walk. Saxon followed her for a bit before deciding he wasn't suited for baby duty and settled down at the door to the kitchen where he could lord over the hallway and the women working to put lunch together. Gwen was pretty sure Bea was asleep as she continued singing softly and walking.

The sound of footsteps over the toddler fussing had Gwen glancing up to find Orin staring at her from the kitchen doorway. Saxon sat next to him, lips curled in a silent snarl as he stared up at the man. The knight ignored her dog, attention solely focused on Gwen and the baby in her arms.

"Hi," Gwen breathed, stumbling to a stop, which had Bea fussing. Gwen shushed the tiny girl, rocking from foot to foot before meeting Orin's gaze again. Grief and an odd look of longing flashed across his face before being replaced by the stoic facade Gwen was used to.

Orin cleared his throat. "You did well today. I wanted to come check to make sure you hadn't done too much?"

Gwen smiled at him as her heart fluttered. She shushed the offending organ as fast as she had shushed the baby. Gwen was sure Orin was simply being nice, and she shouldn't read too much into his question. But, oh man, did she want to. Then she inwardly cringed. Falling for a guy in your dreams had to be the dumbest thing possible, even though Orin stood in front of her now in the flesh.

How much of what Avalon showed of Orin was true? Gwen thought.

She had witnessed his battles and snippets of his life here in the castle. A recurring dream showed Orin, Tor, and a few other knights teaching the squires and pages. From similar dreams, Gwen knew Orin was a patient and kind teacher, which she found endearing. She also knew he could drink most of the men under the table, save for Tor, who as

Caerleon's brewmaster never seemed to get drunk. Countless dreams of Caerleon's feasts and simple meals showed Orin sitting with his close friends in a corner while the rest of the knights grew boisterous.

But at the same time, Gwen didn't know a lot of things about Orin. Did he have a temper? What was his favorite color? Did he have a favorite book? Grief weighed heavy on him from the loss of past lovers; did he even want to fall in love again? Gwen really, really wanted to know the answer to that last question.

Would it be fair, though, to pursue the answer to the question? she wondered. She was going home if she could. Right?

"I'm fine, Orin," she assured the knight, moving to stand in front of him. His eyes dropped to Bea curled up in Gwen's embrace, and he brought a large hand up to stroke the baby's dark, fine hairs. That longing flashed across his face again before he cleared his throat.

"That's good," Orin said, his voice gruff. "Are you settling in all right?"

"For the most part, yeah. It's still really weird being here. I keep wondering about everyone at home. Have they noticed I'm gone? Does time travel differently between the two realms? Has it been only a day since I left or weeks? Is Logan worried about me?" As Orin drew his hand back, Gwen gently turned Bea onto her back and cradled the baby close, drawing her finger across Bea's closed fist and taking a moment to marvel at the sheer perfection of the child.

Orin brushed his fingertips across the back of Gwen's hand, and she looked up at him as he asked, "Who is this Logan?"

"My partner," Gwen said.

Orin snatched his fingers away from Gwen. "Ah, I see," he said, clearing his throat again.

"Are you getting sick?" Gwen asked.

"What? No." Orin asked as he froze, blinking rapidly as he stared at her. "Why?"

Gwen shook her head side to side as she pursed her lips. "You keep clearing your throat. If you're not sick, am I making you uncomfortable or something?"

Orin flushed. "No, don't be ridiculous. I just . . ." He hesitated, then shrugged.

"Uh-huh, okay. Well, to further answer your question, Logan is my best friend and police partner. We work together. Does that help?" She cocked her hip, putting her free hand on it.

"I see. What about your chieftain? Will he miss you? Your parents?" Orin catalogued her facial expressions as they went from pensive to worried then finally rueful.

Gwen gave a quiet chuckle, shaking her head as she shrugged. "Chief is my boss, not my chieftain. Chief Anna Wolfe runs the whole police department. She and Logan will miss me. My parents only will if they need something from me. My mother wanted me to talk to my dad about their divorce last time she and I talked. It was right before Avalon brought me here, and the first time she called me in close to six months."

"Divorce?" His brows scrunched.

"She wanted to end their marriage, claiming irreconcilable differences or some nonsense like that. No doubt Mother found some boy toy who wants to be a kept man and looks better on her arm at social functions than Dad. Then again, a potted plant would look better considering Dad never leaves his archaeological digs to show up at any events." Gwen made a face at the thought of her mother dating someone younger than her. "They're complete opposites of each other."

"I see," Orin said in a voice that told Gwen he very much did not see.

Gwen couldn't blame him. Her parents made no sense together at all. Beatrice Brookes-McMillan was, without a doubt, the most shallow person Gwen knew. At least her father pursued his passion and made a difference in the grand scheme of things; some of her father's discoveries had established a greater understanding of ancient Celtic culture that students could learn at university. It still perplexed Gwen that the Caliburnus's guardianship had passed to her and not her father. With a degree in history that specialized in fifth and sixth century Britain and another in archeology, both from Brown University, he should have been the prime candidate, not Gwen.

"So this friend of yours and your commander are the only ones who will miss you?" he asked.

Gwen blinked at Orin's statement. Was that true? She knew almost everyone in town, but mostly as acquaintances. Would they view her disappearance as weird, and she'd become some cautionary urban legend? Or would they actually miss her? Gwen chewed on her lip, thinking. She honestly wasn't sure.

Isn't that a sad state of affairs? her critical self-doubt whispered.

"I guess," Gwen answered, voice quiet.

Orin lifted a hand and pushed a strand of hair behind her ear, eyes sad as he told her, "That may be all for the good. Avalon does not return what She has taken. I'm sorry, Gwen, but your life will be here now."

"That may not be so bad," she whispered back without thinking, then kicked herself as he winced. When he cleared his throat yet again, Gwen knew she had made him uncomfortable.

Orin's hand dropped as he stepped back. "Right, well, the women will continue to see that you settle in well." He turned on his heel and hurried away.

Gwen stared down at Bea's sleeping face and caressed the baby's soft cheek. "Apparently, I am very scary, Bea. I can make grown men run," she whispered to the child. "Guess we'll go see if your mama wants you back."

"Well, Gwen, that was nicely done. You're obviously a caretaker by nature." Bronwyn stood next to her as Gwen passed Bea back to her mother. Now that the lunchtime madness was over, the kitchen had calmed, and Alodie and Hertha had carried out the dozing twins. Both boys had barely made it through their food before starting to nod off.

Gwen shrugged, looking around the quiet kitchen. Herb bundles hung from the rafters, and one entire wall was covered in pots and pans. "I love kids, so it was my pleasure."

Bronwyn eyed her for a minute. "Can you cook?"

"Basics." Gwen looked around the kitchen. "I'm not used to all of this. We have different cooking techniques back home, but I'd be willing to learn if you need me in the kitchen. Assuming Orin's right, and my chances of getting home are minimal." Gwen wasn't exactly sure how to explain to Bronwyn that she mostly microwaved things or ate takeout. Growing up, her mother had a personal chef for the household. The best Gwen had managed to con the man into teaching her was fancy grilled cheeses.

Would this be her life now? Gwen chewed on her lip again, tapping her toe as she thought. Would she be okay if it was? Her breath started coming rapidly as her mind raced. What if she couldn't make it home? What if she spent centuries fighting fae like the rest of Caerleon? What if . . .

"Sewing?" Bronwyn asked, breaking into Gwen's racing thoughts.

Gwen focused. "Uh, no. That's a hard no. Never sewed in my life."

Please don't make me learn, she thought, wincing.

Bronwyn hummed, eying Gwen with a frown. "Cleaning?"

"Well, yes. I had my own home and kept it clean." At least Gwen could tell Bronwyn that with confidence. Gwen actually liked living in clean spaces.

"Hmm, and you love children?" Bronwyn asked, moving her cooking knives over to the wash bin.

"Adore kids. Saxon and I always took on the community outreach activities like going to the elementary schools to show the little kids what a police dog does." Gwen smiled down at her dog and ruffled his ears. He had come from his doorway perch to see if he could mooch some scraps off Bronwyn. So far, the older woman had resisted the pleading puppy eyes. Bronwyn was obviously made of sterner stuff than Gwen.

"Why don't we put you on nanny duty then? We've got Bea and the twins, Aislinn's four-year-old girl, Maebh's five-year-old son, and a few seven-year-old boys that aren't quite ready to become pages. Let me tell you, that was a busy year when those older boys were born." Bronwyn turned toward Gwen with a smile.

"I'd love that." With that, Gwen found herself embedded in castle life.

"Ready to brave dinner in the main hall?" Eidytha asked, leaning in through Gwen's open door. Gwen realized the other women kept theirs open while they were in them, so she did likewise. It felt like being back in a college dorm.

"Think so," Gwen responded, putting the last of her things away in the wardrobe. She had spent the afternoon trying to settle into the room and determining the best way to keep children out of her firearms when she wasn't there since there wasn't a gun safe. "Do I leave Sax, or can he come with us?"

Eidytha paused, thinking. "Let's bring him. The men will need to know about him anyways, and maybe the threat of Saxon will keep us from being mobbed as the single men try to introduce themselves to you."

Gwen cringed. "I don't know how to say this without sounding insulting, but if any of you ladies are interested in any of them, I'm not interested in any sort of relationship right now." She rocked back and forth on her heels, remembering her jealous freshman-year roommate. Gwen had zero desire to deal with that kind of drama. She also didn't want to admit it, but Gwen had already set her cap toward someone if, and it was a big if, he was even interested and if it turned out she really was stuck in Avalon.

Eidytha's laugh was warm. "No worries, Gwen. You're a novelty, so the men will be interested whether you want them to be or not. We've mostly paired off, and quite frankly those of us without husbands have our pick at any time of male companionship. So you needn't worry one of us will turn into a green-eyed monster."

"Oh, thank God. I like all of you, and I'd hate to inadvertently muck up our friendship by talking to the wrong guy in the hallway if they stop to introduce themselves." Gwen shook her head.

"They will, so best brace yourself." Eidytha looked Gwen up and down. "With the way you dress and how pretty you are, they'll be falling over themselves to meet you."

Gwen wrinkled her nose at that. Sure, she could clean up well. Her mother had drilled that into her since she was six. Gwen could put on flawless makeup in less than five minutes and knew how to put together outfits and style her own hair for almost any social occasion. But her hair wasn't her mother's pretty blond, and she didn't have her mother's striking azure eyes. She wasn't petite and curvy like her mother. No, Gwen definitely took after her father's family, with their dark brown hair, plain brown eyes, and taller, athletic figures. That had always been a bone of contention between her and her mother, as if Gwen could have controlled her genetics in the womb.

Now, she was as ready as she would ever be for what she expected to be a lot of eyes focused on her. Which Gwen hated. So Gwen put on her mother's form of armor, making sure her makeup was on-point, her hair was pinned up in a sleek chignon, and her blouse, leggings, and flats matched the overall casual look she preferred and knew was flattering on her athletic frame.

"All right, let's do this," Gwen said firmly, as if she were preparing to go into battle with the fae. Eidytha threaded her arm through Gwen's and patted her hand.

"It won't be as bad as you think," Eidytha assured her. Gwen looked sideways at her new friend.

Eidytha chuckled and shrugged. "Well, it might be. But Agrona, Blaine, and I have a plan if the men get pushy. We're going to slip in one of the side entrances and sit at the end of one of the long tables in the back. They'll be five or six at the table with us, plus children, so you'll just be one of the group. With luck, no one will really notice us."

Gwen let out a breathy sigh at that. "Works for me. It's already been a day on display, trying to prove myself to Orin and Arthur this morning and staying in Bronwyn's good graces. She's so intimidating. Does she ever stop moving?"

Eidytha laughed again, guiding Gwen toward a closed door. "No, no she does not. If our king ever let Bronwyn out of Caerleon, I daresay she'd have the fae begging for mercy before midday." She went to open the door, turning and winking at Gwen. "Brace yourself and don't worry. We've got you."

They slipped into the crowded room. Long tables in rows were filled with groups of men and the occasional husband and wife couple with their children. The table closest to them was filled at one end with men, then the middle was empty. Agrona, Blaine, Bronwyn, Isola, Hertha, and Alodie and a scattering of children sat at the end nearest them. Gwen thought that they might actually pull off Eidytha's plan as the two of them headed for the empty chairs between Alodie and Blaine, but Stockton saw Saxon.

The little boy's face lit up as he squirmed out of his mother's lap and charged as fast as his chubby little legs could go toward Gwen and Saxon, squealing "Doggy!" in that piercing tone unique to toddlers. Heads turned toward them.

"Hey, my handsome man, careful. We don't touch strange doggies." Gwen caught the gregarious boy under his outstretched arms and tossed him in the air to his delighted laugh. "Are you having a good dinner with your mama?"

"Stockton!" Alodie's voice held both exasperation and mortification as her son's head bobbled in an enthusiastic nod.

"Let's get back to your pretty mama," Gwen told Stockton, popping him onto her hip as she ignored the men looking at them and headed to the chair next to Alodie.

"I'm so sorry, Gwen. He's done nothing but talk about your dog since he saw him in the kitchen door." Alodie fretted, her hands busy with keeping her shyer son from crawling out of her lap.

Gwen let out a soft laugh as she held up her hand to high five Stockton. He slapped it with both of his hands, obviously not used to the gesture. "Well, I'm usually pretty happy to see Saxon too, so I get it."

"Gwen." Cae's cold voice sounded behind her. She groaned a bit as Stockton looked over her shoulder at his father and waved, pointing at Saxon, who now lay beneath Gwen's chair.

The child's delight lifted in the air as he squealed, "Doggy!"

"Why are you holding my son?" Cae growled, arms crossed. His narrowed eyes told Gwen she was still on the man's shit list, most likely due to her friendship with Viviane. Or maybe he still was sore over the fact that she had dumped him on his rump in front of the other knights. Either way, Cae looked less than thrilled at finding his beloved son in her arms.

"Oh, didn't you hear? Bronwyn's assigned Gwen to help however she can, and she and her dog are very good with children it seems." Alodie's cheerful voice soothed as she allowed Athelred to crawl into Bronwyn's lap.

"What?" Cae's voice was a threatening rumble behind Gwen. Saxon growled at the man.

"Easy, buddy," Gwen murmured before twisting a bit in her chair to see the knight. Stockton, clearly smitten with the fact that she owned Saxon, snuggled closer and played with the locket she had put on while getting ready for dinner. "Look, I know we didn't get off to the best start—though I did save your life, if you remember—but I've got a lot of childcare experience. Your boys are fine with me." He scowled at her, so Gwen pulled out what she hoped was her trump card. "Bronwyn trusts me."

Cae cleared his throat as he met Bronwyn's inscrutable gaze. Gwen's guess was right. Bronwyn ruled the keep with an iron fist.

"Fine. Alodie, we'll talk about it later. As for you"—Cae pointed at Gwen—"my boys go nowhere near that fae woman."

Alodie rolled her eyes at her husband before turning back to start planning tomorrow's meals with Bronwyn and Blaine. Gwen simply nodded, plastering an earnest look on her face so Cae knew she was taking his order seriously.

Stockton drew her attention away from his father by placing both his hands on her cheeks and turning her face away from his father. "Doggy," he said very seriously.

Gwen chuckled. "After dinner, little man. Did you know doggies eat lots? Think we can eat lots like the doggy?" She took the trencher Alodie slid toward her and helped Stockton eat the finger foods put on it. When she looked over her shoulder, Cae had disappeared.

"I swear he's not always that bad," Alodie muttered to Gwen.

"Oh yes, he is." Blaine snickered. "You're immune to it by now, Alodie."

Alodie rolled her eyes again but smiled. "Probably true. Sorry, Gwen. I don't know why he's so worried about you."

"I think he was okay with me until I started talking to Viviane." Gwen shook her head and smiled at Alodie, trying to assure the mother that all was well.

Bronwyn leaned around Alodie. "Viviane?"

"The Lady of the Lake . . . the fae that lives in the loch Caerleon sits on." Gwen kept her voice matter-of-fact, hoping the women wouldn't freak out the way Arthur, Orin, and Cae had.

Alodie's eyes widened. "Why ever would you talk to a fae?" Gwen told the women the same story she had told Arthur and Orin about her family and the dreams she had grown up with.

"Gwen, you've been seeing all of this for more than two decades? Including all the battles with the fae?" Alodie asked.

Gwen picked at her own food as she adjusted Stockton's sleeping body in her lap. He had been eating like a champ right up until he passed out, as if someone had hit his off switch. Gwen sometimes wished for a toddler's ability to instantly fall asleep.

"Yep. Not great dreams for a kid, but it probably has helped a bit with me being here. At least I'm not totally clueless like some of the guys who've come before me." Gwen lifted one shoulder in a shrug, making a wry face.

Alodie opened her mouth to say something when Kyla spoke up. "Ah, they've finally worked up their courage."

"Huh?" Gwen swung her gaze to the rest of the room where Kyla was looking with amusement. Two men were walking toward them, their eyes locked on Gwen. She groaned, turning back to the table. "Are they at least nice?"

Kyla chortled into her soup, raising her eyebrows toward the ceiling. "Lamorak and Dinadan. Entitled and sometimes difficult. They'll be pests for a bit, but if you don't want anything to do with them, they eventually get the message if you ignore them. It's because you're new. All the men will probably want to see how receptive you are. Lamorak and Dinadan know we won't give them the time of day unless we're desperate." The woman waved her spoon as if waving away the men.

"Of course it would be them," Isola murmured with a disdainful snort.

"Freaking great," Gwen muttered.

"Ladies." Lamorak flashed a smile at the group, his eyes never leaving Gwen. Gwen pegged him at just under six foot. Even with greasy brown hair, green eyes a touch too far apart, and five-o'clock shadow, the man looked way too smug as he tucked his hands into his wide, brown leather belt. "Care to introduce us to Caerleon's newest resident?"

Blaine looked at Gwen, rolling her lips together to hide a smile at Lamorak's boldness. She raised an eyebrow at Gwen, as if asking if she even wanted to be introduced. Gwen rolled her eyes but shrugged. She'd have to meet everyone eventually, but Gwen hated to do it while the entire hall watched.

"You already know who she is, Lamorak. Gwen's still getting settled in, and as she's brought Caliburnus to Avalon, she has better things to do than deal with you lot. Our king will need her assistance, and you don't need to be a distraction," Bronwyn scolded.

"We'd be happy to help with the settling-in part," Dinadan rumbled in a low voice and winked at Gwen, leaving no doubt he meant settling into his bed. He was roughly the same height as Lamorak, but more heavyset, with salt-and-pepper hair, and a round face lined with wrinkles.

"No thanks." The words were out of Gwen's mouth before she could stop them. The ladies chuckled as Dinadan rocked back on his heels. His eyebrows lowered as he scowled at them and Gwen.

"I have all the help I need," Gwen told them. She gave the type of polite smile her mother had taught her. It meant nothing more than acknowledging the other person's presence. It wouldn't encourage them, or at least she hoped. To discourage further discussion, she turned to Alodie. "Do you need help toting Stockton back to your suite?"

Lamorak opened his mouth as if to say something, but Tor was suddenly behind them.

"Offering to help wash the dishes? That's nice of you two," Tor said cheerfully. His wide smile was a brilliant contrast to his dark skin and short, curly black hair.

"That's not . . . no . . . damn it." Dinadan growled and pivoted to walk out of the hall. Lamorak glowered at Tor and followed his friend. Tor chuckled and grinned at the women before heading back to his seat.

"Well, well. Seems you have a champion," Eidytha commented. She leaned forward conspiratorially. "Tor's one of the good ones. Well worth a turn in his bed. The redhead over there is Bedevere, and he's another one."

"Eidytha!" Bronwyn said, shooting a scandalized look at Gwen.

"What? We can save Gwen the trouble of trying out the men until she finds one to pair off with. That's what friends are for after all." Eidytha rolled her eyes and shook her head before gracing Gwen with an exasperated look, lips pursed.

Gwen placed her head in her hand, shoulders shaking with silent laughter to keep from waking up the little boy in her lap. "I appreciate that, but let me get through a few more days before you start trying to match me with anyone."

Eidytha grinned wickedly at her but left the subject alone throughout dinner. The women batted topics back and forth as they finished eating, discussing everything from planned crop rotation to the need to dye thread for the next round of mending. Eventually the chatter wound down as Cae came over to take Stockton so Alodie could hoist Athelred up on her shoulder and they could leave for the night. Eidytha and Gwen parted ways with the others and made their way back to their rooms.

Day two was done, and Gwen had survived.

CHAPTER EIGHT

ORIN

Bedevere found Orin standing over the gate while talking to Gareth and Bors. It was midday, and they were waiting for the last hunting party to return to Caerleon. A warm breeze threaded around them, bringing with it the scent of wildflowers and damp earth. The sun beat down, warming Orin's older joints. He tracked a lone cloud as it cruised across the brilliant, cerulean sky.

"You took a while on the archery test," Orin commented, raising an eyebrow at his friend.

"Oh, we've been done for a couple of hours. Just didn't come find you right away." Bedevere flashed a cheeky grin at the older knight.

Orin grunted at that. "Well?"

"Well, what?" Bedevere's grin stretched wider. He was deliberately being difficult, damn him.

"Well, how skilled is she with a bow?" Orin huffed, waving his hand for the man to continue.

Bedevere's mouth flattened as he wriggled his hand in a "so-so" motion. "Not the best I've seen but not the worst. She hasn't shot a bow in months, and it shows. but, she started hitting the center of the target by the end of the test. The bow she brought is amazing but not set up for combat shooting. Better for single target hunting. I had her try one of our bows, and she's proficient enough I'd let her on the walls during a fight."

That was high praise coming from Bedevere.

"I'll let Arthur know then," Orin commented while Bors and Gareth murmured quietly to each other, casting glances out toward the forest tree line and the mists they could see in the far distance.

Children's giggles drew all of the men's attention down to the courtyard. Over in the corner where several trees had grown, Gwen stood with the twins on either hip while the other children chattered at her. Saxon flopped on his side in the shade. The children had one of the balls they usually liked to toss to each other, only they had put it on the ground at Gwen's feet as they listened intently to whatever she said. They watched as Gwen set up two stones next to one tree and another set near the wall.

Gwen sat the twins down next to Sax and gave them some blocks from the bag she had slung over her shoulder. Then the woman showed the older children how to kick the ball back and forth between the stones. She seemed to have divided them up relatively equally into teams and let them loose to scrum over the ball while she settled on the ground with her dog and the twins to build block towers. The twins delighted in knocking them over and cheering. As the older children kicked the ball and tried to keep it from the other team, Gwen called encouragement and occasionally got up to show the children some sort of fancy footwork that would allow the children to pass the ball to each other.

"Well, they look happy." Bedevere nudged Orin's arm with his elbow. "Oh to be able to throw off responsibilities and play, eh?"

"Wouldn't mind playing with that one," Gareth muttered, earning him a glare from Orin. "What? You can't tell me you haven't thought the same thing."

Orin's scowl deepened. He was not going to admit he might have had a few passing thoughts on Gwen. Didn't mean he liked the other men ogling her. Gwen was the only woman to be taken by Avalon since their initial arrival. Of course the other men would be attracted to her. It didn't help that she was also beautiful, interesting, and funny.

"Not Stone-Faced Orin," Bedevere teased.

Orin rolled his eyes at his friend. He had his reasons for not wanting to get into anymore relationships, whether they were friendship or romantic. He had suffered enough loss that he wasn't sure he could handle more. The death of his wife and unborn child before he'd come to Avalon gutted him. Once here, he had struck up a relationship with one of the single women a century after they arrived, only to lose her months later to illness. Then there were the deaths of close friends and comrades in fights with the fae. He was going to protect his battered heart the best he could. But damn, he had to admit that the sight of Gwen with a gaggle of happy children made it hard to remember why he needed to keep his distance. He noticed her warm smile even from this distance as she kept the children entertained.

They watched Gwen and the children for a while, which meant they missed the moment that the four soldiers on patrol burst out of the woods and galloped toward the castle. Gareth cursed, swinging his head toward the sound of the men shouting to open the gates. He raised his horn to blow an alarm as a score of harpies rose from the trees, chasing the knights.

"Open the gates!" Orin roared at Cae and Lamorak down in the gatehouse. "Gwen, get the children inside!"

Her head snapped up toward them, and then she moved the children briskly but calmly back to the keep. The twins clung to her, and the children crowded close as men appeared, pulling on quivers. More horns started blaring out in alarm.

Orin took one last glance at the woman and her charges before turning back toward the incoming fae. Bedevere had disappeared into the gatehouse below but was back with a bow and quiver full of arrows for Orin. The four of them spread out across the parapet, limbering up their bows before notching their first arrows and waiting for the harpies to come into range. Other men thundered up the stairs and spread out around the wall, more horns sounding to spread the alarm.

The screeches of the harpies tore at their ears as the flock of fae came into range. Harpies weren't Orin's favorite to fight. Their claws caused serious infections if they inflicted wounds, and they were devilishly quick in the air.

"Fire!" Bedevere yelled.

Around them, the knights and soldiers on the parapet loosed their arrows. Several struck harpies, but most of the flock dodged. Two ran into each other, their wings fowling and sending them plummeting toward the ground until they extricated themselves from each other. The knights kept firing as the harpies drew closer. The fae swirled around flying arrows and dove toward the ground. Screaming their fury, they skimmed up the length of the wall and over the edge of the parapet.

Orin shoved his bow in front of a set of claws as the harpy crawled over the stone edge and slashed at him. Throwing the bow to the ground, Orin drew his sword. He could hear screams and shouting up and down the length of the parapet as the other knights engaged with the harpies.

It was always a jolt, that first sword cut as the blade cut through muscle, sinew, and into bone. The harpy attacking him screeched in agony as he struck it. She lunged back into the air, fanning her wings as her eyes blazed with hatred. An arrow sprouted through the harpy's neck, shot by someone farther down the wall. Her body dropped out of sight as Orin turned to help Gareth.

"Don't let any escape!" Arthur's voice rose above the din of combat.

Then it was all a blur of auburn feathers and sharp claws, harsh breathing, men yelling, and the constant swing of his sword until the surviving three harpies took back to the sky, trying to flee back to the forest. Bedevere swung his bow up, tracking the closest, and let his arrow fly. Orin swung his head to watch as the bolt buried itself between the harpy's shoulder blades, and she fell from the sky. The remaining two swirled on air currents, trying desperately to avoid the arrows being fired at them. One surged up to avoid one arrow, only to fly straight into another. She didn't even get a chance to scream.

"Damn it, bring down the last one!" Arthur bellowed. Bedevere was the most likely to land a hit, but the harpy had managed to almost reach the tree line. It would see the arrow long before it could land and would be able to dodge it easily.

"Shit," Bedevere muttered, lowering his bow. The men watched grimly as the harpy surged above the trees.

Orin blinked as Gwen suddenly stood next to him. He hadn't heard her come up the stairs. He did hear the small exhalation of her breath before a crack of thunder that deafened him. The body of the harpy plummeted into the forest canopy below.

"Well, I'll be damned," Bedevere muttered as Gwen swung her rifle over her shoulder, turned, and jogged down the steps, not looking at anyone.

"Let's get these bodies cleaned up," Arthur ordered, coming over to stand next to Orin. He stared at Gwen's retreating back. "Did you give her permission to come up here?"

"No. She was supposed to get the children inside." Orin watched her disappear into the main keep.

Arthur sighed and scrubbed his face with one hand. "What a mess. They haven't bothered us for a hundred years. Then she shows up, and here we are again, dealing with the fae at our doorstep. I'm beginning to wonder if she's a spy."

"I don't know if it's fair to blame it on Gwen," Orin murmured, still staring at the door where Gwen vanished. Arthur shot his second-in-command a glare. Orin sighed. "Maybe you should talk to her before cursing her name? I know we hate the fae, but while Gwen's presence has been disruptive, she's not been dangerous to us."

Arthur grumbled something uncomplimentary under his breath. "Fine. You're with me. Bedevere, you manage the cleanup effort. See that the injured go to the infirmary. I'll have a couple of the women go there to meet them." The knight nodded and turned to bark orders at the others. Arthur and Orin stood for a few minutes watching the knights haul harpy carcasses toward the gate before the two headed into the keep, the midday sun beating down on them.

Gwen wasn't in her room, nor was she in the kitchen where the women had congregated with all of the children.

"Where the bloody hell is she?" Arthur demanded, voice booming around the crowded, hot room.

"You barely missed Gwen. She headed toward the chapel," Eidytha said, pointing down the corridor.

"Are things all right on the walls?" Bronwyn asked.

"Aye, they're fine. Only some harpies. Bedevere will send in any men who've been hurt, so can you have some of your women in the infirmary?" Orin asked as Arthur's frustration grew palpable. The air practically sparked with his king's irritation. Orin knew if Arthur didn't get the answers he wanted soon, Gwen would never earn his king's trust.

"Of course." Bronwyn turned her steely gaze toward Demelza and Idina, focused on what the injured would need. She dispensed orders to the women, dismissing Arthur and Orin from her mind and the kitchen.

"Arthur, I know things are unsettled right now but charging into the chapel to yell at Gwen won't help anything," Orin told his king as the man stormed down the hall toward the chapel. The sound of Arthur's boot heels echoed off the stone walls.

"This is her doing," Arthur snarled. Orin somehow knew Arthur meant Viviane and not Gwen by the way he said "her."

The knight drew his brows together in confusion, not following Arthur's logic. "The Lady of the Lake? How so?"

"She brought Gwen here, and it wasn't simply to return Caliburnus. She's up to something larger . . . more dangerous. I'd give up this damn sword for another century of peace. We must do everything we can to keep our people safe, even if that means throwing Gwen out. She can try to find her own way home," Arthur growled. Orin frowned but held his tongue. He knew arguing with his king would be useless until Arthur's anger ran its course.

They reached the small chapel buried in the heart of the keep. If the fae ever managed to make their way into the castle, the women and children would retreat here. With only one door in and out of the room, it made for an ideal place to barricade themselves in. A few pews allowed for seating. The wooden benches faced a pale stone statue of a woman holding out her hands toward the supplicants. Whether she was one of the pagan goddesses still worshiped by some of the men and women or the Virgin Mary for those who were Christian was up for debate, but the room offered comfort to those who needed it.

Gwen stood in front of the statue, her hands shoved in her pockets. She must have put her rifle away in her room already. Saxon sat next to her. The dog turned suspicious amber eyes on the men as Arthur barged through the door, Orin more circumspect in his entrance.

"I know. I didn't have permission to be up there." Gwen's admission brought Arthur's advance up short. She looked at them over her shoulder and shrugged. "That's why you're here, right?"

Arthur's scowl deepened. "If you know you weren't supposed to, then why did you? Getting in the way could get my men killed."

Gwen sighed. "I don't know. I felt compelled to." She turned to look at the statue, gazing up at the pale stone woman's serene face. "It was the same feeling that came over me when I first arrived, the one that made me run into the forest to find Orin, Tor, and Cae. Just this need to hurry, hurry, hurry." The woman scuffed her toe on the floor, taking her hands out of her pockets and placing them on her hips. "It's not a great feeling, let me tell you. To be pushed to do something and not feel like you have a choice. Like someone or something huge is standing over your shoulder whispering orders in your ear." Gwen kept her back to them so they couldn't see her face, but Orin could hear weariness in the timbre of her voice.

"So it is her doing," Arthur snarled. "That horrible fae woman. She's cast a spell on you!"

Gwen turned, frowning. "Viviane? No, it's not her."

"Ah, and you are such an expert in the fae, are you? You've been here a mere blip of time compared to the rest of us," Arthur scoffed.

Anger flared in Gwen's eyes. "One of these days, Arthur, your paranoia with Viviane is going to get you and your people killed. You're being a fool for not seeing what's right in front of your nose."

"Which is?" he asked.

"A potential ally in Viviane and also this." Gwen whirled and reached out to touch a small motif at the statue's feet. The sound of a groaning mechanism, one riddled with age, surged through the room, and the floor rumbled underneath their feet as the statue slid back into the wall, revealing a tight spiral staircase beneath its feet.

"What?" Arthur gaped at Gwen.

"By all that's holy," Orin breathed. "How did you know this was there?"

Gwen stomped her foot, glaring at Orin. "How many times do I need to tell you I've dreamed of this place? That includes all the important nooks and crannies of Caerleon." Gwen huffed and grabbed one of the lanterns hanging next to the statue as she and Saxon disappeared into the darkness. "Watch your step." Her flat voice floated back to them.

"Do we follow?" Orin asked, looking at Arthur.

The king grimaced at the opening before growling, "What choice do we have? We need to know what's down there and if it's a danger to us." He grabbed the other lantern and started down the steps.

The spiral was tight so that the steps were weirdly angled, making the going slow as they ended up skipping every third or fourth step. Eventually, they reached the bottom of the stairwell, Orin having the sense they'd descended two or three floors below the castle, and stepped out into a large cavern. Gwen and her dog stood at the far side of the cave in front of a rough-hewn stone backed by an arch built into the cavern wall.

"What is this place?" Orin's soft question echoed around the chamber.

"The spell stone." Gwen ran her hand over it as they approached. "I assume that you've heard the different legends about you and your knights from the folks Avalon's brought over the years? Like the story of the sword in the stone?"

Arthur grunted at that. "Nonsense, all of it."

Gwen graced them with a wan smile. "Well, be that as it may, stories usually start with a kernel of truth. The mortal realm may know some of the right names or details but put them together completely wrong in their stories. This stone is how the fae used to exile their kind. They channeled magic through Caliburnus and this stone to open that portal." She nodded toward the archway. "Avalon moved the stone and the gateway to this cave and buried both underneath the castle when it brought you and Caerleon here."

The men were quiet for a minute, staring at Gwen in growing horror.

"So Mordred will one day want to take Caerleon for good so he can have access to this again?" Arthur asked harshly, pointing at the stone arch.

Gwen shrugged. "I have no idea. Maybe Viviane does. If there was a way to sense it one way or the other, Avalon Herself isn't giving me any clues."

"You speak of Avalon as if it were a person," Arthur accused.

"Avalon is . . . more than She used to be. I told you that the magic in Her soil has become somewhat sentient. I'm pretty sure that's where the compulsions keep coming from, not Viviane. Viviane is simply a conduit for the magic but not the wielder."

"Which means you're also a conduit," Orin said softly.

"Um, I don't know?" Gwen shrugged. "Possibly? Probably." She dropped her hand to Saxon's head as if seeking comfort while she pointed at Caliburnus. "Mordred will want that too. His magic is strong enough to open the gate as long as he has the sword. The blade acts like a key to channel his power into the stone and the gateway. Viviane says the spell requires someone of significant power, and there's only a handful of fae who meet that criteria, like count as a Power with a capital *P*."

"Wonderful," Arthur muttered, brushing his hand against the sword's hilt.

Gwen let out a long breath and stared at the stone above their heads for a long moment before she brought her eyes down to lock with Arthur's. "We need to talk to Viviane. She knows more than I do. She can help."

"No," Arthur snapped.

"Yes." Gwen's quiet, steely voice batted away Arthur's negative response.

Arthur's jaw clenched as his hands formed fists. He slashed a hand through the air. "Absolutely not."

"Yes," Gwen said, as if the choice was inevitable. She stood tall against Arthur's ire.

"Damn you, why? She is nothing but a threat!" Arthur roared, hands thrown toward the ceiling as he whirled to pace.

Gwen pointed at the rough-hewn stone floor. "Because change is coming, whether we like it or not, and she is an ally whether you accept it or not." She clenched at her hair, breath whistling out in an aborted scream. "I know you're king, but why are you being stubborn? Surely you can feel the shift in the air? Mordred is coming, Your Majesty, and Viviane can help us win. Personally, I would prefer not to die. If there is a way home for me after all this, I would like to be able to find it."

Orin flinched at her words but nodded inwardly, tamping down on his chaotic feelings. Gwen didn't want to stay. That made sense even if she was the first woman to catch his eye in years. He couldn't keep her here if there was a way to help her go back to the mortal realm.

Arthur stared at her for a moment before raking his hands through his dark hair, and Orin wondered whether Gwen had finally pushed the king too far. Saxon watched the man warily as if expecting Arthur to attack his mistress.

Then Gwen delivered the death knell to Arthur's refusal. "Viviane gave you Caliburnus back in the mortal realm so you could save your people. She gave you solace when you thought there was no hope. She's not the villain you make her out to be. Viviane's been exiled from her home and family for defying Mordred, used as a conduit for a magic we do not understand, completely isolated from everyone for centuries, and even through all that, she has tried to help you. Trust me, a woman doesn't do that for just anyone." Gwen crossed her arms and shook her head. "Don't let your fear blind you to a power that can help protect your people."

Arthur met her impassive gaze with a desperate look in his. He swung his eyes toward Orin as if pleading with his second-in-command to be the voice of reason.

Well, shit, Orin thought.

Orin cleared his throat as he chose his words carefully. "We know something is happening among the fae right now. Any information could be useful."

Arthur ran his hands through his hair one last time, clenching at it as he let out a long gusty breath. "This is not what I expected for this day."

"Yeah, well, join the club," Gwen muttered and glanced over at Orin then let her eyes slide down to Saxon. "But does this mean you'll come speak with Viviane?"

"Aye, seems like we must. But I want additional knights with us," Arthur asserted. He towered over Gwen as if daring her to argue.

"Okay," Gwen said, a small triumphant smile flitting across her lips. "I'll see you at the gate then." She didn't meet their eyes as she walked between them and headed up the stairs.

Orin looked at his king. "I think we can trust Gwen."

"Is that because you actually think that or because you like the looks of her?" Arthur huffed.

Orin rolled his eyes, temper flaring. Yes, he had to admit Gwen's looks had grabbed his attention. Her body attracted him in a way that had him questioning his self-imposed celibacy, but that's not why he trusted her. Orin knew he could trust her because she had been brazenly honest about her feelings and thoughts since meeting them in the woods, and the way she handled the children told him that Gwen's heart was in the right place. He told Arthur that much, save for the part about liking Gwen's figure. Arthur grunted at his assertions but left Orin alone. With a final glance back at the stone and archway, they left the cavern behind and slid the statue in place over the stairway.

Gwen was exactly where she said she would be, standing in the shadow of the gate and out of the way as the knights continued to clean up from the harpy attack. She looked up at them as they walked toward her—Cae, Tor, Bors, and Henri with them. Gwen raised an eyebrow in surprise, wondering why the men wore full chain mail and had festooned themselves with weapons.

"Mademoiselle! We get to spend more time together. My day is complete now." Henri's bright, mischievous grin flashed.

Gwen's eyes landed on Cae, ignoring Henri for the moment. Orin turned and looked at Cae. Sure enough, his friend's face twisted into an unwelcoming scowl.

Gwen pointed at Cae and said, "No. He's not coming."

"You don't get to dictate that." Arthur dismissed her words, and Orin groaned inwardly. Why was Gwen constantly challenging the king? At this rate, it'd be evening before they even managed to make it to the lakeshore. Arthur hated being argued with. No one dared to do so except Bronwyn. Granted the matron usually went around Arthur instead of arguing, but that was beside the point.

Gwen shook her head, arguing, "Then Viviane won't talk to us, and, quite frankly, I won't subject her to Cae's piss-poor attitude. She doesn't deserve any disrespect from you or your knights. We are asking her for help, Arthur, not declaring war. I know it's been centuries since you had to make alliances, but bringing this much hostility to the conversation is counterproductive. It's clear Cae doesn't want to be within ten feet of a fae."

Arthur flicked his fingers, batting away her concerns. The king waved at the glowering knight. "None of us want to talk to this fae, and Cae is a knight of honor. He won't attack her unless she attacks us."

"His temper is on a hair-trigger," Gwen snapped. She stepped up to Arthur, glaring. Orin made a note to talk to Gwen later about proper etiquette when dealing with royalty. Clearly they did not teach that to people from her time and place.

"Sounds like yours is too, and I'm right here," Cae growled. "I can hear everything you're saying."

Gwen pinched the bridge of her nose and looked at Cae. "Be honest with me. You know you're an ass, yes?"

Cae crossed his arms and glared at her. "I am what I am," he rumbled.

"My point exactly." She looked at Arthur. "Will you please trust me on this? Honor is great but so are manners, and so far, Cae hasn't shown any except toward his wife. Who, by the way," Gwen added, turning to Cae, "you're very lucky to have because Alodie is an amazing person."

Cae's fierce expression eased a bit at the compliment about his wife. "She is." He looked at Arthur.

"Fine." Arthur groaned, dropping his head back with a heavy sigh before scrutinizing Gwen. "Cae, stay here. The rest of us will go to the lakeshore. Anything else?" Arthur's impatient tone snapped out. Gwen ignored his king's derision and glanced at Orin then back at the group before throwing Orin's own words back at them.

"Show Viviane respect." She held Arthur's gaze until he gave a sharp nod.

"Open the gate!" Orin yelled at the men in the gatehouse. Saxon was the first through, running out into the open meadow in front of the castle walls before veering toward the lakeshore at a command from Gwen in a language Orin didn't recognize.

"How many languages do you speak?" Orin asked Gwen as they walked.

"Just English and French, some commands for Sax in German." She shrugged. "My mother loves Paris and spends most of her time there these days. Mother wanted me to learn the language, so she would only speak in French for three years starting when I was seven. Even fired all the household staff and replaced them with people who spoke French. Had to learn the language out of necessity or else I would have starved. Hard to ask for dinner if the cook won't acknowledge you unless you're speaking in the required language."

"You're joking." Orin blinked down at Gwen, mouth slightly open. To have denied a child food based on simply wanting them to learn a different language absolutely boggled his mind.

"Nope. My mother always gets what she wants. Okay, wait here," Gwen said, looking pointedly at the men as they approached the lakeshore. Then she jogged over to the water, Saxon happily trotting right next to her heels.

The lake was still for a few minutes, and Orin could feel his king growing impatient. Based on the way his fellow knights shifted uneasily around him, they were probably feeling the same thing. Still, he had heard the Lady of the Lake tell Gwen to come to the lakeshore and that the fae would come as quickly as she could. So he stood stoically waiting, his hands tucked around his belt and his stance relaxed. Gwen dropped her hand to Saxon's head and ruffled his ears as he sat at her side, looking up at her. The adoration the dog had for his mistress was rather adorable, not that he would admit that to anyone.

The water rippled as Orin turned his gaze back out across the lake, as if something was skimming under the surface heading toward where Gwen stood. She tensed a bit, and Saxon stood, his eyes locked on the waves heading toward the shoreline. Around Orin, the other knights muttered and hands went to weapons.

"Stay calm," Orin told them, keeping his hands relaxed on his belt. He tried to exude the emotion, hoping it would help. If Gwen was sure this would work, well, he was willing to give it a try after everything she had shown him and Arthur this morning.

Viviane walked out of the water. Droplets cascaded off her white-blond hair and deep-emerald dress until she stood in front of Gwen, hair and clothes now dry except for the hemline swirling in the shallows. The fae's smile was bright as she held out her hands to Gwen in welcome.

"Gwenhwyfar, I didn't expect to see you so soon again," the fae woman said, leaning down to rub Saxon's ears. The dog practically vibrated with happiness, his butt shaking with his tail. "And, handsome Saxon, such a good boy." Her eyes raised to look at the group of men, assessing them. She nodded solemnly in greeting, eyes locked on Orin's king. "Arthur."

His king squared his shoulders and walked toward the lakeshore. "Lady," Arthur said in way of greeting.

Viviane's mouth quirked in a small smile even as she flushed a bit at Arthur's terse tone. "It's been a long time. I am glad to see you are well."

"I'm not here for idle chitchat," Arthur grunted. "Gwen seems to think you know something that can help us in regards to Mordred. You will tell me everything you know." He glowered at the fae. Orin rolled his eyes. Clearly Arthur failed to listen to Gwen's warning about respect. It wouldn't surprise Orin if the Lady of the Lake didn't drench the lot of them like she had with the squires. Orin still wasn't sure what had prompted the attack, but knowing the young men, he expected they had been the instigators.

Gwen sighed, pulling her hands out of Viviane's and turned toward Arthur. "Would it kill you to be nice?" she hissed, socking his bicep with her fist. Orin dropped his face into his hand. The discussion on how to treat royalty would be Orin's top priority when they got back to the castle. Maybe Gwen's chief allowed for more familiar treatment between her and her subordinates, but Arthur wouldn't tolerate it.

"What the hell, woman," Arthur snapped at Gwen while Viviane's surprised laughter rang out. The Lady of the Lake hid her wide smile behind a hand as merriment danced in her blue-gray eyes.

Gwen's sigh was ripe with exasperation as she ran her hands agitatedly through her hair. "I swear, every time I turn around, you're grumbling and growling about something. And they say women are emotional. Will you please put your attitude on a shelf for like five minutes and listen?"

"Gwenhwyfar, it's all right. Arthur and I have…history," Viviane said with amused patience. "I would be happy to share whatever knowledge I have. I am bound to Avalon, so I cannot speak to what may be happening in my ancestral lands or beyond in the mists, but I do have contact with those fae who continue to resist Mordred's rule as they seek hiding places here in Avalon. They have shared some news I would willingly tell you."

Orin strode up and patted Gwen's shoulder, trying to get her to stand down from antagonizing Arthur. Not that his king didn't deserve a little prodding. Gwen had told them to be respectful, and Viviane had been nothing but welcoming and accommodating since emerging from the lake, yet Arthur had been nothing but churlish. The odd blush she still held high on her cheekbones did make Orin pause for a minute. Viviane's gaze hadn't strayed much from Arthur since he had joined Gwen at the lakeshore. Orin wondered about that before shaking his head to focus his thoughts.

"We would take whatever news you can tell us," Orin told the fae, eying his king as the man crossed his arms ungraciously. Maybe they had all deferred to Arthur's moods too much, or the man needed to get out of the war room more.

"Well met, Sir Orin." Viviane smiled at him though her gaze stayed riveted on Arthur. She was so tall that she could almost look Orin and Arthur eye to eye, and they both stood just over six feet, versus Gwen, who was a good six or seven inches shorter than they were. He could prop his arm on Gwen's shoulder if he wanted to.

"Mordred has subjugated most of the major fae houses, but there are holdouts from each of the families who have kept the rebellion alive. They manage hit and run campaigns on Mordred's major supply lines, smaller prison camps, and scouting parties." Viviane seemed to weigh her next words, her hands flipping the folds of her dress as she looked away across the length of her lake. "They would be interested in an alliance if such a thing could be agreed to by you."

"You must be joking? Why would I do that?" Arthur sneered.

"They could share with you their information, let you know what Mordred's troop movements are, so that you know when to keep your knights close to Caerleon. Let you know if they see any of Mordred's troops heading your way." Viviane kept a pleasant look on her face, but Orin could hear the exasperation in her voice.

"What would we owe them?" Arthur asked, brows furrowed in suspicion.

"A safe haven behind the walls or the sharing of supplies, potentially," Viviane answered promptly, finally letting her hands go still.

Arthur scoffed. "Like I would let any fae into Caerleon."

Orin sucked in a quick breath. He had to agree with his king. It was one thing to ally with the fae and share intel. It was an entirely different case to let them into Caerleon and trust the fae at their backs. He may trust Gwen's honesty, but he didn't trust her judgment on Viviane that far. Orin refused to risk his men, their home, or the innocents they protected.

Viviane shrugged, continuing, "Think upon it. Should you change your mind, send Gwen here, and we will work out when and where you can meet the rebel leaders. Their latest information is that Mordred will be transferring some prisoners from one of his smaller camps to his main prison camp near his keep deep in the Mist Lands. They will be crossing a corner of Avalon to keep their journey as short as possible. Perhaps you would like to send some knights out to confirm the veracity of this information." She turned and pointed north across the lake. "They are scheduled to cross the northern part of Avalon tomorrow midday. Gwen, may I have a private word with Arthur and Orin?" The sudden change in topic had Orin blinking in surprise at the fae and Gwen's brows pulling together in confusion.

"Uh, sure." Gwen glanced between the three of them then turned to walk over to stand with the knights, Saxon nosing at Viviane's hand for one last pat before heading toward his mistress.

Viviane leaned closer, her voice lowering. "You do not need to like me, nor do you owe me such kindness, but I would ask that you take care of Gwenhwyfar. Avalon has chosen Gwen as Her guardian and change brews around my young friend because of it. Gwen will need your support, not your animosity, disdain, or distrust. I know this woman. What you see with Gwen is how she is. She has a sense of honor to match or exceed yours alongside her good heart. If you let Avalon guide Gwen, we may all be able to seek solace from the threat of Mordred's power."

"What exactly does that mean?" Orin asked, standing taller and whipping a glance over at Gwen. The woman was watching them with interest.

"Mordred has grown impatient with the rebellions that spark across his domain. He will be making one last push soon to crush his enemies, then he will set his sights on Avalon. She does not intend to bow before his might. Avalon will not be owned. If you wish to guarantee your people's safety, listening to the hints that Avalon gives Gwen and seeking allies are your only options." The fae held their gazes as if willing them to believe her. Then she turned and strode into the water, disappearing into the blue depths.

"What the hell," Arthur growled again.

"That . . . is not what I expected," Orin muttered, turning to look at Gwen. She raised an eyebrow at him, as if asking what Viviane's last words were. Orin wasn't sure he should tell her.

CHAPTER NINE

ORIN

"Why now? Why her?" Arthur muttered. He and Orin were ensconced in the war room and had been for several hours. "A guardian? That fae acts like this place has a mind of its own."

Orin settled back into the padded leather chair near the stone fireplace gracing the back wall of the war room, face thoughtful. He steepled his hands across his chest as he asked quietly, "Doesn't it?"

Arthur lanced Orin with a sharp glare. "Explain."

"We've always said that what Avalon takes, She keeps. Isn't that treating the land as if it's an entity?" Orin asked, propping his feet up to alleviate the pain radiating in his knees. He really needed to get better about sitting down more during the day to save his joints.

"I suppose you make a point. I don't like the idea that some power we don't understand or can control is meddling more directly in our lives than randomly dropping new people in our laps." Arthur huffed out a breath, sitting across from Orin.

Orin chuckled, wriggling back into the chair's embrace and grabbing his ale mug to take a drink before saying, "To be fair, bringing Caerleon and all of us here was pretty direct meddling. Maybe Avalon thought we would be needed to help protect Her."

"Protect Gwen?" Arthur asked, brows wrinkling. He scratched at his temple.

Orin shook his head. "No, Avalon. Maybe Avalon brought us here to protect the land. We've always assumed it was magic gone awry or a curse."

"Ah, maybe." His king stared at the hand-drawn maps of Avalon lining the stone walls. Arthur's hand caressed the gem at the top of Caliburnus's hilt where it lay across his lap. "I grow weary of constantly trying to figure out how to keep our people safe. If you were in my shoes, Orin, what would you do?"

Orin took another sip of his ale, letting the golden liquid swish around in his mouth before swallowing. Orin noted that he would have to tell Tor that this barrel was one of the best his friend had brewed in a while.

Focusing back on his king's question, Orin waffled back and forth on the answer. On one hand, Orin failed to see how they could possibly trust any fae. On the other hand, their forces had dwindled over the centuries, and Caerleon lacked the number of men to withstand a full assault on the castle. If there were fae who could be strong allies, his king would be a fool to overlook that opportunity.

Orin ran his hand over his beard, thinking further. Gwen may lack the experience in dealing with the political intricacies of a court, but the Lady of the Lake had been adamant that Avalon's guardianship was no small role. Perhaps Gwen could help bridge the gap between Caerleon and the fae rebels.

"I know our women are precious simply because they are so few, but I think we should give Gwen a chance. She's proven that she can handle herself, and nothing I've seen has indicated she can't work with us. The women certainly helped, but Gwen seems to have seamlessly folded herself into Caerleon life. If she's some form of . . . tether . . . to Avalon, then we should use it to our advantage. I wouldn't mind not constantly looking for the next fae invasion." Orin waved his mug in the air for emphasis.

Arthur sighed heavily. "To think of not being threatened by Mordred after all these centuries? I don't know if I have enough hope in me for that. I am tired of this war, Orin. Deep down-in-my-soul tired."

Orin flattened his lips together before side-eying his king. "We all are, my liege."

"To take the fight to Mordred will cost us so much energy and resources that I daresay we don't have." Arthur's fingers *tap tap tapped* on the table as he thought. "And to ally ourselves with fae rebels? How can we prevent betrayal? What is to say that letting them into our defenses won't end in our slaughter?"

"What's to say that it won't end with Mordred defeated and us free to live better lives than sneaking in and out of the castle?" Orin met Arthur's gaze steadily. He didn't really have much hope either, but the little ember had been fanned a bit by Gwen and Viviane. To not have to worry about losing another brother-in-arms to Mordred? That was very appealing to Orin. They had all suffered enough loss.

"Fine. You and Tor will take Gwen out tomorrow. I trust the two of you to keep her in line. The others are too busy trying to figure out a way into her bed."

Orin grunted noncommittally at that. He wasn't pleased about that either, but he also wasn't planning on pursuing Gwen even if he did feel drawn to her. If she wanted to choose one of the men, that was up to her.

"I'll let them both know and see what we can do to get Gwen kitted out with better armor than what she came with."

Arthur nodded and pinched the bridge of his nose before sharing one last glance with Orin. "Make sure you come back tomorrow. I can't afford to lose you or Tor."

"Or Gwen," Orin prompted.

"Or Gwen." Though Arthur didn't sound completely convinced.

It turned out the women were way ahead of Orin and their king. While the two men had sequestered themselves in the war room to discuss Viviane's revelations, the women had swarmed Gwen and gotten the full tale of their lakeside visit out of her in the kitchen.

Blaine had gone and pestered her husband Griffin, who managed the armory, to dig out some of the squire's chain mail and some thick, dark-brown leather armor. Then the women spent the afternoon and evening hours working to modify the leather armor to fit Gwen.

Orin scratched at his beard, a bit nonplussed by this turn of events. The women were usually more subtle in their machinations behind the scenes. He was man enough to admit that while he and the knights kept Caerleon safe, it was the women who really ran it. They just did it in a way that made Arthur feel in control. Maybe he wouldn't mention to his king that they had taken it upon themselves to ensure Gwen had armor and then presented it like a *fait accompli*.

Still, that would make tomorrow's scouting expedition easier. It was one less thing for him to worry about tonight, so he headed to his rooms, hoping to get a good night's sleep. Orin had a feeling he would need it.

The scent of hay, horse, and manure whirled around them. Overhead, a single cloud skidded along in the clear sky. Orin could hear the men talking quietly on the walls as they patrolled and the shriek of children from inside the keep as they played some form of hide-and-seek. Clearly the children failed to understand that hiding meant being quiet.

Gwen stood in the courtyard, wearing the armor the women had procured her, and looked at the horse the stable boy had led out to her. Distrust was stamped on her features.

"Do you not know how to ride?" Orin asked, adjusting one of the pauldrons slung over his chain mail. If Gwen couldn't ride, that would complicate things drastically.

Gwen flashed him a look he couldn't decipher then frowned at the bay mare. "I do. I just don't trust horses. God put together the most fragile body possible, stuck it on four pencil-thin legs, and gave it a single brain cell to run the whole thing and called it a horse."

Orin's chuckle rumbled deep in his chest as he tried not to laugh. He couldn't disagree with her on that. "Aye, well, we will need them in order to make good time to the other side of the lake, and in the event we need to make a run from any fae patrols."

Gwen's eyes narrowed at the horse as the mare pinned her ears at Saxon and stomped an irritated hoof. "Okay, I mean that makes sense. I still hate having to use something other than my own two feet to get there. You keep your head on your shoulders and feet on the ground, you hear me," she told the horse before swinging up into the saddle. While Gwen found the stirrups with ease and settled into the saddle with a good seat, Orin could see the lingering distrust in the way she handled the reins and used her leg to keep the mare away from Saxon. The dog seemed unconcerned at least.

The new armor looks good on her, as if she was always meant to be a shield maiden of old, he thought. The three of them carried full quivers and small bows while he and Tor had their swords and Gwen her knives, including one long enough that it could qualify as a short sword. She also had the weird-looking small firearm, the one she called a pistol, on her belt. If they ran into trouble, they'd be as prepared as they could be. Orin hoped between Saxon's keen senses, their own experience, and whatever Gwen was supposed to potentially get from Avalon that they'd avoid detection and the fae wouldn't be the wiser that they were being spied on.

The tall, close-grown trees seemed to embrace them as they headed north. While they had cleared the area around Caerleon, Avalon's forest grew right up to the lakeshore elsewhere. The damp, aromatic smell of growing things quickly replaced the scent of the stables.

"This reminds me of the Pacific Northwest," Gwen commented quietly after they had been riding for a while. Sunlight dappled her skin as it danced between the leaves. "It's so wet and the foliage so dense. How do you manage to hunt or keep from being ambushed in these woods?"

"We've had time to get to know most of the forest. We're about to come up on a ridge line. The ground drops down into a wide ravine that the deer like to pass through," Tor told her, looking back over his shoulder and pointing ahead. Orin watched as Gwen stiffened at Tor's words, and he was forced to pull his horse up short as she stopped hers.

"Gwen?" Orin asked, pushing his gelding toward her mare then deciding better of it when the mare squealed and bit at his gelding's nose. Damn mares. Always so bossy compared to the geldings.

"We should go on foot," Gwen answered, her voice oddly monotone. Orin and Tor exchanged a look.

Orin leaned out of his saddle, trying to catch Gwen's attention, but the woman's eyes were focused on her horse's dark mane. "This a feeling you have?"

Gwen hunched her shoulders and scrabbled at her hair with fidgety fingers. "Yes? Feels like ants in my brain."

"All right. On foot it is." Orin tethered his horse to a nearby tree and waited for Gwen to dismount to do likewise with hers. Tor was already waiting for them a little farther up the rise, scouting ahead to the lip of the ravine. Orin grasped Gwen's elbow, capturing her attention as he nodded toward where Tor lay among the foliage. "Stay low."

Gwen nodded and signaled for Saxon to heel. The dog surged to her side, his eyes locked on his mistress. Orin raised an eyebrow at the dog's new level of focus. The three crept up to meet Tor at the ravine's precipice. Saxon settled onto his belly as Gwen lowered herself to lie next to Tor. The ground angled sharply below them, fallen trees dotting the slope.

The knight pointed up the length of the ravine. Five humanoid fae on horseback spread down a line of prisoners shackled together at the neck. The prisoners' hands and ankles were bound in chains, forcing them to shuffle slowly along the ravine floor. Orin counted twelve prisoners total, a mix of humanoid and monstrous fae like the large werewolf at the back of the line.

"We need to help them," Gwen hissed urgently.

"What? Why?" Orin asked as Tor cursed quietly and looked at Gwen like she had lost her mind. This was supposed to be a scouting mission, with no contact required. Engaging with these fae, even if it was to help captured rebels, would be waving a red flag to Mordred that those of

Caerleon were no longer content to sit by and wait for the fae to come to the castle's doorstep. Gwen had no idea of this, of course, but it was Orin's duty to minimize the risk to Caerleon. He would have to tell her no.

"Because I know one of them!" Her eyes were wild as she pointed down at the prisoners.

Orin gaped at her, shocked as he spluttered out a denial, but Gwen's frantic look made him rapidly change his decision. The knight shook his head, cursing under his breath. "Never mind. We'll work it out after. Tor?" Orin jerked his head to signal the man should move farther down the crest of the ravine and ready his bow before turning to the woman practically vibrating at his side. He could feel her anxiety ratchet higher.

"Gwen, you stay close to me. We are going to have to work fast to ensure we hit the guards before they can cast anything, and we have to be careful not to hit the prisoners," Orin told her. "Keep the dog close and stay as quiet as possible as we head down the hill."

Gwen jerked her head down in one quick nod, reaching back to grab an arrow from her quiver. Her eyes darted back to the fae as they drew closer, and she licked her lips before drawing in a deep breath. Gwen's hands steadied as her body relaxed.

"Let's go," Orin whispered, slipping down the hill and keeping behind the fallen logs and brush as much as possible, wincing at the occasional snap of a twig or crunch of bracken under his leather boots. Gwen and Saxon ghosted behind him, surprisingly quiet. Only the occasional pant from Saxon or the crunch of leaves behind Orin let him know where Gwen and the dog were. He held up a hand as they reached halfway down the hill. Orin couldn't see Tor, but he was sure the man had similarly moved closer for a better shot. Then they waited. Sweat rolled down the back of his neck as Orin hunkered down behind a fallen tree propped between two others. The damp, petrichor smell gave way to the muskiness of dog and a lighter floral scent that he was coming to associate with Gwen.

Orin hovered his mouth next to Gwen's ear and breathed, "Take out the front guard. I'll take the middle two, and Tor should be in position to get the two back guards." Her agreement was an almost imperceptible head nod as she notched the arrow to her bow, eyes focused on the guard he had assigned her.

Everything came into focus then as Orin drew a deep breath and let adrenaline flood his system. The guards' horses were jigging along, as if their riders' nerves were infecting them. Something about the prisoners worried the guards. One of them must be powerful. Orin pulled his bowstring back, sighting on the nearest middle guard. They were almost in range.

Almost.

Almost.

Now.

Orin let out the breath he was holding, and then the bowstring twanged as he loosed the arrow. The knight already had another pulled from his quiver as he watched his target fall from the saddle with a yell as the arrow lodged in the fae's chest. Orin switched targets as the guards' horses lunged, reared, or tried to bolt as Gwen brought down her target and Tor his. The other two fae guards saw their brethren fall and slung themselves out of their saddles, using the horses and prisoners as shields.

"Need to move," Orin ordered and jumped over the half-rotten log they were behind and started sliding down the hill, using trees and brush to control his descent. Branches grabbed at his hands and armor as he descended. Orin could hear both Gwen and Tor now that they were going for speed instead of stealth.

One of the guards broke out from behind the prisoners, aiming toward the first fallen guard's horse. Gwen barked an order at Saxon, sending the dog bounding down the hill at a speed much greater than the humans.

Orin finally understood what a trained police canine could do as Saxon barreled into the running fae, the dog's strong jaws snapping closed around the guard's short cape. The momentum swung Saxon off his paws and jerked the fae off his feet. The guard slammed into the ground, yelling as Saxon kept his teeth dug into the cape and growled, pulling on the fabric so that the fae couldn't scramble to his feet.

"We've got him. Go help Tor," Gwen yelled at him, vaulting over the last fallen tree in her way before heading toward her dog.

Orin veered toward Tor, who was battling the final guard, sword drawn. Orin drew his own sword. As Tor moved the fae backward toward him, Orin thrust his sword through the fae's back, low near the spine. The fae looked down at the sword tip protruding from his belly, letting out a strangled breath. Tor sliced his sword across the guard's throat, and the fae slumped off Orin's sword to land on the ground in a bloody, gurgling heap as he bled out.

Orin whipped around, looking for Gwen. She had called off Saxon and was marching the final guard back toward them, his arms wrenched behind his back to control him. Nearing the front of the prisoners, she kicked the guard's left leg from behind, sending him thumping to his knees before her. She put her dagger at his throat while Saxon stood ready nearby.

"Which one of you has the key?" she snarled at him.

The fae's eyes were wide in fear as he glanced at his dead comrades and then the humans. His Adam's apple bobbed as he swallowed thickly and pointed with his chin at the fae Orin and Tor had killed.

Tor turned back to the now-dead fae and rifled through his belt pouches, coming up with a single key made of an opalescent material.

"This it?" Tor asked, waving it at the fae Gwen guarded. The fae's nod was jerky as he kept his gaze on Saxon, who had crept closer, growling deep in his chest. The dog moved back at a firm order from Gwen.

Tor walked over and handed the key to Gwen, his sword replacing her knife at the fae's throat. She snatched it from the knight and flew down the line of prisoners to the large, blond one standing in front of the werewolf at the back. The fae was wearing the same kind of odd garb that they had seen on Gwen, rugged blue pants, shoes that stopped under his ankles, and a short-sleeved, tight black shirt.

He grinned down at her as she fumbled to unlock his wrist shackles. "Hi, Gwen."

"Logan, what the hell?" Her voice spiraled up in disbelief.

"Ah, long story. Funny story actually." He bent down to let her unlock the neck shackle and then took the key to unlock his ankles. "But first, I've got one thing to do." Logan handed the key back to Gwen.

The large man gently brushed by Gwen, patted Saxon's head, and damn, the dog looked ecstatic to see him. Logan strode over to the guard that Tor was watching, flexing his fingers as he went. Water droplets emerged from the air, circling around his hand until finally it was encased in ice that ended in sharp claws. Logan nodded at Tor in respect and waved his hand at the knight's sword. Tor glanced at Orin, as if the older knight knew what was actually going on.

What the hell was actually going on? Orin wondered. But Tor was looking to him for leadership so Orin waved a hand, signaling Tor to step back. His friend did so, and Logan surged forward, his hand snapping out to grasp the fae guard by the neck. The guard let out a frightened whimper as he stared up at Logan.

"Where were you taking us?" Logan growled, the ice from his hand beginning to creep down the other fae's torso.

The guard panted in fear, his hands flying up to his chest as if he could stop the ice from crawling farther down. "Orders were to take you to the main prison camp, near His Majesty's castle. That's where the ones he wants to make into examples go."

"Maybe we should make an example of you, hmm?" Logan asked. The guard's mouth gaped open as Logan closed his hand around the fae's throat, crushing his windpipe. A jagged shard of ice thrust through the fae's heart at the same time, granting him a mercifully quick death. Logan let the fae topple to the ravine floor, flexing his hand to dismiss the ice claws.

"Logan?" Gwen breathed out the fae's name, shock and what may have been horror stamped across her features. Orin couldn't blame her. To be able to draw a weapon from thin air? This fae was powerful.

Logan turned around and shot her a disarming smile while scratching the back of his head and scuffing his toe in the bracken littering the ground. "About that, my name's actually Lancelot."

CHAPTER TEN

GWEN

"I'm sorry, what?" Gwen stared in shock at her partner, hands clapping over her mouth. She took a step back from her best friend, eyes wide. He was Lancelot from the stories she had grown up on? The irony of Lancelot being best friends with a woman named after Queen Guinevere was not lost on Gwen.

"Lo . . . no, Lancelot, I don't even know how to respond to this." She thought back to her time with her best friend in the mortal realm.

Unbidden, an avalanche of memories hit Gwen, and she looked at them through a completely different lens. Every time Logan had picked up anything vaguely sword like—such as a stick or empty wrapping paper tube—and artfully twirled it, or when he had critiqued every sword scene in the movies they watched with such conviction and authority, or when his diction occasionally shifted to something sounding weirdly archaic until she teased him about it.

Gwen pointed at Lancelot, tone accusing. "Wait a minute. You bastard. You lied to me!"

"Now, Gwen," Lancelot started, stepping toward her. "We can talk about this. I didn't lie to you per se."

Gwen skittered back, shaking her head then closing her eyes in frustration and taking in a deep breath before letting it out slowly. When Gwen opened her eyes, worry stamped its way across Lancelot's face.

"I don't suppose we could continue this conversation elsewhere?" one of the other prisoners interrupted, shaking her shackled wrists at Gwen. "Without these on."

Gwen tore her gaze from Logan. No, not Logan. Lancelot. The name change was going to take some getting used to.

"Right," Gwen muttered, shoving her confusion to the side and working to unlock the fae who had spoken to her. She'd deal with her feelings later, safe and sound, tucked behind Caerleon's walls. Maybe with some alcohol to help.

The fae sighed in relief as the last shackle fell, and her body morphed, bark running across her olive skin. She blinked moss-green eyes at Gwen, the breeze sweeping through the ravine ruffling the leaves of her hair. A dryad.

Okay, so the shackles block magic. Got it, Gwen thought, turning to move down the line. She didn't look at Logan. *No, Lancelot,* she reminded herself. Maybe if Gwen couldn't see him, all of this mess would just . . . go away. Gwen snorted at herself. Of course it wouldn't go away. Wishing this was all a dream hadn't gotten her very far yet.

Gwen left the large white werewolf at the back until the end, eying him a bit with trepidation. He tracked her with bright blue eyes as Gwen walked over to him and slowly moved to unlock his wrist shackles.

The werefolk were featured heavily in her dreams, so she knew exactly what those three sharp claws could do as well as the powerful jaws housed in the jackal-like skull. Add in that this wolf was over seven feet tall, and she had to admit to herself, he was intimidating as hell. Gwen hoped he would be happy to be out of the shackles and would leave her alone.

Like Lancelot, the wolf had to bend down to let her unlock the neck shackle. The wolf scratched at his fur as the shackle fell to the ground, then glanced down at Gwen.

"Good," he growled at her.

"Um, sure thing." She pocketed the key and turned back to look at her partner again. Lancelot was watching her carefully while Orin and Tor were watching him. Suspicion simmered in all of their expressions. Gwen couldn't blame them. She had no idea what was going on, but she was going to find out.

"You've got a lot of explaining to do, Lancelot." She pointed at him, her tone harsh.

He nodded. "I do but not here. Perhaps we can head back to Caerleon?" He looked at the other prisoners. "You will be returning to the Mist Lands or . . . ?"

"We would follow the Scion of House Dwyn," the dryad responded, bowing low.

"The what of what now?" Gwen couldn't quite describe the jumble of feelings currently cascading through her as she glared at her best friend. Who even was this man?

"That would be part of the long story." Now Gwen understood why Cae had been so enraged when she had said that repeatedly to the knight. She wasn't sure she had the patience for waiting to understand how her best friend was here or who he was.

"Of course it would," Gwen muttered. She frowned at Lancelot before saying, "That's not my call. It would be Orin's."

"Mine?" The knight looked like she had hit him upside the head.

Gwen sighed, slapping her hands down on her hips while eying Orin with exasperation. "His Majesty put you in charge, right? I'm certainly not the man's favorite. Can you imagine if I showed up with them in tow, and was like, 'hi, here, I found us some fae rebels to adopt?' Your king would kill me."

"Gwen, this is a really bad idea," Orin told her, spreading his hands wide as he beseeched for understanding.

Gwen scoffed. "Oh, I know. We're going to get yelled at. A lot." She crossed her arms over her chest, glaring at Lancelot as if this was entirely all his fault.

"That's not the half of it," Tor muttered, eying the fae who were watching them with a mix of amusement, wariness, or apathy.

Orin rubbed at his temples before tossing his gaze skyward. Gwen felt guilty for being the cause of what she suspected was the beginning of a spectacular headache for the man.

Truly, she had no idea that today would turn into such a cluster. Arthur was not going to be pleased. He might even kick her out of Caerleon. And wouldn't that be the cherry on top of the crap sundae that was her life now? Gran had prepared her for many things, which Gwen was certainly thankful for, but not this. Where were the fae and king-whispering lessons? Hopefully Orin had enough sway to convince Arthur to see reason. These fae were Mordred's enemies and that made them potential allies.

"Fine, but we'll need to leave the group at the edge of the woods and let me go in solo so I can speak to my liege." Orin glowered at Lancelot as if he were to blame for all of this.

"Excellent. Alcina, before we go, can you please dispose of this trash?" Lancelot nudged the body of the guard at his feet. A fae woman with dark brown skin and hair stepped away from the group and moved over to Lancelot. Stopping next to him, Alcina glared at the body then stomped her foot. The ground swallowed the corpse. Alcina repeated the spell for each of the remaining bodies.

"Wonderful. Less evidence of our escape, the better." Lancelot eyed the group of fae. "Alcina and whoever else needs them can ride on the horses so we can move at speed."

Gwen turned to look up the slope. "How the hell are we going to get the horses up that?" She pointed at the steep tree and log-strewn incline.

The dryad stepped forward. "Leave that to me." Her feet glided through the loamy bracken as if she couldn't bear to be parted from the ground. She stopped in front of the nearest downed tree and touched it. The log shivered and then rolled out of the way. "This way."

The fae sorted themselves out, with Alcina riding double with a dark-blue skinned female whose feet faced oddly backward. Gwen wracked her brain, trying to remember what type of fae this could be. She was pretty sure it was a mythological creature from the Caribbean, but her brain had decided it could only focus on the mystery of Lancelot. She'd have to ask someone later.

They crested the top of the ravine and headed toward the horses tethered nearby. Orin and Tor mounted quickly, not looking at the fae anymore. It was like if they didn't look at the rescued prisoners, they wouldn't have to deal with the fact that they were heading back to Caerleon with a group of their mortal enemies in tow like ducklings.

Gwen sighed as she went to her horse, thinking, *Please let this horse have enough brain cells to not freak out about the werewolf.* The mare didn't like Saxon. She could only imagine what the horse would do next to the fae.

"Can I catch a ride?" Lancelot asked.

Gwen eyed her friend. "I don't know. Are you going to do anything new and weird again? Because what the hell, Logan . . . I mean, Lancelot. You know, that's too much of a mouthful. Can I call you Lance?"

His grin was lightning quick, and there was a flash of the old version of her best friend. The one she got coffee with, joked with, and watched action movies with. "Yeah, that'll work. I promise, Gwen, I'll tell you everything once we're safe."

Gwen narrowed her eyes at him, pursing her lips a bit. "You'd better." She glanced up at her horse. "More riding double. Lovely. All right, come on."

It wasn't comfortable having the two of them on the horse, but they made it work. It was odd having Lance snugged so close against her. They were good friends and colleagues, but they most certainly never cuddled.

Who even is this man? she thought again as they retraced their steps toward Caerleon.

"I'll head in. Stay here until I come to get you or you hear the alarm horns," Orin told them when they reached the edge of the trees and lakeshore. Caerleon stood tall and imposing in the distance.

"He seems pleasant," Lance commented quietly next to Gwen's ear.

She hummed an agreement and nudged Lance to dismount. Gwen suddenly needed to talk to Viviane about Lancelot and why Avalon would have brought them both but not together; she could only hope that Viviane would sense her on this part of the lakeshore.

Once Lance was out of her way, Gwen dismounted and thrust the reins into his waiting hands before trotting over to the edge of the water. Saxon hovered between her and Lance; he was Gwen's dog, but Lance was his roughhouse-playing and treat-dispensing buddy. When Viviane strode out of the water, Gwen sighed in relief.

"You would not believe what happened," Gwen started to say, but Viviane's eyes were firmly locked on Lancelot. Viviane's skin blanched as she swayed in place. Gwen reached for her friend, afraid the woman was about to faint.

"Cousin?" The water fae breathed out the question in surprise.

"Cousin?" Gwen gasped, whirling to look at Lance. The familial similarity was noticeable now that the two fae were together.

"Remember that funny part of the story I mentioned?" Lance asked, striding forward to pick Viviane up in a hug. "Yeah, this might be part of it." He grinned down at Viviane. "Hello, cousin. You'll never guess what Avalon did."

Viviane gaped at him. "She brought you as well?"

"Surprise!" Lance's voice was cheerful. "Guess Avalon decided my exile had lasted long enough. We lucked out that Gwen and her knight friends were in the woods. Helped us escape from our jailers."

"We were there because Viviane said there would be a prison transfer. We didn't know that you would be part of it," Gwen told him. She looked between the cousins in bemusement. Here were two of the most important people in her life, save for Gran, who was now just a memory. Avalon had united the people she considered family, and now she didn't feel so alone—confused, yes—but not alone.

Lance kept his arm around Viviane's shoulder as he turned to look at Gwen. "Viviane and I were exiled at the same time. Mordred didn't"—he paused, searching for words—"exactly appreciate the way we protested his rule. When Avalon took Caerleon and Viviane, I thought it best to stay near the sword your ancestress found. It was my only link back here."

"So you've been hanging out around my family for centuries?" Gwen asked, incredulous.

Lance nodded. "Yes, and mostly they didn't notice me, not until your gran. She seemed to have some sort of sixth sense about things. Cornered me one day in a grocery store a few months after your dreams started and she passed Caliburnus to you. Told me over frozen peas and corn to keep an eye on you, that she was doing her best to get you ready in case her fears came true and you were the one Avalon took. I was the one that helped her find you a swordmaster to take lessons from."

"You've been in my life all this time?" Gwen shrieked. Gwen couldn't believe it. Lance was a big guy. How had she never noticed him before they joined the police force together? Surely she would have seen him at some point. Right? *Right!?*

Her best friend eyed her cautiously, hearing the outrage in her voice. "Yes?"

Gwen threw her hands in the air before smacking him in the chest, hard. "So what? You just decided to get on the police force with me? Manage to convince the chief to make you my partner? Jesus Christ, you even joined the same cycling class as me."

Lance flashed a disarming smile at her that didn't quite reach his eyes. "You make it sound stalkerish," he said in a soft voice, rubbing where Gwen had smacked him. When he pouted like he couldn't understand why she was affronted, Gwen's anger spiked.

"That's because it is stalkerish!" Gwen shouted. "Oh my God, so you were my friend because of some . . . some misplaced sense of duty? Or because you thought I was your way home?"

"No," Lance said, voice firm as he let his cousin go and grasped Gwen's shoulders while she glared up at him. "No, I was your friend, best friend

I might add, because you're fun and we get along famously. Also, I like your dog." He winked at her.

Gwen stared at him then socked him in the chest again. Her anger bubbled away still. How dare he think a dash of charm could sway her to forgive a decade of lies. As long as their friendship had been, Lance knew how much she hated being lied to. "You should have told me!"

"Ouch. Really, Gwen? When did you get so violent? Look, I was afraid it would make it weird if I told you," Lance said. He gave her a lopsided smile.

"Oh, and this is better?" Gwen asked before holding up a hand as a thought came to her. "Wait, what about the family you always talked about? The movies you watched with your nieces and nephews?"

"I might have embellished a few things to make me seem more human." Lance shrugged. "Seemed like a good cover story at the time." He took her hands in his. "Gwen, I'm still me, just with a different name. My real name."

"Plus freaking ice powers!" Gwen retorted.

Lance put his arm around Viviane's shoulders again, smiling down at his cousin with fondness as she leaned into him. "Our family's domain oversees all water fae, so our powers obviously lean toward that element. I'm a bit rusty to be honest. I haven't used my powers since my exile. That's why the patrol that found me was able to take me prisoner. It was a bit disorientating to wake up at the border of Avalon and the Mist Lands with nothing but what I was wearing on my way to the pub."

Gwen blinked at him, trying to take everything in. Was this how Arthur and the knights felt when she had arrived? Like someone had hit them in the back of the head with a frying pan and their brain cells were rolling around in their skulls, desperately trying to keep up with everything?

"All right, this is a lot to take in. But I am glad to see you." Gwen punched him again. "But no more secrets! I mean it."

Lance held up his hand. "Scout's honor."

Gwen frowned, not sure she could trust in Lance's promises anymore. Still, what choice did she have? Lance always had her back, and he was right. They were best friends. She loved his humor, all of his dorky hobbies, and simply hanging out with him even if they didn't talk.

"Not to interrupt this touching moment, but it looks like Orin is heading our way," Tor commented. He was eying Viviane, Lance, and Gwen with interest. Gwen sighed. She had brought so much drama onto their poor heads. No wonder they were all upset with her.

Orin's face gave nothing away as he drew closer, and Gwen held her breath. The moment of truth.

"Let's go," Orin growled, throwing a thunderous look at the fae. His eyes paused on Viviane as if surprised to see her with the group. "My king is willing to meet with you at the gates, but don't get your hopes up."

"Oh goodie," Gwen muttered. "He's in a mood."

"Courage, Gwen. If anyone can get it through his thick skull that this is a good thing, it's us." Lance had the audacity to wink at her again, giving her shoulder a reassuring squeeze.

She rolled her eyes at her best friend but went to the horse again. "Viviane, are you coming with us?" Gwen asked.

"She is," Lance said in a tone that brooked no argument. Viviane's mouth opened and closed as she tried to find words. Then she looked at Gwen and gave a little helpless laugh.

"I guess I am. Technically Lancelot is my liege so where he says I go, I go." Viviane fussed with her hair, smoothing down a few flyaways, and then ran her hands down her skirts as if dislodging nonexistent lint.

Gwen raised an eyebrow. Who was Viviane trying to impress? Gwen had a sneaking suspicion but would need to see another Arthur–Viviane interaction to be sure.

"Well, the bossy prick can walk on his own two feet," Gwen said, leading Viviane over to the grumpy bay mare. Gwen made a mental note to ask for Orin's calm chestnut gelding next time. She held her hand out to the fae. "Come on." Now Lance rolled his eyes at Gwen but helped his cousin up behind her.

The motley group made their way toward Caerleon, picking their way along the water's edge as they eyed the forest behind them. The walls were lined with knights as they approached, and the air felt heavy with anticipation.

Will this actually work? Gwen wondered. *Can Arthur and his knights forge an alliance with Mordred's enemies?*

"Here goes nothing," Gwen murmured as she caught sight of Arthur's face. It wasn't the most inspiring look. In fact, he looked like he had smelled something rancid. Gwen helped Viviane dismount and handed the reins to her friend, patting the fae's hand in encouragement before moving to stand with Orin when he motioned Gwen forward.

"You are like a beacon for trouble," Arthur grumbled at her, glaring down his nose and crossing his arms.

"Not usually," she protested. She had once thought being five foot six was quite tall enough, but half of Arthur's knights seemed to be giants. It wasn't exactly fair.

"Let's consider this an acceleration of our plan to ally with people who hate Mordred as much as you do." Gwen tried for a sweet smile but wasn't so sure she hit the mark when Arthur didn't budge. "They have useful skills that could help your men on patrols or if the castle is attacked again. Don't you owe it to your people to find the best way forward?" She waved her hand back at the fae. "You've got to be as tired of Mordred's threats as they are. Why not work together? Please."

Arthur kept his gaze on her, standing quietly for so long that Gwen almost started blurting out more reasons to agree to their crazy plan, but having been pulled up in front of the chief a few times thanks to Lance's antics, she managed to keep her mouth shut. She also knew better than to let her temper get the best of her; Orin had fussed at her about hitting Arthur by the lake the last time she and the king got into it.

Then the king lifted his gaze to the fae waiting behind them. He noted their appearance and how the werewolf had crouched down to look less threatening. While some of the fae's smiles showed off teeth with sharp points, they were all going out of their way to look nonthreatening.

"You will be escorted at all times by guards. You will remain in the areas of the castle we designate for you. After our evening meal, you will be escorted to the rooms we have set aside for you, and you will stay in them until such time as we release you in the morning," Arthur finally, and shockingly, growled.

Gwen let out the breath she was holding. She couldn't believe he had agreed to this. Gwen turned to look back at Lance and Viviane. As she did, Gwen caught a look that passed over Viviane's face as she stared longingly at Arthur for a split second before glancing away.

Aha! Viviane does have feelings for Arthur. Gwen filed that away to ask her friend later, discreetly of course. That would explain so much about why Viviane had stuck around Caerleon for all these years. There couldn't be any other reason except love because Gwen hadn't been impressed with Arthur or his attitude so far. Disagreeable, stubborn man. He needed a serious cranial rectal inversion. How the king had managed to inspire so much loyalty in Viviane and his knights, Gwen would never know.

But that was a thought for another time.

Gwen knew some of the knights had been hurt during the harpy fight. Harpies were the aerial version of the werewolves, shock troopers whose sole purpose was to create as much mayhem and injuries or death as possible. Here was the perfect opportunity to ingratiate the fae and their powers with Arthur. Viviane was a skilled and powerful healer. All Gwen needed to do was look for an opportunity to introduce Viviane to Bronwyn, and the terrifying matron would do all the rest of the work. Once Bronwyn knew that there was a way to heal the injured quickly, Arthur wouldn't be able to deny Viviane the opportunity to showcase her powers.

Or so Gwen hoped.

Gwen eyed the group as they entered Caerleon. The knights on the parapet and the guard of twenty men behind Arthur were silent as the fae were welcomed inside the walls for the first time.

Please take them to the main hall, Gwen thought, crossing her fingers. *Please . . .*

"This way," Arthur instructed tersely. "You'll be in the main hall until your rooms can be readied on the far side of the keep."

Gwen practically danced in place. *Oh, thank God. This might actually be doable.*

"We appreciate your hospitality, Your Majesty," Lance told Arthur smoothly. Gwen's friend didn't bow, but he did grace Arthur with an autocratic nod.

"Who are you?" Arthur asked, eying Lance as if the mortal king found the fae lord wanting.

"Lancelot, Scion of House Dwyn," Lance answered. He waved at the fae behind him. "These are my people."

Arthur gazed at Lance for a long moment, taking in his manner of dress before flicking his eyes to Gwen then back to the fae. Lance seemed to follow the king's thoughts.

"It's a long story," Lance said as a small smile graced his lips. He turned mischievous eyes on Gwen, who shook her head in exasperation. She was sure that Lance would embellish as needed when telling the story.

"That seems to be a common excuse lately," Arthur replied, skin tightening around his mouth as his expression grew stony. Gwen resisted the urge to roll her eyes as Arthur continued, "Mind you don't abuse our hospitality." The king turned smartly on his heels while the knights fell in loose formation around the fae to escort them to the main hall.

Gwen strayed over to Viviane, who scrunched her nose in a grimace. Gwen flashed a warm smile at her friend, trying to soothe Viviane, and linked her arm with the fae's. If she could get into the main hall with the fae without Arthur dismissing her back to her room, Gwen could duck down the hall to the kitchen with Viviane in tow.

"Really?" Cae grumbled, staring at Gwen.

"Oh buzz off, Cae." Gwen scowled at the knight. He was another one who needed to get his head out of his butt. Cae scoffed at her but left them alone.

"What are you up to?" Viviane whispered as they entered the keep.

Gwen patted her hand. "Just go with it." Viviane shared a bemused look with her but allowed Gwen to keep close as they made their way to the main hall.

Arthur and half the knights had entered the large room ahead of the fae, the rest beckoning the rebels toward the wall opposite the door that led to the kitchens.

Drat. Oh well, better to ask for forgiveness later, Gwen thought with a grimace. She took a bracing breath before putting her plan into action.

"Just go with it," Gwen repeated to Viviane, casually sidling them toward the edges of the group once they were in the room.

"Go with what?" Viviane hissed as Gwen tugged on her arm hard, hauling the fae toward the door at an ever-increasing pace.

"Gwen? Gwen!" Arthur's anger reverberated through the room as he caught sight of Gwen determinedly hustling Viviane away from the fae and their guards.

"Can't talk. Woman on a mission," Gwen called over her shoulder and shoved Viviane through the door before Arthur or the other knights had time to stop her.

She slammed the door closed and hurried her friend along the hall but not before she heard Lance tell Arthur, "There's no stopping Gwen when she gets like that."

"Where are we going?" Viviane asked, glancing over her shoulder as if expecting to see the entirety of Arthur's knights charging after them.

"To prove to Arthur that he needs to listen. The only person he listens to other than Orin is Bronwyn, and Bronwyn is here." Gwen tugged Viviane into the bustling kitchen.

All activity ceased as the women and few children looked at them as they burst into the kitchen.

"Doggy!" Stockton shrieked in delight.

"Hey, little man," Gwen said, sweeping Stockton up into her arms as the boy streaked past his mother toward Saxon. While the police dog was well trained, he wasn't meant to be petted.

"Stockton, you scamp!" Alodie fussed.

"Doggy!" The boy excitedly pointed at Saxon.

"Yep, and doggy has a job right now. Can you help him introduce my friend to Bronwyn?" Gwen asked, jiggling the little boy on her hip to get his attention.

Stockton turned suddenly shy eyes on Viviane then leaned close to Gwen's ear and whispered loudly, "Pretty."

Gwen grinned down at the boy. "She sure is." Alodie would have her hands full when Stockton became a teenager if he was already this charming as a toddler.

"Gwen? Who is this?" Bronwyn queried, wiping flour off her hands. She had been prepping her workspace to knead the bread dough that had been rising all morning.

"A healer. This is my good friend Viviane that I was telling you about, Bronwyn," Gwen answered.

"The fae?" Bronwyn gasped.

"The healer," Gwen repeated. "And one of the very best people I know." Gwen's tone was firm. "There are injured from the harpy attack, right? Viviane can help."

"I would be honored to heal your wounded," Viviane told the room, gracing them with a regal nod. Gwen couldn't help but notice yet again how similar Lance and Viviane looked.

Bronwyn blinked for a moment while Viviane held her breath and Gwen continued to bounce Stockton on her hip. He stuck his thumb in his mouth as he peered at the tall fae next to them.

"A healer?" Bronwyn nodded. "Yes, well that's wonderful then. Come along to the infirmary." She waved at Viviane to follow her. "I'm Bronwyn, Lady. It is nice to meet you. We've got one who took a bad wound that I'm worried will get infected. Aislinn, go get the others who we treated yesterday from their posts and bring them to the infirmary. If any argue, tell them I'll put the lot of them on half rations." She turned to Viviane as she led the fae out of the kitchen. "Have to manage these men with a firm hand, like toddlers."

Viviane's delighted laugh floated back into the kitchen as Gwen hugged Stockton then handed him back to his frazzled mother. She should probably go back to the hall and head off Arthur. Gwen turned and ran right into the man's chest.

"Crap," Gwen muttered, looking up at his murderous expression.

"Where," he snarled, "is that woman?"

"With Bronwyn." Gwen waved her hand toward the door leading to the stairs and the infirmary, but he grabbed her wrist in a vise-like grip, expression still thunderous. "Viviane is a healer. You have injured," she pointed out, trying to keep her tone even as she reminded herself of Orin's constant reminders to be respectful. While the urge to smack Arthur was strong, smacking a king was frowned upon, and Gwen had enough problems with Arthur as it was. "It's logical to use her talents to bring your men up to top fighting form. Bronwyn agreed."

"Doggy?" Stockton piped up from where Alodie had set him down. His mother tried to shush him. Arthur flicked his eyes around the kitchen at the women and children staring at him. He dropped Gwen's wrist.

"So much trouble," he growled at her before whirling and heading back to the hall. Gwen sighed.

She couldn't believe she had actually gotten away with her plan and winced. Sometime in the last few days, Gwen realized she had grown overly comfortable with Arthur. Gwen would have to work on remembering to show the king proper courtly etiquette. Or maybe not. The man could use a good shakeup from his current attitude.

Gwen turned towards the child and crouched down. "Okay, little man. If mama says it's all right, you can see the doggy. But no pets."

CHAPTER ELEVEN

ORIN

Gwen had spent the rest of the day trying to stay out of Arthur's line of sight as much as possible. At least that's what Orin assumed, as he hadn't seen any sign of her or her four-legged shadow since she had disappeared with Viviane. Smart woman with a good sense of self-preservation.

At Bronwyn's insistence, Viviane had been allowed to remain in the infirmary and tend to the wounded, a fact that Orin was both shocked by and also, he had to admit, not. Bronwyn could be a force of nature. Even Arthur didn't stand a chance against her, a fact that Gwen had obviously figured out and capitalized on.

That woman. Orin shook his head, his thoughts all a jumble when it came to Gwen. He knew she was trying not to be a bother, even though everything was in chaos now that she was here. The knight was still trying to wrap his head around the fact that not only had they saved fae from some unknown horrible fate in Mordred's prison camp, but said fae were now inside the keep, and it was all Gwen's doing. If there was any way to draw Mordred's ire and his attention, surely this would be it.

Orin blew out a gusty sigh.

Arthur had insisted on staying in the main hall with the knights guarding the fae, which meant Orin had been stuck there for several hours as well. The fae had all been very well-behaved, though that Logan or Lancelot person kept shooting glances over at Orin and Arthur as if he wanted to say something. Or maybe he was affronted at the fact that he wasn't allowed out of the main hall to be with Gwen. Orin didn't care. Something was off about the man. Gwen was as honest as they came, Orin was sure of that deep down in his bones. There was a warmth and openness in her that couldn't be faked. But that Lancelot . . . he was obviously well versed in deceit. Lancelot would need to be watched.

The knight scrubbed his hands over his face as he headed toward the library. At this time of night, it would most likely be deserted. Orin didn't want to return to his empty rooms, too restless now that the fae had been ushered to their rooms in a part of the keep that was rarely used. The knight felt like something else would happen if he tried to go to sleep too soon, as if an energy in the air crawled across his skin. The lure of the new books that Gwen had brought called to him. Maybe he could lose his thoughts in a new tale.

Orin wound his way through the empty halls and up toward the library on the top floor. Arthur had insisted that all of the women and children bed down in the women's hall, as far away from the fae as possible. The knights were taking shifts on guard duty and had congregated in the barracks instead of their individual rooms in order to turn out quickly *en masse* if there was trouble.

That brought him right back to the start of this mental spiral. Gwen was trouble, even if she didn't mean to be. Why couldn't he stop thinking of her? What was her relationship with Lancelot? Could she really take care of herself outside of the keep? What other changes would her presence herald? Would she end up choosing one of the other men, or that dratted Lancelot, as a companion?

Why do I even care? he thought in frustration.

Gwen couldn't be for him. He wasn't ready to open his heart again, was he? He raked his hands through his hair in frustration as he neared the library.

Soft music and candlelight curled out of the cracked library door as he drew closer. Orin's brows drew together. Who could possibly be in the library at this time of night? He pushed the door open quietly with two fingers, sucking in a sharp breath when he caught sight of the library's occupant.

It was Gwen. Of course it was. Fate seemed content to drop the woman in his path as often as possible to tempt his heart. She had curled up on one of the corner benches, out of the way of the main part of the room. Saxon lay on the floor in front of the woman, head on his paws, but his amber eyes tracked Orin as the man opened the door. Gwen's head was lowered, watching her hands strum across the guitar strings as she sang to herself about flames and love in a soft crooning voice. A frown graced her features, but her emotion-rich voice beckoned him forward. Orin found his feet moving him unbidden into the room. The music stuttered to a stop as Gwen's head whipped up to look at him.

"Orin. I . . ." Her voice trailed off as she bit her lip, looking warily at him as she swung her feet down to the floor, putting the guitar down next to her on the bench. Gwen looked as if she was bracing for some form of reprimand, her shoulders already rigid and spine straight. "I didn't expect anyone to come up here. I'll get out of your way." Gwen nudged

Saxon to get him to stand up. The German Shepherd grumbled and rolled over instead, presenting his belly for pats.

"No, it's fine," Orin assured her. "I didn't expect anyone here either." He clamped his lips together and looked studiously at the floor for a moment. "I interrupted you, not the other way around. I'll head out." Orin jerked his thumb over his shoulder at the door.

"No, please don't. God, this is awkward," Gwen said. Her laugh was soft as she rubbed her forehead. "Why are we being awkward? It's been a weird day, right? That's got to be it."

Orin nodded, wanting to put her at ease. "Want to sit with me?"

Gwen lifted her chin, eyes narrowing as if she was assessing his sincerity. As confusing and aggravating as her presence was to Orin and Arthur, this whole experience had to be disorienting to Gwen. He reminded himself of that as she brought her guitar over to the chair he indicated was for her. Saxon rolled over and shot Orin an entirely disgusted look. The look told Orin that Saxon considered the man personally responsible for the lack of belly pats.

What is with this dog? He had more moods than the king.

Orin settled into the reading chair across from Gwen, the seat creaking a bit with age as he sat. He dropped his eyes again to the stone floor, not wanting to stare at Gwen and make her uncomfortable as she relaxed down into her chair, resting her crossed arms on the guitar in her lap. A quiet descended on the room.

"I'm sorry about today." Her voice broke through the oppressive silence as it grew between them.

Orin raised his eyes to her. The corner of her mouth quirked up in a small smile. She gave another soft laugh and shrugged.

"After seeing Logan, who is apparently Lancelot, I get a bit of what it must be like for you guys. I still don't know what to make of him and everything he told me." She tucked her hand under her chin, elbow still resting on the body of the guitar. "Then here I am, bouncing from what must seem like one crisis to the next to you."

He returned her smile gently, sitting back in the chair and crossing his ankles, hands tucked over his stomach. "A little. Bedevere called you a whirlwind." He scratched at his beard as a real laugh burst out of Gwen. She dropped her head into her hands.

"Oh my God, well it could be worse, I guess. I thought I was going to give Arthur an aneurysm when we showed up at the gates today."

This time his grin was bright with humor. "You still might."

"I promise to try not to." She sighed then, meeting his gaze. "Maybe it will be easier to trust me if you know me better? You've got to have some questions. I'd be happy to answer them if you'd like."

What did he want to know? What exactly would be useful? He already trusted her for some reason. She seemed to make that happen naturally with the people around her. The women had accepted her so whole-heartedly that they entrusted their precious children to Gwen's care. Arthur though, he'd want to know more. So where to begin?

"Who saw to your training?" he finally settled on asking.

"That would've been my gran. My mother was always focused on more superficial stuff, making sure I took the appropriate extracurriculars to make her look good, but Gran, she made sure I was given opportunities outside of ballet or ballroom dancing." Gwen's eyes went unfocused as if she was remembering something.

"I grew up extremely privileged. My mother's family is old money. My dad's family though, they're straight-up middle class. They met at university. Dad went to study history, but I'm pretty sure Mother went to find a husband. My parents were never around as I was growing up except for the occasional drop-in visit. Gran, though, she saw that I got everything I needed to be successful. Made me actually earn an education at the snooty private schools my mother sent me to, and every afternoon after school I went to some form of lessons.

"Mondays were violin—Mother insisted on that one, and I actually admit to loving those lessons. Tuesdays and Thursdays, plus the weekends, were martial arts. Wednesdays and the rest of my weekend were dedicated to blade work. Archery on Fridays. Things got moved around sometimes to make room for whatever Mother insisted I do because all the other girls were doing it. Had to keep up appearances, you know?" Orin didn't, but he kept listening.

"But, yeah, the rest was all Gran." There was sorrow embedded in her tone, and a longing that called to Orin. He knew that feeling; it was a bone-deep need to have someone back coupled with a feeling of their loss. It had burrowed down into his own bones long ago, and there it remained.

"She sounds like an amazing woman," he told her quietly.

"Gran was the absolute best." Gwen's smile flashed brilliantly as she chuckled. "If you think I'm a whirlwind, I had nothing on my gran. Gran could look at you and know what you were thinking or what mischief you might be plotting. She was the reason I grew up knowing what family was." Gwen shrugged fatalistically.

"I don't mean to sound all 'poor little rich girl,' but my family's not warm and fuzzy. When I chose to pursue a criminal justice degree at college and then become a police officer, well, my mother pretty much disowned me except for when she needed something from me. Gran saw me through all that before she passed away, but she made sure I kept up my martial training. Worked out well in the job I had, so it wasn't a hardship to do. So yeah, long answer for a simple question." Gwen winked at him. "What else?"

"What exactly is Lancelot to you?" Orin shifted uncomfortably. He hoped Gwen wouldn't be insulted, but he had to know. Lancelot was a potential threat, being a powerful fae. At least, that's what Orin justified to himself as he asked.

Gwen frowned. "Honestly, I'm not sure anymore. We were partners at work. That means we had each other's backs, kind of like you, Tor, and Cae. We clicked when we met. We liked a lot of the same books and music, had the same sense of humor, and had the same career goals. Our friendship came out of working together all the time. But now I'm wondering how much of that was an act so he could stay close to the sword." Her sigh was long and exasperated as her fingers drummed on the body of her guitar. "I mean, he's a great guy. We weren't romantic. Probably could've been if we hadn't agreed not to risk our friendship. Everyone thought we were heading that way, but it's not what I wanted."

"What did you want?" The question was out before Orin could stop it. Gwen's eyes locked with his and something glittered in them he couldn't quite name.

"Someone steady. Someone who I know I can rely on. Someone who won't leave me when the fancy strikes them or they forget about me. Haven't had that in my life other than Gran." Gwen shifted the guitar in her lap and fiddled with the strings, her eyes dropping once again to her hands. "Lance probably would've given me that, except he was always focused on being the fun one, the life of the party. God, he got us into so much trouble with the chief with his silly pranks and jokes. Always figured he'd move on to bigger and better things." She strummed a few chords then, as if grounding herself. Orin wasn't ready to be honest with himself about whether he was pleased or not with her answer.

"So, what do you think of all this then?" Orin waved his hand vaguely around, as if encompassing the whole of Caerleon and Avalon.

Gwen laughed lightly, the thrum of the guitar chords a melodic counterpoint. Orin wasn't even sure the woman realized she was still playing.

"Well, I've accepted it's not a crappy dream if that's what you're asking."

He shook his head. "No, I was asking more so I know where your head's at. If I know that, then I know how best to keep Arthur calm."

Gwen hummed a bit at that. "What's his deal anyway?"

"I don't know what you mean." Orin settled back in the chair, frowning.

"Why's he so opposed to things changing?" Gwen asked. "Mordred's been this looming threat hanging over your heads forever. I would've thought that getting rid of that threat would be super appealing to someone who's supposed to be this great king of legend. He's so angry all the time."

Orin narrowed his eyes, not liking the line of questions. His loyalty to his king warred with his need to be honest.

"It is Arthur's privilege to care for his people. He protected his people when we were in the mortal realm and then when we were brought here to face our worst nightmares. Every death weighs heavy on his conscience. It's made him a bit . . ." Orin paused to try to choose the next words carefully. "It may have made him a bit wary of anything new and obsessive in his need to protect his people. That's what makes him a good king."

She hummed again, the tone changing to a thoughtful one. "Okay, I get that. I didn't see it that way, but when you explain it like that, it makes sense. He's risk averse. So everything he sees in me or Viviane and Lance or the other fae is all a risk, and that's why he doesn't want to take it. He doesn't want to lose anyone else."

Orin sighed heavily, shaking his head. "None of us do, Gwen."

"What if, though, the reward is greater than the risk?" She reached out and touched his knee gently, forcing him to look at her. "What if . . . what if someone else helped share the burden of that risk?"

"Like who?" Orin asked.

Gwen pursed her lips, her eyes darting around his face before she responded. "The fae rebels. Will you help me convince Arthur to at least meet with them? Viviane can get a message to them."

Orin felt torn. He knew Arthur's reaction would most likely be a resounding no, but Gwen had a point. He gave her the barest of nods. "I'll speak to the king."

That's how Orin found himself down at the lakeshore four days later as the sun shone overhead, bathing his temple and the back of his neck in sweat. Standing around for a couple of hours in armor under a merciless sun was not pleasant, even if he had more years than he could count of experience from all of his time up on the walls of Caerleon. He wiped his brow with the back of his hand while watching everyone warily.

Three fae had shown up on the far lakeshore across from Caerleon as requested. Viviane and Lancelot had insisted on attending so they were both here as well. They had spent their time waiting with Gwen, stand-ing farther down the beach from Arthur and Orin. Arthur had spent the entire time waiting for the rebel contingent, scowling at the trio as they talked softly. Occasionally they burst into laughter, and Gwen punched Lancelot's shoulder once while giggling behind her other hand. Orin wondered what was so funny. Then he sighed. It didn't really matter, but knowing would be a nice distraction from the nerve-wracking wait.

Viviane had been clear that only three of the fae leaders would attend and had requested that only Arthur and two more from Caerleon attend. She and Lancelot would help liaise between the two groups if needed. Orin snorted at that. His king considered both Viviane and her cousin a threat, so in his mind, the fae would outnumber them. Arthur and Orin had talked about who the third would be, and after hours of circling around it, they finally agreed to Gwen. She was to bring her firearms because Orin reasoned that would give the humans an advantage that the fae couldn't anticipate. The fact that she was also friends with Viviane and Lancelot mattered too. They'd be less likely to betray Gwen than one of the other knights they didn't have a connection with.

Arthur had agreed only because he wanted to keep an eye on Gwen. He had grumbled uncomplimentary things about chaos creatures and troublemakers, all of which Orin ignored. Maybe Gwen was right and his king needed to learn to be more flexible. Over the last few days, the thought of being out from under Mordred's constant threat had only grown more appealing, especially if the fae rebels took the brunt of the backlash Orin expected to happen once they started tangling with Mordred's forces. Orin had been thinking of ways to convince Arthur to be open to opportunities to protect his people that didn't devolve to simply surviving behind Caerleon's walls. So far, he didn't have many ideas, but he'd keep trying. Orin wanted to actually get back to living, not just existing.

They heard the fae coming before they saw them. Orin suspected that was to put them at ease because most fae could ghost through the woods without a sound. The fae were an odd mix. The first to emerge from the trees was a tall, slender male with dark skin and hair and startling green eyes. He wore green leather armor with leaves sewn onto it. He held a flatbow and had a quiver full of arrows hanging from his belt. Next was a small form that flitted about in the air with transparent dragon-fly-like wings. Orin raised his eyebrow at that. He hadn't seen a fairy for close to three hundred years. This one was dressed all in blue, complimenting her blue eyes, blond hair, and pale skin. The last who stepped out had Orin's hand reflexively going to his sword hilt. Arthur's hand fell to Caliburnus's hilt. Gwen put her hand on Arthur's, looking up at him with a faint frown.

"Wait, Your Majesty, she's part of the delegation," Gwen murmured.

"That is a banshee," Arthur hissed back at her.

"She hates Mordred, so having her on our side is a good thing," Gwen replied softly as if the logic was irrefutable.

"Is it?" Arthur protested as he shrugged off her touch.

"I mean, I don't want her screaming at me, so being friendly seems like a good idea. She hasn't done anything yet to prove she's a danger to us," Gwen responded, eyes wide as they bounced between the delegation and Arthur. Orin couldn't refute Gwen's logic.

"'Yet' is the important word there, woman." Arthur stayed tense next to them. His face flushed red with anger.

Gwen whispered, "I'm kind of new to this whole politics thing, but isn't demanding that one of the ambassadors leave considered rude?" The king huffed a frustrated breath out at her, eyes molten as he glared at Gwen. "I'm not trying to be difficult. It seems like it would be," Gwen added. She turned toward Orin as if looking for guidance. Orin swung his gaze back to Arthur, deferring the answer to his king.

"I can't believe I'm doing this," Arthur grumbled after another tense stare down with Gwen.

"I appreciate that you are, Your Majesty. Viviane, are you handling introductions?" Gwen turned and asked her friend. Orin rolled his lips together to hide his smile. Arthur's gaze could have set Gwen on fire because his exasperation was palpable.

This woman, Orin thought with a soundless chuckle. Gwen could go from friendly to persuasive to feisty all in the same sentence if the mood struck her. She wore her feelings openly, and damn if that wasn't alluring after dealing with everyone's melancholy, apathy, or anger for so long. He rather liked that Gwen bordered on irreverence when talking to Arthur. Over the centuries, Arthur had mellowed in being called "Your Majesty" at every turn but still demanded respect from his subjects. Maybe Gwen was on to something in Arthur becoming more approachable with his potential allies and subjects alike. At least Gwen was trying to be respectful. She might fail two times out of five, but Orin could see she was trying.

"Guthlac, Frideswide, and Aethelflaed." Viviane nodded a welcome to the Green Man, fairy, and banshee. "We appreciate your willingness to meet with us. I wish to introduce to you His Majesty, King Arthur; his second-in-command, Sir Orin; and my friend, Officer Gwen McMillan. We understand that your comrades are planning several strikes against Mordred, and we are potentially interested in supporting them."

"What does this potential support look like?" Guthlac rumbled, his deep voice sounding like the creak of branches swaying in the wind.

Arthur shouldered forward. "It depends. What type of support is needed? What type of strikes are we talking about?"

Frideswide piped up, hovering at eye level with Arthur. "We have had several groups captured by Mordred's forces lately. They are considered minor fae and are in one of the smaller and less guarded prison camps. We wish to free them so that we have larger numbers to harry Mordred's forces. Eventually, we would like to have enough to take one of the larger prison camps and free our more powerful brethren."

Orin stroked his chin then turned to Frideswide. "How much do you know about the prison camp? How many and what types of guards are there? What is their patrol schedule? Do you know where exactly the prisoners are kept? What is your plan for either escaping with prisoners or retreating if something goes wrong?"

"It won't go wrong," Guthlac growled, his eyes lighting with fury.

Orin squared up next to his king, staring the fae down. Gwen's eyes bounced between them, turning to look at Viviane. Viviane pursed her lips and shrugged. Clearly, she didn't know what to do next. Gwen stepped between them and smiled up at Guthlac. Despite being slightly taller than the average woman, Gwen still looked tiny compared to Guthlac.

"No offense intended, sir, but you have to admit they're fair questions. If we don't know the details, we can't plan properly, right?" Gwen smiled and waved her hand as if batting away the tension. "If you were in the position of being asked to help us, those are questions we would expect to have to answer for you. We want to ensure success with minimal injuries for both your forces and His Majesty's knights."

Guthlac's brows furrowed in confusion as Gwen spoke. Frideswide nodded while Aethelflaed smiled despite herself. The expression on the banshee's face seemed incongruous with her ghastly look, but it was clear she was amused by Gwen boldly stepping between Arthur and Guthlac.

"You are charmingly blunt," Aethelflaed whispered, her voice echoing as if from the bottom of a well.

"Charming enough we can get answers to the questions Orin asked?" Gwen asked with hope in her voice. She nodded again, hoping to inspire any of the fae to agree. Aethelflaed chuckled.

"I think that will be acceptable. Don't you, Green Man?" Both the banshee and fairy looked pointedly at Guthlac, who rolled his eyes and sighed in frustration.

"Acceptable, yes," he bit out, and Gwen let out the breath. Orin relaxed as the Green Man continued, "We have scouted the area around the prison extensively. We know that the guard changes at dawn, midday, dusk, and the middle of the night. One of our number escaped from another prison camp and indicated that the prisoners are kept in pits dug into the ground, though the earth fae are kept in wagons. When they're not in their cells, they're forced to work, either farming or crafting items for Mordred's army. Sabotage or any form of defiance is dealt with extremely harshly, so prisoners rarely step out of line.

"We believe there may be as many as thirty prisoners in this prison camp. It's one of the smaller ones, on the edges of the Mist Lands, so if we do this right and kill all the guards, Mordred won't know about the raid for a few days. That will give us time to slip away into the surrounding forests and hide our escape routes. Is that enough information for you?" The last was delivered coolly as Guthlac crossed his arms, standing tall and regal while still glaring at Arthur and Orin over Gwen's head.

Gwen turned to look at the men and took in Arthur's mulish expression and Orin's thoughtful one. A pleading look crossed her face. Orin wondered if she thought getting the fae rebels to work with them was a way to get herself home. Avalon hadn't deigned to return Gwen once the sword was here. Maybe Mordred needed to be defeated first before the magic would return Gwen to the mortal realm? Or would Avalon continue to keep her here? Orin had long ago given up on the chance that the rest of them could return to their mortal homes.

Silence pulsed between the group for a few long minutes until Arthur finally scrubbed his face with his hands. When they dropped, he heaved a heavy sigh and flicked his eyes up to Guthlac. "When are you planning the raid? I must know how quickly to pick from my knights and get them prepared."

CHAPTER TWELVE

ORIN

"No," Arthur stated, shaking his head while crossing his arms.

Bronwyn frowned at Arthur's refusal. She and the other women were on one side of the main hall, wrapping bandages to increase the keep's stockpile ahead of the raid. The fae were on the other side, busy fletching arrows. Arthur, Orin, and nearly a dozen knights stood or sat between the two groups while Lance and Frideswide watched them. Quiet wove ominously through the groups.

"Yes, Your Majesty," Bronwyn said, voice firm. She had come over to speak with them and demand that Arthur let the two groups mingle to strengthen the fragile alliance they had formed with the fae. "You know as well as I, Your Majesty, that people take care of other people better when there's a personal connection. I'd rather have friends at yours and the knights' backs rather than just allies."

Arthur pinched the bridge of his nose. "You and Gwen are going to send me to an early grave."

Orin hid a grin. Bronwyn had always skirted the line of proper respect and power behind the throne. Orin knew it maddened his king to no end, but still Arthur never chided his former nursemaid. She had raised the king from a babe until he had led his first battle. Now the woman ran the household for Arthur.

"Oh, don't be so dramatic," Bronwyn chided. "You've lasted this long. Bless Avalon, but you lot are so moody. It's like dealing with little children half the time. Now, we are going to invite the fae over to our table and some of us are going to theirs so you and the men can either join us or get out of the way."

"Bronwyn," Arthur groaned, looking down at the elderly woman.

"Yes?" she asked, tone dangerously sweet.

"Death of me, I swear. Fine." He dropped his voice to a low whisper. "But no one sits next to the banshee."

"You're a good boy." Bronwyn smiled up from her diminutive height, then patted Arthur's cheek, another familiar gesture that only Bronwyn was allowed with Arthur. She raised her voice as she strode back to the women's table. "Come on, you lot, let's go spread out and about and get to know everyone."

Kyla, Agrona, Brea, and Aislinn all gathered up their work and skirted around the knights, who looked to Arthur and Orin with wide eyes. Arthur waved his hand to show his agreement with the women's plan. Orin tracked them as the women smiled at Lance and Frideswide, continuing on to the table where the fae sat. The fae watched the women approach warily, despite their warm smiles.

"Idina, be a dear and go fetch Gwen for me," Bronwyn said. Orin turned his head, attention caught at hearing Gwen's name. What was Bronwyn up to?

Arthur let out another groan. "Wonderful. Just what we need. The whirlwind herself."

"She's not that bad," Orin muttered, receiving a scathing look from his king. "She's really not," Orin defended, letting out an exasperated sigh. He was only five years Arthur's senior but sometimes it felt like decades. While Orin had conflicted feelings regarding his level of attraction to Gwen, he could admit that the woman's catalytic nature had opened up an opportunity that the Avalonians would be ill-advised not to seize. They needed the fae rebels' help to remove Mordred from power, which was the ultimate solution to the constant threat overhanging their daily lives.

Arthur's dyspeptic attitude started two centuries ago when they had lost more than three dozen knights, squires, and soldiers in a surprise night attack that viciously weakened their defenses. The mourning had lasted for months. Until that attack, there had been some deaths, but they had managed to keep them infrequent once they learned how to fight the fae their first century in Avalon. Now Arthur was paranoid of losing anyone. Gwen had become the lightning rod for that fear. Orin shook his head. He knew Arthur wasn't really mad at Gwen; the king was mad that she had given them hope. Hope could be such a dangerous thing.

Orin raised an eyebrow as the women chatted with some of the fae, and Agrona and Aislinn invited several to join them at the women's table while Brea and Kyla inserted themselves into the vacated seats, introducing themselves and striking up conversations with the bemused fae sitting around them. Lance sidled over to stand next to him and his king. Orin narrowed his eyes at the blond fae, who grinned unrepentant at him.

"Looks like you've got your own steamroller there," he chuckled, nodding at Bronwyn, who was busy ensuring the fae who had joined them were comfortable and introducing everyone.

"A what?" Arthur's brows drew together in confusion.

"Eh, it's a self-propelling wagon used to flatten the ground to make building roads easier. There's this big roller in the front of it, and it mows everything down in its way. Gwen is a prime example of a steamroller personality. Looks like your Lady Bronwyn is another." Lance's smile grew as he crossed his arms.

Arthur blew out a breath. "Aye, that's a fair description then."

Lance nodded at Gwen. "We had this one case where this guy came into the hospital all hyped up on drugs and was threatening everyone with a scalpel. They may be small blades, but they can do a lot of damage, especially if they hit a major blood vessel. Anyways, there we were getting everyone out of the ER waiting room and trying to get him to put down the scalpel. Thought we were going to have to tase him or let the dog loose on him."

He shrugged one shoulder. "Then while everyone's ordering him to surrender, Gwen steps in and, just as calm as you please, asks the guy what his favorite dessert was. We all looked at her like she was crazy, but sure enough, the guy lowers the weapon and answers her. Gwen kept him talking, offering to take him over to the bakery to get something if he would put down the scalpel and chill out. It actually worked. Guy dropped the blade and came willingly to the car, sat in the back, then Gwen made us stop at the bakery where she ran in and grabbed a box of baked goods, and then we drove to the station. He balked at going into a cell before Gwen talked him into going in. Gave him a donut through the bars and that was that. Never seen anything like Gwen when she gets rolling." Lance shook his head, still grinning wide.

"Speak of the devil," the fae said as Gwen strolled in, Stockton on her hip and Athelred on her shoulders. Lance's grin widened into a bright smile at the sight. The twins were babbling at each other and Gwen, who sported her own brilliant smile as she looked down at Stockton. "She should have gone into early childhood education instead of criminal justice, but she wanted to help people," he commented offhandedly.

Orin wasn't quite sure what Lance was talking about, but everyone could see she adored children and they Gwen. It was just another facet of the fascinating woman that he found so appealing.

"Mama, mama!" Stockton yelled, squirming on Gwen's hips to be let down.

"Okay, okay, little man, hold on," Gwen laughed, adjusting her grip to set him down on the floor, her other hand steadying Athelred. Stockton squealed again in happiness and ran full force at his mother.

"Hello, my son. What are you doing here?" Alodie crooned, sweeping the child up in a fierce hug.

"Idina took the other kids for me, but these two became barnacles and wouldn't let go." Gwen tickled Stockton's sides while he giggled in his mother's arms. Gwen grinned up at Athelred, shifting him so they could see each other better. "Ready to come down, little man, and give your mama a hug?"

He nodded furiously, reaching hands toward Alodie. "Yes!" the child said.

"Here we go then." Athelred let out a loud belly laugh as Gwen tumbled him over one shoulder, flipping him as the child came down to land on his feet. Alodie let out a big breath before scooping her other son up into her arms.

Orin glanced around. While the women had at least gotten the fae to start talking, tension had still floated in the air. The sight of the two happy boys, however, had brought out smiles on almost everyone's faces.

"Ah, Gwen, there you are." Bronwyn swept over to Gwen, Alodie, and the twins. "We're getting to know each other while we complete our tasks, but I thought it would be lovely if you grabbed your instruments and played while we worked."

Gwen looked stunned at the request, then shook her head. "Ah, I don't really ever play in front of people."

"Oh, don't be silly. You mentioned you played a lot, so you have to be good. Music will make the tasks go faster. Alodie can look after her boys, and Idina will take care of the others. Why don't you pop down to your room and grab your things then come back?" Bronwyn patted Gwen's cheek with a weathered hand.

"Which steamroller will win?" Lance muttered at Orin. Orin let out a soft chuckle. If it was going to be anyone, it would be Bronwyn. She'd had ages to perfect her persuasion skills.

Bronwyn did indeed win, though it took a few more minutes of terse whispers between the two women before Gwen threw her hands up with a muttered curse and walked out of the room. Bronwyn turned with a serene but satisfied smile on her face as she directed everyone back to work and ordered Alodie and her sons to the kitchen for the midday meal.

"Hmm, I thought Gwen was going to hold out. I never can get her to karaoke night." Lance rocked back and forth on his heels, a thoughtful look on his face.

"To what?" Orin asked, but then Gwen entered again, her guitar case in one hand, the violin case in the other. She shot an exasperated look at Bronwyn as she sat the cases down on the table.

"What would you like first? Guitar or violin?" Gwen asked.

Bronwyn clucked her tongue. "We haven't heard new songs in ages. Be a dear and do something that you can sing."

"I don't really . . . I never . . ." Gwen stopped and huffed a breath out as Bronwyn stared at her. Gwen bounced in place for a minute, showing her frustration before flipping the guitar case open and dragging a chair over with her foot. She muttered something as she sank into the chair, already tuning the guitar.

Orin remembered how she had looked the other night in the library as Gwen moved her fingers across the strings. He had been so flustered to come across Gwen and the way her voice called to him like a siren as she sang. Gwen strummed the guitar now, head bent slightly to avoid looking at anyone, as she softly started singing the same song she had been playing before he had interrupted.

"'I See Fire.' One of Gwen's favorites. Good choice to start with," Lance opined.

Orin didn't pay much attention to the quiet comment. All he could see was Gwen. All he could hear was her velvet voice that curled around the room like smoke. All he knew was that he yearned for her, which scared him half to death. This woman had blasted into their lives, and while he found himself reeling from it, Orin could admit the walls he hid his heart behind were crumbling.

Blinking to break whatever spell the song had woven, he looked around the room as Gwen finished it and moved right into another. Everyone was focused on Gwen even though they continued their tasks. He didn't feel so awkward then. He wasn't the only one surprised by her musical talent.

"Gwen," Bronwyn breathed after Gwen finished seven more songs that vacillated between soft and romantic to more upbeat. "Why ever don't you perform? That was lovely." Gwen flushed at the praise and shrugged.

"Damn, McMillan, holding out on me. We could have beat Jones and the chief on karaoke night." Lance strode forward and beamed down at his partner.

Gwen swatted his belly, laughing. "No one beats the chief at karaoke night. But seeing Jones sweat might have been worth it."

"Would you play some more, dear?" Bronwyn pointedly looked at the violin.

Gwen sighed but dutifully put her guitar away and pulled out the violin. She tucked the chair back in, choosing to stand as she tucked the instrument under her chin. Lance stepped back to give her room as she drew the bow across the strings, making sure the violin was tuned. Then Gwen closed her eyes and let the music soar out of the instrument. Everyone seemed captivated as she coaxed the violin to weep with emotion. Arthur held his breath next to Orin, staring at Gwen in shock.

"Another side of her," Orin muttered. "Always surprising."

"At least she's not being . . . what was that, a steamroller? For once anyways," Arthur murmured back, shaking his head. They stood side by side, captivated by the music as Gwen transitioned from melody to melody. Orin wondered if Arthur was also starting to temper his feelings toward Gwen. Perhaps that was Bronwyn's intention —to not only break down more barriers between the fae and humans, but also to give Gwen a chance to shine.

As with the guitar, Gwen played songs that triggered the heart and others that had people tapping their toes in delight. Her eyes opened as she danced the bow across the strings one last time, finishing the song she was playing. Gwen flushed as she realized all eyes were on her. She coughed uncertainly, moving hurriedly to put the violin in her case.

Gwen looked over at Bronwyn. "That's all I've got in me right now. Need any help with what you're working on?"

"Oh no, we're making good progress. Aren't we?" She looked pointedly at those sitting at her table. Even the four fae sitting with the women nodded. Once again, Orin thought that everything would be fine if they let Bronwyn tackle Mordred. She ruled Caerleon as well as any queen could.

"Why don't you sit with His Majesty and whoever is in charge of the fae and plan this raid we've been hearing about?" Bronwyn's eyes swung over to pin Arthur and Orin in place. Orin locked his jaw to prevent a smile.

Arthur grunted at that, looking over at Lance and then back to Guthlac and Frideswide. "We can retire to my war room if you'd like." His eyes flicked over his knights, deciding who to leave in charge. "Bors, mind the room, will you?" He jerked his head toward the door leading out to the main part of the keep. "This way."

"We insist that young Gwen to join us," Frideswide announced, fluttering up to be eye level with Arthur. "She seems to have a calming effect."

Arthur snorted and crossed his arms. "She has no experience with something of this scale."

Orin sighed. Perhaps Arthur's feelings toward Gwen weren't actually gentling. Orin would need to speak with his king as soon as they had a private moment.

"She's been in tactical discussions as a police officer. We've had to do a few raids on suspected drug houses." Lance's eyes went cold at Arthur's insults.

The woman in question was looking at them as she rolled bandages while listening to Agrona talk with a faun sitting across the table. Gwen raised an eyebrow at Orin. She could obviously hear their conversation. The knight knew it was against his king's wishes, but he gestured Gwen over.

"Orin," Arthur growled.

"My King, both Gwen and Lance have spent time in the mortal world, and they may know unique battle maneuvers that we can use." Orin stared at his liege. Arthur's attempts to ignore Gwen's catalytic and magnetic presence was getting old.

"Fine," Arthur snapped, throwing his hands in the air before turning smartly and striding out of the room.

"This way, please," Orin told the group, catching the way Lance rolled his eyes at Arthur's back before the fae grinned affectionately down at Gwen. She smiled back and let him put an arm around her shoulders so they could walk together. Orin frowned, wondering at their relationship. Then he turned and led the group up to the war room.

They spent the afternoon discussing plans and another two days preparing. Twenty of the knights would be joining them, plus another thirty fae. Guthlac told them that the fae expected there to be only a score of guards, but they would have powers to keep the prisoners in line. To match them with lesser fae and non-magical humans, they would need as many bodies as possible on this mission. Arthur and the fae leaders finally came to an agreement on the assault plan.

They traveled over four hours to get near the prison camp before dark and camped overnight, planning to attack in the morning. Their camp was a thirty minute trek to the prison camp, far enough away that the trees hid their fires. At the camp, the knights and fae shared an uneasy watch schedule through the night.

The next morning, the camp stirred to life as the sun bathed the forest in golden light. Orin watched as Gwen crawled out of the canvas tent she had been assigned to. He had already learned that she wasn't much for the morning, bemoaning the loss of some sort of drink called coffee. Lancelot had regularly joined her grumbling since his arrival. She grunted a good morning at him as she sent Saxon off into the woods for his morning business. The knight handed her a cup of steaming hot tea.

"Ugh, thanks," Gwen muttered at him, hiding a huge yawn behind her hand. Then she put the cup down on the ground to stretch her arms up and behind her. Orin vaguely heard the pop of a couple of joints, but he was trying hard not to look at her breasts as she arched her back to stretch out her spine.

"Sleeping on the ground sucks," she mumbled. He had to agree with her on that. His own joints weren't feeling that great this morning and his back muscles had chimed in angrily as well.

Then he tried hard not to watch as she foraged around in their supplies and found the food she had packed in an oil cloth for Saxon. Or as she sipped at her cooling tea. Or as she looked around at the others waking up and waved her good mornings at them. Or . . . Orin hated to admit that he spent a lot of time trying not to watch Gwen. Except he failed spectacularly every single time.

Saxon appeared as if by magic as she dumped the meat scraps onto a plate for him. While the dog inhaled his breakfast, Gwen disappeared back into the tent with her tea.

When she came out, Gwen donned her leather and chain mail armor and held her packs in one hand and the empty tea mug in the other. Orin continued watching her out of the corner of his eye as she stacked her packs up on the other packs that were lying between their tents and fished out a small bag and a mirror. Gwen nestled the mirror onto the top of the bags, tilting it as she sat down in front of the packs. She was humming slightly as she opened the bag and started pulling out small tubes and brushes, which she placed next to the mirror in haphazard piles.

The rest of the camp buzzed around them, the fae and human knights getting their own gear ready for the mission ahead. They wouldn't be attacking the prison camp until midday so the men and fae were finding ways to keep their nerves under control. Some played cards, others checked their weapons. One of the werewolves looked like it went back to sleep, lucky bastard.

Not Gwen though. She painted gold color onto her eyelids and lined them with black liner with sharp wings then flicked a soft black brush over her eyelashes, making them seem longer and fuller. Then some soft pink blush went on her cheeks and additional rose color on her lips. Once done, she put away her makeup, still quietly humming and started brushing her brown hair.

It had been a long time since he'd watched a woman get ready for her day, and Orin remembered then how soothing it could be. He had always enjoyed watching his wife braid her hair. Watching Gwen braid parts of her hair and then twist it up into some form of messy bun on the top of her head was as fascinating for some reason.

"Why are you bothering with all that?" Cae grumbled at her. "You think the fae care how you look?"

She sighed and made a face at him. Orin had told Gwen that Cae could be more bark than bite, and Gwen and Cae could coexist peacefully as long as Cae kept his mouth shut. This meant there wasn't much peace between the two of them, Orin had to admit if he was honest. His friend was a grumpy bastard at the best of times and downright horrible at the worst. Even Alodie couldn't change that. Orin shook his head to himself. Alodie had more patience than his friend rightly deserved.

"Not that it's any of your business, but this is how I'm dealing with the wait." She nodded at Tor, who was sharpening one of his knives and then at Bedevere counting the arrows in his quiver for the third or fourth time. "It's no different than what they're doing. At this rate, Tor may not have a dagger left if he keeps sharpening it, and Bedevere won't magically find more arrows in his quiver, but it makes them feel better about what's coming. So don't give me grief about how I'm passing my time."

She turned back to the mirror and fixed a few stray hairs and pushed another pin into the bun to hold it in place. "Besides, if I die today, at least I'll do it looking fantastic." Then she winked at Cae and started packing her makeup, brush, and mirror back into her pack.

Orin huffed out a small laugh. *This woman,* he thought, shaking his head. *Does nothing faze her?*

He turned and caught Lancelot watching him watch Gwen. The fae narrowed his eyes at Orin. Orin couldn't help it. He narrowed his eyes right back.

What the hell is the fae's problem? This was going to be an issue if they had to watch each other's backs during the assault. Orin flicked his eyes at Gwen, who was busy prepping her packs to hand over to the small group of fae and stable hands that would return to Caerleon before they began their attack on the prison camp. Good, she was occupied.

Orin stood, jerking his head at Lance toward the horses. The knight stood and casually strolled over behind the tethered horses, expecting Lance to follow him.

"What do you want?" Lance growled quietly once he was in earshot.

"Do we have a problem?" Orin tried to keep his tone mild, holding on to his irritation as best he could.

"Yeah, we do. I don't know what your intentions are for my best friend, but every time I turn around, you've got eyes on her. She and I landed here in the middle of this mess, and while she's done small-scale police skirmishes, this level of combat is new to her. If you're interested in pursuing Gwen, you'll just be distracting her, and she may end up dead because of it if she's not one hundred percent focused on the mission." Lance got up in Orin's face, his fists clenched at his side.

"I'm not interested in Gwen that way. I thought you said she was able to handle this level of plan execution." Orin crossed his arms over his chest, holding his ground, but he winced internally. He knew Lance was right about both the risk of distractions in the middle of a military assault and the larger issue of Orin's attraction to Gwen. How many others had noticed his obsession with Gwen?

"Could have fooled me with the way you keep staring at her with hearts in your eyes. And yeah, I told your king that to keep Gwen close. Stay away from her," Lance snarled back.

"I hear you," Orin returned, trying to keep his voice calm. "Why don't we focus on the fight ahead. I trust you'll have our backs as much as we have yours?"

Lance flashed a shark-like grin at Orin, his eyes glittering with malice. "I'll always have Gwen's back."

Orin sighed at the implied threat. Lance wouldn't have his back, but Orin would need to keep the fae alive. Lance might've been an ass, but he was powerful, and they would need that for the fight ahead. So, Orin swallowed his anger and nodded briskly before turning and heading back to where Gwen, Tor, and Cae were helping to take down and pack away the tents.

Gwen's eyes followed Orin as he headed over to assist Tor, then flicked to Lance. She frowned at them and murmured something to Lance as he came over to her before punching his chest, making Orin think they hadn't been careful enough to hide the tension simmering between him and Lance. The two continued a harshly whispered conversation. Gwen made a gesture in Orin's direction and shook her head at Lance. The big fae's shoulders sagged as he sighed, and he shot Orin a glance before giving him a nod. Maybe the fae would have his back.

CHAPTER THIRTEEN

GWEN

Gwen closed her eyes and breathed quietly, settling her nerves as best she could as she hid with Lance, Orin, Tor, and several fae at the edge of the woods. Her earlier jovial attitude that she used to hide her nerves faded on their trek to where they now lay hidden. The prison camp had short walls patrolled by five to eight guards at any time. The fae had cleared the woods around the camp so that there were clear lines of sight in every direction. Sneaking up close wasn't an option. That's where Gwen came in.

She and her firearms were key to the first part of the attack. It was her job to take out any guards she could see so that the attack party could surge across the field. Gwen had argued long and hard with Arthur, Orin, and Lance about the fact that they wanted her to snipe the guards, but Lance had pulled her into the hallway out of the war room to talk more.

"The guards made their choices, Gwen. It's just like if we had an armed suspect. I know you're proud of the fact you've never had to use your service weapon, but this is war. They're hurting people, Gwen. We swore an oath to protect those who can't protect themselves. You're not a killer or a soldier, but you're going to have to be one during this raid." Lance had raised an eyebrow then, holding on to her shoulders. "I do believe this alliance was your idea, yeah? And you had no issues putting those soldiers down when you rescued me."

"But that was an in-the-moment thing. This feels different somehow," Gwen had protested.

"More premeditated but also just as needed. You can do this." Lance's fingers then tightened on her shoulders before he let go. They had held each others gazes before she gave a sharp nod. Gwen would have to do this. There was no other choice, but it didn't mean she had to like it.

Shoving the memory aside, Gwen opened her eyes to stare across the field. The earth fae with them would create dirt ramps to scale the walls. Once inside, they would battle the remaining guards and work to free the prisoners. Sounded simple, but Gwen knew it wouldn't be. She bore the brunt of the pressure for the first overture. Gwen looked up at Frideswide. The fairy was watching for Guthlac's signal.

Frideswide smiled reassuringly down at Gwen then glanced over to where Guthlac was hiding. Gwen knelt, stabilizing her rifle on the fallen tree in front of her. The air crackled with anticipation. Lance put his hand on her shoulder.

"Ready?" he whispered.

She knew he didn't mean if she was ready for the signal. He was asking if she was ready to kill.

"Yes," Gwen breathed. At least, she thought she was.

"Gwen." The voice came from the fairy commander perched in a tree above her. Gwen looked up at Frideswide.

Frideswide gazed down at her, face serious but calm. "Guthlac signaled. Take out the guards."

"You've got this," Lance murmured, patting her on her back as he moved to the side, ready to attack once the guards had been removed.

Gwen took in a breath and then slowly exhaled, her eyes locked on the head of the guard she could see in the farthest corner of the wall. Her finger pulled on the trigger. The bark of the rifle rolled across the clearing. A collective sigh went up along the forest line as the guard fell backward, disappearing behind the walls.

Gwen moved her sights to the next guard, who was shouting and waving his arms at where the guard had fallen. The gun bucked against her shoulder as she fired. His body jerked before falling out of sight.

The rhythm of finding a target and firing ratcheted the tension in the air around her. The guards were running around now, the shots getting harder. Gwen stood to handle tracking their movements better, bracing her legs to steady her shots. The echoes of each shot blended into the next, creating chaos until the remaining guards dropped below the wall. Gwen reloaded, her fingers flying through the motions.

"Good girl," Lance said softly. "Here we go."

A long wolf howl erupted down the line. That was the signal to charge. Gwen vaulted over the log in front of her, Saxon moving with her. Lance, Orin, and the others ran ahead, their longer legs lengthening the distance between her and them. As the rebels and knights surged forward, the guards popped back up, shouting down into the fort.

Gwen skidded to a stop, snapping her rifle up to her shoulder. This was why she hung back. *Continue to harry the guards. Keep their heads down or take them out if possible.* Guthlac and Arthur's orders drilled into her. They didn't need her in the fort. They needed her to do this.

Two harpies shot up from inside the fort, screeching as they turned to the northeast, toward Mordred's castle.

"Oh, no you don't," Gwen gritted out, swinging the barrel of the rifle to track them. Her first shot missed, but the second hit the nearest harpy in the shoulder. She spiraled down toward the trees, her pained cries mingling with the rumbling of the ground as the earth fae molded the dirt into ramps up against the fort's walls.

Gwen fired again at the same harpy, the fae's body going limp and falling into the canopy below. The second harpy screamed her anger and dove to catch her fellow harpy. With a loud crack of thunder, Gwen's shot hit. The second body plummeted lifelessly after the first.

Panting as adrenaline rushed through her, Gwen whipped around toward the fort. The rebels and knights were already up the ramps and pushing onto the parapet, fighting the surge of guards there. Gwen was out of time to take down any more of Mordred's forces. Slinging her rifle over her back, Gwen looked at Saxon then started running toward the fort with the dog following at her side.

Dirt crumbled under her feet as she rushed up the nearest ramp, but Gwen dug her toes into the earth and powered up, her calves and thighs burning. The breath backed up in her lungs as she drew her knives. Gwen pointed at a guard battling with Guthlac. Fire crackled around the guard's hands.

"Sax, *fass!*" Gwen commanded the dog to attack. The German Shepherd bounded ahead of her and soared over the wall, slamming into the guard who screamed as Saxon latched onto his shoulder. They fell behind the walls as Gwen pushed the last few steps to reach her dog. Over the wall, Gwen took hold of the guard and thrust her long knife into his throat.

"Sax, *aus!*" The dog let go of the gurgling fae at Gwen's order. Guthlac stomped down on the guard's chest, crushing it. Gwen swung her eyes up to the Green Man. "Holy shit."

A feral grin stretched his face. "Keep up, little one." He leaped off the parapet down into the courtyard.

Her gaze locked on two guards battling a werewolf on the opposite parapet. She shoved her knives into their sheaths and rolled her rifle into her hands again. Gwen licked her dry lips, lined up her shot, and pulled the trigger. One of the guards stumbled, and the wolf lunged forward, snapping its strong jaws around the guard's throat.

Rifle thrown on her back again, knives back out. Assess threats. This length of wall was clear with the bulk of the battle moving into the courtyard. Gwen and Sax ran to the nearest stairs and thundered down them as her eyes sought Lance and Orin. She was supposed to stay near them. So much for that plan.

Gwen lunged and thrust her knife up into a guard's back as he battled Frideswide and a group of fairies. Their magic sparkled in the air as the fae guard howled in pain. Gwen kicked at his knee, sending him thudding to the ground. The fairies swooped in, their magic peeling the flesh from his face.

Time to move, her mind shrieked at her.

Everything was chaos. Gwen had no idea where any of the guys were, and the din of battle bounced around the courtyard, bodies thudding to the ground or shoving into each other as groups fought in clusters. Magic sizzled in the air.

Then the roar came.

Silence fell across the fort as what she thought was a large rock against the back wall unfolded itself. Dark red runes ignited across its gray flesh.

A mountain ogre.

It roared again, charging forward. The fae rebels hadn't mentioned the ogre.

They hadn't known.

The fae rebels' screams as they scrambled to get away from the ogre clearly indicated their surprise. Lance, Arthur, Tor, and Orin stood with Guthlac and Aethelflaed acting as a wall between the ogre and the other fae. The guards pressed their advantage as Guthlac bellowed for the rebels to keep pushing forward. The banshee stepped in front of Arthur and Guthlac.

Aethelflaed screamed.

The sound drove Gwen to her knees, hands over her ears while Saxon howled with the wolves as the cry spiraled up and up. Horror, sorrow, rage—all of it was embodied in Aethelflaed's cry. It tore at Gwen's heart, every grief-ridden memory coming to the fore. Tears pricked at her eyes as she gasped for breath.

The ogre stumbled in its charge, rearing back and shaking its head in confusion. It blinked its eyes at Aethelflaed and then roared again, swiping a large, clawed hand at her. Aethelflaed flowed backward as the ogre's fist pounded into the courtyard where she had been standing.

Guthlac and Arthur rushed under the swing, driving their swords into the tough skin of the ogre's underbelly and legs. Their blades skittered off, barely scratching the monster. They danced and ducked away from the ogre as it kicked at them and swung its fists down in a brutal attack. Lance pulled at the water in the nearby well and sent a large ice spike hurtling at the ogre's chest. It shattered on impact.

"Oh, shit," Gwen muttered, running toward her partner. She wove amongst the groups fighting, her breath backing up in her lungs as she lost sight of the men for a moment. An earth fae shoved a column of dirt into the air. The guard on top of it toppled down into the waiting jaws of two werewolves.

"Tor!" Anguish drenched the air as the cry ripped from Orin's throat.

Gwen sliced at the fae in front of her, a rebel finishing the guard off while Gwen continued running. Now Gwen could see her friends clearly. Orin stood over a broken and bleeding Tor, fending off brutal attacks with his shield as the ogre swung wildly at the knights and rebels attacking it. Lance seemed to see her out of the corner of his eye. He raised a hand at the ogre and looked at her.

"Gwen, aim for the eyes!" he bellowed.

She dropped her knives, fumbling for her rifle, but the rifle strap snagged on her armor and refused to come over her head. Saxon snarled and lunged at a guard as she rushed Gwen, lightning crackling between her hands.

"Sax!" Gwen shrieked, her hand dropping down to her service weapon. The handgun jumped in her hand as she pumped five shots straight into the guard's chest. The lightning lanced up into the sky, leaving the smell of ozone lingering in the air.

No time for the rifle.

Gwen approached the ogre, firing at its face. The shots peppered across the ogre's features. It shook its brutish head as the shots pinged off its skin, disorienting it. Guthlac, Arthur, and Lance pressed their advantage, harrying the ogre from all sides.

"Stay away from him!" Orin yelled at a fae trying to kneel by Tor.

"He's a healer!" Lance roared at Orin. "If you want your friend to live, protect them both!" He shoved his hands at the ogre. Ice crawled down its legs from its knees to the ground, trapping it in one place.

Gwen didn't dare look again at Tor. Instead, she shoved her service weapon back into its holster and wrestled her rifle strap over her head and chambered a round. She had tunnel vision on the ogre; a voice in her mind shrieked to be more careful, but the ogre . . . that needed to be dealt with first. Gwen's lungs burned from holding her breath. She forcibly exhaled to relax as she brought the rifle butt up to her shoulder and zeroed in on the ogre's eyes.

The target was so small and constantly moving as the ogre thrashed against the ice.

Gwen fired anyway.

The bark of the gun melded with the scream that ruptured from the ogre's throat. Her shot hadn't hit the intended mark, but the ogre's ear was now gone. Gwen focused on her breathing and the sound of the lever as she chambered another round. Gwen pulled the trigger. Around her, she was barely cognizant of Saxon's rabid growls at her feet; of Orin, the fae healer, and Griffin pulling Tor out of the ogre's reach; of Lance shouting a warning at her. Her entire focus was on the ogre as it broke through the ice holding one leg and stepped back.

Blood sprayed from the ogre's eye, and a weird keening noise spiraled out from its throat. It wavered on its feet, the bright red runes decorating its skin going dull, then black. The earth shook when its body toppled backward, the wet sound of its body hitting the ground rolling through the now quiet courtyard.

"Gwen!"

Her head snapped toward Lance as he hurled himself at her, pulling her hard against his body, his arm protecting her back. Cold ice crackled behind her, sending a shiver down her spine as Lance manifested a thick ice shield. The ice reverberated as lightning struck harshly against it, ozone again tinging the air.

Gwen blinked up at Lance. "Guess some of the guards are alive?" she croaked. He stared down at her, something she couldn't name on his face before he glanced over at Orin.

"Go! I'll protect her," he barked at the knights and healer. "Get Tor to Viviane. She can save him."

Gwen pulled out of Lance's grip, wincing as another spell hit the ice shield. Cracks crawled across the shield. Her gaze snagged on Orin. Concern was etched on his face as he looked between her and Tor.

"Go!" she yelled at Orin. "Save Tor!" Orin's mouth went tight, but he nodded sharply at her. Then he was working with Arthur and Griffin to clear a path for the fae healer and another Green Man to carry Tor toward the gate.

Lance stared down at her, face blank. "There are only two guards left. I'm going to drop the shield. I need you to get the lightning mage. Do you understand, Gwen?"

Gwen licked her lips and nodded. "Stop the person throwing lightning. Good plan."

A ghost of a smile appeared on Lance's face then was gone. Gwen turned, backing up a step so she could raise the rifle one last time. She'd either kill the mage or be struck by lightning. She didn't feel like getting struck by lightning.

"Ready?" he asked.

Gwen licked dry lips. "Yes."

The ice dissolved instantly, water raining down into the blood-drenched earth at their feet. Gwen's eyes snagged on the single guard that still lived. His tall frame and bright blue hair stood out amongst the knights and fae. Lightning lanced into the ground around him, creating a shield that the rebels couldn't breach. There was nothing between him and her and Lance. The mage's gaze locked with hers. She pulled the trigger.

Lightning arced at her, Lance, and Saxon as the mage's body fell backward. Gwen stumbled back as Lance grabbed her again, throwing up his arm in front of her. Another ice shield formed an inch in front of her face; the lightning that hit it seconds later blinded her.

"You okay?" Lance whispered hoarsely as she blinked away the spots dancing in front of her eyes.

Gwen sagged in his arms, the adrenaline dump ripping away her legs' ability to stand. "Yeah?" Gwen wasn't sure if her answer was a statement and a question. "Was that the last one?"

Lance looked around the courtyard, still holding her tucked against him. "Looks like it."

"Thank God." Gwen breathed out as Lance squeezed her tightly. "Prisoners next?" Lance nodded then released his hold on her, something in his body language showing his reticence at letting her go. Gwen wasn't sure what to think about this overprotective version of Lance. She steadied her legs and looked around, taking stock of the chaos in the prison's courtyard.

"The prisoners feel like they're in chambers below the courtyard," Alcina said, trotting over to them. The three healers wove their way from injured fae to injured knight and back. Gwen wondered how many they had lost.

Lance nodded, standing straight. "Then let's go liberate them." His eyes roved over the courtyard, alighting on Frideswide. "How many dead, Frideswide?"

The fairy flitted over, hovering in front of him. "One of my fairies, two wolves, and two more from House Keithia. Several severely wounded, including some of the humans. They've already been sent to Caerleon with King Arthur and his knights so that Lady Viviane can tend them." Frideswide's eyes flicked to Gwen then back to Lance. "It seems removing the first wave of guards made as significant a difference as we had hoped. Aethelflaed's scream as well. Those of us prepared for the banshee's attack kept our feet and used the advantage to kill several guards while they were incapacitated. We are already moving the other wounded out."

Gwen let out a little sigh, pressing the heel of her hand to her forehead. Her head throbbed from Aethelflaed's wailing onslaught. Saxon leaned hard against her leg, and she knelt, running her hands all over her dog. There was blood, but none of it was his. Gwen held Saxon's head and pressed her forehead to his.

"You're okay, Fur Face." Gwen didn't even mind the dog's hot, panting breath in her face. Relief washed over her. They'd both made it.

"We need to keep moving," Lance said quietly, offering his hand to Gwen. She scratched quickly behind Saxon's ears then let Lance pull her to his feet.

Alcina waved them over to a large, flat stone in the middle of the courtyard. She and two other earth fae knelt, placing their hands into the dirt.

"There's a ramp beneath this that leads to the prison below." Her voice dripped with exhaustion as she dug fingers into the packed dirt, the earth parting slowly for her. The rock quivered as the three earth fae pushed their magic into it. Slowly, so slowly, the rock inched across the ground, revealing a tunnel with a ramp leading down into the darkness.

"Gwen, Arthur ordered us back to Caerleon." Griffin stood next to her.

Lance's hand landed heavily on her shoulder, his warmth suddenly behind her back. "You can go, but Gwen is critical to this mission. She stays with me." He paused, then continued as if correcting himself, "With us." Gwen turned, squinting up at him. Her partner shrugged and tapped the rifle hanging off her shoulder.

"This changes the tide of battle," he told her. "We need you here in case another nasty surprise pops up while we're finishing the prisoner extraction or making our way back to Caerleon."

"Hmm, okay." Gwen looked at Griffin. "Maybe we split up? Some of you guys stay with us? The rest make their way back to Caerleon?"

The knight shook his head, brow furrowed in a frown. "Arthur was clear. We've done what we promised we would. The fae need to escape and hide on their own."

The earth rumbled under their feet. The stone slid until the way into the prison was clear.

"Griffin, we need to make sure there's nothing else down there preventing the fae from escaping," Gwen argued, holding the bridge of her nose. After all of this, how was she still arguing with them about helping the rebels? "I'm staying."

Griffin huffed out a long, heavy breath. "Arthur isn't going to like this."

"Yeah, well what else is new?" Gwen muttered, following Lance and Alcina into the tunnel.

Griffin hesitated then shouted a few names and followed. The knights appeared shortly behind them as they stopped at the bottom of the ramp.

"Thanks, Griffin," Gwen whispered to the knight as he caught up. She smiled up at him. The knight patted her back and peered down the tunnel where Lance and Alcina were already trying to get the doors open.

"Guess we should help." Griffin sighed. "Let's go, boys." He shouldered past Gwen, Agravaine, Bedevere, Gawain, and Caradoc following.

Saxon sat at Gwen's feet, panting and looking up at her as she scratched his ears. "Let's see what we can do to help, huh, Fur Face?"

The answer was clear as a female fae staggered out of the door Lance had wrenched open. She had dusky blue skin, darker blue tattoos across her face, and white hair, and she was clothed in grime-covered rags. Gwen wasn't sure what type of fae the woman was but caught her as the fae faltered.

"Easy, I've gotcha," Gwen said, pulling the fae's arm across her shoulders and bracing against the fae's weight. The fae blinked at her.

"A mortal?" Her voice spiraled high in surprise.

"My name is Gwen." Gwen started walking toward the tunnel entrance, pulling the blue-skinned fae along.

"Gwen?" the fae asked, perplexed.

"Yeah, and you are?" Gwen helped the fae stumble into the daylight.

"Artemisia," the fae whispered in a cracked voice.

Gwen smiled at the fae. "Let's get you out of here, Artemisia."

The rebels and remaining knights split up into smaller groups as they left the prison. Guthlac demanded Lance, Gwen, and the knights to come with him and a few other fae. They trudged through the woods for several hours, doubling back on their trail and walking through whatever water they came across to hide their tracks. With the sun setting in an hour, they didn't have time to make it back to Caerleon. Navigating the dark, misty forests meant dealing with the darker portion of Mordred's forces. No one wanted to run into the ogres, aswangs, pugots, or gorgons that roamed the forests and fields of the Mist Lands once night blanketed the land. Finally, Guthlac told the group they were close to their destination, and a sigh of relief swept through them.

Guthlac led the small group to a giant tree clinging to the side of a small, steep hill. As they approached, Guthlac put his hand on the exposed roots, and they crawled out of his way, exposing a dark hole surrounded by long, gnarly roots that formed an organic doorway. The fae waved a hand for them to follow him. As the last of them stepped inside, the roots creaked, curling in on themselves so that the entrance was once again hidden. The knights kept their hands on their sword hilts, but Gwen focused on holding Artemisia up. The fae was barely able to stumble forward, even with Gwen's assistance. Both Gwen and Artemisia sighed in relief when the tunnel opened into a large, dirt-walled chamber. More roots twisted over their heads, creating a wooden roof that held up the space.

Eight fae moved around the chamber, serving up something from the large pot bubbling away in the center of the earthen room. The smoke dissipated on its own as it spiraled up toward the roots. They stilled as the group trudged in, Guthlac striding in first.

"We have reinforcements joining us tonight, including our human allies." His head swung from side to side until it fell on a small, wizened figure. "Richella, see to the wounded and to those we freed from the prison." Guthlac turned back to Lance, Gwen, and the others. "Be welcome. We will rest here tonight then escort you to Caerleon in the morning to ensure your safety."

"Thanks for that," Caradoc muttered, sarcasm lacing his words. Griffin's hand thumped hard on the man's chest. Caradoc glared at Griffin and rubbed at his chest.

"Manners," Griffin hissed. "Unless you wish to get us killed." Caradoc blanched and nodded, pressing his lips together.

"We have her, mortal." The voice belonged to a cold-looking female fae who glared at Gwen.

Gwen blinked. The fae's icy-blue eyes shone out of a golden-skinned but wrinkled face, surrounded by a mess of dark black, unkempt hair. A scar split her lip, causing a permanent leer. A small dryad with pale green hair and pale skin that reminded Gwen of birch trees stood next to her. The dryad offered a timid smile.

"Okay, Artemisia?" Gwen asked, her legs shaking as she continued to hold up the fae's weight.

"Thank you, Gwen." Artemisia patted the hand Gwen had wrapped around the fae's waist. "Lorna and Lyonesse can help me from here." She staggered out of Gwen's hold and into the other faes' grip. Lance immediately surged into the empty space and put a protective arm around Gwen's shoulder.

"Let's get some food and rest," her partner told her. Lance looked at the knights and nodded his head to an empty corner. "We can bed down over there," he said, steering Gwen and Saxon in that direction.

The knights hesitated then followed. Gwen let Lance guide her over; at this point, she couldn't care less where they sat so long as she wouldn't have to move anymore. Exhaustion pressed down hard on Gwen, and she pulled out of Lance's hold to flop down on the floor and lean back against the wall. Saxon shoved himself halfway in her lap, forcing her hands to stroke his bloodstained fur. He would need a good scrubbing when they got back to the castle.

"What?" she asked Bedevere as he shot her an amused look.

"Making yourself at home?" Bedevere asked.

"I'm tired, thank you very much," she replied, voice prim. Gwen narrowed her eyes, looking over the knights. They may have thought that they were hiding it, but they were exhausted too. It showed in the slight slump of their shoulders, the lines of pain around their corners of their mouth, or the barely noticeable waver. "Feel free to join me."

Bedevere chuckled and slid down the wall to sit next to her, propping his arms up on his bent knees. He knocked his shoulder into hers lightly. "You did well today. Very well. I'm glad Avalon brought you."

"Yeah?" She bumped his shoulder back. "Well, you would be one of the few."

Lance sat on her other side, pulling her against him. "Rest. We leave at dawn to go back to Caerleon."

"Do you think Tor made it?" Gwen asked, chewing at her lip as she melted into her best friend's side.

Lance nodded, staring up at the roots above their heads. "If they got him to Viviane in time, then he did. My cousin's healing powers are some of the strongest in the fae houses. Sleep now. Dawn comes quickly. Then we can find out when we get back to the castle."

"Okay." Gwen sighed, letting her dog stay draped across her lap. She snuggled farther into Lance's large, warm frame, trusting him to keep her safe, and drifted into sleep to the sound of low murmurs as the fae moved about and settled down.

Chapter Fourteen

Gwen

"Almost there," Guthlac rumbled as the trees began to thin and the telltale lap of water sloshing against a shoreline drifted to their ears.

"Yay," Gwen breathed without enthusiasm. After spending the night sitting up while sleeping, she didn't have the energy for it. While she wasn't a fan of horses, Gwen missed the grumpy mare she had ridden only a few days ago. Her feet screamed at her as did her back and neck. No more sleeping on the ground, she swore to herself. Saxon's head hung as he plodded next to her. Bedevere chuckled right behind her.

"A hot bath, some food, and sleeping in a real bed will have all of us set to rights," he told Gwen.

She hummed an agreement as Caerleon came into sight. While Gwen still wished she was back in her farmhouse, cuddled with Saxon in her own bed, at this moment, she had never been so happy to see that damn castle. Gwen could see forms patrolling the wall. Then she heard the horns as the group was spotted.

Guthlac continued forward. Gwen raised an eyebrow at that. She had been sure he would leave them at the tree line. The fae kept marching toward Caerleon, with her, the knights, and Lance trailing after the Green Man. The gates groaned open as they plodded up to them. Knights swarmed out, slapping Bedevere, Agravaine, Griffin, Gawain, and Caradoc's backs and shoulders.

Henri welcomed Guthlac and Lance. "My liege will want to talk to you. I'll take you to him."

Griffin and Bedevere extracted themselves, joining Henri, Guthlac, and Lance as they headed toward the keep's main entrance. Gwen peeled off from everyone, aiming toward the small entryway that would lead to the kitchen and then her room.

"Gwen, where are you going?" Griffin jerked his thumb over his shoulder. "Arthur will most likely have questions for you."

"I'm not interested in hearing Arthur's wrath," Gwen told them, still walking. "There's enough of you to answer whatever questions he has."

"Gwen!" Griffin barked.

She drowned out whatever else was said as she firmly shut the heavy wooden door behind her and Saxon. Gwen rolled her eyes, looking down at her dog. He looked worse than yesterday, and Gwen reckoned she did as well.

"Bossy men," she muttered to Saxon. He huffed, his stride picking up as they neared the kitchen. It was noisy again, the sound of clanging pans and pots, raised voices, and toddler screeches smashing into Gwen. "Full house. Maybe we can snag something quietly and avoid all the questions." She held off telling the dog that they were going to get baths, otherwise Saxon would hide under the bed and she'd have to physically drag him to the bathing room and wrestle him into one of the copper bathtubs. Gwen had experienced enough physical exertion in the last twenty-four hours, thank you very much.

"Doggy!" The toddler screech turned into a wild whoop of enthusiasm.

"Stockton, no!" Alodie snapped, snagging the two year old as he pelted past his mother. The woman tossed a glance at Saxon and then looked down at her son sternly. "The doggy is filthy. No touching!" Stockton burst into tears, his tiny toddler heart devastated at the news. Alodie sighed and swept him up in her arms before hustling out of the room, shouting over her shoulder. "I'm so glad you made it home, Gwen!"

Gwen blinked at that. Home? Did she consider Caerleon her home now? She realized she hadn't thought about how she was going to get back to the mortal realm in the last few days at all.

With Lance here, what did she have to return to? Her parents probably didn't care if they ever saw her again. The chief and others at the office would miss both her and Lance, but while they were friendly, they weren't friends. Gwen scrunched her nose up, admitting that her only true friends had been Lance and Saxon. Add in the fact that she had finally met the literal man of her dreams, and he seemed to be softening toward her. Did she want to go home?

Gwen wasn't sure. It wasn't her choice to be stuck in Avalon, and that rubbed her all kinds of wrong. Gwen hated not being in charge of her own life. She'd have to think about it later when she didn't reek of soured blood, offal, and sweat.

"Gwen!" Bronwyn rushed over, her hands hovering around Gwen's shoulders and arms as she looked for wounds. "Thank goodness you're all right. We were so worried when everyone else made it back but you, that hulking fae of yours, and the others."

"Tor?" Gwen croaked. She cleared her dry throat. "Is Tor all right?"

"Lady Viviane saved him and the other two who were badly hurt. But she did say that expending that much magic to keep them alive drained her, so while they're alive, they still have some wounds that must heal on their own time. She has all three of them under a magical sleep in the infirmary so they don't make their injuries worse."

"Thank God." Gwen rubbed her eyes as they prickled suspiciously, and she cleared her throat again. "Can I go see them once I get cleaned up?"

"Of course, of course, come along. Let's see to you first. Maebh, you're in charge while I make sure Gwen is unharmed." Bronwyn steered her through the other kitchen door, heading toward Gwen's room.

"I'm not hurt," Gwen protested.

Bronwyn clicked her tongue, making a tsking noise. "We won't know until we get you out of this bloody armor. There's dirt everywhere down your back. If you're wounded under all of this, the last thing we need is for an unknown wound to get infected." She ushered Gwen into her room, closing the door brusquely before pointing at the new armor rack in the corner. "I had some of the men find one for you, and the weapon rack too in case you needed it."

While the room had been sufficient for Gwen's needs, it was a bit empty. Now though, the armor and weapon racks graced one corner, a new rug was on the floor, and colorful wall hangings softened the walls.

"Um, what?" Gwen waved at everything as she divested herself of her rifle, service weapon, and knives and placed them on the table. "No, Sax, don't get up on the bed. Out you go," she ordered, shuffling the dog out into the courtyard.

Bronwyn started to peel Gwen's armor off. "Well, we thought it would be nice for you to come back to something cozier. Now let's make sure you're all right then get you into the bath."

Bemused, Gwen let Bronwyn fret over her, feeling a surge of warmth for the somewhat overbearing woman. This felt like being taken care of by Gran, so she allowed Bronwyn to help remove her armor, groaning a bit as she shucked off her boots.

Lord, I must stink to high heaven, she thought.

"Well, no wounds, that's wonderful. You're much better at keeping yourself in one piece than the men. I'll leave you to get yourself and the pup clean and bring some food so it's here on your table when you're done." Then Bronwyn was gone, bustling out and down the hall back to the kitchen.

Getting clean sounded like a wonderful idea so she found some clothes, called Saxon to her side, and slowly made her way to the bathing chamber. When she emerged, both she and Saxon were clean, their hair damp. Saxon grumbled and looked at her with disgust.

"What? You were gross. No, not on the . . ." Gwen groaned as Saxon hopped on the bed. "You did that on purpose." The dog shot her a look then turned three times and dropped down onto the blanket. "Fine," Gwen huffed, grabbing the bread and cheese that Bronwyn had left for her and hastily consuming it. "You can stay here." Saxon stretched, implying he was fine with that as she closed the door behind her and locked it.

Gwen made her way up to the infirmary, avoiding everyone by ducking down back halls and winding her way up to the third floor. Viviane looked up from a still form as Gwen slid into the room.

"Gwenhwyfar!" Viviane was across the room and sweeping Gwen up into a tight hug before Gwen could greet her friend. Viviane grasped Gwen's head between her hands, searching her eyes. "How fare you?"

Gwen couldn't stop the heavy sigh. "Exhausted, a few bruises here or there that I found while getting clean, but otherwise, I'm whole."

"How does your heart feel?" Viviane asked, still gazing at Gwen with concern.

Gwen drew her friend's hands down, swallowing hard. "It really sucked. I don't like killing." Viviane nodded at that, her eyes sympathetic. "How is Tor? Who else was injured?"

"A man named Lamorak and another named Erec. Come, I'll show you." Viviane drew Gwen over to Tor's bedside. The dark-skinned, large man looked much smaller without his vibrant energy carrying him around. Gwen felt the prickle in her eyes again, fighting back tears. This was her fault. She had convinced Arthur and Orin that this was a good idea. If Tor died, everyone would be devastated, especially Orin and Cae. He had to live.

"With some rest, I think I can further accelerate their healing, but piecing Tor back together, dealing with Lamorak's stomach wound, and Erec's blood loss plus the wounded fae has drained me."

Power smashed up from the floor through her feet and flooded Gwen's body. Gwen's heart skipped a beat as her chest tightened. It felt like the one time Gwen had accidentally stumbled into a live electric fence while chasing a teenager who had stolen two chickens from one of Littleton's farmers. Golden light danced in front of her eyes, creating a sparking haze. Gwen's fingers tingled as she fumbled for Viviane's hand.

What was happening? Gwen wondered, swaying on her feet as the onslaught rushed through her. As the power swelled, Gwen could have sworn she scented petrichor and growing things, the smell she had grown to associate with the woods around Caerleon.

"Gwen?" Viviane's eyes widened as Gwen's clutching fingers tightened until they were white knuckled. Then the fae jolted as the energy surging through Gwen flowed into Viviane.

"Heal them." Gwen's voice was toneless, her eyes locked on Tor. Fog swirled around the edges of her vision, tinted by the odd golden light that misted over her eyes. Her feet wouldn't move. She could do nothing but channel whatever this was.

Avalon, she thought.

That must be what this was. Avalon was bestowing a gift on them, and Gwen would not waste it. Viviane rushed to put her other hand on Tor's chest, the air growing cold around them as the fae woman fed her power into the knight's body. The torrent continued. Gwen wavered on her feet, but she gritted her teeth to stay upright and focused on keeping the energy flowing into Viviane.

Tor's eyelids fluttered.

Wake up, Tor. Wake up, Gwen thought desperately.

His eyes blinked open, and Viviane snatched her hand off his chest. Tor looked at them in confusion. "What happened, and why do I feel like shit?"

"You had multiple broken . . ." Viviane started to say, then gasped as Gwen pulled her away from Tor's bedside. "Gwen?"

"Heal." That was all Gwen could grit out as the fog curled more around her vision. The pressure on her chest doubled, as if both Stockton and Athelred were sitting on her. A moan pushed out. The staccato beat of her heart hurt so much.

"Right." Viviane nodded, putting her hand now on Erec. Viviane directed the energy into the man, prompting his body to create more blood as water droplets gathered on his skin before being absorbed. Once done, Viviane led the way to Lamorak.

The flood of energy was waning. Gwen thudded to her knees next to Viviane when the fae touched Lamorak's stomach, the chest pressure and arrhythmia redoubling. Was she going to die like this? It sure felt like it. Now the fog turned black, with white spots dancing across her eyes. Gwen knew she was seconds away from passing out.

"Gwen! Gwen." Viviane had her hands on Gwen's shoulders, stabilizing her as Lamorak groaned and sat up, holding his stomach.

Her tether to the energy snapped, rocking her head back as she felt the ping of it ripping through her mind.

"Ow." Not the most eloquent response to Viviane's question, but it was the best Gwen could manage. The fog whipped away from the edges of her vision, and she blinked up at her friend. "Well, that's new . . ."

Gwen's joints felt like they were on fire as she trudged to the war room. She could only assume Arthur and Orin would be there, maybe still with Guthlac and Lance. They would want to know that the men had woken up, their wounds mostly healed though Viviane thought that they wouldn't regain their energy anytime soon. The body could only take so much. While Avalon had gifted Viviane with enough energy to fuel her spell work, that energy hadn't transferred to the knights.

Male voices rumbled out of the war room's cracked doors. Perfect. She wouldn't have to go much farther, and there were chairs in that room. Wonderful, wonderful chairs that would welcome her drained body. One of the doors squeaked loudly as she practically fell into it, pushing the door open far quicker than she had expected. Heads whipped around to stare at her.

"Tor, Erec, and Lamorak are awake," Gwen rasped as she staggered to the nearest wooden chair and sank into it. Wonderful, wonderful chair. She gripped the seat to keep from sliding out of it and straight to the floor.

"They're awake?" Arthur snapped to attention, halting his harsh words with Guthlac and Lance. Griffin and Bedevere stood at his back, but it looked like the others had been dismissed. She wondered where Orin was; he would want to know his friend was not only alive but well on his way to being fully healed.

"Yep." Gwen emphasized the *p* sound at the end of the word.

"Hey, what happened? You all right?" Lance dropped to his heels in front of her, grabbing one of her hands.

"Avalon gave us a gift. She fed some weird energy through me into Viviane, and I guess that was enough so Viv could finish healing the guys. I'm just tired. Turning into a human magical fire hose was not on my lifetime bingo card." He chuckled at that. Gwen shifted her focus, locking gazes with Arthur. Something crossed his face, but she wasn't sure what it was. Surprise, maybe? Relief? Plus, he wasn't scowling at her. That was weird. Arthur always scowled at Gwen.

"They're still going to need time to heal. Their bodies used up a lot of energy as new blood was made and skin cells were forced to replicate, or I guess that's what happened? Viviane uses the water to force the body to fix itself. Did you know up to seventy-five percent of the human body can be made of water?" Gwen realized now that she was babbling, but she couldn't seem to stop. "Anyways, that's all I wanted to tell you. I'll get out of the way. Can you help me up?" Gwen said the last to her partner, who rose and pulled her to her feet by her elbow.

"Do you need help getting back to your room?" Lance murmured, eyes darting around her face as if assessing her fatigue.

"Nope. I think I will be okay." Gwen patted him on the chest. "Hope you're being nice to each other," she called back into the room as she shuffled into the hallway. Gwen winced. She knew she shouldn't have made that last parting shot toward Arthur, but she was tired, damn it. The mind-to-mouth filter never worked when she was exhausted.

After wobbling her way through more back halls, Gwen dragged her exhausted self to Orin's closed door and raised a heavy hand to knock. She used that same hand to prop herself up on the doorframe while she waited. If Orin wasn't here, Gwen would have to sit outside his room until he reappeared because getting back to her room seemed like too long a journey to make right now.

Gwen frowned at the door. It was still closed. The rooms beyond sounded quiet. One more time, then she'd have to decide on sitting down or trudging back downstairs.

She raised her fist again and knocked louder, calling through the door, "Orin, it's Gwen." Gwen thought she heard rustling. "Orin?"

The door was wrenched open, Orin suddenly looming over her.

"Hey, I was just—" she started to say then squeaked as Orin yanked her into a hug. While Gwen had spent enough time watching Orin to know that he watched her right back, heat and interest in his eyes, he had never once tried to touch her. The ladies had told Gwen that Orin had stopped trying for romantic relationships centuries ago, avoiding heartbreak, but Gwen had hoped he might be softening toward her. It was one of the reasons she regularly sought him out, to get him used to spending time with her so she could cautiously flirt with him.

"You're all right," he mumbled above her head.

She leaned back a bit to see his face. Harsh worry lines snaked across his face, dark circles below his eyes. It looked like Orin hadn't slept last night. "I'm all right," she told him, licking her lips. His gaze dropped to follow the glide of her tongue, and he lowered his forehead to hers, hands clenching her closer.

"You're all right." His mouth was a breath from hers.

Gwen brought shaky hands up to his face. "Yes." Her heartbeat picked up, and she bit her lower lip in anticipation. Was Orin going to kiss her? Oh God, she hoped so.

"Thank Avalon," he growled, tilting her face up more so he could slant his lips against her.

Oh . . . my . . . God. The thought pulsed in her mind. *This man could kiss.*

Gwen wrapped her arms behind his neck and kissed him back. She poured all her feelings for Orin into the kiss. This was the man she had been in love with for a decade, the dreams letting her know him in a way that he probably wouldn't understand. So she'd show him.

But the kiss ended abruptly. Orin wrenched himself out of her embrace, looking horrified at her. Gwen blinked at the sudden separation, her brows drawing together at his expression.

"Orin?" she asked, voice tentative as her breath caught in her chest. Oh no. Her heart sank.

"I'm sorry. I shouldn't have done that," Orin said, his frame stiffening. He ran a hand quickly over his face then leveled her with a mournful look.

"Okay . . ." Gwen drawled, tilting her head while keeping her gaze on him. "Well, I guess I should apologize too, then, though it wouldn't be sincere."

Heat flared in his eyes again as he repeated her words. "Not . . . sincere . . ." Orin seemed to be trying out her words as he said them.

"Orin," she responded with a resigned but exasperated sigh. "As much as I catch you looking at me, I don't know how you missed how much I look at you. Jesus, I've flirted with you every chance I could as long as I thought you wouldn't be uncomfortable."

Orin blinked at her. "Oh." A flash of something that might be hope crossed his face before it shuttered again.

Gwen huffed out a little laugh. Orin had kissed her stupid, and now he looked like shed hit him upside the head with a frying pan. The women's words about Orin's former heartbreak and caution toward recent relationships bubbled back up and reminded Gwen she'd have to be patient with her continued pursuit of the man. For now, it was time to put Orin out of his misery. Gwen took a step back out of the doorway, working to hide the way she was shaking.

"I came to tell you Tor is awake. Viviane was able to make progress on healing him. I didn't think anyone had told you yet, and I thought you might like to go see him. I'll catch you later." Gwen turned on her heels and shuffled away. She'd definitely have to make it to her room now.

As thrilled as she was to see Caerleon earlier this morning, that feeling paled in the face of her pleasure at unlocking her door and closing it behind her. For a little while, she could hide from everything—her feelings . . . Arthur . . . Lance . . . Orin—in sleep. Gwen toed off her shoes and shoved Saxon over. The dog grumbled at his mistress but settled again at the foot of the bed so she could crawl in and drift off immediately to sleep.

The dream slammed into her. The woods outside of Caerleon teemed with small groups of armed fae. Gwen couldn't tell if they were rebels or Mordred's forces. She also couldn't tell if this was something from the past or something happening now. What was Avalon trying to show her? The forces seemed to clash. Okay, so it must be the rebels and Mordred's army. Blood soaked into Avalon's soil, and the earth trembled with pain. A pale fae with dark hair sat on a black horse as he stared up at Caerleon. She knew that face. Mordred.

Gwen moaned in her sleep as the dream shifted, showing the front of Caerleon. Her view zipped through the gate, then into the keep, down the hallways, into the chapel, and finally the hidden cavern. The spell stone pulsed with a soft, blue light. The power beat in the same rhythm as her own heart, tugging at her, demanding she stand before the stone.

Gwen shot up in the bed, her heart pounding, with Saxon standing over her legs and whining at her. Sweat beaded across her body.

"Ugh, boob sweat," Gwen grumbled, peeling her damp shirt off her clammy skin. "I'm fine, Fur Face. Back up some." The dog sat down next to her legs instead. "That works, I guess."

Gwen drew her legs up to her chest and said, her voice quiet, "The dreams came back. It wasn't a bad one compared to some, but I guess we need to go see what's up with the spell stone. Get down. I'll feed you, maybe myself, then we can go." She glanced out the window. It was still daylight, but it must be the afternoon. The courtyard was bathed in shadows now.

"We'll go as soon as I clean up," she told Saxon, letting him out into the darkened courtyard. Minutes later, they crept through the halls, hoping to avoid running into hyperactive toddlers, grumpy knights, or Bronwyn. Gwen was glad the shakes had passed and that her back, neck, and feet had stopped complaining. The nap had done her some good though she figured she'd go right back to sleep once she had a chance to grab dinner.

The air felt dense and heavy as Gwen stepped into the chapel, Saxon snuffling along the ground ahead of her. He whined as he stopped at the base of the statue, pawing at it. Magic thrummed across her skin, making Gwen gasp as her feet were pulled unbidden to stand next to Saxon. One of his big paws hit the decoration that activated the stair mechanism, and it groaned again as the stairs were revealed.

"Sax, wait!" But it was too late. Her dog shot down into the dark. The magic kept pulling at Gwen, but she resisted enough to grab one of the ever-burning lanterns. She hadn't survived yesterday's madness to break her neck today falling down some steps.

As she wound her way down, the blue light from her dream filtered up the stairs. Maybe she hadn't needed the lantern, but Gwen kept her grip firmly on it anyway. Saxon waited for her at the base of the stairs, frozen in place with his eyes locked on the spell stone. Gwen gulped as the magic danced across her skin and drew her across the rough-hewn floor until she was in front of the glowing stone.

"Now what?" she whispered. Tentatively, Gwen brushed her hands against the stone, thinking to herself *stupid stupid stupid*. Hadn't she watched enough horror and suspense films to know touching weird, glowing things always ended badly?

Apparently not.

It was like the magic snatched her hands, forcing her palms against the warm stone. As she cursed and struggled, power slammed into her, sending Gwen thudding to her knees. Brutal agony washed through her. It felt like the magic was ripping her apart, cell by cell, remaking her. Gwen threw her head back, screaming, as the magic consumed her.

Gwen floated in a sea of pain as she was altered into something . . . more. Avalon bound her to every grain of sand, every plant and tree, and every body of water in Her domain. The binding was weak but persistent, like a barely healed bone. The bond could be easily broken. Something else was needed.

The sword, the magic pushed at Gwen. The sword needed to be bound back to the stone. But how?

Hands grasped her shoulders, bringing Gwen back abruptly to the feel of her body. As the hands ripped her away from the stone, Avalon pushed one last vision.

The sword, drenched in Gwen's blood.

CHAPTER FIFTEEN

ORIN

It took a while for Orin to get his head around his encounter with Gwen. He could still feel her lips on his, her body pressed against him. What was he thinking? He pulled at his hair, hoping the pain would stop his downward thought spiral.

Surely she hadn't meant what she said. Did she really watch him? As much as he watched her, Orin had never caught her looking back. She was too young for him. Then again, she was too young for any of the men by a magnitude of centuries. He couldn't keep using that as an excuse to stay away from the woman. Orin wasn't sure he was ready to get close to someone else. Could he handle the possibility of losing her one day?

He scrubbed his hands over his face, pushing out of his room to go see Tor. The thought of losing his brother-in-arms gutted Orin. When they fled the fae prison, Tor was clutched in one of the Green Man's arms as they rushed back to Caerleon. The sound of Tor's bloody, rasping breaths would haunt Orin for a long while. The Lady of the Lake met them at the gates, pouring magic into Tor's broken body even before the Green Man lowered his friend to the ground. Hearing from Gwen that Tor was going to live sent Orin's emotions spiraling. That was the only explanation for the madness that had caused him to kiss her. Surely that was it.

Only he knew it wasn't. He wanted Gwen. The woman had snuck under his skin from the moment he saw her.

Viviane met Orin at the infirmary's entrance, letting him know that Tor and the others were asleep but doing much better thanks to Gwen and whatever spell Avalon had wrought through the woman. That didn't stop Orin from checking for himself that Tor's breathing and color was better. He should let Arthur know. With that thought, he bid the fae healer goodbye and made his way back to the war room. He found his liege having an intense debate with Lancelot and Guthlac. Orin sidled in, half listening to the discussion and occasionally answering a question thrown his way.

He needed to talk to Gwen. Orin had no idea what he would say, but it was clear that they needed to see where this went. Now that he'd had a taste of her, he couldn't let that slip through his fingers. If the last few weeks had taught Orin anything, it was that Gwen was a woman who could stand with him against whatever the Mist Lands threw at them. If they survived, maybe she might even be the woman he could find forever with. The fact that she had chosen him over any of the others still baffled him. What did she see in him? At the moment, he didn't care. He wanted her.

The scream that ripped through Caerleon jolted him out of his own head as the others in the room cursed and grabbed for weapons, looking around in shock as the agonized cry echoed through the keep.

"What the hell was that?" Lancelot growled, shooting a suspicious glare at Arthur.

"How would I know? What did you do?" Arthur snapped back. Behind him, Griffin and Bedevere's hands dropped to their weapons.

A gut feeling had Orin shaking his head. "Wasn't them."

Eyes darted to Orin before the stare down between the fae and the knights continued. Orin didn't have time for this. He strode out of the room, feeling the need to head down to the chapel. Footsteps fell in behind him. Orin glanced over his shoulder to see Lancelot. The fae looked shaken.

"You feel it too?" Orin asked.

Lancelot nodded, voice grim. "Gwen. Avalon isn't done with her. Where would Avalon call her?"

Orin's feet were already carrying him down the stairs as he answered, "Below the chapel."

As they hit the ground floor, they could hear frantic calls from the courtyard asking what was going on and where the scream was coming from. Bronwyn, Idina, and Demelza hurried toward them from the kitchens.

"Orin, what is happening?" Bronwyn asked, her eyes wide with fear.

"It's fine, Bronwyn. Just tell Viviane to come to the chapel," Orin ordered, picking up his pace. "And you stay away from there! Avalon is doing something, and we don't want to risk you."

"Orin," Bronwyn spluttered, but he and Lance were already far enough down the hall that she couldn't say anything else to stop them.

His heart sank as he barreled into the chapel, seeing the open entryway and one of the lanterns missing. Orin snatched the other lantern as Lance grabbed his shoulder.

"Is that Saxon?" Lancelot asked. The man's shoulders were rigid, knuckles white as he peered into the darkness.

Orin cocked his head, listening. Sure enough, he could hear the dog whining in the depths below. Holding the lantern up, Orin charged down as fast as was safely possible on the narrow, winding stairs. Even the eerie blue light filtering up from the cavern didn't stop his haste or that of Lancelot behind him.

If the fae loses his footing and falls, we'll both break our necks, the knight thought irritably as he hit the final step and made his way into the cavern.

"Gwen." Her name was ripped out of his chest against his own volition. The woman knelt in front of the spell stone, her hands pressed against it. White light pulsed around her. Saxon crouched a few feet away, the hair on his entire body standing up as he whined at his mistress. Orin rushed toward Gwen, Lance right behind him. The knight reached for Gwen but paused. She looked locked into some spell, her head tipped back with tears streaming from open but unseeing eyes. Orin looked at the fae. "What do we do?"

Lancelot's wild eyes met Orin's. The fae shook his head, saying, "I don't know. We might hurt her more if we break the connection, or she may die if we let it continue. Look. It's like Avalon is sucking her life force dry."

Orin dropped his gaze, noting the color leaching slowly out of Gwen's skin, her breaths growing shallow. He wasn't about to lose anyone else. His hands dropped to her shoulders, and Orin pulled with everything he had.

There was a moment of silence. Energy burned through the air as if a bolt of lightning was about to strike. Then, the light around Gwen flashed so bright that it blinded him and Lance. Orin blinked his eyes clear, finding himself on the ground with Gwen in his lap. He wrapped his arms around her as Gwen's body slumped into his. Saxon whined again, nosing Gwen's face as the dog snuffled all over her body. Lance knelt next to them, taking one of Gwen's hands.

"Gwen," Lance said quietly. He reached out to tilt Gwen's face up with a gentle touch to her chin.

"Lance?" she croaked out then turned to look up at Orin. "Orin?" Her face was awash in tears and pain.

"We've got you, darling," Orin told her, his arms involuntarily tightening around her as the endearment slipped out.

"What happened?" His heart plummeted as a strong sob rattled her thin frame. Orin made small shushing noises as Lance looked over Gwen, searching for injuries. Saxon continued to get in the way until Lance ordered him to lie down.

Lance met Orin's eyes, shaking his head. "I don't see any injuries," he said as Gwen continued to weep. Tremors crawled through her body, causing her limbs to jerk in Orin's hold. "We need to get her to my cousin."

"No need. I'm here." Viviane knelt gracefully next to them, her knowing gaze flowing over Gwen just as Lance's had. "She's been fully claimed now. Before, she was just a tether. Now, she is part of Avalon."

"What the hell does that mean?" Orin growled, shifting Gwen a bit in his lap so he could wipe at the tears streaming down her face. She stared at him with blank umber eyes. Fear surged through him. She looked completely broken.

"Gwen, I need you to come back to us. You're scaring us," Orin crooned as his heartbeat ratcheted higher. He pushed a lock of hair behind her ear, then cradled his palm against her cheek.

Not again, Orin thought. He couldn't lose someone again. In that moment, he knew that if Gwen made it through whatever this was, they were going to talk about these burgeoning feelings between the two of them.

"It's all right, Orin. Lance, I need to hold her hands, so let the poor woman go." Viviane peeled Gwen's hand out of her cousin's and shifted so she could kneel in Gwen's line of sight. "Gwenhwyfar, let the magic go. Let it flow through you as water flows down a mountain, disappearing back into the soil. Let Avalon have Her magic back for now. You will remain a part of it, but you must let it go."

"How?" Gwen sobbed, scrunching her eyes closed. Agony etched fine lines across her face.

"Imagine yourself as the top part of an hourglass," Viviane commanded. "The magic is the sand. Let each grain of sand flow out of you and down into the portion of the glass that is Avalon. You can do this, Gwenhwyfar. Now take a deep breath and let it go. The power will go with it."

Gwen's chest expanded as she did what Viviane bid, taking a deep breath and slowly letting it out. The frenetic energy rippling through the air around them diminished.

"Good. Again." Viviane's calm voice curled around them.

Gwen took another deep breath then blew it out slowly. As she did, the energy in the cavern disappeared and her sobs slowed, the tears beginning to dry on her cheeks. Orin felt his anxiety soar higher as she let out one last breath and went limp in his arms. Unconsciousness claimed Gwen.

"Gwen?" Panic had Lance's voice hitching on her name as he grabbed for Gwen.

"She's fine, Lancelot," Viviane said, batting his hands away. "Orin, can you bring Gwen to her room? She needs to rest."

Orin cleared his throat, making sure his voice would be steady as he glanced at the fair fae. "She'll be all right?"

Viviane's smile was sad as she nodded. "With what Avalon may have in store for her, I don't know if I can answer that fully. I can, however, say that what she went through hasn't permanently harmed Gwen. Rest and then some food should have our Gwen back on her feet by sometime tomorrow, the day after at the most."

Viviane patted his knee and then held out her hand to Lancelot to help her up. "I told you and Arthur that day at the lake that Avalon had chosen Gwen as Her guardian. Until now, Avalon has been gentle in Her claiming. Danger must be on the horizon if Avalon has accelerated Her binding with Gwen. We must be ready for whatever may be coming, which means we must let Gwenhwyfar rest and continue down this path that has been chosen for her."

Orin listened half-heartedly as the men and fae standing around him completed their preparations for the scouting mission they would conduct today; it would be another three to four hour ride to the scouting location from Carleon. He, Lance, and Viviane had taken Gwen to her room yesterday evening; the healer then shooed the men out of the room, promising to keep an eye on her. Both Lance and Orin argued, but Viviane held firm. Gwen had only been here a few weeks. Why did it feel like he was leaving his heart in her room when he walked away?

"Orin? You ready?" Bors asked.

Orin shook his head to clear his woolgathering. "What? Right, yes, ready." Bors's gaze was assessing, making Orin frown. "Problem?" he growled.

Bors's eyes widened at Orin's terse tone. "No, no problem." Bors nudged his horse away as the scouting party began trickling through Caerleon's gate.

"My cousin will keep an eye on her." Lance's voice filtered through Orin's thoughts.

Orin grunted at that. Lance didn't sound convinced. Orin wasn't convinced either, but he had no choice but to leave both Gwen and his worry for her back in Caerleon. They'd be in the saddle for several hours, meeting up with smaller scouting groups the fae rebels were providing. Then they'd scatter up and down known supply routes between Mordred's prison camps, training camps, and the fae houses. Orin tapped his heels against his horse's ribs, and the mare ambled forward, falling into place at the end of the long trail of scouts with Lance directly ahead of him.

That was one more thing to worry about; what exactly was Lance's purpose in all of this? Was he trying to reclaim his ancestral home? Did he want to step into the leadership vacuum that would occur once Mordred was defeated? Or did he want something . . . or someone . . . closer to home? Orin frowned at the fae's back. Whatever the answers were, he'd have to work with the fae today. Gwen obviously trusted Lance with her life. Orin hoped he could do the same.

"We'll leave the horses here," Lance murmured to the group of fae and knights. "The forest fae will keep them safe and hidden so we can continue on foot. Guthlac says he expects a supply caravan to pass by in an hour, which gives us time to get in place." There was a brief wave of murmurs across the group. "Scatter up and down the road, either side. Focus on how much and what type of supplies they have. Do not engage. After the caravan goes by, we can regroup and report back to the human and fae council."

"There's a council now?" Orin asked, raising an eyebrow.

Lance rolled his eyes. "You're part of it, being Arthur's right hand."

"So that's what we're calling it then these days?" Orin crossed his arms, not liking the sneer in Lance's tone.

"Let's get in place," Lance huffed, shrugging a shoulder to situate the sword on his back more comfortably as he nodded at two of the fae. They fell in behind him as he strode across the road and disappeared into the woods.

"Maybe we can just . . . accidentally lose him?" Bors muttered next to Orin.

Orin snorted a laugh. "Gwen and Viviane would probably miss him."

"Would they? Would they really?" Bors asked, raising an eyebrow.

Orin sighed. "Unfortunately, they would. Let's find our places. I've no desire to tangle with a fae patrol."

Bors held up a hand as he listened. "Hear that?"

Orin cocked his head, listening. Hoof beats. Orin pointed back at the tree line, hustling with the other knights to blend into the forest. A lone rider on a chestnut horse with a bold, wide blaze and four white stockings came into view, trotting at a lazy pace. The fae wore black and red livery and held a small horse bow. A quiver full of white-fletched arrows graced his back.

Bors started to whisper "A messenger. Wonder what he's—"

A bolt of ice zipped out of the opposite tree line. It sliced across the rider's throat, sending his body thudding into the dirt. The chestnut pranced away, head raised while it snorted nervously.

"Really?" Orin grunted, moving toward the fae now drowning in his own blood as Lance emerged from the other side.

"We haven't even been here a full ten minutes, and you're already going rogue?" Orin growled at Lance, who flicked a bored look at the man.

"Scouting a supply caravan is one thing, but being able to intercept a message from what looks like one of Mordred's personal messengers? That's worth something." Lance held out his hand as the shorter of the two fae handed him the messenger's belt pouch. Lance opened the pouch and rifled through the contents. "Dispose of the body well away from the road and cover up the blood. The horse is yours."

The two fae nodded, one shuffling over to force the earth to absorb the evidence of Lance's attack. The other wrapped the cloak around the messenger's neck to prevent a blood trail as he dragged the body off into the woods. Once all traces of the messenger were removed from the road, the earth fae grabbed the horse's reins and followed his fellow fae into the forest. Orin could only assume the earth fae would hide the body the same way that Alcina had disposed of the others.

"Well, well, this is interesting. Letters written by Mordred himself for the heads of each of the houses, and it looks like my younger brother is vying for a larger holding than the current House Dwyn is entitled to. Mordred is promising him House Keithia." Lance skimmed through the pages.

"Which is?" Bors asked.

Lance spared a quick glance at Bors before returning his attention to the papers in his hand. "The creatures and fae of the forest and earth fall under House Keithia's banner. Guthlac used to be one of the Keithia's lieutenants. I was not aware that the Lord and Lady of their court were rebel sympathizers. If their holdings are at risk, we may find ourselves with a powerful new ally if we can convince them this threat is real. We should talk with Guthlac. He'd have a better feel for whether or not his Lord and Lady would be interested in speaking with us."

"Well, we need to either head back to Caerleon then or hide and wait for the supply caravan. My vote is to return to Caerleon. This information is too important to risk us ending in an altercation with Mordred's people," Orin said, crossing his arms and leaning toward the tall, blond fae.

Lance shot Orin a sidelong look then sighed, shifting the messenger bag between his hands. "Yeah, you've got a point. The others can wait here and see what's up with Mordred's supplies. I'll let the others know." He turned to follow the fae that he had tasked with body disposal.

"You're not taking that bag out of our sight," Bors snapped.

Lance raised an eyebrow and squared his stance. The air around him grew frigid. "Are you threatening me?" he growled.

"You may have Gwen's unwavering trust and loyalty, but you haven't earned ours." Orin narrowed his eyes. "We don't need to make threats. Bors is merely stating a fact, which is that the bag stays within our sight."

Lance held Orin's gaze for a long moment before thrusting the bag at him. "Hopefully this earns some brownie points." He whirled and strode across the road.

"What are brownie points?" Bors asked.

Orin shook his head. "I have absolutely no idea."

CHAPTER SIXTEEN

GWEN

The lake stretched out in front of Gwen. Its placid surface reflected the bright cerulean sky while the white-and-gray pebbled beach sparkled like diamonds. Across the breadth of the lake, the dark green trees rose like silent sentinels, watching, waiting. The gentle waves lapping against the shoreline murmured a soft symphony that settled across Gwen. A red-breasted, brown bird circled over her head then dipped low to skim over the water and disappear into the forest's shadows.

Despite the tranquility, the ground under her feet and the air circling around her hummed with Avalon's power. It sparked along her skin, raising the hairs on her arms before she smoothed her hands down them in a jerky motion.

Was this going to be her life from now on? Gwen thought, gritting her teeth. When she first arrived in Avalon, Gwen had visions of returning home. Keep the sword safe and return it to Arthur; that had been her family's mission. Well, check and double check. She'd done that, but still she lacked agency in her life. Instead of returning her home, Avalon had decided to not only keep Gwen but claim her.

Avalon's magic thrummed through her very bones. The sheer unfairness of her lack of choice in the matter took Gwen's breath away. The fact that this was the first time she'd had a moment away from everyone and out of Caerleon's shadows meant she couldn't keep these feelings locked tight inside anymore. A single tear trailed down her face, and she swiped it away with a fierce grimace. She hated being an angry crier.

Saxon's hot breath fanned across her arms where she had them propped up on her knees. He dropped a stick at her feet. His amber eyes focused on her expectantly as his paws did an adorable tippy tap that seemed incongruous for a dog his size.

"If I start throwing that, you won't ever let me stop," Gwen murmured to Saxon, but she took the rough, lichen-covered stick anyway, standing up and brushing off the seat of her pants. Turning away from the lake and its tranquil spell, Gwen flung the stick as far as she could, Saxon letting out a happy bark before bounding off.

Gwen sighed. This was her home now. The power thrumming under her skin was her new normal. She ran her hands through her hair and growled in frustration, trying to let her anger go. Having a meltdown wasn't going to make her situation any better. At least here she had people she'd actually consider friends, not just colleagues. Then there was also Orin to consider. Now that their feelings were out in the open, would he consider pursuing them with her? Gwen turned and gazed at the impressive edifice of Caerleon. Could her future be there behind those walls?

Viviane came out through the gates and walked toward Gwen, the sun turning her bright golden hair almost white. Saxon's tongue lolled out of his mouth and his paws danced in place again while he waited for Gwen to throw the stick. The dog's energy hadn't seemed to wane, but Gwen was about done with the game.

"Does he ever stop?" Viviane asked with a small laugh. Her delighted gaze followed Saxon as he raced away again.

Gwen shook her head, scrunching up her nose. "No, sadly. Eventually I have to be the bad guy and tell him no."

"I thought you might still be resting." Viviane turned to look down at Gwen. "You should be resting."

Gwen frowned and turned to go sit back on the log. She let Saxon drop his stick to the ground and patted his head instead of throwing it again.

"See, I'm resting." Gwen waved at where she sat.

Viviane smiled as she sat next to her human friend. "Mmmm, I can see that. What is bothering you, young Gwenhwyfar?"

Gwen let out a hefty sigh, her hands stilling in Saxon's fur. He pawed at her knee, but she continued to stare unseeing across the serene lake.

"Gwen?" Viviane prodded.

"What? Oh, sorry. I'm kind of spacey. I can . . . feel so much more now. It's really hard to sift through all the sensory input." Gwen leaned down and tapped the ground. The grains of sand near her finger shivered. She glanced at Viviane. "Also, I can do this now, which is super weird."

Viviane raised a thin, expertly shaped brow. "You're already starting to learn how to manipulate your magic? That's wonderful."

Gwen snorted, unamused. "Sure. Like I'm not weird enough." She propped her elbows again on her knees, chin cradled in her hands. "I have to wonder, why me? Looking back, I can see what Gran did. She made sure I learned things that would be useful here. I thought it was cool that I got to learn how to use a sword instead of ballroom dancing like Mother wanted. I kept up with it and the martial arts because I liked how they made me feel, powerful and in control. Not to mention, the martial arts is sometimes useful as a cop. Makes me wonder what exactly Gran knew though. Did you talk to her about it in her dreams?"

Viviane stared across her lake, busying her hands by braiding her hair. "I did, but they were never very clear conversations, not like ours. She was always cryptic, but most everything we discussed eventually came true in some way. I wondered sometimes if your familial line didn't have some fae mixed in. Maybe an ancestor married one of the exiled fae? It would explain your grandmother's seeming clairvoyance."

Gwen grunted at that. Gran's ability to know when Gwen was guilty of some trouble as a child and teenager had shaped Gwen's moral framework. Gwen vividly remembered the one time she snuck out of their house in the Hamptons to attend a beach party when she was underage. Gran had waited for her when she stumbled back into the house well after midnight. Gran never punished her for her transgressions, but there were a lot of discussions and lectures on right and wrong. Luckily, neither of her parents knew about that night, not that Gwen was one hundred percent sure they would have cared.

"It's strange, you know. I thought by now I would have found 'the one' and have a family." Gwen chuckled with sardonic humor. "I've always dreamed of a big family. That's why I bought that farmhouse. I wanted to fill it with kids. Instead, here I am in a place that shouldn't exist, talking to a literary figure that also shouldn't exist—no offense—with powers I have no idea how to control, and committing acts of war even though I don't want to kill anyone."

"The deaths you've caused weigh heavily on you." Viviane's words weren't a question.

Gwen nodded. "They do. I've never even had to discharge my service weapon while on duty. That's the nice thing about being a small-town cop; you know pretty much everyone and can mostly talk them out of doing stupid stuff. Just because half of the fae I've shot didn't even look human doesn't matter. They were sentient beings. What if they had a family? Kids?"

"This is war, young Gwenhwyfar," Viviane chided, but her voice was gentle.

Gwen grimaced. "Yeah, well, I never wanted to be a soldier. It fucking sucks. I'm not cut out for it, to be honest. I can't put my feelings aside and trot into battle, snuff out lives, then happily continue with mine. I know there's no other way. Mordred isn't someone we can negotiate with and be BFFs with. Still, I'm mad about all of this."

Viviane nudged Gwen with her elbow and offered a soft smile. "Which is probably why Avalon chose you as Hers."

Gwen groaned, rubbing the heels of her hands into her eyes. "Because I don't want to be the Chosen One? That's fantasy book shit, not real life. I keep thinking I'm going to wake up and this will all be a dream. Or I'm in the hospital in a coma or something. No one person should make that much of a difference."

"And yet you have," Viviane said.

"Sure, yeah, having the rifle definitely helped during the prison break," Gwen scoffed. "You don't bring a knife to a gunfight, right, but the inverse; I don't have that much ammunition. I didn't have much at the house when I packed everything, so my usefulness there will soon wane. Moving a tiny bit of sand around won't be of much use either. Unless you know someone who can help teach me to do something more with it?"

Viviane tapped a finger to her chin, thinking. "Some of the earth fae like Alcina may be able to help. Can you manipulate the water?"

Gwen leaned forward and poked at the small waves hitting the shore at their feet. The water split away from the gesture for a moment before falling back into rhythmic lapping.

"Well, then we will be spending time together." Viviane beamed at Gwen. "I haven't had the opportunity to teach in a millennium. This will be fun!"

A slight edge of hysteria lined Gwen's laugh as she looked up at the sky. "Yay for training montage?" Then she cocked her head, her eyes getting a faraway look again. "I think some of the scout groups are coming back early. They just crossed into Avalon."

"Interesting," Viviane murmured, casting a thoughtful look at Gwen. "Then let's go prepare to meet them."

Gwen tilted her face up to look at Orin and Lance as they rode into the courtyard. "You're back earlier than expected. Was there trouble?"

Orin threw an exasperated look at Lance as the knight swung out of his saddle. "Just your 'friend' taking matters into his own hands."

Lance scowled. "I never make trouble. What? I don't," he said.

Gwen leveled him with a skeptical look. "How many times a week were you in the chief's office because of your shenanigans? Trouble is your middle name."

Lance gasped. "Bestie, you wound me." He brought his hand over his heart while giving her an exaggerated appalled look in return.

"Lance," Gwen fussed. "You know how to work as a team. Come on, man."

"Yeah, well, we're a team, you and me. Jury's out on the others," Lance retorted, shooting Orin a glare. "But we've got interesting news for the council, so let's get up to the war room and see who is available to discuss it with us."

"Council? What council?" Gwen asked.

"That's what I said," Orin grumbled as the stable boys took their horses away.

"There's always a council," Lance said with a shrug, slinging his arm around Gwen's shoulder and steering her toward the keep. "Like in *The Lord of the Rings*, right? When it comes to standing up to great evil, there's always a council leading the way. Come on, you know this." He shook her shoulder a bit as he grinned down at her.

"Okay, whatever, but this isn't a book or movie, Lance. What made the Fellowship work was the fact that they worked together even when they came from different backgrounds." Gwen poked him in the side. "Everything started falling apart when they split the party."

"Right, well, we didn't really split the party, other than being on the opposite sides of the road. I saw an opportunity and had to take it." Lance shrugged his big shoulders then winked.

Gwen groaned at his playfulness and pulled Lance into a hallway to let the others pass. Orin slowed but continued when Gwen jerked her head toward the stairs.

"What's up?" Lance asked as she stood in front of him. Shrewd eyes inspected her even while he kept the easy grin on his face.

Gwen wasn't fooled by his nonchalance. "Lance, are you all right?" she asked.

He tucked a strand of hair behind her ear. "What's bringing this on? Of course, I'm all right. I'm home. We're making progress in taking back power from Mordred. We're still partners. Why wouldn't I be all right?"

Gwen sighed. "It's just . . . well, you've been vacillating between the friendly, jocular guy that I know and this, no pun intended, cold and ruthless autocratic bastard. You don't sound like yourself when you're that version of you. It's giving me whiplash, and it's not endearing you to anyone here in Caerleon, which worries me. They need to have your back as much as they need to know you have theirs."

"I promise your new friends can trust me," Lance said with another shit-eating grin and mock salute.

Gwen huffed and stomped her foot. She crossed her arms and glared at Lance. "But you need to show them that."

"I'm bringing this message to Arthur and not Guthlac or Frideswide, aren't I? Doesn't that earn me brownie points?" Frustration meandered across his face, and he dropped the grin, propping his hands on his hips.

"Well, sure," Gwen told him, sighing again. "Stop poking at the other guys, please?"

"Well, that's no fun, but since you asked nicely, I will. Now, come on, let's go discuss our next steps with the others. We may have lucked out and found a way to gain a powerful ally today." He pulled her back into the main hall and up toward the war room.

Gwen could hear the rumble of voices as she and Lance turned the corner toward the war room. *They don't sound happy, but then again,* she thought, *what else was new.* She shook Lance's arm off her shoulder and sidled into the room while he strode confidently toward the table where Orin and Arthur were talking with Bors and Frideswide. Gwen smiled as she watched the fairy wave her arms for emphasis and glare up at Arthur.

Gwen settled into a chair. Like the sand grains sifting outside on the lakeshore, Gwen felt like something was filtering through her, leaving tiny sparks in their wake that made it hard to concentrate. Saxon plopped his head in her lap, nosing at a hand. She automatically started petting him, forcing her attention back to the council discussion. Her skin tingled in random places, and her joints buzzed with low-level pain.

"We should see if Guthlac can get an audience with our Lord and Lady and feel them out for support," Frideswide commented.

"Are they that likely to stand against Mordred?" Arthur inquired. "Or would they need to be more covert in their support of the rebellion?"

Lance crossed his arms and shook his head. "Most likely covert until we gained further traction against Mordred. We would need to at least show we are powerful enough to topple some of his other prison camps and outposts before they openly defied his rule. We will also need to be cautious of my younger brother. Aberlin always was ambitious, and with me out of the picture, he finally has what he always wanted as Lord of House Dwyn. Our lands border Avalon so if Mordred were to move his army in, it would be across our land with Aberlin's full support. House Dwyn's land stands between us and House Keithia, which can be both a good and bad thing. We can potentially crush Aberlin's forces between ours, but it also means House Keithia is blocked from our support if they need it swiftly."

"Who do the wolves normally work for?" The words slipped out before Gwen fully formed her thoughts. Everyone turned to look at the woman.

"The wolves?" Frideswide asked.

"Yeah. They're shock troops, right? You have several who have defected and joined your ranks. I can't imagine that the wolves are cool with Mordred throwing their lives away. What about their pups? Are they going to be forced to grow up to be soldiers even if they don't want to? I guess I'm trying to figure out which court they belong to. Is it Keithia?"

"No," Frideswide answered slowly. She tapped a finger to her chin, blue eyes focused on Gwen. "They bend knee to Morganna of House

Mors. Where she stands with Mordred is anyone's guess. The darker fae are ruled by her iron hand. She provides Mordred with not only the werewolves but the more monstrous of our kind—the vampiric, trolls, harpies, spirits, etcetera. Aethelflaed defected from Morganna's court."

"Why don't we ask the white wolf if more of their kind would be interested in joining us? We can offer safety for their families in exchange for them spying on whatever they can." Gwen shrugged. "Just a thought. I get the impression they're often overlooked unless they're getting right in your face." Her eyes flicked to the scars on Orin's face then back to Frideswide.

"You want to work with the wolves?" Arthur asked, tone aghast.

Realizing that continuing to talk to Arthur in front of the group would be like talking to a wall, Gwen made a quick decision. "Would everyone mind stepping out for a moment, please?" Gwen asked, standing. Her eyes never left Arthur. "I need to speak to Arthur in private for a moment."

"Gwen," Orin started, warning in his voice. Gwen pointed toward the door.

"Now, please." The crack of command in Gwen's voice surprised Orin and Lance both, forcing them both to take an involuntary step toward the door. Gwen kept her gaze locked on the High King as power raged in her chest before dissipating. Questions abounded on Lance's face as he strode out of the room, Frideswide fluttering behind him. Bors and Orin hesitated, but Gwen waved imperiously at the door, blinking away flashes of color dancing in front of her eyes.

"Arthur and I have things to discuss relating to Avalon," Gwen told them. The knights looked to their king, who nodded as he crossed his arms. They followed the fae out the door, Orin shooting one last questioning look at her. Gwen pushed the door closed.

"What is all this about?" Arthur growled.

"Can you come join me at the window?" Gwen asked, tapping the panes of glass. Arthur narrowed his eyes but stomped over. The lake spread out in front of them, the water devoid of any ripples. The few clouds in the sky reflected against the mirror-like surface.

"What am I supposed to be looking at?" Arthur griped, arms still firmly crossed.

Gwen kept her voice soft, hoping that Arthur would listen. "You remind me of this lake."

"What?" he asked, jaw tightening. Gwen knew she was on thin ice but forged carefully forward.

"Quiet facade with so much life raging beneath it, trapped under the surface." Gwen tapped the glass to emphasize her point. "But every now and then, something causes ripples. Those ripples cause your emotions to slam against everyone around you, chipping away at your friends, subjects, and allies just as the lake's waves chip away at the shoreline. You're a protector, a leader, but you've lost yourself in fear. You can't be afraid of the waves and still be able to lead your people."

Gwen took a bracing breath and turned and put her hands on his wrists, slowly forcing Arthur to drop his arms. She was surprised he let her, but she was thankful he seemed to be listening. Gwen knew the irony in what she said next as she herself hadn't really had time to process her own emotions on the situation.

Gwen continued, "You need to be able to let these emotions out; you need to face them. You can't hide away in here, bottling up your rage and fear. It comes out against the wrong targets and blinds you to possibilities."

"I need to protect my people," Arthur protested, voice fierce and his eyes unwavering on her face.

Gwen let go of his wrists. "You do, and you're trying. But the way you're doing it isn't working anymore. Mordred is coming. We don't have enough forces to withstand his army. You know this. You have to let your fear go and let something else in. You have to drop your defenses and trust."

Arthur glowered. "Trust is earned."

Gwen let out a low chuckle. "I know. I told Lance that out in the hallway. I also told him to stop being an ass and poking at you and the others." She wrinkled her nose at Arthur, merriment dancing in her eyes. "I was trying to be more polite with you, but I'm basically saying the same thing." Saxon nudged at her hand again, and she ruffled his ears.

"Trust can't be earned, Arthur, unless you give them a chance. We've had one successful foray together. We could have more," Gwen said.

"My people were hurt waging their war!" His shout ricocheted around the room. Arthur slammed his fist sideways into the stone wall.

"Your people were hurt fighting *our* war; we face a common enemy. As I was recently reminded, war means risk, even death," Gwen said. "As a commander, you do everything to minimize loss of life, but with Mordred coming, you won't be able to save anyone unless we start trusting and working with Frideswide and the others. When Mordred takes Caerleon, and he will if it's just us, he will slaughter everyone and raze the castle to the ground as he seeks the spell stone and gateway."

Gwen took a deep breath and dared to take Arthur's hand, giving it a comforting squeeze. "Be the leader your people need. You once brought so many disparate people under your banner and successfully protected them back in the mortal realm. It's why you're a man of legend even after a millennium. Use that skill to negotiate with House Keithia and other potential allies so that you can protect your people here."

Arthur looked at their joined hands, pain etching lines into his face as he abruptly changed topics. "You're nothing like her, you know."

"Like who? Your Guinevere?" Gwen asked, trying to follow his non sequitur.

He nodded sharply.

"No, I'm not. She can never be replaced in your heart." Gwen hesitated, wondering if she should nudge his thoughts in Viviane's direction. Her friend hadn't stuck around Arthur all these years because she hated the man; no, Viviane yearned for Arthur.

The hell with it, Gwen thought. Might as well hit him with this information as part of the intervention while he was open and actually listening to her. "I don't have feelings for you. Someone else does, but you need to stop looking inward to notice." She squeezed his hand one last time before letting it go. "Be the king your people need. Work with the fae. Protect Avalon. I have faith in you. Your people have faith in you. Lean on that faith and lead us. Please."

Arthur glanced at the placid surface of the lake. Gwen closed her eyes and reached out to the part of her soul that swirled like the lake and pushed. Her brow furrowed as she willed the water to move, pain lashing the back of her eyes.

"Ripples," Arthur murmured.

Gwen blinked her eyes open, a weird sense of being both here in the room and also down in the water disorienting her. "Ripples," she repeated, shaking her head to gain her bearings. "Small ripples can become big waves. Big waves change the shoreline. Change is what is needed right now. Let's go cause some waves, High King."

A small smile quirked his lips. "Lady Viviane said your presence was a sign of change. I suppose I owe you an apology. Change meant danger to me, and I haven't treated you well because of it."

"You don't say," she responded dryly. "I thought you were a raging asshole until Orin tried to change my mind. You're very lucky you have him, by the way."

Arthur snorted out a laugh. "Avalon help me, but you're so forward in your language and bearing."

"I do what I can." Gwen tossed a cheeky grin and wink at Arthur. "But apology accepted."

"I still think you're trouble," Arthur said, voice gruff.

Gwen frowned. "I'm not. That's Lance's job."

"All right, Trouble." He shook his head in amusement, waving at the door. "Let's let the others back in so we can plan our negotiations with whichever fae will listen."

Gwen stayed out of the discussion. She had no experience with negotiations on the scale they were working. Sure, she could handle one-on-one interactions well. It was something she prided herself on. The chief had always praised her ability to talk down suspects or break up bar fights with a few pointed words or jokes. Gwen knew that most people thought she was crazy or mercurial. Perhaps she was both. She found herself content with that assessment if it meant Arthur could collaborate now with Lance and Frideswide without a hint of animosity. Bors and Orin stood behind their king, both throwing the odd look at her where she once again sat near the door.

"Then that will be the plan," Arthur said, reaching across the table to shake Lance's hand.

Gwen shook herself out of her rumination, wincing a bit at the flare of pain that coursed up her spine. It pulsed in time with the waves now crossing the lake. It was definitely time to take Viviane up on those lessons. Yay for training montage, indeed.

"Arthur, would you like to join us for the discussion with Hearne?" Lance's voice brought her focus back to the room.

"Sorry, who is Hearne?" Gwen asked.

Lance shook his head. "Spaced out again, huh? That's the white wolf."

"Shame his name's not Geralt. That would be fitting. And no, I wasn't being spacey. I was just . . . trying to figure out how to detangle myself from the lake. I'll tell you later," she told him as his eyebrows winged up in confusion. "Welp, glad you all have a plan. I need to go find Viv."

"I'll escort you there." Orin strode to the doors, opening one for her.

"That's not necessary," Gwen protested but stopped as Orin put a hand low on her back.

"I'd like to," he told her softly.

Gwen felt the rush of blood to her cheeks. Dear God, she was blushing. Why was she blushing? She had wanted Orin's attention and now here it was. "Okay." Gwen refused to look at the others and ducked out into the hallway, Orin following and closing the door.

"Are you all right?" he asked, keeping his hand on her back. Gwen wondered if this meant he had thought about what she had said outside his door earlier this week.

Gwen chuckled at his question as he fell in step beside her. "That seems to be the question of the day. Is anyone ever all right with the threat of war hanging over their heads?"

"No, not really," he replied, glancing up and down the hall before he herded her into a small alcove, looking down at Saxon. "He's not going to attack me, is he?"

"Why would he attack you?" she asked, raising an eyebrow.

"Because I'm going to do this," Orin told her, eyes intent on her face as he pulled her body flush with his. His fingers slid into her chocolate hair as he leaned down and kissed her.

Gwen's eyes fluttered shut, her own hands grabbing on to his shirt to hold herself steady. Orin kissing her was the last thing she expected. Like before, Orin commanded her body, tilting her head back to deepen the kiss. He broke away and smiled down at her.

"Holy crap." Gwen gaped at him. "What was that?"

"I'd like to see where this goes if you feel the same," he said, voice quiet. "I admit I'm a bit scared to try. I can't . . ." His voice broke, then he cleared his throat before continuing, "I can't handle losing someone close to me again, but you've pulled at me from the moment I laid eyes on you. I think about you constantly. Obviously watch you." He chuckled at that and brushed her cheekbones with his thumbs. "You are the most intriguing woman I have ever met. Why the hell you like me is a mystery, but I'm not going to let go of this opportunity."

"Holy crap," Gwen repeated. She stared at the man she wanted with wide eyes. She was sure it would take months of pursuit, maybe even longer, to break down his walls.

Orin's brow furrowed. "Is that . . . a yes?"

Gwen popped up on her toes and gave him a quick peck, before beaming. "I can't believe you're serious, but yes." She patted his chest. "I don't handle loss well either, but I've always figured trying to find the right person is worth the risk." Her bright smile turned shy. "I think you're worth the risk."

"Good." He nodded as his hands circled her waist and pulled her more flush with his body. He tipped his head to the side and kissed down her neck. Gwen felt like one of her romance book heroines, ready to swoon. A small moan escaped as he kissed back up her neck.

He buried a hand in her dark hair and tilted her head back to kiss her again, this time slowly but firmly. "Can't seem to stop touching you," he whispered, "but Arthur needs me to rally some of the men for an expedition. We can take this slow. Maybe we can have dinner together sometime soon?"

"I'd like that," Gwen said, breathless as she continued to clutch at his shirt. She blinked at him as her brain scrambled to catch up.

He glanced down at Saxon, who sat stone-still, amber eyes focused on the man. "I'll bring something to bribe your dog with."

Gwen let out a hushed laugh. "He'll like that. Okay, I guess I'll see you later." She let go of his shirt. Orin ran his thumbs one more time across her cheekbones before dropping a gentle kiss on her forehead. Gwen almost melted. Why were forehead kisses so damn good?

"You will." He winked, backing up and turning to walk down the hallway. Saxon huffed at the man's retreating back before turning an accusing look on his mistress.

"What? Don't judge me." Gwen shook her head at her dog and stepped out of the alcove, heading toward the infirmary. If Viviane was anywhere, that was the most likely place.

A smile spread across her face as she rubbed over her heart. Gwen still couldn't believe that Orin was willing to take a chance with her. She took light steps as she turned the corner and bumped into Lance. He put steadying hands on her shoulders before stepping back and crossing his arms, glowering at her.

"What's that look for?" she asked, the somewhat-dreamy smile on her face fading. Lance pointed in the direction Orin had taken.

"Gwen, you need to watch yourself with Orin," Lance warned. "He's a broken man, and broken men crack under pressure at the wrong time. He won't be there when you need him to be. Trust me on this. I've seen it time and time again in my very long life. As your best friend, I don't want to see you get hurt."

Gwen rocked back on her heels at the unexpected vehemence then scowled at Lance. "Well, I'm sorry. I don't remember asking your opinion on my love life. Orin's a good man. He won't hurt me."

Lance scoffed, a mulish expression on his face. "You haven't been here long enough to know that."

"Yeah, well, my dreams and what time I have been here in Caerleon say otherwise. Orin is steady. He has a dry sense of humor that I like. He's gentle. He's so freaking loyal that it's ridiculous, and you know that's important to me because of my family. He won't be constantly looking for the next best thing. He makes me feel like I'm enough." Gwen thumped her chest. "That is everything for me."

Lance reared back as if she had slapped him. He couldn't stop the hurt crossing his face before he whispered, "You've always been enough, Gwen. I don't know why you think you're not. Because it's not what I think." He pivoted and strode away, hands in his pockets, head bowed.

"Lance," Gwen called after him, shaking her head. Gwen huffed out a long breath, feeling the flush of anger still burning her cheeks. She had no idea what brought this on or how to fix it. Gwen screamed quietly, fisting her hands at her sides, and whirled to find another way to the infirmary.

Chapter Seventeen

Orin

Orin stood on the parapet and stared out at the broad expanse of cleared land in front of Caerleon. From the low swales near the lake to the mist-backed tree line, he could see odd groups of fae walking around, waiting for orders. Members of both House Keithia and House Mors milled around with the fae rebels that had been liberated from the prison camp. The three wolf packs stood out the most, not only because of the adults' heights but also the bundles of small fur running and tumbling around their elders' feet.

"They're really cute," Gwen commented, grinning up at him as she put her arm around his waist. He put his arm around her shoulders, tucking her in close. He basked in the novelty of being able to do so. Saxon huffed and shoved his body between their legs. Orin shifted his weight to accommodate the dog.

It had taken two painstaking weeks of negotiations and finding pockets of dissonance hiding among the fae to bring more forces under the rebel's banner. Orin thought he used the time well, mainly in courting Gwen. Or perhaps she was courting him. All he knew was that they had spent every moment they could learning about each other's likes, dislikes, and dreams. He knew her favorite color was orange, that she hated being outside in the rain, and she would try any food if it was related to cheese. In return, she learned that he preferred to spend his evenings reading books while drinking a mug of ale; he hated the green, leafy vegetables that Bronwyn insisted they all eat; and that he missed being a farmer.

The corners of his lips tipped up in a small smile. He had also learned that Gwen's sense of humor was . . . odd, but entertaining . . . and occasionally dirty. She seemed to whip the dirty humor out when he was drinking something, then she would walk away, peals of her laughter bouncing off the walls. It was now his life's mission to make her blush in front of others in retaliation.

"The pups? I suppose so." Orin bent a little to catch the drifting scent of her soap and lotion.

Gwen's smile widened in sheer happiness as she bounced on her toes. "Apparently I get to pup-sit when I'm not in lessons with Alcina and Viviane. It'll be interesting to see if werewolf kids are like human kids. I can only imagine what type of mischief they can get up to."

Orin felt his smile slip away, not enamored with the idea of Gwen being near the werewolves in any capacity. "I'm not sure I'm comfortable with that. Surely one of the fae remaining here can handle that task?" He felt her shrug and looked down at her. Gwen was still gazing across the open space. She looked completely unfazed by the prospect of managing the pups. "Does nothing bother you?"

"It does. I told you I don't like being a soldier, though I understand the necessity of it right now, and this weird insistence you all have that

I'm this special Chosen One." She held her hand up and made quotation marks with her fingers as she said those last two words with disgust. "Having Avalon deluge me with magic definitely knocked me for a loop." Gwen sighed heavily, shaking her head, but her gaze remained fixed on the young fae playing in the meadow.

"We don't think you're the Chosen One. It's more that you're just . . . you." It was his turn to shrug. "There's something about you that helps bridge the gap when people aren't listening to each other." He nuzzled her hair. "Avalon brought you here for a reason. You belong here, with us."

Gwen tossed her hair back as she looked up at him. "I'm so happy to hear you think that. As for pup-sitting? No need to get spun up about it. I'm not going to be in danger, unlike you." She snuggled even closer, sandwiching Saxon between them tightly. The dog grumbled and squeezed his way out to lay down by their feet instead. "I'm worried about you and Lance and the others. Hitting that outpost is a big jump up from a small prison camp, and look how the prison camp turned out. The troll was a surprise, and you know we got damn lucky with the limited casualties we had. What are you going to find at this outpost? What happens if Mordred sends reinforcements?"

Orin turned her so he could fold her into his arms, tightening the embrace as he murmured in her hair, "It'll be fine, darling. Mordred won't even know what is happening until we are long gone, and his outpost is a smoldering ruin."

"God, I hope that's the case," she muttered back. Orin grinned as she grabbed his collar and pulled him down for a smacking kiss. "Now go be a badass and get back here. You owe me another dinner."

As sweat dripped down his forehead into his eyes, Orin wasn't sure he was going to make it back to that dinner he promised Gwen. The attack on the outpost was fast becoming a prime example of the saying, "Plans only last until the battle starts."

"Mordred's sent reinforcements," Frideswide told him and Lance as she hovered in front of them. "My scouts just saw them in the woods, and Mordred's with them." She wrung her hands together, panic in her eyes.

Orin cursed under his breath. Mordred's presence changed everything. If they wanted their forces to live, retreat was the only sane option. Orin glanced around at his comrades and allies, gnawing at his lip in worry. They were all dead if they didn't get out of there immediately.

Around them, rebel forces tore into the outpost's battalion. The bulk of the rebels infiltrated under the walls, the earth fae creating tunnels that gave them access to the main courtyard. The wolves and flying fae went over the walls, and Orin was shocked to find the wolves were excellent climbers, using their three clawed fingers to find cracks in the stone wall. If they made it back to Caerleon, that was going to be the first thing he discussed with Arthur to prevent Mordred's wolves from tackling Caerleon's walls.

"Mordred's with them?" Lance repeated, his head swiveling back and forth as he assessed the courtyard and the parapets. "He'll have his troops trap us in here and slaughter us if they can get through the gates or lay siege until we surrender. Either way, we lose. Signal for everyone to fall back. We need to make it into the woods before they can flank us. Have the fire starters keep torching the outpost on our way out."

Orin raised the horn dangling from his belt and blew three loud notes. Others around the outpost picked up the call, the rebels disengaging from the remaining soldiers struggling to keep the outpost out of their hands. Frideswide swirled up above the fight before diving down into a cluster of rebels backing quickly toward the gate. Orin ducked as a huge fireball flew over his and Lance's heads out of the clustered fae.

"Careful!" Lance yelled as the spell singed the air around them. The fireball burst across the wooden portions of the tower, quickly eating away at the supports. Another fireball screamed overhead, and Orin could feel the heat of the flames on his face.

"Let's go," Orin gritted out, leaning down to pull a wounded dryad off the bloodied courtyard. She blinked, her gaze unfocused as he clutched her close to his chest and head toward the gate. He had to trust Lance would cover his back as more fire rained down across the far side of the outpost, leaving the gate intact for now. The screams of the soldiers and wounded rebels mixed together in the air while the metallic stench of blood and foul smell of exposed intestines made him gag. He could only hope someone was helping his knights get out.

Orin stumbled as he focused on getting to the gate. The bloodied corpse of Griffin lay just inside the courtyard. Griffin's blank eyes stared back at him. Something had wrenched the armorer's cuirass off and cracked his chest open. A low growl of pain and grief rumbled in Orin's chest. Not again. Not another loss.

"Regroup at the tree line," Guthlac bellowed. The rebels surged into a loose formation. The earth fae pushed at the dirt, forcing it into crude fortifications. Lance and Orin tumbled over the top of one of the earth barriers as they brought up the rear, Orin passing the dryad over to someone who hustled her away into the forest. *Hopefully,* Orin thought, *the healers will help her.*

"Here they come," a feminine voice yelled.

"Let them have it!" Guthlac's voice reverberated through the air. Spells and arrows followed, slicing into the oncoming soldiers wearing Mordred's black and red colors.

"Stay alive," Lance muttered to Orin. "Otherwise, Gwen will have our heads."

Orin coughed out a laugh. "If we're dead, I don't think that will be a problem." Irony lay heavy in his voice as Orin raised his own sword and shield, bracing for the onslaught.

Mordred's forces slammed into them, the burning fort creating a hellish backdrop. Orin caught a blade on his sword, knocking it away. The fae bashed her own shield into his, and they grappled over the rounded crest of the earthen works. Lance pulled at the moisture in the air around Orin's opponent, then pushed ice over the soldier's eyes to her screeching horror. Orin thrust his sword up into the soft place where her neck met her jaw. Mordred's soldier gurgled, clawing at her neck while falling back only to be replaced by another soldier stepping over her corpse.

They came in waves, breaking against the crude earthen works that Guthlac's forces erected. Orin could do no more than stand shoulder to shoulder with Lance and . . . something. It seemed vaguely humanoid but had green skin, some form of shell on its back, and webbed hands and feet. Orin had no idea what type of fae it was other than vicious. More than a few of Mordred's soldiers fell to the claws at the ends of those webbed fingers.

The sun was merciless as it beat down on them. The cries of the wounded spiraled into the sky, melding with battle cries. Still, the rebels held Mordred's forces back, the earthen works creating a barrier they couldn't move past. Orin focused on the burn in his muscles, the weight of the shield on his arm, and the brutal reverberation up his sword arm as the blade dug into flesh.

"They're falling back," Lance panted next to him.

Orin blinked sweat out of his eyes, watching warily as Mordred's soldiers retreated. "Mordred's about to make an appearance."

"He is," Lance nodded, face grim. He looked at where Guthlac stood. The Green Man urged the fae and knights around him to rally and close the gaps where their comrades had fallen. "Guthlac! Brace!"

The Green Man's head swiveled to meet Lance and Orin's stares before snapping to face Mordred's soldiers. A collective intake of breath swept up and down the rebel line as Mordred rode through his forces. The bright jingle of the dark kelpie's ornate pelham bit was a discordant note above the sound of the wounded and the crackling fire still sweeping through the outpost. The kelpie threw its head up as if in protest at the way Mordred yanked on the reins to halt its forward jigging trot. A crack of power echoed out from Mordred, and silence blanketed the battlefield.

Cold green eyes swept over the rebel line. Mordred's black armor seemed to absorb the sunlight as he shifted in the saddle, his focus homing in on Lance and Orin. Orin was fairly certain Mordred was solely focused on Lance, but he still felt the punch of power from the fae's gaze.

A corner of Mordred's mouth lifted in a sneer. "Never thought I'd see the day when fae would slum with mortals, but here you are. And the exiled Scion of House Dwyn. Never thought I'd see you again either."

"Surprise," Lance growled. Orin grunted as the air around him suddenly felt too dry to breathe. Ice coalesced along Lance's arms and chest, adding a layer of armor over his chain mail breastplate.

"I see you've retained your attitude," Mordred said, shifting in his saddle.

"I see you've retained your megalomania," Lance shot back. A twitter of laughter ran up and down the rebel line.

Mordred's sneer morphed into a crooked smile. "I look forward to killing you this time."

Lance scoffed. "You can try. Shields up!"

Orin wrenched his shield up to align with the ice shield Lance manifested. The weird fae next to him didn't have a shield, but it readied its claws instead.

Mordred lifted his voice to his soldiers. "Take them, but the exile is mine."

"Here we go," Orin muttered, sliding a foot back to brace for the oncoming onslaught.

The fae soldiers swirled around their stationary king, like water whirling around a rock midstream. The wave of soldiers broke once again against the rebel's shield wall, curling back and then pushing forward again. Over the top of their heads, Orin could see Mordred calmly sitting on his mount as it chewed agitatedly at its bit, flipping its head until Mordred yanked on the reins. The kelpie reared, sunlight catching on the scales interwoven into its black coat. Diseased water plants trailed from its mane. Orin captured all of this in a quick glance as he batted away a spear.

"Look out!" someone near Orin and Lance shrieked.

Mordred charged through his soldiers, the kelpie's shoulders pushing fae out of the way as he rushed toward Lance and Orin.

"Shit," Lance cursed, shoving Orin into the amphibious fae as Mordred's mount sailed over the earthen barrier where the knight had been standing.

Lance whirled to face the fae king, leaving Orin to cover his back. The turtle fae growled and worked in tandem to keep the soldiers from following their leader over the dirt wall. The temperature behind Orin plunged, leaving the knight gasping at the cold.

Mordred's steed screamed in pain as Lance shouted behind him. Hissing at their allied fae to cover their backs, Orin turned to find Mordred charging toward Lance, sword drawn. The kelpie moaned, sounding almost human, and thrashed on the ground, covered in ice.

Lance and Mordred clashed, spells flying, as Orin ducked under a fireball. Down the line, a roar came up, and Orin shifted his gaze toward the sound. He sucked in a breath as he watched fae soldiers swarm Guthlac. The towering Green Man bellowed in pain, disappearing from sight in the melee.

"Damn it." Orin rushed Mordred. Lance blasted ice toward Mordred, who batted it away with his hand. That moment of distraction was all Orin needed. He shoved his sword through the area Mordred's armor didn't cover—right between the cuirass and pauldron and deep into the shoulder muscles under the clavicle.

Mordred met Orin's gaze as the knight wrenched out his sword and snarled, "Do you think a mere mortal's weapon can kill the one true king?"

"Oh, fuck off with that bullshit," Lance spat. A spike of ice jutted out of Lance's hand as he drove it into Mordred's cuirass, trying to pierce the flesh beneath. It lodged between the punctured metal before Mordred brought his elbow down, shattering the spike. Blood oozed from the wound.

"Do you think the Mist Lands would let its king die so easily?" Mordred rumbled, a laugh erupting from his throat. He bared bloodied teeth at the two. "Nothing can kill me." As they watched, the wound stitched itself closed.

"Retreat!" The cry went up and down the rebels' line, preventing Orin and Lance from their next attack.

Mordred's laughter grated on their skin as he stepped back, sneering. "Go. Run. Tell the others their king will be at their door in the morning, and they should be on their knees ready to beg for forgiveness."

The rebels' line collapsed as the fight turned into a rout. Fae and knights fled into the forest, heading toward the Mist Lands and Avalon border. Lance blasted a wall of ice behind them to protect their backs from Mordred's forces. Mordred stepped back, waving a sardonic hand at the forest. Orin grabbed at Lance, pulling him along into the trees with other fae on their heels.

"Why is Mordred letting us go?" Lance asked as he ran besides Orin.

"Because he knows he can beat us." Orin's expression was grim. He glanced around at the others scrambling toward Caerleon. It would take them hours to make it back to the safety of the castle's walls. "They're coming for us."

CHAPTER EIGHTEEN

GWEN

Gwen blew out a harsh breath at the sweaty strands of hair hanging in her face. While Orin and the others were executing the planned outpost attack, Viv and Alcina had vetoed the plan for Gwen to pup-sit (and wouldn't that please her boyfriend) and instead dragged her to the far side of the lake. It turned out that Viviane, her nice, sweet friend, was an absolute merciless taskmaster when it came to learning to control her new powers. Alcina was worse.

"You're absolutely useless at this," Alcina commented.

Gwen wrinkled her nose at the snarky tone. She didn't believe in teaching via insults, but Alcina one hundred percent did. Gwen refused to rise to the bait.

"All right, Gwen. Move the water again and then scoop out the wet sand," Viviane told her.

"Fine," Gwen growled, bouncing on her toes and shaking out her hands. Her hairline wasn't the only place where sweat gathered. She could feel a drop roll down her spine. Gwen felt like she had gone several rounds back at the MMA gym she trained in; her muscles quivered, and her head was starting to ache. Every attempt felt like stretching a new muscle she didn't know she had. It bloody hurt.

Okay, move the water and scoop the sand. Move the water and . . .

She felt that weird string-like connection with Avalon vibrate beneath her feet as she embedded her consciousness into the lake. It felt different than when she inadvertently managed to cause the ripples while talking to Arthur. Then, the lake had overwhelmed her. Gwen had lost herself in its depths so that she felt an odd juxtaposition of being in Caerleon whilst simultaneously being submerged in the deep water. Now, though, Viviane had at least taught Gwen how to keep herself separate from Avalon while she manipulated the world around her.

"This is simply learning a new skill. I can do this," Gwen muttered as she strained to split a small patch of water and shovel some of the beach sand toward Alcina's feet.

Like with all new skills, she was going to suck at this at first. The only problem with that was the knowledge that Mordred's attack was imminent. Gwen felt that heavy weight on her shoulders. Everyone acted as if her connection to Avalon was going to be some form of Hail Mary, but what the hell was she going to do with this newfound ability to Moses a bucket full of water and make a foot-sized hole in the ground?

"Well, that's something I guess," Alcina muttered as she watched the waves rippling against the shoreline split. Her brows drew together as the exposed beach sand quivered but nothing else happened. "You need to feel the earth, like a second skin almost. It's an extension of you, and you need to tell it what to do, like when you tell your arm to move or your hand to pick up something."

"That's easier said than done, you know. My arm is finite. I need to segment the earth and move small sections. Moving my arm versus moving pounds of earth are not synonymous," Gwen told Alcina. Her focus wavered and the water splashed back over the wet sand. "Well . . . crap."

"We still have at least an hour of daylight left," Viviane mused, looking up at the evening sky.

"We don't actually." Gwen's eyes went unfocused as she turned her attention to what she was feeling down her bond with Avalon. "They're coming back. But in small groups. That can't be good, can it?" She lifted her eyes to meet Alcina's and then Viviane's gaze.

"No, it's probably not," Viviane said, already moving into the lake. She disappeared from sight, and a small wake of waves surged across the lake surface, heading toward Caerleon.

"Well, that's rather rude to leave us," Alcina groused. "Let's get back and you can work on moving the earth in front of us as we go."

Gwen groaned at that. "Of course." She trudged toward the castle, focusing on making the ground quiver ahead of their feet. She mostly succeeded.

Gwen stayed in the courtyard as rebels and knights stumbled into Caerleon, waiting for Orin and Lance, while helping Alcina to assess the wounded to send them to either the infirmary to be tended by Viviane or the great hall to be helped by less powerful healers or the Caerleon women. This was so far beyond her experience with Search and Rescue.

While she knew basic first aid, Gwen had never seen this type of bodily trauma. She didn't even like gory movies.

"If you're going to lose your stomach, do it over in the corner of the courtyard," Alcina snapped as Gwen stumbled away from the stretcher holding Louis that Henri and Caradoc had hauled back from the outpost. Louis had a long, oozing wound across his stomach that showed layers of flesh beneath. Gwen pointed toward the infirmary, grabbing Louis's hand to give it a quick squeeze of support. He had huffed out a breath at the contact, his pain-glazed eyes meeting hers before closing again.

"I know, I know." Gwen gagged, swallowing harshly and breathing in through her mouth and out her nose. She licked dry lips then froze as she saw Lance and Orin slough into the courtyard. Saxon made it to Lance before Gwen, so she peeled off and threw herself at Orin. He grabbed at her, arms tight, and she sighed in relief.

"Are you hurt?" she murmured, leaning back to run her hands over his chest and arms.

"Bumps and bruises, maybe some small cuts, but nothing major," he assured her, grabbing at her face with both hands. His hands were gentle on her cheekbones but his lips claiming. Gwen couldn't help the small moan as Orin changed the angle of the kiss to sweep his tongue into her mouth.

"Fuck," he whispered, pulling away before dropping his forehead to hers. "We lost too many."

"I'm fine, thanks," Lance snarked. Gwen turned to look at her best friend, squeezing Orin once more before detangling herself to go to Lance.

"I'm glad. I need my bestie," she joked, noting Lance's wince. "Are you sure you're not hurt?" She grabbed his arm, turning him around, trying to find what was paining the other important man in her life.

"I said I was fine, didn't I?" Lance's cold tone had her rearing back.

"Um, okay. Arthur is waiting upstairs for you then." She stepped back into Orin as Lance stomped off.

"What happened?" Gwen murmured, eyes locked on Lance's retreating back.

Orin sighed, rubbing his hands up and down her arms as if to confirm she was really there. Or perhaps grounding himself. "Mordred and his soldiers appeared right as we were making progress on the outpost. We managed to burn it to the ground, which may or may not gain us favor with that one fae house Lance is focused on allying with." Orin shook his head. His focus drifted across those still in the courtyard or the stragglers entering the gate. "Mordred must have been close. He brought his soldiers against us, though we held him off at the forest's edge. Then he got involved. Smug bastard. Didn't even wait for his troops. He went straight after Lance."

"But you both are okay?" she asked, peering around Orin to where Lance had disappeared.

Orin sighed. "Mordred was toying with us. Lance cast what should have been a fatal spell, and I managed what could have been a lethal blow, but Mordred shrugged the attacks off. We watched his skin knit back together as if we hadn't even touched him." Orin bared his teeth, looking over her shoulder toward the wall, not seeing the concern on her face. "Bastard can heal mortal wounds. No wonder he's not concerned with taking to the battlefield. We're nothing but a nuisance to him. He said he'd be here tomorrow with his army."

"What—" Gwen started to ask when she heard Blaine's voice call out.

"Has anyone seen Griffin?" The woman hurried toward Orin and Gwen, calling out, "Griffin!"

Orin expelled a deep breath, shoulders slumping, before he stepped away from Gwen toward Blaine.

"No. No." Blaine shook her head at the look on Orin's face. The woman held her hands up as if to ward off a blow. "No!"

"Blaine." Orin shuffled toward her. "I'm . . . sorry."

Gwen grabbed her friend as the woman let out a loud wail and collapsed. Gwen cradled Blaine against her chest, helping them both sink to the ground so that Blaine was leaning against her. Orin stood over them, tears in his own eyes. Gwen unwound one arm from Blaine and grasped Orin's hand. Connected, the three of them grieved the loss of a great man.

"Come on, ladies," Orin rasped, his voice raw from holding back his tears. Gwen wasn't sure how long they had been in the courtyard, but her right leg was going numb and Blaine's heaving sobs had dwindled to hiccupping whimpers. The light in the courtyard was deepening toward dusk, and somewhere along the line, Saxon had settled against Gwen's hip, opposite of Blaine. His blocky head lay in Blaine's lap. Gwen swept a light hand over his soft fur before encouraging Blaine to stand up. The woman swayed, her face ravaged with tears and emotions.

"You can stay with me tonight," Gwen whispered.

Blaine's answer was a ragged sob.

Orin left them at the kitchen, Gwen nodding to him before leading Blaine down to her room. The quiet hall grated on Gwen's ears. She knew it was quiet because the others were still tending to the wounded. Gwen unlocked the door, ushering in Blaine and letting Saxon out into the courtyard before turning back to her friend. The woman collapsed on the bed, and Gwen helped her remove her boots before tucking the woman under the covers. She sat with Blaine, holding her hand and wiping tears off Blaine's face until the woman gave one last sigh and fell asleep.

This is bullshit, Gwen thought at Avalon, fury drenching her mind. *What good is this power you've given me if you won't teach me how to use it!* Gwen railed at the semi-sentient entity.

Trying to be quiet, Gwen tiptoed around the room, throwing irritated glances at the floor. Her head ached something fierce. She was ready for bed, but energy jittered through her system. Saxon didn't seem to have that problem, hopping up on the bed and draping across Blaine's feet. He gave her an exasperated look and flopped over on his side, grumbling a low moan.

"Fine, fine, Fur Face. Sleep it is. Just wish I knew what to do." Gwen lay down on the top of the blankets, rolling over to give her dog and Blaine her back. Then she let her own tears fall quietly into the pillow.

"Oh, come on!" Gwen yelled at the spell stone. Somehow, she was standing in front of it, only she wasn't in the cavern underneath Caerleon. Her hands clapped down on her hips as she glared around the glade and then at the stone arch behind the stone. The foggy forest of the Mist Lands swirled behind it. The stone should have been in the cavern, but prior dreams let her know this was the original setup before Avalon buried the stone and gateway beneath what would become Viviane's lake. The gate archway had originally straddled the border between Avalon and the Mist Lands, bridging out to the mortal realm.

Gwen whirled, throwing her hands up at the trees. "What am I supposed to do now? Huh?"

The ground shuddered, nearly throwing Gwen off her feet.

She blew hair out of her face. "Well, that was rude."

This time the ground rolled under her feet. Gwen yelped, landing on her butt.

"Really? That's what we're going with now?" she growled, slapping the grass. A rock bumped her left butt cheek. The sharp pain had Gwen hissing. "Fine. I'm listening. Why are my dreams suddenly interactive?"

The trees rustled at her.

"Oh," Gwen griped, dragging out the vowel, "is this where I'm supposed to be learning something? Usually, you make me a passenger princess." Gwen draped her arms over her knees, staring up at the verdant canopy overhead. A small, red-brown pebble hit her cheek. "Ouch! Okay, okay, show me! I'm listening."

Another pebble pinged off her face as if to say, "About time."

"Bossy pants. Do you know how hard it is to lose your entire life, then try to figure out how to use these new powers while watching people you've come to care about die horrible deaths because some old white guy with pointy ears and magic has decided he wants to run the world?" She huffed out a breath. "Speaking of the prick, did you know he apparently can't be killed? What's up with that?"

The ground under her butt wriggled as if to remind Gwen she was here to listen.

"Right, right, okay, listening." Gwen sat quietly, waiting. She tapped her fingers on her knees, thinking that she was far too cognizant in this dream to actually be getting rest. Then she cocked her head to the side, actually listening. Sounds were coming from the mist on the far side of the spell stone and arch. Gwen scrambled to her feet as two fae dressed in

Mordred's black and red colors dragged a bound man into the clearing, Mordred striding in after them.

"Crap, crap, crap," Gwen mumbled, staggering back toward the forest. She paused as Mordred walked by her. "Right. A dream . . . he can't see me." She placed her hands on her hips again, pursing her lips.

What is going on? she wondered as the guards shoved the bound fae to his knees.

"Well, Uther," Mordred drawled. "You'll finally be of use to me."

Uther snarled. "You miserable whelp. You wouldn't even be alive if it wasn't for me."

"Now, now, Father, let's not get testy." Mordred tsked. "You killed Mother, now I kill you. Seems somewhat poetic to me."

"This won't get you what you want." Uther struggled against his bonds.

"If the spell works as I think it will, the sacrifice of your blood should allow me to tie my life force to the Mist Lands through this blade." A smile stretched Mordred's mouth, and Gwen shuddered at the cruelty in it. "With that level of power, the other fae houses will bow to me. I will be unkillable as well as immortal as long as the magic resides in the blade."

"You got him monologuing," Gwen whispered to Avalon. The leaves rustled behind her. "So what you're saying is, if we get his sword away from him, he won't be able to heal? Ow!" She rubbed at her head where a branch slapped it. "Okay, not that." The branch slapped her again. "Not just that? We have to undo the spell in the blade?" The branch tapped her on the shoulder this time. "How do we do that?"

Gwen flailed her arms as the earth moved under her again, ripping her away from Mordred as he raised his sword over his father. The world blurred around her, and she found herself back in the cavern underneath

Caerleon when she gained her bearings. The spell stone pulsed sulkily in front of her. Gwen started in surprise as she realized she was holding Caliburnus. Magic wrapped around the blade in thin threads, tying it to the stone.

"So Caliburnus is tied to you, got it. Are you saying it's the only blade that can hurt Mordred? Because it's tied to you like his blade is tied to the Mist Lands?" Gwen asked.

A rumbling overhead seemed to be Avalon's agreement.

Gwen looked at the blade, turning over her thoughts with slow precision. "What happens if Caliburnus is tied to someone?"

The ground groaned again, encouraging this line of thought.

"So we need to tie Arthur to Caliburnus and you?" Gwen asked.

This time the rumble that reverberated through the cave seemed aggravated.

Gwen frowned. "Not that. You need someone else tied to the blade. I'm already tied to you. So it's not me, right?"

A blast of magic erupted from the spell stone and smacked her in the chest. The sharp pain had Gwen grabbing at the place of impact.

"Is that a yes or a no? I can't tell!" she yelped as the pain spread down her sword arm. Her hand muscles spasmed, clenching the hilt hard enough that her knuckles turned white.

Gwen looked down at the blade. Blood smeared Caliburnus a rusty red, the same red that she realized now covered the palm she had used to clutch at the pain in her chest.

"Oh. I have to tie myself to the blade? So it's tied to you better?" Gwen asked, feeling the blood drain from her face.

The creaking of the rocks around her softened into a comforting purr. Gwen swallowed hard. Avalon's agreement with her statement caused a lump to form in her chest.

"Is this the only way?" she whispered.

The spell stone shone brightly for a moment, then Gwen woke, gasping and covered in sweat. Saxon whined next to her, shoving his muzzle in her hair and snuffling at the sweaty strands.

"It's okay, Fur Face," Gwen muttered, shoving his nose out of her ear. "That feels gross." He gave a soft whuff at that, his nose moving right back into her ear. "Saxon! Off." The dog gave her a betrayed look before slinking to the foot of her bed.

Gwen pulled herself off the bed, padding toward the door. She glanced back at Blaine, who slept on, before slipping out into the hall to head to a corner of the parapet where she could get some fresh air away from the others.

Despite thinking she'd manage to get some time to process her dream alone, Lance found her as she stared up at the stars. He had changed out of his armor and was wearing a soft linen shirt and a midnight-blue tunic along with dark-brown leather pants and boots.

"How's it going?" he asked, sliding down the stone wall to sit next to her.

Gwen rolled her eyes, grimacing and tilting her head at him.

"Right . . . pretty sucky." Lance sighed and banged his head back against the wall. Torch light glinted off his bright, blond hair. "I got cocky, and it cost us too much."

Gwen shook her head, putting a hand on her best friend's shoulder. "It was a joint decision, Lance. The whole council agreed to it."

Lance grunted, shrugging. "Yeah, but I figured Mordred would still be sitting pretty in his castle, not out with his forces. Should have sent the scouts out farther afield. Now we've lost critical resources, and morale is shit."

Gwen wrapped her arms around his, leaning against his warm bulk. "We can only make decisions based on the information we have and try harder the next time."

"Maybe." He patted her hand on his arm, looking down at Gwen. "How'd the lessons go with Viv and Alcina?"

"The best I've gotten so far is moving a bucket-sized amount of dirt or creating some waves in the lake." Gwen sighed, leaning harder against Lance's shoulder. "I don't exactly think that's going to help us."

Lance chuckled quietly. "I don't know. *Mold Earth* is a good cantrip."

"Cantrip?" Gwen's brows drew together as she sat up straighter.

Lance sighed and leaned his head back against the wall, staring at the stars. "It's like a base level spell in Dungeons & Dragons. Sometimes the simpler spells in the game are the most useful." Lance scrubbed a hand over Saxon's head. The dog grumbled his pleasure, nosing Lance's hand when the fae stopped scratching.

Gwen leaned away to give her best friend a look. "Wait a minute. So you, a fae—a powerful one, I might add—played a human game where people pretend to be elf wizards and dwarf fighters?"

"Only in the early nineties. I was bored, and it seemed like it could be fun. And it *was* fun so long as you had a good group. Otherwise, someone was yelling at someone else so they could be in charge, messing up the math, or arguing over the rules, which wasted a bunch of time."

"So, not unlike what we've got going on," Gwen commented, placing her elbows on her knees and dropping her head into her hands. "I don't understand how the outpost was such a disaster, and now everyone is pointing fingers. Trust is back to where we were a few weeks ago, which means basically at zero." She cast a glance at her partner, dropping her hands and sitting up again. "We are going to have to force everyone to listen again, which means you're going to get Frideswide and the others to chill out while I tackle Arthur and the others."

Lance slung an arm around her shoulders. "The outpost was such a cluster that I don't know if we're ready for Mordred even if we get everyone to listen. But, yeah, let's see what we can do. As for Mordred, I don't know what to do there. The man took an ice bolt to the chest, and Orin stabbed him. Mordred should be dead. The healing powers he has . . ." Lance's voice trailed off before he shook his head. "He didn't have those when I was exiled, at least I don't remember him having them. The others are just as shocked. Our only option may be getting him wounded enough to try to cut off his head."

Gwen dropped her eyes to the floor, watching Sax's tail sweep lazily across the stones as her dog practically melted into Lance's lap. "There may be one other way." She winced as she said it. Gwen felt Lance go rigid next to her. Lance and his Spidey-sense always knew when she was about to tell him something he wouldn't be pleased with.

"What's that?" Lance's voice was a low rumble.

Gwen sighed, swiping her hands over her face. "I've had dreams since coming here. Not as many as when we were back home, but each has been more about Avalon and my connection to Her than about Caerleon or the fae. In hindsight, the first one helped me realize that being connected to Avalon meant I could feel who crossed over her borders. Plus, it made me go down to the spell stone to initiate the connection with Avalon. I had a dream tonight."

Gwen risked a glance at Lance. Her friend stared at her, concern etched on his face. She knew he wouldn't like what she had to say next.

"Caliburnus is the key, not just to opening the portal to the mortal realm. It's the key to unlocking a tighter connection with Avalon, and if I'm interpreting things right, I'm pretty sure Caliburnus is the only blade that can hurt Mordred. But the sword's power has to be fully unlocked first."

"Exactly how do we unlock it?" Lance asked, keen eyes focused on her.

Gwen grimaced. "With blood."

"Whose blood, Gwen?" Lance growled, twisting to look at her fully. She could already see the refusal in his face and the rigidity in his body. He had a guess at what the answer was, and no, he was definitely not going to like it.

She swallowed hard. "Mine."

CHAPTER NINETEEN

GWEN

"Absolutely not. I forbid it. There has to be another way!" Orin roared at her.

She had been right, not surprisingly. Lance had taken the news about Caliburnus with the same aplomb he usually did, which meant ironically with no chill at all. He yelled at her first, pacing back and forth in front of the bench they had been sitting on before dragging her into the war room and blurting out everything to those in attendance.

"I'm not losing you, not now that I've found you." Orin's voice was as rough as his hands on her arms. Gwen braced herself for him to shake her, but it didn't come. Instead, he dropped his forehead to hers. "There has to be another way, darling. I can't lose you. This is too much of a risk. Maybe the vision meant something else."

Gwen swallowed hard. "Avalon was pretty insistent." She looked around the room. Aethelflaed and Frideswide stared back at her, grief etched on their faces. Guthlac had perished back at the outpost, leaving the two in charge of the fae forces.

"While the outpost expedition didn't end the way we wanted, we learned critical information about Mordred. We need to keep taking risks like the prison camp and outpost in order to finish this war. I don't think it's a coincidence that Avalon finally told me how Mordred empowered himself. She doesn't want to belong to the fae king."

"Yeah, well you don't belong to Her," Lance snapped.

Gwen scowled at him. "Yeah, I don't like it, but I kind of do. My whole life was set up so I could be here. You even helped with that, may I remind you." She rubbed tired hands across her face. "Look, it's clear Mordred is more formidable than we anticipated, and we already knew beating him was going to be challenging. If Avalon is willing to help us, then this may be the only way to untether Mordred from the Mist Lands and remove him from power.

"Orin, I know you're worried about losing me, but at this point, any of us can be lost to an arrow or a blade or anything else that comes out of the mist. If there is a way that we can win with minimal bloodshed, we should take it."

"I don't want it to be your blood, darling. You are worth so much more than that. We need you," Orin pulled her tight against his chest, hiding his face in her hair. "*I* need you," he whispered.

"Perhaps . . ." Frideswide stopped. Sorrow carved harsh lines on her delicate face.

"Perhaps what?" Arthur muttered, staring down at the maps dotting the table in front of him. His tense shoulders bowed low.

"Perhaps we should run. We thought ourselves so clever, and yet our very first encounter with Mordred nearly wiped out our forces. He let us escape. He would have no other reason to do that other than he feels his victory is assured. Mordred is playing with us."

Aethelflaed's dark, wispy voice echoed around the room. "My Lady is not interested in supporting us. While she detests Mordred, she's not willing to step in on either side. The monsters in Mordred's ranks willingly left the House to join his army."

"Why does he allow that?" Orin asked, brow wrinkled in confusion. "Surely he would have brought your Lady to heel."

"She allows those who want to bow to Mordred to do so, and he foolishly believes that those traitors are her tithe to him," Aethelflaed said.

"What are you and your rebel kin to her?" Arthur looked up at the banshee.

She gave him a wispy, dry smile. "Traitors."

"Wonderful. So we can't run to her. We most certainly can't find refuge in my cousin's lands. House Keithia is pretending we don't exist so we can't run and put a target on their backs. That leaves us nowhere else to go." Lance's stride ate up the width of the room as he paced back and forth, agitation clear in the way he ran his hands through his now disheveled hair.

"Or we could stop dithering about and make sure that today's sacrifices are worth something." Gwen's voice curled through the room. She kept the tone soft but firm as everyone swung their heads back to look at her. "We started this because we know this is the right thing to do. Mordred has terrorized the Mist Lands and Avalon for centuries simply because he can. He has used blood sacrifices to outstrip the normal bounds of fae magic, and he has cost all of us thousands of lives in his quest for power. Running away is not an option. He will follow us. He will try to destroy us, and if he succeeds, he has an open path to the mortal realm. I will not allow that to happen. You call Avalon a gateway. If that is the case, then I am the Gatekeeper, and as Gandalf said, he shall not pass."

"Who is this Gandalf?" Arthur asked.

Gwen waved her hand, batting the question aside. "That's unimportant. The point is that losing one battle doesn't mean we lost the war." She turned to Lance. "You saw human history. How many times did it look like one side would win but the other rallied? Like the Allied Powers in World War II."

"Yeah, well they didn't have to deal with magic," Lance scoffed.

"No, they had the atomic bomb. Come on, Lance!" Gwen scowled at her best friend. "What happened to 'Never give up, never surrender!'"

Lance grunted. "Dumb movie quote. We aren't going to win this with bravado and movie quotes."

Gwen shook her head. "No, we're going to win this by getting our heads out of our asses and making sure that we're ready for the inevitable invasion. Caliburnus is the key. We need to—"

"Come up with another plan, because yours isn't happening," Orin said firmly. "I forbid it."

"You what?" Gwen gaped. "Look, I don't want to die, but Avalon was pretty clear that Mordred is tied to the Mist Lands through the blade, and Caliburnus can cut that connection if it is empowered. So what else are we going to do?"

"I don't know. Something. But not this. I'm not losing you. I'm not losing anyone else," Orin said.

"You can't wrap me in bubble wrap to keep me safe. If we aren't going to empower the sword, then that means we have to fight. I could lose you or Lance in battle. Or die myself and then there won't be anyone tied to Avalon. So what are the alternatives?" Gwen asked again.

"I don't know," he gritted out again, glaring at her.

After Orin finished speaking, it was a jumble of contradicting arguments rolling over top of each other.

"Run."

"What about—"

"Let the fae handle—"

Then accusations started flying. Gwen tried to talk over the jumbled conversations and raised voices but shook her head. No one was going to listen to her.

"Which is fine," she told Saxon after shuffling out into the hallway. Gwen swung down to her room and bundled her violin case under her arm. When in doubt, her go-to thinking mechanism was playing music. There was something about focusing on the notes and the draw of the bow across the strings that allowed her subconscious to work in the background on the problem without her stressing over it.

Her dog stayed glued to her hip as she wound out to the courtyard. The gates were thrown wide, leading out to the bright campfires of the camped fae. Knights patrolled the walls, but none stopped Gwen as she and Saxon trotted out into the open gloom, heading toward the water.

"Let them wear themselves out, am I right?" she asked Saxon, thumping down on the log next to the lake's edge where she and Viviane had first discussed her new powers. Placing her violin case on the ground, she hung her arms over her knees, watching the moonlight dance with the ripples wavering across the dark water. Saxon flopped down beside her, rolling over to show his belly. Gravity drew his lips back, showing a derpy canine smile. Gwen couldn't help the chuckle that wound its way out of her throat.

"Doofy dog," she murmured, rubbing his stomach and under his collar like he loved so much. "All right, so let's think this through. I don't want to die. You don't want me to die because then who would spoil you with treats, and don't say Lance because that ruins my argument. Obviously, Orin, Lance, and Viv don't want me to die. Jury's still out on Arthur and Cae. Who knows what the fae think." She sighed. "I'm not good at this." Gwen rubbed Saxon's stomach a little more vigorously to his rumbling pleasure. He flopped over onto his side, and she shifted to rubbing under his foreleg.

"Never once did Gran find me someone to learn strategy from, and small-town cop life isn't conducive to helping win a war. So, what now?"

Saxon huffed at her.

"What's with the bombastic side-eye, huh? I'm having an existential crisis on the possibility of dying. That was not a paltry amount of blood on that blade. Mordred killed his father to cast his spell. That implies that I have to die to make this spell work. Since that's not going to happen if I have any say about it, we need to get creative.

"Not to mention, I don't want to risk my relationship with Orin. He is going to be so pissed if I take this risk. Never mind the fact that if I decide to go on the battlefield with him, I'll still be at risk." She sighed, staring at the moon. The moon stared back with no answers. "I like it here. I like the people here. I feel like we're finally home. And what good am I if I can't protect my home?" Her dog's chest rumbled under her hand as he groaned in pleasure from her continued scratches. "So what do we do, huh? Risk everything and piss our new family off? Or risk everything on the field?"

Saxon huffed again as if asking which she preferred.

"I have no idea. But we have a few hours before daylight to figure it out." Gwen gave a gusty sigh and pulled her violin out, fitting it beneath her chin. The notes shivered out and melded with the lapping waves.

Saxon snored next to her as the sun peeked over the trees, illuminating the lake in crystal gold. Gwen's butt had long gone numb, but she couldn't find it in herself to go back to the keep and face another lambasting, not until she was sure she had a different idea.

Unfortunately, her music hadn't bothered to give her any new ideas, though it did garner her some attention from the fae camping in front of the castle. Several had come by to compliment her, then one had stomped over to tell Gwen to shut the hell up because she was trying to sleep. Gwen was pretty sure it was the same female fae who had glared at her back in the tree hideaway.

"This would be a lot easier with coffee," she told her snoozing dog. "The brain cells are not braining."

Diamonds dotted the tops of the soft waves covering the lake as a breeze swept in over the trees. The sharp, verdant smell of trees blended with the damp of the lakeshore as mist folded out of the forest and carpeted the blinking water ripples.

"I'm going to have to do this," Gwen continued. "I'm going to have to risk everything and let Avalon have Her blood sacrifice. I can't see any other way out of this." She pushed hair out of her face. "I don't need to convince Orin or Lance, just Arthur. He'll do anything to save his people and probably be happy to see me go." A tear dripped down her cheek, and she chased it away with her hand. "Gran, I wish you were here. You'd know what to do. Did you know this is where I'd end up? Spending a life preparing for a role only to have to die to fulfill it?" A sardonic chuckle erupted from her chest as Gwen's head dropped back, letting the dawn light bathe her face.

"Well, I'm not going to figure out anything else out here." She leaned down to rub Saxon's belly. Saxon rolled over, grumbling before standing and shoving his butt high in the air while he stretched his front paws out. "Let's grab some breakfast, tea, and maybe a frying pan in case we need to wallop someone in the war room and see if we can't convince the crew to get creative. Maybe they'll have a better idea where I don't have to give up everything I've finally found."

Saxon bashed into her legs, sending her stumbling before she righted herself, laughing. "Breakfast first, I promise."

Gwen started striding toward Caerleon but stumbled again, only this time it wasn't due to Saxon. A flash of awareness zipped through her. Mordred's army had just crossed the border between Avalon and the Mist Lands.

"Well, shit. The bastard is prompt."

Chapter Twenty

Orin

Mordred gave them a day as his army assembled in the woods facing Carleon. Orin watched with the others as the enemy set up camp and stood shoulder to shoulder for hours on the far side of the field, trying to intimidate them. Arthur, Orin, Gwen, and the fae leaders had worked hard to combat their smaller force's nerves. When the sun set, they had set watch and sent others to bed to rest, anticipating that Mordred would attack the next day.

When morning finally dawned, Orin pulled his body out of his warm bed. His knees groaned in protest.

"Getting old is hell," he growled, scrubbing his hands over his beard. If he survived the day, he would need to trim it soon. Orin's back cracked loudly in the silent room as he stretched. No matter how much he worked to stay in fighting shape, his body still reminded him how old he had been when Avalon had absconded with them.

Which was rather unfair, he thought. *If Avalon was going to give them immortality, the least She could have done was remove the aches and pains from being perpetually forty-two.* He grumbled his way through pulling on his armor and kitting out his gear. Today was going to be a long day, assuming he didn't die in the upcoming battle. Mordred would no doubt bring his might against the walls of Carleon today. Yesterday's intimidation tactics had been merely a performance.

Orin sighed. His thoughts were distinctly morbid. He needed a hit of Gwen's cheery attitude. He doubted she was ready for the battle ahead of them, but he bet she would still have her humor firmly in place. Then again, she might still be in the mood to hit all of them with a frying pan.

Orin chuckled at the memory of her snarling that threat at Lance yesterday when he had warned that he would completely sideline her from any fights with Mordred if she didn't give up the crazy idea regarding empowering Caliburnus. She had finally agreed to stand with the archers on the parapet with her rifle to take down any aerial attackers or the larger monsters.

Orin shook his head at himself; it was the first time he had wholeheartedly agreed with Lance, and Orin wasn't going to make a habit of it if he could. Lance's arrogance, growling threats, and dark looks frayed Orin's patience. Gwen was Orin's. Lance could keep his opinion to himself. If the fae had wanted Gwen, he should have made his intentions clear to her sooner.

The blood rite was a worry he was glad to leave behind so he could focus on the plans for today. The earth fae would create barriers to try to funnel Mordred's forces so the rebels and knights would face smaller groups. The water fae would try to counteract Aberlin's forces that were embedded in Mordred's Army. The forces on the wall, including Gwen, would handle the harpies and whatever other flying surprises showed up.

Arthur, Lance, and Orin planned to focus on Mordred if the fae king ever took to the battlefield.

Orin strode into the Great Hall, delighted to find Gwen already there. She wore the leather and chain mail armor that Griffin had modified for her. Orin flinched at the memory of his friend, a sad twinge hitting his chest as grief welled before he ruthlessly stuffed it down.

Gwen's dark hair was twisted up in two braids wound around her head and pinned in place. The same fierce eyeliner she had sported at the prison camp graced her eyes, along with a bright, bold red lip color. Gwen looked like a fierce warrior goddess, one he'd happily worship for all time if they survived.

"Hello, darling," he whispered, bending down to kiss her good morning. She smiled wanly up at him, face pale and uncertain despite the makeup.

"Good morning." Gwen forced Saxon to move so Orin could pull out a chair. The dog glared at him. Orin barely refrained from glaring back.

"Do you think the beastie will ever like me?" Orin asked, curling an arm behind her shoulders while he sipped from the cup of tea Gwen had thoughtfully procured for him.

"T-R-E-A-T-S," Gwen spelled, "are a great way to try."

"Duly noted." Orin smiled at her and twirled a loose curl of her umber hair around his finger. "You hanging in there all right?"

"No?" Gwen gave a soft laugh and tucked her head onto his shoulder, wriggling her chair closer to his so she was leaning against him despite the fact both were in armor. "I'm terrified. This is so much worse than the prison camp. I don't know how you and the others look so calm."

"It's all a front. If someone tells you they're not afraid, they're already as good as dead. It's good to be afraid. Fear is what keeps us sharp, keeps us alive." Orin stroked a hand up and down her arm. "You stay up on the wall. We'll do everything we can today to repulse Mordred's attacks. You and the archers will be key to keeping the skies clear so we don't have to watch over our heads and can focus on the ground assault. I think it would be best if you kept Saxon in your room. He'll be underfoot on the wall."

"That's a good idea," Gwen murmured, running a hand over Saxon's head. The dog had wormed around to the far side of Gwen and now had his head in her lap, staring intently at Orin. The knight moved to pet the dog but pulled his hand back as Saxon's lips curled.

"Don't need him biting someone he shouldn't," Orin said, voice dry. He reached for the plate of food that Gwen had gotten him. He noticed hers was barely touched. "You need to eat something, darling."

Gwen sighed. He felt it shudder through him, the movement heavy through her body as she picked at the food.

"I've tried, but my stomach says no. I'll be okay, Orin." She turned her head and kissed under his jaw. "I need to go. Bedevere asked me to be up on the wall as soon as possible, but I wanted to spend some time with you first."

He smiled at that, kissing her temple. "I'm so thankful for you, Gwen." Orin admonished her with a stern look. "No heroics. Be safe."

"You too," Gwen replied as she stood, throwing her rifle over her shoulder and grabbing a quiver and bow that had been tucked under the table. "I expect to see you at the end of the day."

Orin nodded. "You will. We have too much to live for."

He watched her walk out the door, his heart traveling with her. He shook his head. *How had Gwen come to mean so much to me so quickly?* Orin wondered. After everything was settled, if they lived, Orin was going to explore the answer to that question and the life he hoped they could lead together.

"Hold your positions," Arthur roared to the fae and knights shield-locked with him, including Orin. "Pikes and spears up! Hold!"

Orin followed his king's orders, hefting his pike up higher. Their plan to funnel Mordred's forces to them had worked. Mostly. Alcina led the earth fae, working in groups to raise earthen works or dig deep ditches, forcing Mordred's soldiers to scramble over those obstacles or choose the more open paths that the rebels created. Either way, this meant that Mordred's soldiers couldn't throw overwhelming forces at them, a fact which Orin was grateful for. He had a promise to fulfill. He was going to make it back to Gwen.

Behind him, archers on the wall loosed their arrows overhead, keeping harpies, raven shifters, griffins, and even a roc at bay. Gwen's rifle barked out at regular intervals, creating large swaths of open air as his love focused her fire on large clumps of winged fae. Orin was fairly certain she had been the one to bring down the roc, though it had been riddled with arrows and singed by multiple fireballs. The smell of burnt feathers still rankled in the air.

Centaurs and mounted cavalry charged toward them. The ground rumbled beneath Orin's feet to the galloping drumming of hoof-beats. Mordred's soldiers rammed into their defensive line. The force reverberated down the line of Orin's spear as a centaur tried to bat it aside with a small round shield, but the blade skittered off the metal and plunged into its chest. He dug his feet in as the centaur's momentum tried to drive the knight backward to break the shield line.

A deafening crack of sound ripped through the air, and the centaur fell heavily, dragging Orin's spear with him. Lance stood next to Orin, Gwen's service pistol in hand, shield on the other arm.

Lance grinned through bloody teeth and a split lip at Orin. "Got to get you back to Gwen, otherwise she'll kill me." He shifted his aim, and a rapid barrage of bullets sent both riders and horses—and a few centaurs—to the ground directly in front of them.

Orin nodded his thanks to the blond fae, his eyebrows raised at the comment. Lance had made it clear enough that he didn't approve of Orin and Gwen's relationship. Then again, Orin doubted Lance wanted Gwen upset. Orin appreciated the assist either way.

Mordred's calvary broke against the rebel's line, peeling back to re-group while foot soldiers clambered in uncoordinated groups toward where Orin, Lance, and Arthur stood. The few strong magic users that the rebels had left worked together to harry these groups. The rebels moved the terrain or, in the case of the one remaining fire mage, lobbed balls of fire to keep their foes' heads down in the trenches. The archers continued to harass the flying fae, who had all but given up under the steady threat. Some of the archers sniped at the ground forces in the trenches.

"Alcina! Trap them in those trenches," Arthur yelled at the dark-skinned fae woman standing near the gates. The ground under their feet trembled again as Alcina and the five other fae with her pooled their magic together and, with abrupt hand movements, closed the ground on top of the nearest enemies.

Lance whooped his excitement at the maneuver. "That'll do it. We might actually have a chance."

Orin nodded but kept his focus on the tree line where Mordred's reserved forces remained hidden. Getting cocky would get them killed.

Horns sounded from the forest, and Mordred's forces fell back. Sweat rolled down Orin's neck and back, his arm muscles trembling as he watched them retreat. Bodies littered the field in front of Caerleon, and the mud turned crimson from blood. The stench assaulted Orin's nostrils. Up and down the line, the rebels shuffled to fill in the holes left by their own dead and wounded. The gates creaked open behind them, and several archers scuttled out, stretchers in hand to whisk the wounded away to the Great Hall. Orin watched as Gareth and Caradoc were both shuttled into Caerleon on stretchers. He couldn't tell if their wounds were mortal or not. Orin cursed low under his breath.

"So did we actually give them pause, or does Mordred have something else more unpleasant up his sleeve?" Lance murmured.

"Our experience lends itself to the first. Mordred's forces have always gone for brute strength when they've attacked us." Arthur grunted in disgust. "Why wouldn't they? They have the numbers, and he doesn't care how many die so long as he gets his victory."

"Movement in the trees," someone yelled down from the parapets.

Orin shrugged his shoulders back and lifted his shield to reform the barrier, shoving his worry about his comrades to the back of his mind. Lance dropped his shield and pulled out the holstered service weapon, pulling out one part and slamming a replica in its place. He reholstered it, grabbing at his shield and pike.

Lance saw Orin's curious gaze and gave Orin another wild grin. "Reloading. We're going to live through this. Just you watch and see."

Orin dragged his exhausted body through the gates as twilight settled across the field. The sounds of the dying echoed across the field, melding with the moans of the wounded. Their own wounded and dead had already been moved into the keep during the lulls in battle that had occurred throughout the day. Lance had made a comment about a Pyrrhic victory as they surveyed the sheer number of bodies scattered across the field in Mordred's red and black livery. Orin wondered if the losses would shift Mordred's attack strategy for the next battle, or, as Arthur stated, Mordred's confidence would lead to further sacrifices.

Gwen's and Lance's firearms had come in handy. Gwen had taken down another roc and then a large troll before it could lumber across the field to Caerleon's gates, but the sound of the rifle had cut off midday as Gwen ran out of ammunition. Lance likewise had to keep the service weapon holstered once he ran out of ammunition. If Gwen didn't have any further ammo for tomorrow's fights, that was going to leave the rebels at a significant disadvantage.

Orin glanced around the courtyard, taking in the knights and fae slogging their way toward the Great Hall and the fresher individuals moving up to the wall to keep watch in the event of a night attack. Exhaustion, sorrow, and a touch of desperation blanketed everyone moving around the courtyard. Today hadn't been a victory for either side.

Got to get to Gwen, he thought, head swiveling as he looked for the woman he was falling in love with. Gwen slammed into Orin from the side, saving him the trouble of finding her.

"You're okay," she breathed. Her arms encircled his waist, winching closed so tightly that he almost wheezed. His woman was so strong.

A grateful smile wandered across his face. "I am," Orin told her, voice rough from barking orders throughout the day. "You did good today,

Gwen. We would have been in real trouble if some of those larger monsters had made it to us."

"We all did good," she retorted, turning him toward the kitchen entrance. "Let's get you settled, take care of your wounds, then get you some food. I expect Arthur will want you and Lance back in the war room soon enough. Where is Lance?" she asked, swiveling her head.

"He should be around here." Orin turned her toward the gate and pushed her forward with a light smack on the rear. Gwen shot him a surprised and somewhat scandalized look. He chuckled. "Go find the bastard. He's the reason I'm still here."

"Are you sure?" Gwen asked over her shoulder even though she was still walking away. Then she stopped as Lance swung through the gate, a slight limp in his stride. She hustled over to the tall fae, looking up at his blood-spattered face. Orin nodded as Lance met his eyes then turned and headed into the keep. He knew Gwen would come find him. His trust in her was absolute.

They had survived the first day of Mordred's invasion, and Orin needed to find out how many of his friends were injured or had not made it off the field. Then they needed to figure out how to keep surviving.

CHAPTER TWENTY-ONE

GWEN

Gwen stared at the lights dancing among the trees from where she stood on Caerleon's parapet. She had left Orin and Lance in the war room with the other leaders and escaped out to the walls of Caerleon. Gwen knew the dancing lights were Mordred's forces sitting around their campfires. The forest looked like it was hosting a firefly rave with all the lights twinkling through the trees.

Below her, she could feel the rough shift of the grass in the wind, the way blood from today's battle had seeped into the soil, tainting it. Gwen lifted her face to the moonlight.

This was what war really meant. Blood and pain. Bodies mangled beyond repair or recognition. The metallic scent of fresh blood followed by the acrid scent of it hours later as it soured in the sun. The smell of bowels sliced open or vented at the time of death.

But it was also the small things. The tears tracking down a child's face at the loss of their parent. The hurried steps of a healer rushing by with bandages for the wounded. The low murmur of warrior's voices as they checked their weapons. The palpable weight of fear hanging over Caerleon and the rebels camped in front of the gates. Today's losses could have been so much worse, but they'd be burying so many friends and allies after just today's battle. Who knew how many they'd lose in the morning.

She turned her head at the sound of footsteps. Arthur strode toward her along the parapet and came to stand next to her. His gaze followed hers, and he leaned against the stone wall. Saxon shoved himself between Gwen and Arthur. The dog obviously still wasn't sold on the man despite Arthur starting to thaw towards Gwen.

"Everything will be decided tomorrow." Exhaustion saturated his voice. Gwen knew it wasn't just from today's battle. This was exhaustion driven by the weight of centuries.

"What do you want to do about Caliburnus?" Gwen murmured. "Shouldn't the decision be made with all the variables in play? Mordred may have borne the brunt of the losses, but we lost a quarter of our forces today, and we didn't start with many. We need something powerful to help us win, Arthur. If we don't empower the sword, you won't be able to take down Mordred, and he will keep coming until none of us are left. I don't have any more ammo, which means that the guns are out of play. The fae who can wield magic are exhausted. They did amazing today, but what happens tomorrow if they're not able to rest tonight?"

"What if your interpretation of the dream is wrong? We lose our tether to Avalon, and your sacrifice will mean nothing." Arthur huffed out an exasperated breath.

Gwen couldn't take her eyes off of Mordred's encampment. The lights blurred as tears pricked her eyes, but she blinked rapidly. She wasn't going to let them fall, not in front of this man. "My interpretations so far haven't been wrong, have they?" Gwen demanded, voice sharp.

"Look, Trouble—" Arthur started to say.

"Don't call me that!" Gwen turned to look at the king, her hands striking his chest, giving him a rude shove. "Do you think I want this?" Her breath hitched. "I had a perfectly good life back home. I never asked to be the guardian of your sword, nor connected to a land that claimed me as Her own without my consent. Yet here I am, and this is my home now. Your people are my people. If the choice is for everyone to be slaughtered by a power-hungry fae, then sacrificing one person sounds like a good fucking deal to me!"

"Even if you are that person?" he hissed.

"Why the hell do you even care? You barely tolerate me," she snapped back.

"Because you are important to Viviane! And Viviane is important . . ." He trailed off, rocking back on his heels.

But Gwen thought she knew what he was about to say.

"Because she is important to you?" she asked, hoping that Arthur had finally seen what was in front of him.

"Yes," he ground out. "You are important to me. You are important to all of us!"

Gwen blinked at him. "Come again?"

"Stupid, stubborn, blind woman. Yes, you are important to all of us. You've been the bridge between everything and everyone. I will not let you sacrifice yourself unless it is absolutely necessary," he spat, his hand slapping down onto the stone next to hers. "The very best man I know has opened up from his grief and has fallen in love with you. Do you think that I would sacrifice that love? When you've brought him out of the darkness? When you've brought *me* out of the darkness? When you've turned my eyes toward a possible chance at finding love again?"

"Well, I can assure you that I don't want to die, but we may not have a choice, Arthur." Her breath hitched on a sob, and she curled her hands into fists, charging on. "So if you're not going to do this unless absolutely necessary, we still need to have a contingency plan in case we have to spill my blood to unlock Caliburnus's power. What can we do to make sure I don't die? Because whether you want to accept it or not, you're going to need a fully empowered sword tomorrow. I bet Mordred will take the field with his army. He will have to. We put on too good a showing today. He will need to crush us to prove to his forces how strong a king he is." Gwen's expression was fierce and challenging as she looked up at the king.

He sighed, running a hand through his dark hair as he glanced out at the lights flickering from the forest. Then Arthur dropped his gaze to hers. "Let's go find Viviane. Perhaps she will know."

Arthur guided Gwen to the infirmary, collecting Viviane there, and ushered the women up to the library. It was one of the few rooms in the castle that was likely to be empty. The war room brimmed with Arthur's knights and the remaining fae leaders. The infirmary held the wounded, as did the main hall. Other rooms had been repurposed to host the families and non-combatants that supported the rebel fighters.

"Gwen, how does it feel when you are connected to Avalon?" Viviane asked as she settled into one of the leather chairs, her hand smoothing down her green skirt as she flicked a quick glance at Arthur.

"Overwhelming, if I'm not careful. When I focus, it's like I'm an extension of something much more powerful and primal than me," Gwen replied, dropping her head into her hands. She felt like she had been doing that a lot lately. It ached from suppressed tears and the overwhelming fear of what lay ahead.

As much as those around her fought this plan of action, Gwen knew deep in her bones that this path was inevitable. She was going to have to accept—no, she was going to have to submit—to her connection with Avalon. That was the crux of the matter, wasn't it? Gwen knew the path she had been put on would lead to something outside of her control, and she hated being out of control. But for Orin, Lance, Viviane, and the others she now called friends, Gwen would give up that control willingly.

"It takes a lot of energy to force changes, not as much with assessing what is going on," she continued. "When I first got here, my connection with Avalon felt more like I was barely brushing fingertips with someone. I could barely feel it. Now it's more like a hand clasp, but one with someone way bigger than me. They can pull me all around, but it takes significant effort to pull back."

Viviane tapped her chin, eyes soft as the fae was lost in thought. Gwen picked her head up out of her hands, noticing that Arthur's eyes stayed locked on her blond friend.

"So in theory," Viviane began, "we believe that Mordred is possibly tied to the Mist Lands just as Gwen is tied to Avalon. Caliburnus and Mordred's sword seem to be the focal point of those tetherings. If Mordred is able to pull energy from the Mist Lands to heal himself from mortal wounds, then it's likely Gwen should be able to do the same."

"Except I can barely control any of my new powers," Gwen muttered. "Mordred inherently knows how to handle them because he was born a fae. The dozen or more centuries he has on me probably doesn't hurt either."

"I have a feeling that Avalon won't throw you away." Viviane leaned forward and covered one of Gwen's hands with hers. "But I can also be there to help. I reached some of my limits today, but with some rest tonight, I can see what I can do to keep you from slipping away from us." Viviane's knuckles turned white as her grip tightened around her younger friend's hands.

"Then that's all I can ask for," Gwen choked out. She cleared her throat, looking up at Arthur. "When it's time, I will be there to empower Caliburnus. The blade will help you break the tether Mordred has to the Mist Lands, and you should be able to land a killing blow. I assume if he falls in front of his troops, they'll be weaker, right?"

Arthur held her gaze for a moment before nodding. "With luck, yes. Many may feel pressured into his service and even break and run. Lancelot indicated his brother's forces were those most dangerous. Apparently this Aberlin is angling to gain more power as Mordred claims Avalon."

"Yes, but my cousin hasn't been seen yet, only his forces. If Aberlin is anything like he was when we were young, he's staying close to our ancestral lands. He was always a bully, but a cowardly one. He will want to stay near his power base." Viviane shrugged. "There was a reason why Lancelot was favored to take over House Dwyn's holdings. Lance is a much better leader."

"So we have a plan then? If things are going poorly on the battlefield, Arthur will fall back, and the three of us will go to the spell stone to finish unlocking Caliburnus's power?" Gwen asked. She buried her hands in Saxon's fur to keep the other two from seeing them tremble.

Arthur nodded, rubbing his hand across his heart as he first peered at Gwen and Viviane. Then he nodded. "Yes, though let us hope it won't come to that."

Except Gwen knew deep in her gut that unless a miracle happened, the blood rite would be required.

Gwen stayed quiet as Arthur escorted first Viviane back to the infirmary, a subtle brush of their fingers the only sign that they didn't want to part, and then Gwen to the war room. Gwen smiled to herself as they walked. Arthur's stubbornness was legendary; she wondered when he'd make a more public move on Viviane. Then she sobered. Gwen hoped he would have the chance. Both he and Viviane deserved a happy ending.

While Arthur strode into the room and straight to the table, Gwen sidled into the room, assessing the mood of the room. A weird mix of despair and gritty hope mixed in the air as discussion volleyed back and forth between the room's occupants. The knights held court over one side of the tapestry lined room while the fae stood on the other side of the large wooden table burdened with piles of maps and books. The other smaller tables had been pushed into the corners to make standing room for everyone. Large pillar candles flickered in black iron wall sconces as people paced.

"We will need to funnel Mordred and his forces back through the defenses. It worked well today. It'll give us a better chance of holding them off." That was Frideswide. For all that she was the tiniest being in the room, the fairy could command everyone's attention.

"Not that it did us much good today," Cae muttered. "We lost a lot of our good warriors and your magic users today."

"It could have been worse," Aethelflaed pointed out. "We have other attacks we can use tomorrow that we didn't wield today," she continued sagely. "There is myself and one other banshee, albeit she's not quite as powerful. If we deploy her and I as Mordred's forces move on us, we may be able to send some running, which will break their ranks."

"We could muddy up the ground if we draw on Viviane's loch and try to swamp their flanks as they try to flee." Lance tapped the edge of the lake on the map they surrounded. "Viviane may be required since the lake is her realm, for all intents and purposes, but she and the House Dwyn fae loyal to me can stand here. A tidal wave of lake water should dampen the enemy force's attitude a bit. Once done, our water fae can fall back to the castle, leaving House Keithia's rebels to move the muck around and make other portions of the battlefield impassable. Today's battle proved that there aren't nearly enough earth fae as expected within Mordred's forces, and ours are powerful enough to stand toe-to-toe with them despite the number discrepancy."

"What about Mordred?" Orin demanded. "These plans may handle the average fae, but he's a force unto himself."

"We keep him at bay. If we can keep him off the battlefield, we may be able to break his force's spirit."

"Easier said than done." This was Cae again. Arthur shot the man a frustrated look, and the knight settled back against the wall, his lips thin and arms crossed as he held back anything further.

"This is the best we can do. Our plans will change as the battle unfolds," Arthur told everyone. "But tomorrow will be the day we either free the Mist Lands and protect Avalon, or we die trying. Our forces need to know this. Everything balances on this, so be prepared to make sacrifices and to fight fiercely." His eyes flicked to Gwen at the word "sacrifices," but he swung his gaze away so fast that she was pretty sure she was the only one who noticed.

Arthur knocked his knuckles against the table, pinning everyone in the room with his stare. "Tonight will be about rest. Tomorrow will be about outlasting our enemy. See to your assigned forces and make sure they are prepared."

Murmured agreement swept through the room before everyone filed out. Orin caught sight of Gwen and moved over to her. Lance followed on his heels.

"You've been hiding," Lance said, putting his hand on her shoulder.

"No, not really." He lifted an eyebrow at her rebuttal.

"I wanted to see," Gwen told them, curling her arms around herself.

"See what?" Orin asked, his brows furrowing.

"The stars," Gwen whispered. It might be the last time she would see them. The constellations weren't the ones she knew from the mortal world, but seeing the shapes drawn in the sky were somehow . . . grounding. Then Gwen had made the mistake of looking at the forest, and her thoughts had spiraled from there.

The men's manners softened, then Lance glanced between Orin and Gwen. A pained expression crossed his face, but he squeezed her shoulder and stepped back.

"I will see you in the morning." Strain and something else blanketed Lance's tone, but he nodded to them both and turned on his heel, striding away.

The silence in the room caused Gwen to shiver. Despite Orin's presence, there was a loneliness that descended upon her. She grabbed his hand, looking up at the man she had dreamed of for so long. His presence grounded her as much as the sight of the stars.

"Can we spend the night together?" Gwen dared to ask. Was this too soon? They had spent weeks together, shared kisses, started exploring each other's bodies in stolen moments but never shared a bed. Orin's eyes flared with surprise then heated interest before he nodded. Without a word, he took her hand and drew her out into the hallway to lead her to his room. Saxon trailed behind them, a fact that had Orin glancing over his shoulder.

"Will the protective beast let you stay?" he grumbled. The man and the dog had not quite come to an understanding with each other.

Gwen chuckled, the first full laugh she had let loose that day, and tucked her arm around Orin's waist, drawing herself closer to him. "He'll live."

"He can stay out in the main room then," Orin told Gwen as he pushed open his door, sweeping her inside. "Are you hungry? I can scrounge up something to eat."

She shook her head, staring up at him. "No. I just want to spend time with you."

Orin smiled at that, its brilliance blinding her. It was rare for the stoic man to show true happiness, but it always seemed to be directed at her. His happiness was something she would always treasure. Gwen stepped forward into his embrace, determined to have one last happy memory with this man.

Orin's kisses were soft and tender as she pushed him back into a nearby chair and sank into his lap. His fingers tangled in her hair, pulling Gwen's head back to expose the line of her throat; his lips whispered along the soft skin as he breathed in her scent, seemingly struck with wonder that she wanted him. Gwen combed her fingers through his salt-and-pepper beard and then down to his shoulders, locking her legs around him and the chair, her breath coming in quick gasps as she shuddered under his featherlight touch. She let her hands roam down, tugging at Orin's shirt as he brought his mouth back to hers.

Finally, he was hers.

"I want to see you," she murmured in desperation, pulling his shirt up and over his head. Gwen gave a satisfied sigh at the exposed muscles and ran her hands over him.

"If you continue to do that," he told Gwen gruffly, "we won't be able to get very far."

That would be a damn shame. She kept her hands to his shoulders and a few teasing touches.

His hands were conducting their own exploration, lingering over her curves. Gwen wriggled enough to get her hands free and pulled her shirt over her head, dropping it to the floor. Orin's gaze dropped to her breasts, his breath expelling at the sight as he brought his hands up to cup them.

"Damn me, but everything about you is small." The tone was reverent.

Gwen smiled slightly and bit her lip as he rubbed his thumbs over her breasts, replying breathlessly, "I'm not sure if that's a compliment or not."

Orin smiled back. "Small but perfect."

"Okay, that's a good compliment." Her voice broke on a moan as he slipped the bra straps off her shoulders and bent his head to nip and kiss the exposed flesh. "It unhooks in the back," she told him, twisting her arms back to do just that. Orin caught her hands again.

"No, I like looking at it for a bit," he told her, savoring the pale flesh exposed above the black lace. "The ladies I remember didn't have quite the wonderful clothes . . . or underclothes that you do."

"Mentioning other ladies probably isn't conducive to our going much further," Gwen said dryly, pulling her hands out of his grip to send them roaming back over his torso.

"Talking at all probably isn't conducive to going much further," Orin replied with a cheeky grin, returning to kissing her. He stood, picking her up, and turned toward his room, taking her to his bed. Orin kicked the door closed in Saxon's face, and Gwen could hear the dog grumble at that. The two fell onto Orin's bed, Gwen's legs still locked around him.

"God, please, hurry," Gwen moaned, her hands worrying at his pants.

"I've waited this long for a woman," he told her. "I can wait a bit longer."

That wouldn't do. Gwen wanted him right now, distracted for a moment as he brushed more kisses along her neck. Her hands started roaming again, but he trapped Gwen's hands in his to keep her from touching him.

"Not yet," he told her again and went back to exploring her body. "Let me love you."

So she let him, and Gwen loved him in return.

When they lay tangled together afterward, Orin rubbed his hand up and down her arm, staring down at Gwen as if he couldn't believe she was in his bed. Then his fingers drifted to the tattoo inked under her left breast.

"'I was not built to break'?" he asked.

"It seemed like a good reminder," Gwen told him sleepily, then shivered as his hand drifted over to the flower-ringed tattoo on her right hip.

"And this?" Orin lifted up on his elbow to get a better look.

Gwen stretched under his touch. "The compass rose. So I always remember to keep finding my true north."

"Have you found it yet?" Orin's eyes flicked up to Gwen's.

Her smile was soft but small, a little unsure. "Maybe."

Orin held her gaze, the quiet stretching between them for several moments. Then he cleared his throat. "Do you still want to stay the night?"

"Yes," she whispered, her hand over his pounding heart. Eventually, she felt it slow from its frantic pace.

"Good," he said, closing his eyes.

Gwen reached down and pulled the blankets over them. She slipped into dreams while Orin held her, his fingers still brushing across the words etched into her skin.

Chapter Twenty-Two

Orin

The warm darkness of his room cocooned Orin and Gwen where she lay wrapped around him, arm and leg thrown over his torso and legs. If he thought getting up yesterday had been hard, leaving Gwen's embrace this morning was torture. He shoved his face into her dark hair, hiding from the inevitability of the battle ahead. He had just found her. Orin wasn't going to lose her.

"I don't want to get up," Gwen yawned into his shoulder, snuggling down farther. "Tell Mordred to go away. We have better things to do."

Orin chuckled. "Like what?" he asked, then grunted as her hand meandered down to his groin. He could feel her wicked smile against his skin. "Oh."

"Mmmm, yes, oh." Her sultry tone twined about him, and Orin banged his head a couple of times back into his pillows.

This. Was. Torture.

Orin told Gwen as much, smiling at her giggle, then sighed as she rolled onto her back and rubbed at her eyes before sitting up. The sheets pooled around Gwen's waist, and Orin wound her hair around his fist, pulling it to the side so he could trace the flower-bedecked longsword tattoo on her spine with his eyes. Orin's skin shivered as a chill swept over the knight. Something about the blade etched in her skin had dread curdling in his chest.

"You'll be careful?" he asked, voice gruff.

Gwen turned and planted a quick peck on his lips but didn't meet his eyes. "Of course."

"Gwen." She looked up as Orin said her name. "You are everything for me, my true north. And I'll always be yours." Orin slid his hands around his lover's jaw, pulling her to him for a passionate kiss that left both of them breathless. "Do *not* do anything heroic that puts you at risk. I can't lose you."

"You won't lose me," Gwen whispered to him. "Please be careful out there. I don't want to lose you either."

"I will. Let's get ready. I'll check your gear to make sure you're good to go before you report to Bedevere."

That kiss carried Orin through the dawn preparations and out onto the field, where he joined Arthur and Lance to form the center of the shield wall. Water fae lined the beach of Viviane's lake; the Lady had spent time the evening prior ensuring the water would respond to their magic. Alcina and Frideswide ordered about members of House Keithia, strengthening the earthen barriers and encouraging tangling roots to grow from the ground while creating new trenches. Aethelflaed and the other banshee stood directly behind them, an eerie chill wafting off both that made his skin crawl.

The tree line wavered as Mordred's forces rushed back and forth, forming their own shield line. Orin watched the flash of dark armor and red accents with a grim smile. There was a certain satisfaction after all these centuries in knowing today was the end of worrying about what would happen next. Either he would be dead or they would be victorious, and he had every intention of starting a new life with Gwen if they won. If they survived this, Gwen was going to move into his rooms with him. Granted, she didn't know this yet, but she would. Orin was done waiting for his life to begin again.

"Look alive!" Arthur ordered, his voice booming up and down the line. Someone on the parapet picked up the order and sounded their horn, the deep melody carrying out across the field. A brassier sounding horn answered from Mordred's forces. Arthur and Lance stepped aside so the two banshees could move in front of the shield wall.

"Here goes nothing," Lance muttered beside them as the forest rippled, and the first few rows of Mordred's soldiers marched out. More followed, stacking up behind the front line as the front runners ran into the first defenses, breaking the line as they struggled to cover thorn-and-vine-wrapped ground or slog through newly formed trenches.

"The plan will work." Aethelflaed seemed so calm, her whispery voice strong as she stood with her hands hanging loosely at her side as if she didn't have a care in the world. The other banshee fidgeted, shifting from one foot to the other. "Peace, Nyla. Our focus is key. Once we scream, we fall back to Caerleon."

Nyla nodded, her head bobbing up and down with manic energy. "Yes, Aethelflaed."

"You're going to get your chance sooner rather than later." Lance looked toward the water fae, bellowing, "Be ready!"

Mordred's forces picked up their pace, breaking into a trot then charging forward at a run. No calvary today, which Orin thought was odd, but meant they stood a better chance of surviving this first wave. The enemy soldiers flowed down the easier paths that the rebels had created, funneling toward the two banshees, Arthur, Lance, and Orin.

Orin slapped his hands over his ears as the enemy closed in. Everyone up and down the line followed suit as the banshees' jaws unhinged, their screams bursting out. Even through Orin's hands, the muffled scream evoked so much. Sorrow. Grief. Melancholy.

But most of all . . . fear.

The enemy broke, soldiers tossing themselves to their knees as emotions weighed down their shoulders. They turned and tried to flee, only to run into their compatriots and wreak havoc on the close-knit formation. Mordred hadn't seemed to learn his lesson yesterday. Sheer numbers weren't going to win this battle. Arrogant bastard.

The banshees stumbled back toward Caerleon, the strength of their magic draining them. A sloshing sound had Orin looking toward the lake. Lance's water fae worked together, their arms swinging in time with the large wave that they were creating in the lake. Orin sucked in a sharp breath as the wave crested halfway up the height of Caerleon's walls. The water fae parted, turning en masse to point toward Mordred's forces struggling to detangle themselves from each other.

One of Mordred's soldiers saw the wave coming and screamed in terror. The dark water raced across the ground, picking up detritus, fallen weapons, and dead enemy bodies from the prior day's battle. The wave's shadow fell over the enemy.

Silence blanketed the battlefield for a brief moment as the wave curled up higher, then crested.

The water crashed down, slamming into the soldiers scrabbling to get away. The sheer force of the water broke bones, sweeping battered bodies into the trenches that House Keithia rebels had created. Lance slammed his foot down. Immediately, the water froze over, trapping those still alive in long troughs of ice. The soldiers that could still run fled back toward the tree. In the distance, Orin spotted Mordred on his kelpie mount barking orders inside the tree line.

Lance chuckled darkly. "Doesn't look happy, does he?"

"No, he doesn't. Shields up!" Orin barked. A fresh wave of troops broke out of the woods, Mordred joining the charge. It looked like Mordred's patience had run out, and he was ready to join the battle. Next to Orin, Arthur grinned with a savage energy.

"Finally," his king growled.

Orin's chest heaved with exhaustion as he looked around for his king, but he couldn't find Arthur among those fighting nearby. Where was the man? Orin's gaze swiveled around the battlefield. It was a rare lull in the fighting, with Mordred's soldiers struggling to reach them through the mud and terrain challenges. Even Mordred had fallen back to the tree line. Despite their best efforts, the rebels had failed to break the will of Mordred's army. At this rate, Mordred may indeed outlast them.

Orin wondered if his king might be injured but didn't see Arthur's body. Maybe Arthur had already been taken into Caerleon?

"Where's Arthur?" Orin panted, looking at Lance. The fae was sucking in great lungfuls of air, his hair matted to the side of his head with sweat and blood. He looked terrible. Orin figured he did too.

"Saw him pull back some but lost track of him during the last charge," Lance said. "Shit, here they come again."

Orin grunted, changing the grip on his sword. Arrows flew over his head, an angry, buzzing rain. The archers were still keeping the skies clear, and now they focused on peppering the leading edge of Mordred's charging soldiers. Mordred had joined three of the charges, but now he sat on his mount again at the tree line. Apparently, his bravery only extended so far.

Lance followed Orin's sight line, then his lips curled in disgust. "Bastard is a coward. Won't even face us directly, even with his powers. What's he waiting for?"

"I have no—" Orin choked on his words as power erupted out of Caerleon, rippling through the ground. Mordred's forces tumbled and flew into each other, driven back by the pulses of magic until they were flung into the woods. Mordred's mount reared, throwing him to the ground.

An eerie blue magical barrier speared up from the ground, forming a ring around Caerleon and capturing Mordred in with the rebels, his forces left on the outside and unable to help their fallen king.

"What the hell?" Lance breathed, turning back to look at the castle. He clutched at his chest, gasping. "Something's blocking my magic."

"Mine too," a fae warrior next to him confirmed, eyes wild.

Orin followed his gaze, the dread from earlier once again slamming into him. *What the hell was happening?*

Chapter Twenty-Three

Gwen

"You have to promise me you won't tell Orin or Lance until everything is done. They have to stay focused if they're going to make it out of this final battle alive. They won't if they think something is wrong with me," Gwen asserted as Arthur strode into the cavern.

Viviane and Arthur looked at each other before Arthur nodded. "Done. This is . . ." His voice trailed off as he shifted his wrist. Azure light from the spell stone created a kaleidoscope of colors on the blade in his hand, the sapphire gem in the hilt deepening in color.

"This is the only way," Gwen said softly. "But I need you to do this. Once my blood is on the blade, stab the sword straight into the spell stone to activate the connection with Avalon. Then the sword will contain Her magic, enough to end Mordred and his connection to the Mist Lands if you can get in a killing blow."

Viviane laid a soft hand on Arthur's arm as he stared at Gwen. Sorrow was stamped on his face as Viviane assured him. "I'll do what I can to heal her if that is possible. She is bound to Avalon. As Mordred draws strength from the land he has claimed, she can draw strength from Avalon." She turned to her mortal friend and swept Gwen into a hug. "Brave, brave girl. You humble us with your sacrifice."

Gwen twisted her hands in her friend's gown, her skin growing clammy with sweat. "I don't want to die," she whispered so softly that she wasn't sure even Viviane could hear her. Gwen's muscles clenched involuntarily before she stepped back, taking a long breath. It filled her lungs, and she wondered idly if this would be the last time she did so.

"Let's do this," Gwen told Arthur, stepping up and placing her hand on the spell stone. Magic pulsed beneath her fingertips, a living heartbeat of power that synced with her own rapid heart's rhythm.

He gave her a curt nod, placing his hand on her shoulder, and ducking his head down so he was eye to eye with her. "Thank you, Trouble."

She hated that he called her that. Why couldn't she have a kick-ass nickname? Trouble sounded so . . . preschool. That was her last thought as he thrust the blade up and into her stomach, his strength making the stroke smooth and swift.

Gwen gasped as fire erupted in her abdomen, her knees immediately giving out. Eyes streaming tears, she stared up into Arthur's face as he pulled Caliburnus free of her flesh and took the hilt in both hands. Gwen's world tilted, then she was sliding down the spell stone, leaving a bloody trail in her wake. Beside her, Arthur plunged the bloodied blade into the stone.

Everything stopped.

Arthur stood frozen, his face a ravaged mask of anguish. Viviane was caught mid-kneel, arms reaching for Gwen to begin the healing process. The only thing that didn't seem to stop was the blood seeping out of her wounds.

Gwen stared down at the rapidly growing crimson puddle, her cheek leaning against the cool, rough stone.

Funny how quickly life drains away.

The heartbeat she had felt mere moments ago thrummed in her head, a bass melody that twined with her thin, panting breaths. She clenched her teeth, putting her left hand down in her blood. The warmth of it shocked her cool skin. Lifting heavy limbs despite her darkening consciousness, Gwen gave into the compulsion battering her mind.

With the last of her strength, Gwen raised her arm and placed her sanguine palm against the sepia-colored stone. Gwen pushed at her connection with Avalon, binding the thread that tied her soul and the land to Caliburnus where it lay entombed in the rock. Like a spider, she wove a gossamer web of power around and into the blade. She watched as the magic settled into the metal, pulsing softly. With a soft whine of pain, she ripped her hand off of the stone, knowing her work was done.

The blue light from the spell stone pulsed once, twice, as her heartbeat slowed and the powerful rhythm in the stone accelerated. It *beat, beat, beat* so hard that Gwen could do nothing but feel it down to the marrow of her bones.

Time flowed again as Arthur wrenched Caliburnus out of the stone. Her blood was gone from the blade. In its place, power shone from the sword, matching the cadence of Avalon's power.

"It's done," Arthur rasped, mesmerized by the changes in the blade.

"Go," Gwen whispered, slumping farther down the spell stone.

"Hang on for me, Gwen," Viviane whispered, placing her hands gently over the oozing slit in Gwen's belly.

"'Kay . . ." Gwen mumbled.

"This is going to hurt," her friend warned her.

Gwen quirked one side of her mouth in a wan imitation of a smile, feeling something seep out of it as she coughed. She fought to bring one listless hand up to swipe at her chin. Her hand came away with fresh blood.

"Alrea . . ." She gurgled out a breath. ". . . dy . . . does."

"No more talking," Viviane admonished.

Gwen closed her eyes as pain ratcheted through her middle from whatever spell her friend was casting. It felt like fire tore through her, and lightning danced in her veins. What was Viviane doing to her? Why did it hurt so much? Gwen's vision wavered, blackness creeping along the edges like a soft mist.

Orin is going to be so angry with me, she thought. The unfurling mist and the burning blade were the last things she saw before darkness took her.

"Gwen. Gwen!"

The voice was very insistent as were the hands grasping her shoulders. It sounded like . . . Eidytha? Gwen fought to open her eyes. Her damn eyelids were so heavy, but her breathing seemed easier. She took in a tentative breath. No scorching pain. That was a welcome improvement.

Eidytha stood over her, wringing her hands. "Gwen, they need you on the walls. Arthur is fighting Mordred."

"I've only just healed her. She almost died. She's weak!" That was Viviane's voice. Huh. Viv sounded upset. Not the usual tone for her friend.

"Then we will have to help her. Come on, Viviane, help me sit her up," Eidytha ordered. Gwen hauled her eyelids open as she saw Eidytha's and Viviane's hands grasp her shoulders and arms to draw her into a sitting position.

"Not dead?" Gwen asked.

Viviane huffed out a small laugh, grabbing at Gwen's face to wipe away tears that Gwen hadn't even realized she was crying. "No, my brave girl. But it was close. I lost you twice before I was able to bring you back and keep you." Then Viviane hugged her.

"You're . . . stronger than you look," Gwen muttered, but the bone-deep pressure helped stabilize her further. She dropped her head listlessly onto Viviane's shoulder. "What's . . . what's happening?"

"The armies have been cleared from the field. I don't know how, I just know Arthur, Orin, and that fae friend of yours are fighting Mordred. If it's any time for Avalon's guardian to make an appearance, it's now." The urgency in Eidytha's voice had Gwen assessing her body.

"Not sure I'm up for moving," Gwen said. She tried to get her legs under her, but they felt like overcooked noodles. Saxon shoved his snout under her chin. "Where'd Sax come from?" Gwen was sure she'd locked him in her room for safekeeping.

"The beast wouldn't stop barking, so I brought him with me," Eidytha told her, maneuvering Gwen so she wasn't slumped against the stone but instead against the woman's skirts. Eidytha's strong hands shoved under Gwen's armpits. "On three, me and Viv are going to hoist you up. Got it?"

"Uh huh." Gwen's mind was muzzy, but beneath her, she could feel a huge well of power. Gwen tried to draw on it, but it came to her in a trickle. It was enough, though, to clear her head a bit.

"One . . . two . . ." Gwen groaned as Eidytha hauled most of her weight up, Viviane keeping her from pitching forward.

"That wasn't three." Gwen swayed, leaning against Eidytha.

Eidytha laughed as she snarked, "No, it wasn't but got you up all the same."

"So I'm up; now what?" Gwen blinked as the cavern wavered. *Is the ground moving?*

"Now we get you to the wall," Eidytha said. Viviane and Eidytha propped Gwen's arms on their shoulders and helped her stagger out of the stone cavern and up to the parapet where archers continued to pepper Mordred's forces to keep them at bay. Saxon padded after them, his nose practically pressed to Gwen's knee.

"You can't be up here," Bedevere barked at the women as they crested the top of the stone steps and edged over to the wall to peer across the open field.

Despite what Eidytha had said, Gwen had expected to see the battlefield teeming with fights, but Mordred's forces were being held at the edge of the field by both some form of magic and the occasional arrow from the wall whenever one of the soldiers tried to skirt around the magical wall and get closer to Caerleon.

"Never you mind what we're doing, Bedevere," Eidytha shot back. Gwen was appreciative of her strong friend, and not just because of the fact she carried so much of Gwen's physical weight right now.

"Arthur," Viviane breathed next to her as all three women focused on the only movement on the field below.

Mordred clashed with Arthur, Orin, and Lance, fending off their brutal strikes. Their grunts and yells echoed around the cleared area in front of the castle as they slipped on the muddy ground, hammering blows into each other.

"Why isn't Mordred using spells?" Eidytha wondered, her voice quiet.

"My cousin and others on our side infused Arthur's armor with spells this morning before we went to battle," Viviane told her. The tall fae woman shook her head. "It's enough to give Arthur an even playing field."

The words hit Gwen. "No, that's not quite right," she said, feeling the magic thrumming under her feet. "I think Avalon has created a magical null field within the barrier. Mordred can't cast spells, but that means Lance can't either. Except Mordred's still tied to the Mist Lands, so they can't kill him. We need to level the playing field more."

"What are you going to do?" Eidytha asked, wrapping her arms around Gwen's waist to steady her as Gwen dropped her hands to the stone wall.

Gwen looked out at the fight between Mordred and her friends grimly. The men and fae had equal fighting skills. The winner would be determined not by training but by endurance or a lucky blow. They needed to make sure all factors worked against Mordred's favor. If Mordred died, his forces might scatter.

Beneath her feet, she could feel the thrumming of magic interwoven through Avalon's soil in a way she hadn't before. The trickle of power she had pulled on below Caerleon widened until it was a constant flow, and for the first time, she didn't feel like an overwhelming force was grabbing her and throwing her about or pushing against her. Now she felt as if she clasped hands with an equal.

"Mold earth," she murmured.

"What?" Viviane and Eidytha chorused.

Gwen didn't focus on her friends' questions. Instead, she concentrated on the ground beneath the men's feet, watching, waiting. She could feel the oozing mud as if it was beneath her feet instead of the stone parapet. Gwen pushed magic forcefully where she expected Mordred to step.

Except she was wrong.

A sharp gasp rose from the ranks as Arthur stumbled into the divot Gwen had created. Mordred battered at Arthur, shoving the mortal king with his red-and-black shield while raining blows on Arthur's dull gray shield with his dark blade. Arthur's shield clattered to the ground, leaving his side exposed.

"Shit, shit!" Gwen hissed, swaying. This was all wrong. If she was the reason Arthur lost . . . If the blood ritual was for nothing . . .

The women watched as Lance lunged in front of a cutting slice aimed at Arthur's exposed side, blocking Mordred's blade with his own. Arthur staggered, righting himself. Mordred's cursing rose about the clanging din of swords as Orin harried the fae king from the side.

Gwen gritted her teeth. She knew that moving the ground was the answer. She just had to get it right.

As Mordred's left foot stepped back to brace for Arthur's next strike, Gwen punched at the ground with her magic. A small sinkhole opened beneath Mordred, his shout echoing across the battlefield as he flailed for balance. In a move eerily similar to when Arthur had bathed his sword in Gwen's blood, Arthur brushed past Mordred's shield and slammed Caliburnus up and through the fae king's chest. Orin lunged forward, toppling Mordred to the muddy ground where the fae king lay skewered with Caliburnus sticking out of his chest.

Gwen manipulated the ground again, wrapping mud around Mordred's limbs and freezing it rock hard, keeping the tyrant pinned to Avalon's earth. Power flared from Caliburnus, wracking across the battlefield and sending everyone tumbling to the ground.

Everyone but Gwen.

Gwen let Avalon's power wash over her, seeing the faint shimmer of magical threads wrapped around Caliburnus fanning out in every direction to blanket the entirety of Avalon. Darker threads wrapped around Mordred's blade and tied it to him, leading off in the direction of the Mist Lands and where she knew the sacrificial grove stood. Now she knew why Mordred hadn't used his powers as part of the attack; it was all tied up in the spell that anchored his life force to the Mist Lands's magic. He wasn't on his lands, which meant he lacked access to magical reserves. No, the fae king was on *her* land.

Gwen's mouth crooked in a small smile. "Gotcha."

As Avalon absorbed Mordred's blood, Gwen wound Avalon's magic around the fae king's blade, snipping through the black strands of the Mist Lands magic with the silver-gold ones of Avalon's. Just as she knew what to do in the cavern, Avalon guided her here. The dark magic blasted across the field, snapping back toward the Mist Lands like a rubber band pulled too tight. People on the periphery of her vision toppled back to the ground at the second release of power. Gwen had severed Mordred's life tie to the Mist Lands.

Gwen gritted her teeth, her head pounding as she wavered on her feet. Avalon wanted to claim Mordred's dark blade, not just sever its tie to the fae realm.

Greedy bitch, Gwen thought.

She knew somehow that she didn't need to bathe Mordred's sword in her own now that she was tied so tightly to Avalon. No second life-threatening sacrifice needed, thank goodness. The magic welled up beneath the ground, waiting for an outlet. Gwen reached for the magic, spinning it into tight laces before interweaving them into the caliginous metal. The magic burned hot in her brain, lancing the backs of her eyes, but the work was done. Avalon and Gwen were now tied to the second sword, and Mordred was cut off from reclaiming his ties to the Mist Lands's life force or trying to meld himself with Avalon's magic.

Arthur leaned forward, grasping Caliburnus's hilt, and wrenched the sword from Mordred's chest. Gwen barely dared to breathe, letting it out slowly as Mordred finally bled out on the battlefield. In the end, the fae king was still only a man, and he died as one, staring blindly at the cerulean sky.

A roar of triumph came from the men, women, and fae rebels scrambling to their feet. Gwen swayed at the sound and sight before her.

"Gwen, you did it," Viviane breathed, hand pressed to her mouth, tears in her eyes.

"Tired," Gwen murmured, sagging into Viviane and Eidytha before her legs folded and she slammed into the stone at their feet. Her last thought focused on the woods standing at the backs of Mordred's forces. Shoving her still bloodied palms against the stone beneath her, Gwen jetted one last surge of power into the ground. In the shadows of the parapets, in the arms of her friends, she listened to the ground rumbling and the cracking of tree trunks as Avalon's magic answered her request and brought the forest crashing down onto Mordred's fleeing soldiers.

CHAPTER TWENTY-FOUR

ORIN

Orin blinked sweat and blood out of his eyes as his chest burned with exhaustion. He stared down at Mordred's limp form, his brain unable to process that the villain who had terrorized them for a millennium now lay dead at his feet. If he was honest with himself, Orin hadn't been sure he, Arthur, or Lance would walk away alive from this fight. He stared at his comrades-in-arms, taking in their injuries. Lance's shield arm hung weirdly while blood drained from a long, open wound. Bruises shadowed the side of Arthur's face where Mordred had bashed him with his shield. Orin's body ached, and he could feel the slow ooze of blood under his armor from numerous small wounds.

Did we win? Orin thought as the spell barrier fell. The knight watched fae rebels and Arthur's men surge out of the castle to chase groups of Mordred's retreating forces. At this pace, the enemy's retreat may even turn into a full rout. He stood in the shadows of the gate into Caerleon.

But how did Arthur manage to empower Caliburnus? Last Orin knew, Caliburnus was a normal sword, and Arthur definitely didn't have any magic. Which meant . . .

"Gwen!" Orin bellowed, whirling and lurching back into the courtyard. Lance and Arthur limped behind him.

"Orin! Up here!" Eidytha screeched his name. He whipped his head up to her, in time to see Viviane hurrying down the nearby steps, russet skirts in hand so as not to trip. She ran towards Arthur's open arms. Eidytha held Gwen's limp form in her lap.

"Gwen!" Orin rushed up the steps, his breath catching in his throat at the sight of the blood covering Gwen's shirt and pants. "No, no, no."

"Orin, she's alive," Eidytha soothed. She held a hand up to stop Orin from grabbing at Gwen. "She's just unconscious. Viviane has already healed the wound. Gwen lost quite a bit of blood, and I think whatever magic she used with the trees pushed her to her limit."

"What happened?" Orin snapped. He knelt down next to the women, his hands curling under Gwen and pulling her onto his own lap. Gwen's head lolled back until he shrugged her into a better position so that her head rested against his shoulder. Orin pushed strands of mahogany hair out of his lover's face. Gwen was so pale. Saxon whined where he was standing sentry beside Eidytha while Lance loomed behind them, face grim.

"I'm not sure. You'll have to ask Viviane or Gwen. Can you help me get her to her room?" Eidytha asked.

"No," Orin said, voice rough. "I'm taking her to mine. Come on, Saxon. You're coming too." He lumbered to his feet, keeping Gwen cradled against his chest. Lance moved out of Orin's way as he made his way towards the steps. His trembling, strained, and cut muscles screamed in protest. He would need to tend to his wounds once he cleaned up

Gwen and got her settled in his bed. "Lance, you're welcome to come with me. If you're magic is back, maybe you can see if you can help."

"But Viviane said she was fine," Eidytha protested as she scrambled to her feet.

"The Lady may have healed Gwen's wound, but what if something else is wrong? Please move, Eidytha," Orin growled. Eidytha reared back at his brusque tone, but she shuffled out of the way.

"I'll be right behind you," Lance murmured as Viviane stomped up the stairs and glared at her cousin. "Viviane will wish to heal me first."

Without a quick nod at Lance, Orin turned and carried Gwen down the steps and into the keep. His limp made the journey twice as long as it should have been, but he sighed in relief as he shouldered his door open and strode to his bedroom.

"Gwen, darling, please come back to me," he whispered as he lowered her to his bed. Orin looked at Saxon as the dog hopped onto the bed and nosed at Gwen's slack hand. "I'm going to get her cleaned up. You behave yourself." Saxon stared at Orin, and the man wondered how much the dog actually understood as the German Shepherd chuffed out a breath and settled next to his mistress. "All right, then. I'm glad we've come to an accord."

"Here." Lance handed Orin a glass tumbler. Amber liquid swirled in it. The tall fae settled his bulk down in the chair opposite Orin as the two stared into the fire.

It had been two days since the battle, and Gwen still hadn't awakened. Both Lance and Viviane, along with some other fae healer whose name

Orin couldn't remember, had assured him that his lover was fine, that her body was fatigued from the blood loss and expenditure of magic. They weren't quite sure what Gwen had managed to do, but the current theory was that she had somehow removed the spell keeping Mordred immortal. Eidytha and Viviane had confirmed that Gwen had been responsible for literally changing the battlefield by molding the earth underneath Arthur and Mordred.

A knock came at the door. Tor ducked his head in. "Any news?" he inquired. Tor tossed a concerned look at Orin's closed bedroom door. He and Gwen had hit it off immediately, and his concern was clear on his face.

"No," Orin's dull voice responded.

Tor appraised Orin, worry in his eyes. "Do you want to hear the report I gave Arthur regarding tracking down Mordred's soldiers?"

Orin opened his mouth, about to deny the request, but Lance beat him to it.

"What's the word from the woods?" Lance asked.

Tor sauntered into the room. A sling cradled his arm from a wound he had received during the second battle, and he would bear a small scar on his cheekbone. Tor snatched the tumbler out of Orin's hand with a wink and downed the contents. Orin couldn't find it in himself to care.

"Well, your little brother is nothing but persistent, Lancelot. While most of Mordred's force have either surrendered or slunk home, we've had some run-ins with clusters of House Dwyn. They're still pushing at our boundaries, looking to expand your brother's territory, I wager. House Keithia has shown up in an official capacity a few times to help. Guess now that the danger is passed, they're willing to make a statement." Tor waved the glass at Lancelot, indicating he wanted another round. Lance obliged, filling the tumbler as Tor continued.

"We've had several score throw down their arms and surrender or show up at the gates requesting mercy. The banshee is helping to coordinate connecting Mordred's deserters with members of the rebel forces that may be friends or family." Tor gave a low, small laugh and shook his head. "Who would have thought such a scary person could have such a soft touch?"

"Just goes to show that you shouldn't judge a book by its cover," Lance murmured, sipping at his own drink.

Tor's brows drew together. "Right. Well, we've got patrols on the border between Avalon and House Dwyn. The fae rebels are getting ready to withdraw and either head back to their Houses to reaffirm their loyalty to their lieges, or they've pledged themselves to you, Lance."

"Wait, what?" Lancelot's head whipped up to stare at the knight.

"Showed up at the gate a little while ago. Lady Viviane is entertaining them in the Great Hall. I've come to fetch you at her request. Come along, we can finish our drinks on the way there." Tor bestowed a look of pitying comfort on Orin. "I'll send someone up with food for you to eat. Gwen wouldn't want you neglecting yourself while she heals. She'll wake up. She's too strong and stubborn not to."

Lance gave a low chuckle as he stood. "Her first words will probably be to rag us about being such sad pandas."

"What's a sad panda?" Tor asked, turning to head back out in the hall.

Lance gave a nod to Orin then clapped Tor on the shoulder. "I'll explain on the way downstairs."

Orin watched them go with listless eyes. He knew how pivotal this time was to stabilize things, but he couldn't bring himself to care. All he cared about was the woman sleeping in his bed.

It took four days before Gwen's eyes opened. Four days while Orin wondered if his heart had finally stopped beating. Four days, he and Saxon held watch, occasionally joined by Viviane, Lance, Eidytha, Bronwyn, and even Arthur. When she finally awoke and looked over at him, weak and still pale, Orin and Saxon were alone in their vigil. Orin lurched out of his chair to sit on the edge of his bed next to Gwen. Saxon whined his excitement, wriggling up the other side of Gwen to lick eagerly at her chin.

"Hi," Gwen croaked as she patted Saxon with one hand. She brought her other hand up to Orin's cheek and ran her fingers through his salt-and-pepper beard. "You okay?"

Orin's rusty laugh crawled out of his chest, full of irony. He kept his fierce gaze on her face as he said, "No."

He knew his tone was harsh, but her wince drove it home. Still, Orin couldn't find it in himself to feel bad about it. Before Mordred's initial attack, he and Lance had forbidden Gwen from sacrificing herself, and yet she had still done it. Knowing now that it had been the only way to truly defeat Mordred didn't dull the anger throbbing in his blood.

Sad brown eyes stared into his as she murmured, "I'm sorry."

That was it. Two simple words.

"I . . . lost you," he ground out, straightening up to tower over her. "I. Lost. You. I thought we had an understanding. I told you that I couldn't lose you, that I have lost too much already. That losing you would break me. You did exactly what we told you not to do, even knowing the heartache your actions would cause."

"I'm here. You didn't lose me." Crystal tears glimmered on Gwen's lashes as she struggled to sit up. Orin didn't help her as he watched Gwen's weak struggles. His chest heaved with the effort to hold back his anger, but it escaped him anyway.

"You *died*! Twice!" Orin roared, his face flushing red as his hands clenched into fists. "If Viviane hadn't been able to bring you back, you would be gone, and where would I be? Grieving with a shattered heart again! Then what good would I be to Arthur, to our people? How could I protect them as a broken man? Let's not forget that your powers are needed to keep Caerleon safe! Mordred's forces are scattered, but Lancelot's brother is making moves that may threaten us all."

Saxon surged to his feet where he had been lying next to Gwen, the dog's fangs on display as he snarled at Orin. Orin tossed a glare at the dog. They had come to a tenuous understanding over the last four days, but that peace could easily fall apart with a harsh word or sharp nip of Saxon's canines.

"Easy, Fur Face. It's okay," Gwen whispered, sagging back onto the pillows. "I'm sorry, Orin. Arthur, Viviane, and I thought we were doing the right thing." She turned her face away from him. "I hurt you. I know I did. I didn't want to, but I did anyway." Her hand came up and swiped at the tears dripping down her cheeks. "I . . ."

Gwen sighed. "We're both broken people, Orin. You struggle to let people in, and I want to matter to people too much. You took a chance on us, just as I took a chance on you. I knew what possibly losing me would do to you based on your history." Gwen turned back to look at him. The tears still fell, but Gwen kept her face fierce as she met his gaze. "I apologize for hurting you, but I don't apologize for doing what was needed. Mordred had to die. Viviane thought she would be able to save me, and Arthur agreed that the risk was worth taking. We knew no one else would agree, so we went ahead and did it anyways. We won, but I don't want to lose you." Her intense tone wavered back to a whisper. "Did I lose you?"

Orin whirled to pace, his hands dragging through his salt-and-pepper hair. He ground his teeth together. He had no idea what to tell Gwen. He loved her. He loved how brave she was. He loved that she was such a strong caretaker. He loved how funny she was, how witty she could be, and how fierce she could be. He both loved and hated how independent she was. Over the last few days, Orin had vacillated between wanting to continue this relationship with Gwen and stepping back to protect himself. He still wasn't sure what the right answer was. He told Gwen as much.

Gwen hiccuped through her sobs as she worked to get her tears under control. Her eyes tracked him as Orin continued pacing. "I could have lost you too, you know." Her hushed, watery tone stopped his frenetic movements.

Orin blinked at Gwen. "What?"

"It's not like you're invincible. You were out on the battlefield, facing unfair odds. You fought *Mordred*. The last time you faced him, both you and Lance couldn't hurt him, yet you went out there anyway not knowing if you could make a difference. I told you before. I could have lost you to a sword or an arrow; we both knew it was a risk for you to be out front on the battlefield. You took it anyway. I would have been devastated to have lost you, but I didn't stop you or forbid it. We did the ritual with as much risk mitigation in place as possible. Viviane was at her most rested, so she was at her strongest, standing right there. Arthur aimed Caliburnus to try to miss internal organs. I know the enemy didn't give us that courtesy when they were trying to kill our people."

He hated to admit it, but Gwen had a point. Before the battles, she had told him as much, but he'd brushed it off. He was a soldier. Soldiers risked themselves. He just didn't want Gwen to. If he could, Orin would keep her inside Caerleon, safe from all harm. Orin deflated, coming back to the chair he had placed next to his bed. Slowly, he reached out and took her hand, looking at her heartbroken face.

"So where do we go from here?" he croaked, tears soaking his voice. Orin refused to let them fall.

Gwen shrugged, dashing the last of her tears away. Her voice was weary. "We either accept that life is a risk and keep trying, or we accept that our traumas are too much and call it quits. I'll be honest; I'd prefer the first choice. I'm not ready to lose you." It was a sincere answer.

Orin let out a heavy breath, then cleared his throat. "Don't . . . don't do something like that again. Please. I don't like to beg, but I will."

Gwen gave him a wan smile. "Luckily, there was only one Mordred. I think this was a once-in-a-lifetime sacrifice, and I am A-OK with that." She leaned toward him, cupping her hand next to her mouth as if she was telling him a secret. "I'm not a real fan of dying."

Orin chuckled, snatching at her hand to bring it to his lips. He kissed the fingertips. "I'm still mad at you."

"Understandable." Gwen sighed, deflating back into her pillow.

"But I still love you," he told her.

Her eyes sparkled. "Also understandable."

A reluctant laugh boomed out as Orin shook his head. This woman. She had dropped into his life like a whirlwind, and even after all these weeks, his head was still spinning.

"I love you too, Orin." Gwen pulled at his hand, asking him to come closer. He did, and she planted her lips on his in a somewhat uncoordinated but still passionate kiss. "Now, I have one other really important question for you."

"What's that, love?" Orin asked.

Gwen grabbed his face, staring into his eyes and asked in a very serious tone, "What are you going to feed me?" Her stomach growled to emphasize the need.

Orin chuckled, answering, "Whatever your heart desires."

Chapter Twenty-Five

Epilogue - Gwen

Two Months Later

Gwen leaned against the warm stone of Caerleon's parapet, arms crossed to brace herself. Saxon lay at her feet with his paws in the air so she could rub his belly with her foot. He grumbled and groaned appreciatively, tail thumping in slow beats. She was so glad Avalon had brought him with her. The fact that Lance was also here lifted her heart. Besides Orin, Lance was the second most important person in her life, followed closely by Viviane. Saxon held his own special place. Mommy and daddy issues aside, she felt blessed with the people in her life. The fact that it took being in a mystical place that was a literary writer's dream to find her family was beside the point.

The field in front of Caerleon looked so different from the battlefield two months ago. Members of House Keithia, with the help of Viviane and a few others from House Dwyn, had dried the earth out enough that other nature fae could encourage long green grass and purple, blue, and yellow wildflowers to cover the scars of battle. Then they buried their dead, mourning the loss of their comrades. She and Alcina had raised a six-foot-tall, gray granite monument at the edge of the forest to commemorate those that they had lost.

Gwen smiled to herself. The field now rioted with color, with fae children and wolf pups running in small packs with the Caerleon children. Clumps of adults gathered to chat and watch over the younglings.

Arthur and Viviane were walking along the lakeshore, her hand held in the crook of his arm. Ever the gentleman, Arthur stopped to pluck some flowers and presented them to Viviane. Gwen was so pleased that the king had finally seen what was right in front of him. To say she was also thrilled for her friend Viviane to receive the fairy-tale love story of her dreams was an understatement.

Gwen shook her head, grinning. Little had anyone known that while Gwen was quietly courting Orin until he openly courted her back, Viviane had taken a page from Gwen's book. The Lady of the Lake had likewise acclimated Arthur to having the fae woman around. Viviane had dropped meals off for the king in the war room, sought his advice on stocking the infirmary, and simply been available for questions whenever Arthur had them about the fae. In a surprise to everyone, Arthur had apologized to Viviane for his behavior toward her and started taking meals with the Lady of the Lake. He was now courting her, taking Viviane on walks like the one they were on or sitting in the library and reading with her. Gwen thought they made an adorable couple.

"Enjoying the sunshine?" Orin asked. Gwen glanced up at Orin as his deep voice rumbled at her back. He caged his body around her, elbows resting on the wall while he laid his chin on her shoulder. Gwen was wearing jeans and a plum-colored T-shirt, and Orin's linen shirt scratched lightly against her skin. He wore a deep-green tunic over-top the linen shirt, belted with a wide brown belt, and black leather pants. Gwen admired how the green looked against his tan skin. The sunlight picked out the gray glittering in his hair and beard.

She melted back into him. Every now and then, Gwen caught Orin looking at her with fear in his eyes, as if he was worried she would disappear. Because of this, Gwen relished the times when the weight of his grief was light, and he allowed her to love him fully. Gwen knew how blessed she was to have someone like Orin in her life. After pining after a dream man for a decade, Gwen wasn't going to squander a chance to enjoy the real thing. She knew, however, that their love was fragile. She would need to take care of it and of Orin.

"I am. Aren't Arthur and Viv cute together?" Gwen pointed at the two still walking slowly down the shore. Arthur kept bending down to add more flowers to Viviane's growing bouquet.

"Never thought I'd see the day to be honest," Orin murmured into her ear, his beard scraping along her neck, before pecking a quick kiss on her cheek. His hand smoothed over her shirt right where the scar was emblazoned across her stomach. He had been doing that ever since he found out what she, Arthur, and Viviane had done during the final battle with Mordred.

A shiver wracked her body, and Orin's arms tightened around her. Gwen had thought she was going to lose Orin when he found out that she had gone against his wishes and performed the blood ritual to tighten Avalon's hold on Caliburnus. The sheer bleakness in his eyes when he hoarsely told her he couldn't lose her . . . her heart still ached at the thought. Gwen wrapped her arms over Orin's. She would do anything to stay with this man.

"So, what's next?" she asked. Gwen tipped her face up to enjoy the warm sunlight, closing her eyes as the giggles and shrieks of happy children drifted up to them.

Orin hummed, settling his weight more against her and pinning her to the stone wall. "What do you mean?"

Gwen shrugged one shoulder, looking over her shoulder at her lover. "Mordred is gone, but if I know my history—and I do because Dad kept dumping info on me anytime he remembered I was around—falling regimes don't end in happily ever afters. Someone always tries to fill the void. Do we have to worry about that?"

Orin grunted, shaking his head. His scruff scraped gently against her neck again. "Not our problem. Let the fae fight it out amongst themselves. I'm thinking Lance and Lady Viviane will be enough of a banner to pull members of their house away from that cousin of theirs. House Keithia may be content to stay allied with us. Arthur is already in talks with them." He turned his head slightly to graze his lips against her neck with another kiss. "In the meantime, you and I have a very important task ahead of us."

"Hmm, we do?" Gwen tilted her head to the side to give him better access as goose bumps erupted on her skin. She loved Orin's touches, but he usually wasn't this amorous in public. She wondered what he was up to.

"Mhm," he murmured, "you need to gather your things and move you and that shadow beast of yours into my rooms." Orin chuckled, pointing at Saxon with his toe but not touching the dog. Saxon rumbled a low growl, rolling over to stare at the two of them.

Gwen whirled in Orin's arms to look up at him in shock. The sharp edge of the wall ground against her back. "I need to do what?"

Orin smiled down at her, pulling her close with his hands on her hips. He hooked his fingers through her belt loops, effectively trapping her further. "I'm not spending another minute without you, darling. I want you with me."

"This isn't too fast for you?" Gwen peered at his face, trying to discern if this was what he really wanted or if this was the lingering fear and anger from the last few months talking.

He bent closer, touching his forehead to hers. "It isn't. I love you so much, woman. Never expected anything to hit me the way you did, but it's a fight I'm happy I lost. You're worth the risk." Orin kissed her before continuing, "Please say yes."

The sounds of the children and the feel of the sunshine faded as Gwen's entire focus shifted to the man she loved. Gwen blinked, tears brimming. He loved her. She loved that he said it so freely, reaffirming her.

"I love you too." She let out a watery laugh as he brushed away a tear with his thumb. "Happy tears, I promise. I love you too, Orin. You're one of the very best men I know. I'm so honored that you call me yours."

A blinding smile flashed across Orin's face as he straightened. "Does this mean you'll move in with me?"

Gwen nodded, chuckling. "Yes. Shouldn't take that long. I don't have that much stuff even with Bronwyn shoving clothes at me whenever she can." Her hands circled his waist as she hugged him, leaning into the warmth of his chest. The fact this man chose her was . . . everything. Apparently dreams could come true.

"Let's go then. I want you sleeping in my bed tonight and every night going forward." Orin grabbed her hand, pulling her toward the steps. Saxon huffed and surged to his paws, glaring at Orin. "The beastie can come as well." He grinned at her. "Maybe one day he'll eventually like me."

Gwen's laugh burbled out of her. She was pretty sure no matter how much Orin tried or how many treats he offered, he'd never measure up to Lance in Saxon's mind. The dog had imprinted on her and her police partner and no one else. Still, it was a nice thought. The three of them as a family. She clutched at Orin's hand a bit tighter as they walked into the keep and headed to her room.

"Maybe later we should take our own walk around the lake," Orin said.

"I'd like that," Gwen said as she opened her door but staggered back into Orin, shocked by what lay before her. The room was piled wall-to-wall and floor-to-ceiling with things from her house. It looked as if Avalon had played an excellent game of Tetris as she spotted her favorite turquoise reading chair wedged under her bed and bolstered on the sides by her multitude of bookshelves. The books were still neatly organized on the shelves. She turned wide eyes to her lover, who stared back in surprise. Scattered throughout were piles of clothes, knickknacks, photos, and what looked like her EMT supplies. How the heck they'd get everything out of the room, Gwen had no idea.

"Well," Orin finally managed. "It appears Avalon also wishes for you to be comfortable here."

Gwen looked over her shoulder, blinking. "But . . . why?"

"Maybe she needs you for something else?" he said, voice cautious. The two looked at each other, Gwen's face paling.

"What else could there be?" she asked.

"I don't know, love," Orin said, kissing her forehead. "But whatever it is, we'll find out together."

Chapter Twenty-Six

Epilogue - Lancelot

Lancelot watched from the courtyard shadows as Orin and Gwen headed into the keep before letting out a dejected sigh. He ran his hands through his hair, twisting it up into a small man bun at the nape of his neck while cursing silently. Neither the sunshine nor shrieks of happy children penetrated his frustration.

Lance had missed his chance. Gwen was taken, and he hadn't even gotten a fair shot.

For the last decade, Lance had relegated himself to the best friend role, knowing that loving Gwen would lead to nothing but heartache since she was a mortal and he was a fae. She'd die long before him in the mortal realm, leaving his heart shredded. So Lance had tried redirecting his feelings into their friendship to such an extent that he had even deluded himself into thinking he didn't love Gwen as more than his best friend.

Only, everything had changed when they landed back in Avalon. This world was timeless, which meant Gwen's lifetime would closely match the length of his. Lance could have her as his beloved. Except she only had eyes for Orin. Lance kicked at a small rock with his boot.

"Oh, I know him because of my dreams," Gwen had told Lance.

Yeah right, Lance scoffed. Orin was a mere blip in Gwen's lifetime. He didn't care how many dreams she'd had about the mortal knight. Lance had been the one to watch over Gwen her whole life, who had been there since her early twenties as her friend, confidant, study buddy, and police partner. Orin may think he knew Gwen, but Lance knew the man's knowledge was all surface-level things. Orin didn't know or understand the heartache Gwen had grown up with in an emotionally neglectful and abusive home. The mortal didn't understand Gwen's dreams of having her own large family to love on. He didn't understand her fear of hurting people unnecessarily. Orin just didn't understand . . .

Lance closed his eyes and sighed heavily. Orin may not understand yet, but Gwen would see that he did. She would trust the man with all of her secrets, secrets that Lance already knew. Lance had well and truly lost her.

But if Orin ever hurt Gwen . . .

Lance growled at that. He'd end the knight, plain and simple. He stared at where they had disappeared one last time before shaking off his anger and stomping toward the stable. Lance needed to leave Caerleon. Gwen may not need him now, but his people did. House Dwyn still struggled under his brother's heinous rule.

It was time Lance reclaimed his birthright. Lance just wondered how he would do it with a broken heart.

Read Lance's story in Burdened by Mist and Sorrow

CHARACTER GLOSSARY

Main Characters:

- **Gwenhwyfar "Gwen" McMillan** grew up in an emotionally neglectful and abusive but wealthy family that afforded her a unique set of skills that melds well with her responsibility to protect Caliburnus. She is vivacious, mercurial, and intelligent who loves athletic hobbies, reading, and music. Avalon has chosen Gwen as the guardian responsible for returning Caliburnus to King Arthur now that Mordred threatens Avalonian soil and the gateway to the mortal realm. Gwenhwyfar is a Welsh name that means "fair or pure spirit."

- **Orin** started his life as a farmer before becoming a soldier for King Arthur. He is one of the individuals taken by Avalon and now acts as King Arthur's second-in-command. Orin was in his forties when he arrived in Avalon and has three distinctive scars on his face courtesy of a werewolf attack, dark hair and beard sprinkled with gray, and a stocky build. He is wary of creating additional connections as he feels grief deeply but is instantly drawn to Gwen upon her arrival. Orin is an Irish name that means "dark-haired."

- **Saxon** is Gwen's police German Shepherd with an all black coat, amber eyes, and a judgmental personality. Saxon adores both Gwen and Lancelot, but the jury is still out on everyone else when it comes to this opinionated canine. The name Saxon means "dagger."

Caerleon Characters:

- **Agrona** is one of the Caerleon women. She aids Kyla with creating and mending clothes as well as helps the mothers with child care. Agrona is a Celtic name based off the Goddess of War and Strife.

- **Aislinn** is one of the Caerleon women and the mother of a four year old girl. She is one of two midwives and healers at Caerleon. Aislinn is an Irish name that means "dream or vision."

- **Alodie** is a sweet, soft spoken Caerleon woman who is mother to Athelred and Stockton and works in the kitchen with Bronwyn and Eidytha. Her sunshine personality is a direct contrast to her broody, antagonistic husband Cae. Alodie is a French derived name that means "wealth."

- **Arthur** is the famous king of legend and owner of Caliburnus. After centuries of leading his people, the responsibility and grief has worn down the man, making him paranoid when it comes to their safety and firmly entrenched his hatred of the fae, especially Mordred. His bitterness and brusque attitude is a challenge for Gwen and others to handle while convincing the king to give trust another chance and to step out from the shadows of Caerleon's walls. The name Arthur means "strength and courage."

- **Athelred** is Alodie and Cae's son and is the more reserved of the two boys. This Old English name means "noble counsel."

- **Avina** is one of the Caerleon women. She is responsible for managing the gardens. Avina is a Latin derivative that means "from the oat field."

- **Bedevere** is one of Arthur's knights and is a master archer. He is a good friend of Orin's. Bedevere tends to be quiet but has a good sense of humor with those close to him. This Welsh name means "birch man."

- **Blaine** is one of the Caerleon women who helps Bronwyn in the kitchen. Blaine is married to one of Arthur's knights, Griffin. Blaine is well known for her bold and snarky sense of humor. The Gaelic name means "thin" or "yellow."

- **Bors** is Tor's brother and one of Arthur's more senior knights. Bors is a German derived name that means "bear."

- **Brea** is one of the Caerleon women responsible for managing and reporting on the castle's different supplies. Brea is an Old English word that means "hill."

- **Bronwyn** is the power behind Caerleon despite what Arthur may think. This elderly woman is extremely efficient, kind, and stubborn. Lance refers to Bronwyn as "the nicest steam roller you'll ever meet." Bronwyn is critical to forging the alliance with the fae along with Gwen. The Welsh name means "white raven."

- **Cae** is one of King Arthur's knights and part of Orin's scouting team. His grumpy demeanor is off putting, but he is fiercely loyal and protective of his family. Cae is an alternate spelling of Cai or Kay, which is a Welsh derived name that ironically means "happy."

- **Caradoc** is one of Arthur's knights, well known for his impertinent sense of humor. Caradoc is a Welsh name that means "amiable."

- **Demelza** is one of the Caerleon women and acts as a midwife and healer. Demelza is a Cornish name meaning "fort on the hill."

- **Dinadan** is one of Arthur's knights who is pushy and one of Lamorak's cronies. This Old English name means "knight."

- **Eidytha** is a vivacious but fierce Caerleon woman who immediately befriends Gwen. Eidytha is one of the single women in Caerleon and helps Bronwyn manage the castle's kitchen. The English name means "prosperous warrior."

- **Fiona** is one of the Caerleon women and is responsible for the castle's weaving. Fiona is a Gaelic or Irish name that means "fair."

- **Gareth** is one of Arthur's knights. While he has a crude sense of humor, he is also loyal and watchful, often leading sentry duty. Gareth is a Welsh name that means "gentleness" and "modest."

- **Griffin** is one of Arthur's knights as well as the castle's black-smith. He is also Blaine's husband. Griffin is a Welsh name that means "fierce leader" or "strong chief."

- **Henri** is a French mountain man taken by Avalon in the early eighteen hundreds who has joined those at Caerleon as a soldier who specializes in guerrilla warfare. He is a helpless flirt but still respectful of the women. Henri is a French name that means "home ruler."

- **Hertha** is one of the Caerleon women and helps with either childcare or in the kitchen. Hertha is a German name that means "strength."

- **Idina** is one of the Caerleon women. She is a multi-talented woman and helps around the castle wherever extra hands are needed. Idina is an Old English name meaning "prosperous friend."

- **Isola** is one of the Caerleon women and mother to infant Bea. Isola helps in the kitchen, the gardens, or with childcare. Isola is a Celtic name that means "island."

- **Kyla** is one of the Caerleon women who is responsible for creating and mending clothes. She is an avid reader. Kyla is a Gaelic name that means "slender."

- **Lamorak** is one of Arthur's knights who is both arrogant and pushy. He tends to rush into battle, which often results in injury. Lamorak is an Old English name and can mean "Brother of Percival" from the Arthurian legends.

- **Louis** is a Frenchman taken by Avalon from the seventeen hundreds. Louis has a boisterous personality, who often speaks before he thinks. He is an excellent swordsman with a rapier. Louis is a French name meaning "famed warrior."

- **Maebh** is one of the Caerleon women and is the mother to a five year old boy. Maebh is Bronwyn's second-in-command. This Irish name means "the cause of great joy."

- **Stockton** is Alodie and Cae' other son and is the more exuberant and outgoing of the two boys. Stockton is enamored with Gwen's dog Saxon, a feeling which is definitely not mutual for the dog. This Old English name means "from the monastery settlement."

- **Tor** is one of King Arthur's knights and Orin's best friend. He has a vivacious personality. Tor is an excellent swordsman and knife fighter. He acts as a foil for the normally dour Orin. The name Tor is an Irish name that means "from the craggy hills."

Fae Characters:
- **Alcina** is a rebel from House Keithia with mid-level power to manipulate earth and move it around as necessary to create trenches, ramps, and holes that the rebels leverage in their attacks and defenses. Alcina has dark brown skin and hair and is a no-nonsense and driven individual who helps train Gwen in her new powers. The name Alcina means "strong willed and intelligent."

- **Aethelflaed** is a banshee rebel that hails from House Mors. She is soft spoken with a dry sense of humor. Aethelflaed has extremely pale skin, sunken black eyes, and limp gray hair. She is one of two banshees within the rebel forces and is by far the more powerful of the two. Aethelflaed 's banshee wail causes both auditory pain as well as emotional pain by forcing victims to relive their worst sorrows. The name Aethelflaed means "noble beauty."

- **Guthlac** hails from House Keithia and leads the rebel forces with Frideswide and Aethelflaed. The Green Man is a tall, slender male with dark skin and hair plus startling green eyes who wears green leather armor. He is gruff and easy to anger, but fiercely protective of his rebel forces. The name Guthlac means "battle."

- **Frideswide** is one of three rebel leaders, a former member of House Keithia. The fairy has transparent dragon-fly like wings, blond hair, pale skin, and blue eyes. She is charismatic, strong-willed, and powerful. Her name means "peaceful strength."

- **Lancelot** is an exiled fae who has kept tabs on Caliburnus' guardians since arriving in the mortal realm. Gwen's Gran befriended Lance, leading to him becoming both Gwen's best friend and police partner. Lance is in line to take over House Dwyn but has been usurped by his brother, Aberlin, when Mordred exiled Lancelot and his cousin Viviane to the mortal realm. Lance's fae powers allow him to manipulate water, which he does so as part of his fighting style. The name Lancelot can mean "land" or "servant."

- **Viviane** is the mythical Lady of the Lake from the King Arthur legends. She is Lancelot's cousin and an exiled member of House Dwyn. Her fae powers center around controlling water but, unlike her cousin Lancelot's battle tendencies, her powers lean towards healing. While being exiled, she stole Caliburnus, effectively ending Mordred's ability to open the gateway to the mortal realm. Viviane then gifted the sword to Arthur to help protect his people in the mortal realm. Avalon claimed Viviane back from her exile when She brought Arthur and his people through the gateway while leaving Lancelot back in the mortal realm. Arthur and the people of Caerleon blame Viviane for their troubles, and it takes Gwen's efforts to bring them around to realizing that Viviane is a strong ally. The name Viviane means "lively."

Antagonist Characters:

- **Aberlin** is Lancelot's younger brother, Viviane's cousin, and the current Lord of House Dwyn. Aberlin is known for his power hungry but cowardly ways and is rarely seen away from House Dwyn lands. Aberlin is one of Mordred's inner circle and provides the bulk of soldiers for Mordred's army. The name Aberlin derives from a multitude of cultures, and can mean "marshy place" or "river."

- **Mordred** hails from none of the established fae courts. He is one of the very rare fae who can control and manipulate multiple types of magic. He has leveraged this unique skill set to establish a power base over the centuries and tie his life force into the Mist Lands, effectively making him invincible. Mordred's ultimate goal is to crush the final rebel forces, take over Avalon, and move into the mortal realm. The fae tyrant is well known not only for his power but also his arrogance. The name Mordred ironically means "controlled" or "restrained."

Places, Groups, and Items of Importance:

- **Avalon** acts as the bridge realm between the mortal world and fae realm. Avalon's magic is partially sentient and chooses who becomes the guardian for the key sword, Caliburnus.

- **Caliburnus** is the legendary sword of King Arthur. Caliburnus is the original name for the sword, which eventually became more well known as Excalibur. Historians still disagree if Caliburnus is derived from Latin or Welsh, but do agree that this is the name for the sword in the earliest literature related to King Arthur.

- **Caerleon** is the traditional Welsh name for Camelot, based on early writings indicating that King Arthur ruled "The City of Legions," which was originally a Roman settlement that became an important trade and political site.

- **House Dwyn** is the court of the water fae. The name is derived from the Welsh word "dŵr," which translates to "water." Lancelot is the rightful heir for the House, but he has been usurped by his brother Aberlin after Lancelot was exiled by Mordred. Fae that can either control water or whose secondary forms require water (e.g., the Kelpie) fall under this House's mantle.

- **House Keithia** is the court of the forest and earth related fae, led by Lord Adair and Lady Aveline. They are rebel fae sympathizers, and the bulk of the fae rebel forces are from this house. The name Keithia is derived from English origins and means "forest."

- **House Mors** is the court of the monstrous fae, led by Lady Morganna. Lady Morganna is a highly independent fae ruler and remains as neutral as possible in the Mordred-rebel conflicts. The name Mors is derived from the Latin noun for "death."

- The **Mist Lands** are the fae realm, which is ruled by three main fae courts delineated as Houses. These courts bow to Mordred, who has leveraged his level of power to dominate the courts. Based on the types of magic that the individual fae may wield, both minor and major fae types live within their designated courts. As king, Mordred has built a castle nestled between the three fae court lands.

Creature Glossary

- **Aswang**: Filipino shape shifting ghouls.

- **Banshee**: Irish creature most often depicted as an old woman or ghostly female figure whose wailing cry heralded the death of a family member.

- **Centaur**: Greek mythological creature that is half human and half horse known for their savagery.

- **Ciguapa**: Dominican mythological creature that takes a human female form with skin that is usually dark blue or brown. Their notable features are backward facing feet and long hair that covers their bodies.

- **Fairy**: European creature found across multiple cultures. Fairies usually appear as small humans with wings and have some form of magical powers.

- **Faun**: Greek and Roman mythological creature that is half-human and half-goat known for leading travelers astray or alternately helping them, depending on the myth.

- **Green Man**: British creature who wears armor or clothing adorned with leaves.

- **Griffin**: Legendary Greek creature with the head of an eagle, body and tail of a lion, and wings of an eagle.

- **Gorgons**: Greek mythological female creature who has snakes as hair and can turn people to stone with a look.

- **Harpy**: Greek and Roman mythological creature that is half-human and half-bird, often female.

- **Kappa**: Japanese creature with a dish-like head that retains water, the source of the kappa's strength. Depicted as human-like beings with a turtle's shell, webbed hands and feet, and green skin.

- **Kelpie**: Scottish mythological water spirit that inhabits lakes and shape shifts into a horse-like creature.

- **Manananggal**: Filipino mythological creature with a winged vampire-like appearance that can separate its torso from its lower half of the body.

- **Ogre**: Mythological creature that appears in myths and stories worldwide. They are often depicted as large, brutish figures with immense appetites for human flesh.

- **Pugot**: Filipino mythical fiend that can take various shapes, including headless, black beings.

- **Redcap**: Scottish mythological creature known for soaking his cap in the blood of his victims after luring them into his lair.

- **Roc**: Large, legendary eagle from Middle Eastern mythology.

- **Werewolf**: European mythological creature that is a person who can shape shift into a wolf. Depending on the country and the interpretation of the myth (e.g., through a religious lens), the werewolf can appear very different, with some walking on two legs and others looking like traditional wolves.

ACKNOWLEDGEMENTS

I want to acknowledge a handful of folks who were instrumental to completing Legend of Mist and Blade and supporting me in my author journey.

First and foremost, I want to thank my parents. They've always encouraged my writing and have been the best cheerleaders in the world since I was little. This book is the end result of all the times you told me to keep writing and dreaming. Love you both so much.

Secondly, a huge thank you to my amazing and supportive husband. You kept the kids from burning the house down while I worked and brought me all the coffees. I love you so much.

For my writing girlies - Danielle, Michelle, and Jessica - thank you for keeping me sane through this whole process, for being my sounding board and beta readers, and just in general being the most amazing friends.

Thank you to my fantastic editors. This book is the best it can be thanks to your help.

And you, dear reader, thank you for taking a chance on my debut novel. Your support means the world to me.

About the Author

I've been an avid reader and writer since I was a child, devouring books from the school library and writing my first short story at age seven. Growing up as an Army brat who moved around the country frequently, I found books to be the one constant in my life.

With as much reading as I did, I eventually found myself creating my own characters and worlds that have evolved through the years, and now I want to share them with readers.

Realizing that stories with women in their late thirties (or older) as heroines were few and far between, I wanted to capture the power, strength, and beauty of women my own age in my books. I hope readers can experience the nostalgia of the fantasy stories they loved growing up, only this time, with heroines secure in themselves finding love, going on adventures, and healing old wounds.

When not reading or writing, I love painting tabletop miniatures, spending time with my large, chaotic family, or cooking traditional Southern or Italian recipes.

Find me at amrosswriter.com

www.ingramcontent.com/pod-product-compliance
Lightning Source LLC
Chambersburg PA
CBHW071346300726
48976CB00006B/1781